S0-ANO-110

EXACT CHANGE YEARBOOK

Sala au rocher de la Vierge, Biarritz, August 1927 by Jacques-Henri Lartigue © Association des Amis de Jacques-Henri Lartigue

EXACT CHANGE YEARBOOK 1995

no.1

EXACT CHANGE * BOSTON * USA
CARCANET * MANCHESTER * UK

Published in the United States by Exact Change.
ISBN-1-878972-17-0
ISSN-1051-1717

Exact Change
P.O. Box 1917
Boston, MA 02205 USA
Distributed by D.A.P. (Distributed Art Publishers)
1-800-338-BOOK
N.B.: Unsolicited manuscripts will not be returned.

First published in Great Britain by Carcanet Press Ltd.
ISBN-1-85754-173-1
A CIP catalogue record for this book is available
from the British Library

Carcanet Press Ltd.
402-6 Corn Exchange
Manchester M4 3BY England
Carcanet Press Ltd. acknowledges financial assistance
from the Arts Council of England

PRINTED AND BOUND IN HONG KONG

CONTENTS:

ON THE CD

publisher's note:

WHEN New Directions discontinued its annual in 1991 we felt the loss of one model of literary publication — a large miscellany of avant-garde work, both contemporary and historical, chosen less to represent a particular "school," and more in the spirit of learning what's out there. Of course some editorial point of view is unavoidable, and also (we believe) necessary toward making an interesting book. But one can hope, at least, for a perspective that is not too strictly limited by one's own short-sightedness. And in a large book one can include a lot — even the strictest ideologue runs out of canonical work at a certain point, and blurs the boundaries.

For this issue we asked Peter Gizzi to help us find a range of contemporary work that draws on the tradition we publish in our books of Surrealist and other early twentieth-century experimentation. He in turn asked for help and advice from many others, in the U.S. and abroad, our "correspondents" for this issue. To what came back we added work by Exact Change authors (Stein, Cage, de Chirico, Aragon), as well as a few other discoveries we were eager to share. All is herein enclosed.

— DK & NY

LETTER *from* EDWARD

Letter from Edward to the Scientific Community

THE MOUNT WILSON Observatory lies a short distance northeast of Pasadena California at an altitude of 5,704 feet above the sea. Established in 1903 by Dr. George Ellery Hale, by 1908 the observatory possessed the largest actively used telescope then in existence. Beginning in 1905 the Observatory regularly published the results of its research in a number of scientific journals, and almost immediately certain of the observatory's findings began to trickle down to the lay public through the popular press.

As early as 1911, the astronomers at Mount Wilson began receiving letters from people all around the world, people from all walks of life, educated as well as uneducated. Many of the letters were simple expressions of appreciation and awe for the work that the astronomers were accomplishing. There was, however, another class of letter. These letters were by individuals who felt, often with a great degree of earnestness, that they were in possession of understandings or information that should be shared with the astronomers.

The information contained in this class of letter was typically of astronomical or cosmological concern. These individuals had gleaned the information they wished to communicate either by experimentation, observation, or intuition, and invariably felt a strong sense of urgency in their need to communicate with the observers at Mount Wilson.

In the 1940's the letters were collected and organized by Joe Hickox, chief solar observer. Eventually the letters were passed to the current solar observer at the Mount Wilson Observatory, Larry Webster, who brought them to the attention of the Museum of Jurassic Technology. In 1993 the letters were placed on exhibit at the Museum, and a book was published by the Museum entitled *No One May Ever Have the Same Knowledge Again* (distributed by Brico Press) which provides exact transcripts of the letters, and includes photographs and relevant background information. The following is an excerpt.

— SARAH SIMONS

LETTER FROM EDWARD
TO
THE SCIENTIFIC COMMUNITY THRU
THE MOUNT WILSON OBSERVATORY

CAT. # 0024

1

To the scientific world Thru the Mt. Wilson Observatory Mt. Wilson Calif.

To whom it may concern:

This is to certify, That I have found the Key To all Existance. And all I ask of any one Is for them to read What I am about to say. Because it is not my purpose to tell What you already know. And consequently the proof Shall follow and establish My work to make it law.

For the key to all existance Is the key to the Law By which all things Come into existance and therefore my word Is the key to that law to be verified by proof Listen therefore to what I say As follows:

2

The Moon Is practically all Water frozen or Ice It was formed By water evaporating From the earth Which arose and gathered Between the Earth and Sun It is hollow Like a pumpkin The inside is composed of that part of the air known as Nitrogen And very very cold Consequently its water is frozen.

If the crust of the moon Was removed, it would be a Sun bright enough To destroy the earth. There is no life upon the moon, but Without the moon There would be no life upon the earth.

3

There is no land upon the moon Except what has been made By falling (debris) from the sky But without the moon There would be no land Upon the earth, and consequently all life Would be in the water. and Therefore we say that there is no life Upon the Moon by reason of atmospheric conditions. But There is an abundance of life In the Moon or in the waters Of the Northern half.

There is no rain there The light is always the same and the temperature has not changed One degree in a million years The water is H20. The Ice is as pure as snow and consequently the air is N40 and To make a long story short. That is a physical paradise.

4

Upon the (Southern) half however The sun has never shown, Except (thru) the reflections of The Earth and stars Which is approximately Five times greater Than the light of the moon Upon the earth. Where the days and nights are equal. Fourteen days of night and Fourteen days In the light of the earth. And not a very (—) place For life of any kind, and First to be explored by man.

Which will be done in time. These facts I will prove. In part, thru the Moving Picture World, by speaking a few words to them which will enable them to make a moving picture of the Moon in which it will appear to fall Upon the earth, and apparently come Within the reach of human hands.

5

The Earth, upon which we live Was created between the sun and the worlds center of gravity and fanned by the burning of Oxygen in the center (—) and made by the remains of life and the mixing of the elements From above and from below. And it lies in the (—) of Equal attentions and resistance Between the center of the Earth and the lines of Equal attractions and resistance above the earth. And consequently it is a hollow shell filled with Nitrogen.

Even as Nitrogen exists above the (earth) and the attraction and resistance From the center of the earth Is equal to that above the earth and an object placed below the crust of the earth, would fall upwards Even as it would fall downward If placed above the earth and with the same rapidity.

6

(Escaping) that the one (force) below would (loose) in velocity And the one from above would grow in velocity And so it is with the (line) of Equal attraction and Resistance above the earth. Where a common ball would flote like a feather and if two balls were liberated together, one above and one below The one above would go away From the earth. With the same increased velocity as the one below would gain In returning to the earth.

The Moon rests, or floats In that line of equal attraction and resistance — The Corona of the Earth and it cannot fall to the earth By reason of the earths resistance and it cannot fall from the earth By reason of the earths attraction and consequently it moves and floats In its orbit around the Earth.

7

If the crust of the earth was removed, a Sun would be revealed with such powerful Resistance, that it would Be cast out of the Solar System If the crust of the earth was doubled in weight It would sink Toward the sun One half the distance It is from it to day. And therefore by this Information, I will prove The thickness of the crust of the earth.

By the worlds great mathematitions, which will also determine the composition of all the (solar) planets and even that of the sun itself. First however I will tell them Their composition, that by (These) figures, they may prove the veracity of my (word).

8

The Moon moves in its orbit Of the earths resistance and the crust of the earth Moves in its orbit of resistance which in earths case is From the center of the earth and therefore it is not necessary for the earth To have any particular Thickness. And in fact there is no land at all covering the North Pole And if a common (ball) was (lessened) of the Earths Center of gravity, between

Them and the North Pole It would leave with such velocity that it would come To the surface of the water of the North Pole, providing The Ice was cleared away when it would have arrived and then it would sink and rest above the lower edge of the Earths Crust

9

and that is the substance of that universal Law which is given to all solar planets thru the sun. They were all created by him and (thus) they maintain his law and that same law came from the center of universal gravity (sh —) fourth In many generations — Many Suns in the center of as many systems. And therefore a careful study of our own Solar System means the comprehention

(To a certain extent) of the vastness of the universe. But at the present time, a thorough understanding is too strong For the human mind. Suffice it to say however That these few words will pave the way that leads to all understanding which lies within my hands.

10

In the spring of 1904, at the age of 29 I was admitted to the study of that Law and for thirteen years I carefully followed That voice which called me Son of Man. And since the month of June 1914 I have written many chapters which As yet are held in vain by Those to who I wrote. Therefore I have turned to those of scientific Research to give to them what I have by writing Ten chapters. and whenever I am recognized There will I abide To draw all men to me.

Know you therefore all of you That seek the truth in any capacity that I stand upon the foundation of the law from whence all things sprang And that I am able to deliver you From all misunderstanding. and In that capacity, I speak, not the Words of man but of Him That made All Things. I thank you Very Kindly.

12

Etholeum — The base of all existance — it is One with Electricity and There is no place where It does not exist. It is the conduit of The Light between all of the planets and thru the telephone and the radio and without it There would be no Earth Because there would be No sound. to be transferred between

The planets and Life upon the earth Etholeum, therefore is the Mother of all planetary existance and In her all things are begotten To be concieved and born of her (Providing they have not already Been born) the last of which Is human understanding.

13

Electricity the spirit of all existance. Is one with Etholeum and the positive extreme of all things made between it and Etholeum. And therefore the universe Is charged with Electricity By the center of universal gravity Thru all the (planets) Even as a battery is charged From the elements Than a (—) and the planets are (strange —)

By which they move and have their (—) In their regular orbits and therefore there is places in the universe where Some things do not (exist) but there is no place where these two extremes do not exist.

14

Nitrogen the first Form of creation between Electricity and Etholeum, (In which the light (opposed) In the center of universal gravity and Therefore it sprang to all Planets when then centers of gravity was formed.) Is that element that envelops The earth and the center that lies beneath the crust of the earth. Pure Nitrogen beneath and Oxygen and nitrogen above the crust of the earth.

Mixed to the consistency of Life above and death below, the crust of the earth And so it is within and upon all of the planets of heaven, (—) that hydrogen exists In sufficient quantities upon Them, there is Life, but the center of them all is Pure Nitrogen.

15

Oxygen that element of the Air and water that envelopes the earth. In all the planets was created by Electricity in the midst of Nitrogen. and to day it is created By the light of the sun upon the surface of the water Between the air and the water. And so (perfect) is this (—) of creation that oxygen is always the same in the air and in the water.

Regardless of how much may be consumed by fire. and in fact the water and the air could not be without oxygen For in their primitive forms they were Hydrogen and Nitrogen and it took oxygen to make The water and the air, which was and is by the rays of the sun.

16

Hydrogen, was created by Electricity between Nitrogen and Oxygen and the three forms the Trinity of Life Even as Electricity, Nitrogen and Etholeum form the trinity of all planetary existance. Electricity the (passtime p) thru Nitrogen the passtime Entrance (—) Hydrogen between Nitrogen and Oxygen and these (—) forms the air and the water with the surface of the earth and that of the water between which is the trinity of the worlds existance. By the gathering of the water below and above to form the firmament which in the beginning God called Heaven, and wherein we live.

17

And Life was created in the water Before the earth was formed And there it grew in great abundance Between the Air and the water and each atmospheric condition Brought forth new forms of Life (Until) the land appeared to support another form of life which came in the air (above) the same as it came in the water below the firmament. The (end) of what was found in the electrical radiance of the sun and

(Thereby) planted in the water and upon the land and there it grew and passed away according to atmospheric conditions thru out the ages that led onward toward the earths (perfection) until the present times.

18

Man was created at the end of the day of imperfect atmospheric conditions and his birth created a (Kingdom) to rule the earth and How man endowed with the possibility of Thought Knowledge and Understanding which is the (—) of human perfections When the three are one. But until the present time the truth has been withheld By reason of human ignorance.

and the inability to grasp it when it appeared in sufficient strength to reveal the creation of the earth and universe and the human mind never would Have been sufficiently strong, had it not Have been for astronomical and scientific research, and therefore I hereby commend you all to them.

19

The Father, the Son and the Holy Ghost In human creation means the same as Electricity The Sun and Etholeum In Solar Creation With the throne in the Sun The Center of the Solar System Even as the Son of Man Is the (Throne) of Human (Existance) In the midst of Men Then to overcome all Mankind, even as the Solar System is (ruled) by the sun God, the Father, in all forms of Creation Is that same, (power) Father or God, that First came into the center of Universal Gravity

The Sun or Son of God Is His throne whether physical or mental and due to prevail upon the earth Even as the Sun prevails in the universe the Holy Ghost is the possibility of Creation, the negative (power) to receive the passive spirit, in order that the created may arise between the Holy and the Unholy.

20

Thought, Knowledge and understanding Is also the (—) Those ancient words. Which is the trinity of that Kingdom To rule the Earth and therefore the same condition Exist to day among men, that did exist in the beginning Before the sun was born. We have the two (entrances) But Knowledge has not arisen between Thought therefore in every human mind is simply another word meaning God within us

Knowledge means the return of The son of man and understanding means that he will draw all men to him By the proof he holds within his hands Because the Father, the Son, and the Holy Ghost, or Spirit is to every human mind the same, as Thought Knowledge and understanding which is divine.

21

Government, of by and for the people Is another trinity to (—) the forward stride of civilization By making laws to be obeyed by some and disobeyed by others. For the (—) of some and the destruction of (others) and Founded upon the propositions of Equal Liberty and Justice for all. Government of all people, is of those that make the Law By those that obey it.

And for those that (brake) it. And when the Fathers are one with the Sons, by obeying the laws they make, the law will be inforced in the far extreme and the human race will be one Indivisible people with Liberty and Justice for all.

22

The Election of Law Officials by the people for the purpose of Inforcing the Law Is the transforming of Government From the hands of the people to (—) of a few and therefore If the officials of the Law are obedient to it, To begin with, the Law is inforced by a two thirds Majority, (—) the election should terminate, In the honesty of Alfred E. Smith who made this Immortal Statement: Hoover is the not the president of the Republican Party But the president of the United States Like the Father and the Son he (tries)

To these convictions and the Law to begin with, Is Inforced by a two thirds majority And it shall prevail In the far extreme Until Crime shall vanish from all the Earth Never to return of any great consequence and never in the majority Beyond the power of the law to (—) it.

23

And now I must conclude My words to you By saying that the constitution and its Eighteen Amendments shall never fall But by these four last chapters 19, 20, 21 & 22. It shall be transformed From a mighty oak tree to a royal palm. Because these four chapters are four more amendments To it, to grow thereon. Which I hereby Trust to you of the Astronomical and the scientific world.

Because you have used the talents of your minds (—) and Have not hid them in the and consequently you are (worthy) to receive my words. In witness where of I set my hand and affix the (seal) of (—) By signing my name — Edward.

THE END

ORIGINAL: CHINESE LANGUAGE-POETRY GROUP

TRANSLATED BY JEFF TWITCHELL

ORIGINAL, not in the sense of unique, but because of their interest in the earlier meanings and associations that can be read in the Chinese written character, an effort to recover vitalities repressed by the degradation the language has endured in recent history. So, too, the recuperation of the original impetus of poetry as the play in language. *Yuányàng* might also be translated as "prototype" — experimentation, the trying out of possibilities for further work.

The Original poets are from Nanjing and Suzhou in the heartland of classical Chinese culture. They belong to the more radical wing of the so-called Third Generation poets, a very diverse range of poets throughout mainland China who are only defined by their mutual concern to go beyond the seminal early work of the Misty (or Obscure) poets. In the late 1970s, the youthful group who became known as the Misty poets — adopting the tag hung on them by their official critics — decisively broke with the banal political verse that defined the entire field of poetry throughout the reign of the great poet-leader of the Revolution. Younger poets quickly saw the enormous prospects that had opened up and the 1980s saw an explosion of new poetries — as if a century of modernisms were compressed into a decade.

Of this poetry very little has been translated aside from that of the major Misty poets — Bei Dao, Shu Ting, Yang Lian, Gu Cheng, Meng Ke, Jiang He, Duo Duo — and even in their case, most of what is available is their early and relatively immature work. At present it is impossible for a Western reader to have much idea of what is going on poetically in China, but it is hoped the following will offer some inkling of the possibilities happening at one coordinate of a crowded map. Of particular interest has been the development of the long poem, almost unheard of throughout the history of Chinese poetry, and it is regrettable that examples of the more extended works of the Original poets, especially Che Qian-zi and Zhou Ya-ping, cannot be presented here.

What follows is a small selection from an anthology of poetry and essays by the Original poets published as a special issue of the poetry journal *Parataxis* 7 (1994) edited by Drew Milne at the University of Sussex, Brighton, England. Many people ought to be thanked for making these translations possible, but especially the remarkable young women Zhen Zhen, Wang Yi-man, Xu Yang, Sun Yi-qian, Jia Yun, Jiang Li, Wei Yan-mei and Zhao Yue-li.

— JEFF TWITCHELL

CHE QIAN-ZI

A SONG

When I write a poem
I think of you
Feel there is some coincidence
I want to write a poem
But do not know what will happen later

Even if naked the body
Will not let others understand more
I think as I write
Hoping to discover something
You sit on a mountain, body
Like math in a primary textbook
1+1=2

I often don't know what to do?
Cross out make changes, have to start again
Five people ten people
Only five ways to write a word
And ten ways to write
Rules, or
Too illegible to discern
I think as I write
I have never imitated anyone
If someone's shadow appears on me
Then, it is only because
My life comes several years too late

ORIGINAL: CHINESE LANGUAGE-POETRY GROUP

"CLOTH" NO. 2

A piece of cloth makes the body mute and silent
When it, when it acts a piece of cloth
Will turn into
Another piece of cloth, and a third

Cloth
Flies throughout the days, when I see
Cloth has already turned into
Another piece my other half
Rides on it

Cloth has brought shame

No, horror, cloth, wall of cloth
It is coming here, cloth wall
wall of cloth
Cloth-brick cloth-cement
Cloth-sky cloth-
uncommon road
Cloth has brought mankind's shame, shame
has brought the latest evil

On the cloth-water surface cloth-beard
Cloth political economics, aesthetic theories,
cloth metric ruler
Cloth

Cloth is concrete, cloth does not possess
abstract thinking
Fiber woven into cloth
Cloth is the ultimate end of "cloth"
Cloth-warmth and iron
Cloth-ice cloth-tree
Go everywhere, the life of a person
however wrapped by cloth

Cloth, number 2, flies over the tree tips of days
hovering
Cloth wings are people I am wearing
Clothes, have taken
Cloth across the Yellow River
A big piece, cloth, cloth, cloth
I stapled on it
An anti-allegory book that happened to be at hand
100 pages
Punish virtue advocate evil

H

(also titled "if, symmetry: touchable smoothness")

Sacrifice the wind you want, it blows on the garden
balsam
If the wind is blowing the white balsam flowers
I will feel very good
Revealed nature of water, skin, and so on
Sleep naked but don't feel cold
If I feel very good, the Ganges
India if I were there India India
Again to see the oriental moon
Again with you: cinnabar the size of an egg

Stitches of shimmering waves, on some white flowers
A mirror or love I still have
I think this poem, if
Really written by me is then my most elegant composi
tion of late
The places your hands touch are all very smooth
And empty
And not to the point
A place the size of a piece of cinnabar
I put up down

CHAIR, AN EXTRACT

Gray water, and matter. Gray water, and matter
The side in shadow, I pinken birds that don't fly
Vast and mighty pond, loud washing sounds
A house passed through a door destroyed
Washing sounds that don't fly, objects overlook

Chair one chair a set of chairs
Again the yellow house. Side in shadow, I resolve to
adopt another kind of
View: the sky is blue half of a dead bird
Mouth protrudes, bright, destitute and vicious
Again the yellow house, I can't leave

Give him a bit of green grass so as to return to the
world of mortals
A blade of green grass to enable them to return
Fleshy sky weak column top
Darkness in the heart: edged with gold on four sides
Jewelsmith, silversmith, give him a bit of gold
Holes and hunger, I have committed a crime
Read in the night a village barber
Cuts short the hair of a fish. It is simpler
In the long stretches of water a body sticks out. Stand up
straight
Fish bladder has foreseen the lying bowl

Wood-block edition, revolver
Hello! Village barber
Give me a story K or G
The razor stops in the mouth of the scarecrow
Sensitive, trample on oneself

Countenance in the water, people in the water
Big river flows through flesh, like light penetrating glass
Carrying silt toward the lower reaches
And boats, loaded with goods
Mathematics, flowers of anti-allegory

Forging gold rings for nipples
Pink human body. Jewelsmith
The village detective raises donkey skins under lamplight
A paper horse treads the candy-counter, 11:20
Nipple, the eye of the candle sweltering, about to drop

The village detective, in the middle of the puddle
Solved the problem that the dead were unable to solve
The barber clamors for the living
(Everything disappears from here)
In the past, he cut my hair

Four legs, human solidarity, man and man
Put into order by the surface of the chair
Accept metaphysics, the Lord of Creation, then
If a chair has five legs
The fifth leg expounds the rules of decoration

You hold birds' eggs, your face
The flesh deducted from the torso
It is "the soul" I gradually figure out
I sometimes am rotten like technique
Holding birds' eggs, I witness your rebirth

ZHOU YA-PING

VULGAR BEAUTY

(I)

I write down the two words "vulgar beauty."
Fingers skim over flames, surprisingly like
Drawing out darkness, the edge emits deep green
  flames.
A black pear, placed near a flower vase
Its light yellow epidermis, clear and light
Enticing moment. This is because a snake
From the vase's thin neck sticks out
A reddish brown tongue.

(II)

A crude shriek, pierces a flower garden.
The only crudeness, is on the paint.
Already bluish smoke rises. Ox horn comes from the
  northwest
Herdsmen have removed its fresh filth and foulness.

Two fruit stones blossom on a light green sphere
On its chin is stuck a braid-like beard.
Amid rosy clouds is the sun
Mingling red and yellow
The brilliant rays appear purple-blue.

(III)

An afterbirth is unfolded, taking the shape of an umbrella.
The ridges of an umbrella along yellow lines.
A fetus like a coal cinder has long been reared in it,
Lit by me, it will give off light.
A white crane, unexpectedly covered by a black string-net
A snake, bound with copper wire, body
Like a tightening spring, soft parts flashing.

ORIGINAL: CHINESE LANGUAGE-POETRY GROUP

(IV)

Facing sunset clouds, on Buddha's face
Appears a genuine blush. At first I had doubts about
A mistaken metaphor. Buddha's face trimmed as
Passionate green grass. Let it flourish in spring.
Flowers have blossomed. Large broad-leaves against
  dark brown,
Open the human skull, there too is an orange berry

(V)

Vulgar beauty is required. Southern flame
Just like a rotten battery, green rust stuck to
Its lower part, tossed on a coal-pile.
"Breathe" or "perish"? These are
The spat-out words of the robust trunk

(VI)

A woman opening a window, at the top of the building.
At last the wind will present you. But I can't see clearly
The lobes of your lungs. On a blue sponge
Are reflected threads of loess yellow. A man
Strikes ebony, water stains marked the floor
Craftsmen making ornaments for silver flower gardens
Do not know the early morning (turns out to be)
  kingfisher's harsh words.
A murder takes place in the holy temple on Jinfan Road
A priest plays the part of lawyer. Mouth
Swallows and spits leaves, like a plastic sack wrapping
  beef jerky
I do not know what attitude to take toward flower
  gardens

(VII)

I write down the two words "vulgar beauty,"
Transparent wooden comb, on the teeth
Are left tiny specks of blood red. Seem like
The fresh pulp of a pomegranate. Flames burn inside a
  sphere
Cold and gorgeous epidermis, only incantation
  corrodes
Tables and chairs, mirrors, birds feel pain on the skin.
Sensuous shoulder blade, turns away
The outline of the base, is in turn green, dark green,
  black and dark black.
Southern wood crack, revolving
Soaked with venom, can light the will-o'-the-wisp.
What else?
More vivid than eyes painted with vermilion
Inflated balloon, filled with milky white
Floating to the left side of the skull, a dagger
In its sheath, like a snake trapped in the grass
Exultant with the black pear's glow.

STORY HORSE · RED FIREWOOD

Riding provided me with a story. He was 3-6 months old. Speaking a beautiful language. His expression displayed an astonishing fluency and deductive ability:

He (I) was not asleep at the time. The huge horse was killed on the snow. Chopped to death on the snow. When the huge horse 马 fell to the ground, Riding (he) must have heard the last sound it uttered *"ma"* [horse]. The simplified Chinese character can be written as "马" (in orthodox characters "馬"). I (Riding, he) thought, the death of the huge horse, should have at least two settings. He made a gesture. The first one was (omitted). Then the second one was (omitted). The snow must have started falling between 8 and 9 o'clock. I was rather sober-minded before 8 o'clock, I wound up my watch, put it in a glass. At the same time, Riding recited the most important lines of poetry at that moment: "Something falls, it is snow. / And teeth glimmer in the sky" (Zhou Yaping). Therefore, it was 8 o'clock when it snowed. Now it is 9, the snow has just stopped.

The person who passed by, why did he (she) say: "*Love* is the reason, I will feel very satisfied." I (Riding, that is, he) did not understand at all. I was holding an ax — because of nervousness and threats, I went back and got this three-nine ax — , intending to chop him (her) up. But perhaps I couldn't. He (She) was only one fortieth big. I (He) was afraid.

But the watch spring was held in her (his) hand.

"I will feel very satisfied."

The cry of the watch spring is faint, revolving.

"Revenge is a reason."

Revenge!?

When he (I) turned around, the huge horse had already been piled into a stack. It tried its best to emphasize logic. But it was still confused. Riding (I, He) pointed out, it could only be a minor trick of structuralism.

Huge horse huge horse huge horse
The ax brandished a knife and beat it violently.
The red firewood gave out a sound that shook the
sky.
Huge horse huge horse huge horse
Huge horse is strength

YI CUN

A CRITICAL SKETCH ON "STORY HORSE · RED FIREWOOD"

I met Riding in Zhou Ya-ping's room.

I asked Riding: Who is Riding? He answered: I am Riding. But before the snow fell, Riding wrote sentences like these: "Go to bed, have a look at the huge horse's body. Riding. Polysemous. The alienated caught unprepared. Repeatedly coming on stage in changes, inverted, ambiguous. When Riding was me, I was not on the spot. I left Riding. I, Riding, these two terms make up each other."

Let me disclose the identity of Riding.

The story provided by Riding is not under his control. It is fragmentary. Incoherent. Interfered with by genius, forever beyond expectation. In addition, the sign of genius is interfered with by blunt nonsense, language is being put on stage. I went on: "Language revolution, overthrow the reformist qualities on paper, let them go mad."

"Story Horse · Red Firewood." A creative writerly text. "It can conceal the relationship between signifier and signified in a special way, disrupt and tighten, even abolish the signified, enter into a game with signifiers." This text injured some readers' confidence. This can be expressed as: I will die for faith in convention. h. End. "The huge horse was killed on the snow, and was chopped up on the snow." horse/3. I am aware, Zhou Ya-ping's ax cannot chop me up. She says to herself, I do not mean to be unfaithful, how come my personal relations with the gods fail to work out?

On the other hand, however, "Story Horse · Red Firewood" as an event is in process. First, the snow, has no ability not to fall at 8 o'clock sharp, at the same time, "The huge horse was killed on the snow, chopped to death on the snow." "The Chinese character can be written as "[illegible]"." "[illegible]" is horse reversed. (Note: here the signified vanishes in a flash.) The two settings of the death of the huge horse are revealed in this text as: "The first one was (omitted). Then the second one was (omitted)." Riding has recently disclosed to me the settings of the killing of the huge horse. Here is an excerpt from his letter: "At 8 o'clock, I was reciting the two lines of the poem that came to you without thinking, I had every reason to believe that Riding was creating a writerly text, it was almost an ode or a manifesto. Therefore the snow fell. Therefore language performed the killing of the huge horse. After that the second was (again omitted)." About the second, it does no harm to introduce it into this text, you are the second. Also Riding. It can be anyone at any moment. He (Riding. Zhou Ya-ping or you. That is, I) starts with the huge horse, "Love is crazy talk / I love you three times a day." As for the red firewood, it was cleared away before 8 o'clock.

ROLAND BARTHES.

(About the writerly text, reading is writing). "Huge horse is strength." The huge horse decided not to die. The shadow of the huge horse $(pvq)^2$ was chopped dead on the snow, but the huge horse went mad. The huge horse ran across its own body, leaving no room. The huge horse shouted: "You can manipulate me as you like, but I know you like the palm of my hand."

PARABLE

Beat the shepherd, the sheep scatter
(excerpt from Food)

Neither opening the wasteland, nor cultivating the land
Whose boy tends the sheep on the hillside
Take care that the crops in the fields not be eaten
Whose shepherd keeps silent
Looking at my sky
Dazed for a moment
I realize the whip leaning against the rock
Used to be a branch heavy with fruit
Leaves grew silently in its reminiscing
A crazy flock of sheep surrounded it
Over and over again
Chewing up the leaves

Pan Gu said: Let there be an ax, and there was an ax

A wound cannot grip an ax
This is the worsening news
The ax high above, startles an expanse of wild mountain trees
Their attempt to become lumber
Is exposed
By one word of the ax

9/3/89

[Note: Pan Gu created the heavens and the earth by splitting open the cosmic egg with his ax.]

HONG LIU

NUDE

Coming from an imaginary corridor
You are a nude in a black castle
Your hair is gaily-colored but you are at a loss
Mouth wide open with no trace of pretension
Oh, hello, hello,
People nod, greeting you
Red is no longer needed to express the powerful night sky
Stars like three hundred matches lying in an exquisite box
A baby's wail is heard from a distance
You don't know this is a pleasure in itself
If you pay a big enough tip
A taxi also can take you to your destination

ORIGINAL: CHINESE LANGUAGE-POETRY GROUP

VANISHING

What hangs on and refuses to go   only our soul
Strolling along the street getting stirred up by a quarrel
Modern-dressed men and women tread on my arms
A stench always rises out of moisture
In the eyes' expression your and my shadows
Rise and fall upon pouting lips
Here there is no sea
A desert oasis vanishes in the sun

Oh   beloved
White is a color
Certain to hear the heel's tearing while lying on it
Frail life floats out
This is just another start
The lucky escape of the world shines in a black hole
Like the unevenness of a bed sheet
Vanishing is the sacrifice of doing nothing
Like a knocked out window   cannot be replaced

TELEPATHY

I grew up in a city in water
Eastern enchantment waters me into perfection
The so-called refreshing rain
Troubles me I want
To open the gate of sunlight
Sweet words soften my life
Held hands sway with faith

Though blinking eyelids
Stop the blood from flowing
At the feet lies only an eyeball in the rain
A way of life is a cry for help
Anxiety and maturity make life changeable
The only memory is of God's caress
A feather-clothed body drills a hole into the heart
The fairy tales you have told all belong to me
Tightly embrace the house in the mirror
All time stands up straight
Welcomes you to push back the wordless tide

HUANG FAN

RECOLLECTION

Daytime rain. The rain's sturdiness, durability.
I pass under a tree, seeing rhythm.
Unfavorable conditions made me grow up, sturdy speech.
Before me a bird skims over the treetops,
Flashing is its solemn proposition.
At that time the rain submerged my ankles.
The drought-stricken rice paddies, already grave labor,
Trust in the rains sustains this vast plain.

Afterwards they bring beauty, freshness.
Rice stalks, I also see the temporary wound,
Step by step sweat that crowds around.
I walk under another tree,
Thinking of the invisible country and distress.
At that time like a bird I loved the sound of rain,
Until the rains force the wheat fields to come up differently.

ORIGINAL: CHINESE LANGUAGE-POETRY GROUP

THE DRAMA OF OUR GROWTH

Three people use salt to stride
Again using iron's example, toward wheat fields with heads hanging
Yearning for more than growth's good luck
Some kind of gentle beauty, again tradition shines red

Again some good luck's kindness
A succinct as well as swift abyss
Again some superfluous flowing
A changing of subjectivity, a change in the flash clock tower

Forever, the whole winter in dire straits and making concessions
Worthy of a blind molded injury
Choose a cavalry rifle, list complex expectations
At the consecrated zenith, remains of a touching trace

For 27 years possessing without discriminating the real from the fake
Accompanying music by the three's ex-Taoist priests
Until now an undiscovered paralysis
That's a kind of freedom that can bury you

INDICATOR

The design that comes from faith's childhood
Its critical shadow is returning to the city
Red light, The world's most beautiful voyage
Launches for the rewarding frontier
Unusual accent, Chinaman,
Break away from love, Nobody cares

Through one wound after another reaching to harmony
Avoid heroics, Never betray technique
One night of careless love produces responsibility, Worthless commodities
The flag rises to the height of recovery
Enriched sleep drops to the depths of the landscape

Resplendent birthrate, Acuteness,
Poverty, No one disappears, Many flowers bloom
Toward withering success, Such well-preserved
Success, Between symbol and expression
More prudence than forgiveness and love

XIAN MENG

WALKING THE HORSE IN THE SHADE OF A TREE

Lead the horse away
Tie it in the shade of a tree

Then sit down
Take off the straw hat
Lean against a green slab stone
Reclining
Looking at the sunshine
Sometimes bright
Sometimes dim

Over there the grassy slope is quiet
There is no one
A goat
Stands lazily
Over there the grass
Grows lushly

The horse tilts its head
Leaves rustle
Through the shadows of the leaves
See
You holding the straw hat
The wind blows
Lazily

Time passes quickly
In an instant
Summer has come
Wheat seedlings growing so green
Peasant women
Sturdy and pretty

Rest here
For a while
Then hurry on their way
Walking past the village
See women reaping wheat
Red-cheeked
Standing in the fields

Lead the horse away
Tie it in the shade of tree

ORIGINAL:

MANIFESTO of SPRING 1988

WE OBJECT to localist and ethnocentric — in a word, to nationalistic writings. Our writings are of the world (an open box): through writing, we hold conversation with contemporary art of global significance and with modern Western art in particular. We pay particular attention to the Chinese written character because we know: it will grant us the right to a firm individuality. Therefore, we are at the same time creating and developing a localist and ethnocentric, namely nationalistic *modernist* art.

When the poet's consciousness shifts to *language,* this is in fact the preparatory stage of modern artistic experiment. We think the first step of such experiment is: the written characters alone (the code of recording language) is the starting point, only in this way will the exploration of human spiritual phenomena and especially of individual phenomena be possible. Compared with spoken language, written characters are less polluted and pre-judged. We do not avoid the phrase "word games" which already has aroused great misunderstanding. We even like it. "Game" [*yóuxì*] is a word, connoting the profound, eerie spirit of art and philosophy. Because of our involvement, it constructs the only cross during the last decade of this century.

+

We say: "swim" [*yóu*], the horizontal line. Getting in touch with reality or linking with reality.

We say: "play" [*xì*], the vertical line. Comes from the heart or points directly to the human heart.

Nevertheless, all of this is related to the written characters, that is to say it is practiced within the possibilities the written characters offer. The intersection of these two hypothetical/imaginary/fictional lines is precisely our concrete and perceptible poetic activity.

This is a type of real dream	These two make up an antithesis,
This is a type of abstract matter	

Which is the "spot":

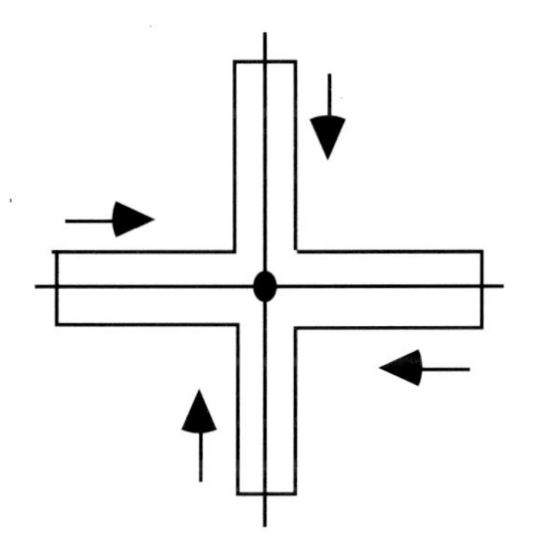

Our ideal poetry will put the art, which it abstracts from contemporary poetry, into the place of abstract poetry—

We invent it!

Written characters are the labyrinth of the poet's home. But poetry is by no means the movies where readers entertain themselves.

Change! Change! Change!

We are the poet who uttered the word in *Parable of the Palace!* With head cut off, we come to you again!!

Note:
Parable of the Palace relates that the Emperor showed a poet around the Imperial Palace, this was not only a palace, but also the entire universe. The poet recited a poem, this consisted of only one line or a single word, but also contained the whole palace, namely the entire universe. The Emperor became furious, killed the poet, hence all trace of the poem was lost.

The author of this parable [*yùyán*] is Borges.

We do not need allegory [*yù*], only words [*yán*]!

AFTERWORD

WITHIN the great aquarium of language the light refracts variously and can bounce by inclinations not previously observed. Some of the codes will unfold with merely adept connivance, others will swim vigorously into and by circulation inside their own medium. If you can imagine staff notation etched on the glass you can read off the scales, *da carpo* and mirror-folded. "The fish of writing melts into the face of the water" — thus the iconic boundary features declare, by difference and by movement of an intense register, shifts of focus that will skim and can turn about on the smallest coin. The colour force suffuses a diagram, there is a play within the box which says "play carefully" on the outside cover. Energy prevails by conversion about the axis of activity, the object-perimeter tingles with our hues, your readiness to jump ahead. This is a "world" all right, the rules for civil adherence percolate into a grammar made iconic by gaps and outbursts of intense writerly variance. The history of contradiction lies in the ground of the body image as a co-ordinate of written sound-play, so calibrated with signifying exchange that every part offers an assembly "in the swim."

I first met the kernel pair of the ORIGINAL collective near to the banks of the Imperial Canal in the eastern city of Suzhou, during the summer of 1991. We had intent discussions and readings in both directions. The exotic remoteness of that location at once bids to compose an allegory of displacement, which in turn demands a fully prepared resistance. Plants grow in the same way, upwards. People eat lunch, eye each other, words fly out of mouths. Does the subject-position bind to the life-world by a different syntax? Well, these poems and writings set out a composite text of investigation into such ponderables. Zhou Ya-ping's *Shadow* essay speaks of Wang Xu-bing's paintings, and this prolific oeuvre (which he showed me, again in Suzhou, in the summer of 1993) reveals the vigour of a remarkable astuteness, reckless and specific: "extreme abstraction should contain emotion and enthusiasm" — and perform also the trace of such containment, as these pictures do. This group of writers and artists and critic-theorists has devised by circulation and interchange an intense life of creative production, which this anthology demonstrates.

I find the combination of analysis and ardent obliquity in these writings very powerfully enabling. What cannot be resolved by working out ideas and pushing them forward can often be deployed into writing which already exceeds and tests its own devices, so that the interchange between modes is intensely energetic. The western reader also has some work to do, here. If oriental art and its solicited application is part of "our" imperialist iconography, then "their" sense of our art-world (renaissance, expressionist, surreal) fits obversely into a differently hegemonised frame of exterior possibility: not too much limp plum-blossom or spiritual pathos, but to hold in place a sense of explicit object-horizons, as a tacit intertext interleaved into daily life. There's still no free lunch, though anyone can write the word for it who can hold the pen.

Or the brush. This language of the written character is painted on to the paper, abstracted from the world-surface, whatever now is the more abbreviated practice. Its iconic deployment by stroke play and contexture makes a traffic with the eye worked by a different ground-plan. There is lexical transference and collocation, but also the sense of the occasion ramifies within the stroke-field itself: not by symbolism or imitation or assigned convention but by homologies intricately linked to the affective diagrams of social consciousness and activity. The writing in this collection resides and disports itself very intently within the field of language-presence and language-process. The routine wiring of the circuit to external devices has traditionally proceeded by what's described here as "allegory" and "parable," and by such old chestnuts as "the music of poetry" (not to mention "direct treatment of the thing"). Of course, anti-allegory and beast fable are sarcastic examples of language trapped within, or artfully escaping from, the demands of a forced outcome, reminding the reader how such transposed devices have traditionally adopted the constraints blocking off other options. But the tail does not wag the dog, even when it barks all night.

To prevent the leakage of energy into pre-determined frames of control, several ancient Chinese traditions of wit, skepticism and cantilevered invention have been brought into newly explored relations with western iconography and the art-slogans of selfhood. Not only the ellipsis of lyric epigram but also the exuberance of the *fu* or rhyme-prose join up with the frequently deflected currents of Chinese poetic experiment in the twentieth century; here, to centralise the contingent via its force for total candour, or "to drive out all lyricism" by rapid cross-talk and studious hooliganism. Or indeed, both at once. All this is likewise also decoy manoeuvre, reclaiming the margins by transferring their negligence back into spirited invention. There is a running stream half-visible alongside, but for those not tuned into these features the inter-play of this writing in its English form can still provoke analogous recognitions. "The world is small" opined Confucius, standing on top of Mount Snowdon and chewing a banana. The English text can disclose to the English reader one truly essential feature: this writing moves about its native element with a good deal of unusual compression and exhilaration but it is not *exotic.* This is the language of a world, not a fancied ping-pong utopia, and its living currency is what makes abstraction and invention into such considered forms of daring. Much is not said and much has been folded back into the components of character-writing, by intense punning and lexical wit and adoptive idiomatics; but the sound-plays of counter-active ceremonial fizz and lurk and conduct intellectual experiments right up on the surface of this swirl of signification. The thought-play within the colour registers and utterance forms sets out vividness as an exploratory instrument.

I put up these thoughts and comments myself, because I have an extremely strong confidence in these translations. A very extended and focused labour of attention has attended their coming-to-be. How to get inside the detail of the play and the run of a local *progression d'effet* has had to be balanced with how to maintain an appearance of naturalism that won't deceive the close attention of a reader for a moment longer than is useful. I think these versions show a sustained brilliance, of intelligent, patient alertness and formal energy, mediated through layers of detailed discussion and comparison with native speakers so as almost completely to submerge this process of consultation beneath the texture of performance and its prosodic exactness. No translation will exhaust its originals, even though it may tire them out; but there are many forms of connivance with tacit sideways compromise, and the committed good faith of Jeff Twitchell's accomplishment gives the non-Chinese-speaker an altogether fair chance of finding in the ensemble of this collection an interaction that is specific and hyper-active. At one stage we thought to include some of the Chinese text, maybe even brush-written, but the ORIGINALS themselves have countered this idea, because it would suggest exoticism or extraneous willow-pattern ornament; to them, *we* are the exotics, with our credit-card view of the speech act.

Angus Graham wrote of the philosopher Zhuang-zi (c.320 B.C.) that "in one of his many aspects he is himself a true sophist, fascinated by the subversion of received opinions and intoxicated by the plunge which imperils rationality in the course of discovering its possibilities. He is also, even in the flow of reason itself, a poet who changes course as new insights explode, elliptical even when most logical" (*Disputers of the Tao*). The roots of the ORIGINAL anthology are tangled in much contemporary contradiction which exerts a certain pressure; but they also run deeply into the ancient substrata and continuities of the language culture, and this too makes up a vigorous presence that I believe the close reader of the English version can draw energy from, and acute enjoyment.

— J.H. PRYNNE

Before the Flowers of Friendship Faded Friendship Faded: gertrude stein & georges hugnet

IN THE SUMMER of 1930 Gertrude Stein "translated" the French poet Georges Hugnet's *"Enfances."* It is difficult to call the poems Stein wrote translations as she does not preserve much of Hugnet's original text. Often small parts of *"Enfances"* appear, at times a word or an image, but Stein made no effort to preserve line breaks or length or content. Instead of translating *"Enfances,"* Stein poaches from it, rewrites what she has stolen with little concern for Hugnet's intents. It is this interactive model of reader/translator that makes "Poem Pritten on Pfances of Georges Hugnet" an important work in Stein's oeuvre. Stein actively opposes translation's normative impulse to make another culture discernible and digestible; while Hugnet's poems are often concerned with heterosexual sex, male genitalia, and onanism, these are all absent in Stein's poems. Stein wrote in a letter to Hugnet quoted by their mutual friend Virgil Thomson, "The translation is more like a reflection, a true reflection."

After reading Stein's versions, Hugnet wrote to Thomson, "Really I have friends too strong for me," but nonetheless wrote to Stein: "Admirable Gertrude, what joy you give me in my solitude of sand and rock! I laugh at the sea which breaks out into white laughter all along the shore. This isn't a translation, it is something else, it is better. I more than like this reflection, I dream of it and I admire it. And you return to me hundred-fold the pleasure that I was able to offer you. . . ." The poems were first published, side by side as they appear below, in the American journal *Pagany,* and were also to be published in Paris as a lavish edition overseen by Hugnet with illustrations by Picasso, Marcoussis, Tcheltitcheff, and Tonny.

Gertrude Stein and Georges Hugnet in Bilignin, c. 1930

But in December 1930, Stein saw a subscription page for the proposed Paris edition and protested the fact that Hugnet's name appeared first, followed by the title *"Enfances"* and then beneath this in smaller letters the words *"suivi par la traduction de Gertrude Stein."* Stein complained about the size of the type and suggested the words "adaptation" or "transposition" instead of *"traduction."* But Hugnet would agree only to the words "free translation." This was not good enough for Stein and she withdrew her text from the publisher and the illustrated book never appeared. Stein also wired *Pagany* in an attempt to stop the face to face publication but was only able to add the title "Poem Pritten on Pfances of Georges Hugnet" to her poems. *Pagany* is the only place these poems have appeared together until now. A version of Hugnet's *"Enfances"* was published as a book in 1933 by Editions Cahiers d'Art. Alice Toklas published "Poem Pritten on Pfances of Georges Hugnet" in the Plain Edition series under the title *Before the Flowers of Friendship Faded Friendship Faded: Written on a Poem by Georges Hugnet.* The title is supposedly something Toklas overheard one woman saying to another over lunch.

While "Poem Pritten on Pfances of Georges Hugnet" has gone mainly unnoticed and when noticed often disliked (Richard Bridgman calls them a "creative abortion" and Marianne DeKoven writes that they are "just plain silly" and also argues that these poems "fail to offer anything to a reader"), this work initiates Stein's prolific period of the 1930's. These years, as Ulla Dydo has often pointed out, are crucial ones for the radical Stein. The poems written during this period are undeniably dense, abstract, and lacking in some of the more sing-song lyrical qualities that defined Stein's work before 1930. Instead the work of this period tends to utilize an iambic-esque line with Shakespearian undertones and romantic imagery. This form reaches its fruition in *Stanzas in Meditation.*

Poems based on a reading (or a rereading) of another text are able to generate a number of questions which a work that hides its own readings, or insists that its reader should be reading it as translation, can at best approach only fleetingly. Stein's personalization of her reading of Hugnet's poem demonstrates the manner in which, as Proust writes in an often quoted passage from *Past Recaptured,* "In reality, every reader is, while he is reading, the reader of his own self. The writer's work is merely a kind of optical instrument which he offers to the reader to enable him to discern what, without his book, he would perhaps have never perceived himself." Moments like these, in which the writer/translator is also reader, are radical ones. Such moments, for example, allowed Stein to pursue her own political, cultural agenda and to abandon the poems' heterosexism and replace it with her relationship with Toklas. As she writes, "I love my love with an a/Because she is a queen."

Stein's final lines, "By all of it in case/Of my name./What is my name./That is the game," are ironic in light of the fight over the size of the names on the subscription form. But the irony is doubled by the way they speak to an authorial confusion. Through the game of reading to translate and write a whole new series of poems off Hugnet's work, the name becomes confused. This is the way of writing and reading for Stein. While never negligent in areas of public relations (as her concern over the size of her name demonstrates), authorship is still repeatedly confused in Stein's work. Emphasis throughout her work is on multiplicity. As she writes in "Poem Pritten": "It is whatever originally read read can be two words smoke can be all three."

Reproduced here are the versions of *"Enfances"* and "Poem Pritten on Pfances of Georges Hugnet" as they appeared in *Pagany.* When Toklas reprinted "Poem Pritten on Pfances of Georges Hugnet" as *Before the Flowers of Friendship Faded Friendship Faded,* a number of minor changes were introduced: some lines were merged, punctuation marks changed, and space added. There is one change of some importance. Stein added the lines, "George Hugnet/By Gertrude Stein" at the very end of the poem.

— JULIANA SPAHR

Enfances

Georges Hugnet

1

Enfances aux cent coins de ma mémoire
si ma mémoire est l'oeuvre de la passion,
enfances décimées par les nuits
si les nuits ne sont qu'une maladie du sommeil,
je vous poursuis avant de dormir, sans hâte.
Sans hâte, mais plié sous des tâches ingrates,
tête nue et transpirant du fièvre,
je vous mesure au trajet de la vie
et vos insoumissions, enfances, sont muettes,
enfances si l'enfance est ce silence
où gravement déjà s'installe la mort
et si ma main n'a pas retrouvé sa solitude,
et c'est avouer que je vous laisse libres
hors de mon destin que d'autres voulurent court,
à vos robes d'indienne, à vos plaisirs sanguins.

2

Enfance dans la laine
en dépit des semaines,
enfance dans la rue
sans adieu et sans mal
et jouant avec le hasard,
au rire des cotonniers
comparez vos corps nus,
enfance dans la cour
avec des oiseaux comme des chiens
annonçant les voleurs sans talent,
j'ai vécu cette enfance

Poem Pritten on Pfances of Georges Hugnet

Gertrude Stein

1

In the one hundred small places of myself my youth,
And myself in if it is the use of passion,
In this in it and in the nights alone
If in the next to night which is indeed not well
I follow you without it having slept and went.
Without the pressure of a place with which to come unfolded folds are a pressure and an abusive stain
A head if uncovered can be as hot, as heated,
to please to take a distance to make life,
and if resisting, little, they have no thought,
a little one which was a little which was as all as still,
Or with or without fear or with it all,
And if in feeling all it will be placed alone beside
and it is with with which and not beside not beside may,
Outside with much which is without with me, and not an Indian shawl, which could it be but with my blood.

2

A little a little one all wooly or in wool
As if within or not in any week or as for weeks
A little one which makes a street no name
without it having come and went farewell
And not with laughing playing
Where they went they would or work
it is not that they look alike with which in up and down as chickens without dogs,
Coming to have no liking for a thief which is not left to have away,
To live like when
And very many things
Being with me with them

et tant d'autres encore,
ayant du sang mêlé de nord
et de midi, ici et là,
où je naquis et où je voyageai
et tous les noms sont là
au courant de l'invisible
et de ce que l'amour n'a pas brouillé

3
J'ai parlé de tant d'années
que la mémoire a ornées
de ce qu'inventèrent leurs complices.
Mes souliers n'étaient point usés
d'une course au soleil
dans les places où seules
les ombres des arbres prouvaient des arbres
qui ne cachaient pas du soleil.
Alors on criait et la main alors
réfléchissait et se sentait cruelle.
Je joue, je suis fort,
ma faim me donne raison.
L'amour déjà et ses dons
naissaient avec le sang.
J'ai battu mes pensées et les bois:
partout les filles trouvaient des prétextes
à ne rien passer sous silence,
des prétextes à lever leur jupe pour apprendre
et leur rire était donné au mauvais élève,
gagné par lui au temps du premier tabac.
Restait à prouver l'irrémédiable:
le visage masqué par l'inconnu, sans peur,
des heures elles restaient à genoux
devant les garçons déculottés

with which with me
whoever with and born
and went as well
Meant,
Five which are seen
And with it five more lent.
As much as not mixed up,
With love.

3
I often live with many months with years of which I think
and they as naturally think well of those
My littlest shoes which were not very much without that care left there
where I would like the heat
and very nearly find that trees have many little places that make shade.
which never went away when there was sun
In a way there were cries and it was felt to be the cruelest yet
I am very happy in my play
and I am very thirsty in hunger
Which is not what is always there with love
And after all when was I born.
I can touch wood and think
I can also see girls who were in finding
and they will laugh and say
And yes say so as yes as yes with woe
And now they with me think and love love that they told with hide and even
It is as if all fields would grow what do they grow, tobacco even so,
And they will not delight in having had,
Because after no fear and not afraid,
they have been having that they join as well,
And always it is pretty to see dogs.
It is no double to have more with when they met and in began who can.
There is very little to hide,
When there is everything beside

et les chiens ne s'en allaient pas.
Mon sexe se souvient ici
de ses premiers soupirs.

Rien à cacher,
je le dis à tous:
mon sexe a respiré
entre leurs mains moites.

4
Je suis dans mon droit,
on m'a trahi si fidèlement.
J'ai payé le prix des mots
et ce n'est pas un amusement.
Un oiseau, m'a-t-on dit,
a passé entre le ciel et moi.
On ne m'a pas parlé de toi,
j'ai cessé d'écouter, j'ai feint
de découvrir un incendie
dans la substance de ton oeil.
Les animaux sont beaux
parce qu'ils sont nus.
A l'intérieur aussi.

5
Tout ce que j'ai tu,
le partage de la conscience,
tout ce qui s'est dérobé,
le perpétuel et le visible,
et quelque adieu nocturne,
notre premier dialogue,
la croissance des graines,
tu n'avais rien d'autre au front
que le sable de la mémoire

And there is a well inside
In hands untied.

4
I follow as I can and this to do
With never vaguely that they went away
I have been left to bargain with myself
and I have come not to be pleased to see
They wish to watch the little bird
Who flew at which they look
They never mentioned me to it,
I stopped to listen well it is a pleasure to see a fire which does not inspire them to see me
I wish to look at dogs
Because they will be having with they wish
To have it look alike as when it does

5
Everything is best of all for you which is for me.
I like a half of which it is as much
Which never in alone is more than most
Because I easily can be repaid in difficulty of the hurry left
Between now not at all and after which began
It could be morning which it was at night
And little things do feed a little more than all
What was it that was meant by things as said
There is a difference between yet and well

au fil de l'eau où j'ai lavé
ma pensée et ainsi de suite,
à tes pieds l'histoire de la terre
et quelque chose de très rare
que je ne connaissais pas,
enfance prédite par la magnésie.

And very well and when there was as much which is as well as more
And it is very likely made away again
Very nearly as much as not before
Which is as better than to have it now
Which it is taken to make my blood thin.

6

Dénombrée l'éxigence,
dénommée la fallace,
les grands se sont trompés
en fondant une famille.

L'enfance est née de l'enfance
dans l'indifférence surmontée
et longuement vécue
sortira sa parole.

Quelque erreur insolite.

6

It is very likely counting it as well
Named not alas but they must lend it for
In welcome doubt which they need for deceit
They face a little more than most and made it.
They will be born in better than at least
with not at all relieved and left away a little said
Which is not with made not useless.
Unless is used with where like what.

7

Ai-je longtemps rapproché
de mon appétit
ces empereurs qui cachent
leur tendresse peinte?

Recouvert de mon sang
ces livres d'enfants fouettées?
Et tout ce plaisir avec feu
puis bien plus vite

avec une écolière sans devoir
ou les copiant sur l'ennui,
noire des taches de l'écriture
et blanche de percale,

7

A very long a little way
They have to have
In which array
They make it wring
Their tendering them this.
It is whatever originally read read can be two words smoke can be all three
And very much there were.
It is larger than around to think them little amiably
What is it said to incline learnt and places it as place
as which were more than the two made it do.
Remember not a color.
Every little boy has his own desk.

à cause de l'amour
qu'on joue sous les tables,
tapis jusqu'au sol,
par les après-midi sans mère.

8

Tu doutais de toi à compter les jours
qui te séparaient d'un ennui habitable
et tu te criais avant de courir:
j'ai ma tête et j'ai ma voie.
Il ne faut pas répondre à l'enfance.
Enfance, il y avait des mots et des présences
que tu n'osais pas t'avouer
et l'ombre t'accablait de ses malédictions.
Le soleil t'avait donné cette ombre
cette ombre pour aimer et pour te conquérir.
Tu chantes pour oublier cette conquête,
ton départ et celui des clartés nomades.
Mais alors, tu te couchais des semaines
en feignant d'être malade
et si l'on criait comme aux révolutions
tu étais sûre de ta fièvre puerpérale:
le doute s'installait en toi magnifiquement
avec l'amour.

8

Who leaves it to be left to like it less
which is to leave alone what they have left
They made it act as if to shout
Is when they make it come away and sit.
Nobody need say no nor yes.
They who had known or which was pressed as press
They might with thought come yet to think without
With which it is to like it with its shell,
A shell has hold of what is not withheld
It is just as well not to be well as well
Nevertheless
As when it is in short and long and pleasure
It is a little thing to ask to wait
It is in any kind of many chances
They like it best with all its under weight
And will they miss it when they meet its frame,
A frame is such that hours are made by sitting
Rest it in little pieces
They like it to be held to have and hold
Believe me it is not for pleasure that I do it.

9

Me voici lourd de circonstances,
profond dans mes appétits
et mon intelligence est animale.
J'avais compris d'une façon ou d'une autre
qu'on pût rester des heures devant l'amour.
Les promenades devant le dernier train

9

Look at me now and here I am
And with it all it is not preparation,
They make it never breathless without breath
And sometimes in a little while they wait.
Without its leaving.
It is mine to sit and carefully to be thought thorough

n'empêchaient pas d'aimer et davantage.
L'enfance et l'enfance de la poitrine,
les belettes en parlent entre elles.
Je ne capitule pas devant vos avantages,
j'appelle et ma voix va droit,
où tu m'entends, m'entends-tu?
J'ai quitté ma chemise ancienne
et nu devant mon âge je sais,
je sais que tu m'entends
comme tu dois m'entendre, avec joie,
parce que je parle de ma solitude
et de ma solitude à la tienne
et qu'entre l'une et l'autre de ces cités infaillibles
il y a une houle qui va et qui vient,
tout ce que le parole désenchante.
Devant témoin je parlerai de cela
et de ceci qui me tient au mouillage
malgré le vent, les courants et la marée.
Mon tangon est ta pensée,
ta pensée un manie étrangère à la séduction.
J'ouvre de mes audaces brûlées
la pulpe du silence, cent fois par nuit,
je contourne l'édifice de notre dédain
et j'entre par la porte de l'accident.

Let it be said that it is said let me alone,
You alone have a way to think and swim,
Leave it as well
And noises have no other.
It is in their refrain that they sing me.
It just can happen so.

10

Enfance apprise dans les livres d'aventures,
enfance en but au miracle des mécaniques,
enfance sans lecture des mauvais livres,
enfance sans rêve et préférant la vie
où tu mettais ta lumière d'anarchie,
enfance montée dans l'amour des batailles
et dans la haine des règles et des soldats,
enfance silencieuse dont la rébellion

10

Did he hear it when it was as said
And did he sing it when he sang a song
And did he like it when it was not said
And did he make it when he went along
There is a little doubt without which meant
That he did go that he went that he was not sent,
Who could send whom
Which went which way where

si blanche s'augmentait de blancs calculs,
enfance qui complotais un théâtre
où jouait la peine de mort son rôle
de gestes graves appris par la révolte,
enfance qui contenais la beauté des déserteurs,
enfance que dire de plus de ton enfance,
sous le front des inductions, ferme,
je te vis en moi et n'ai point changé
et je puis médire de mon angoisse,
maudire toutes les tares du désespoir.
Ma poitrine si blanche contre le cauchemar
et cette inégalité font que je puis vivre.

It is alike that they say that this is so
In any little while more may be most
Most may be most and best may be most best
It is at once a very little while
That they eat more when many are more there
Like it alike
Every little while they twitch and snore
It is a hope of eating all alike
That makes them grow
And so say so.

II

Voici que la maladie me donne une voix plus forte:
je suis malade, je suis grand: on m'a volé,
tout le monde est là et je suis en colère,
les splendeurs de la maladie battent contre mes côtes.
Mes bras ont bruni et l'enfance sent la viande.
Dans une ville lointaine ma tête solitaire,
par delà les murs ma voix qui frappe,
au-dessus de ma tête mon bras veineux,
mes amis furent jugés au tribunal de l'enfance.
L'indifférence des victimes pèse sur l'injustice
et celles qu'on n'exécute pas nous méprisent.
Mais la maladie me rend invulnérable,
lâchement j'aurais pu rire ou me tuer moi-même.
J'ai appelé les noms, puis à bout de coeur
j'ai craché sur le reste ne valant pas ma violence,
sûr alors d'avoir de droit de parler et de vivre,
le droit d'être dans mon tort par plaisir,
comme la peste et la famine.

II

Here once in a while she says he says
When it is well it is not more than ill
He says we say she says
When it is very well it is not more than still it is not more than ill
And all he says it is and all and very well and very much that was of very ill.
And anyway who was as strong as very strong with all and come along,
It is a height which makes it best to come to be a matter that they had
Alike in not no end of very well and in divide with better than the most,
And very well who knows of very well and best and most and not as well as ill.
It could be made as curly as they lie which when they think with me
Who is with me that is not why they went to be just now.
Just now can be well said.

In imitation there is no more sign than if I had not been without my filling it with absence made in choosing extra bright.

I do mind him, I do mind them I do mind her,
Which was the same as made it best for me for her for them.

Any leaf is more annoying than a tree when this you see see me she said of me of three of two of me.

And then I went to think of me of which of one of two of one of three of which of me I went to be away of three of two of one of me.

Any pleasure leads to me and I lead them away away from pleasure and from me.

12

Ma faim est large, mon appétit démesuré.
Je peux parler longtemps sans médire
mais tout me blesse et je sais haïr.
Ce pays que je vois pour la première fois
à ma timidité confie les soins du voyage,
tout ce qu'une absence crée d'incertitude,
tout ce que la surprise a gagné sur l'amour,
et c'est si haut que je pense à mon orgueil
qu'aucun regret de mes humiliations subies pour toi
n'exerce mon enfance à redouter la nuit,
la nuit et ces dons que tu m'as faits,
ces dons où se tatoua ton indifférence
sous la forme et le chant d'un regard particulier.
Enfance, je te nomme au centre du monde,
au centre de mon coeur tu te nommes toi-même,
tu te nommes la course à l'exemple de ma faim,
enfance homicide à l'exemple de ma faim.

12

I am very hungry when I drink,
I need to leave it when I have it held.

They will be white with which they know they see, that darker makes it be a color white for me, white is not shown when I am dark indeed with red despair who comes who has to care that they will let me a little lie like now I like to lie I like to live I like to die I like to lie and live and die and live and die and by and by I like to live and die and by and by they need to sew, the difference is that sewing makes it bleed and such with them in all the way of seed and seeding and repine and they will which is mine and not all mine who can be thought curious of this of all of that made it and come lead it and done weigh it and mourn and sit upon it know it for ripeness without deserting all of it of which without which it has not been born. Oh no not to be thirsty with the thirst of hunger not alone to know that they plainly and ate or wishes. Any little one will kill himself for milk.

13

L'imprudence a dérangé les simples,
déjoué les mesures de la honte.
L'enfance se décrit et se plaît
dans les maisons de bois où dort le charbon,
derrière les palissades dont on fait les bateaux.
Du doigt elle invente l'équilibre du repos,
l'orgueil du regard avec de frais contrastes
et nourrit son plaisir du repos des marées,
quand la mémoire file au plus près du vent,
ce sont les souvenirs d'un voyage en projet.
Ailleurs s'en va l'enfance et la table vacante

13

Known or not known to follow or not follow or not lead.
It is all oak when known as not a tree,
It is all best of all as well as always gone when always sent

In all a lent for all when grass is dried and grass can dry when all have gone away and come back then to stay.

Who might it be that they can see that candied is a brush that bothers me.

Any way come any way go any way stay any way show any way show me.

They ask are peas in one beets in another one beans in another one,

They follow yes beets are in one peas are in one beans are in one.

They hear without a letter which they love, they love above they sit and when they sit they stare.

So when a little one has more and any one has more and who has more who has more

de l'eau, du sel et du pain reste embarrassée
et des artichauts et du lard, du fromage et des abricots.
Elle bâtit sa maison sur l'heure de nos mots,
se prête au jeu des phrases où jeune l'oubli,
où tournent les prisonniers et les esclaves du hasard,
tandis que s'exilent l'inconstance et la perfidie.

when there can be heard enough and not enough of where.
Who has more where.

14

Que me disent amour et ses tourelles?
J'ai perdu la plus belle en ouvrant la main,
en changeant de pas j'ai trompé le silencieuse,
rira l'éternelle en tuant la plus belle,
la morte a su garder son domaine,
en refermant les bras j'ai tué l'éternelle,
l'enfance a renié, renié la souveraine
et c'est ainsi que vont les semaines.

14

It could be seen very nicely
That doves have each a heart.
Each one is always seeing that they could not be apart,
A little lake makes fountains
And fountains have no flow,
And a dove has need of flying
And water can be low,
Let me go.
Any week is what they seek
When they have to halve a beak.
I like a painting on a wall of doves
And what do they do.
They have hearts
They are apart
Little doves are winsome
But not when they are little and left.

15

De quelle couronne légère
fleurir l'adultère?
Jamais les jours, jamais les nuits
n'ont donné de preuves à la terre.
J'aurais résolu le problème,
en saurais-je plus de moi-même?
J'ai faim et soif à vie,
à vie purge ta peine,
en pure perte.

15

It is always just as well
That there is a better bell
Than that with which a half is a whole
Than that with which a south is a pole
Than that with which they went away to stay
Than that with which after any way,
Needed to be gay to-day.

16

La louange a choisi parmi vos corps ensemble
la méthode qui rectifie vos brusques chagrins
et toutes celles, enfances, toutes celles qui sont mortes
portent un ruban clair et la manie de la danse.
L'onaniste se souviendra-t-il de cette fille en deuil
drapée d'un deuil si limpide et qui l'excitait tant
après les robes soulevées en visite, en secret
et qu'il vit pâlir devant une image obscène.
Chaque jour, elle pâlit davantage, chaque visite,
jusqu'à mourir à l'ombre sure le jeune homme nu.
Dormir où tu dors, Angélina, si Angélina
que le bain réveille au milieu de son parcours
ton collier de sommeil et l'infidèle pensée
d'où ta solitude descend vers nous de si loin,
comme tu dors, Patricia, dois-je le dire, Patricia,
dont l'obscurité recule à chaque outrage,
au mépris des rêves, c'est dormir avec soin
sur ton jeune amour solitaire et sans vêtement,
où d'autres ne verraient que de l'herbe.

16

Any little while is longer any little while is shorter any little while is better any little while for me when this you see then think of me.

It is very sad that it is very bad that badly and sadly and mourn and shorn and torn and thorn and best and most and at least and all and better than to call if you call you sleep and if you sleep you must and if you must you shall and if you shall when then when is it then that Angelina she can see it make it be that it is all that it can have it color color white white is for black what green which is a hope is for a yellow which can be very sweet and it is likely that a long tender not as much as most need names to make a cake or dance or loss or next or sweetening without sugar in a cell or most unlikely with it privately who makes it be called practice that they came. They come thank you they come. Any little grass is famous to be grass grass green and red blue and all out but you.

17

Sans sortir de l'enfance tu as vingt-trois ans
et tu traverses une rivière sans penser à moi.
Si tu dormais en vérité, quitterais-tu si vite
cette tête et ce bras lancés contre ton mensonge?
Et me voici sur ta table au secret de mon malheur
parce que je ne puis croire, je ne puis croire à tes robes
et parce que je n'ai pas menti décidément
et que tu pars pour longtemps sur un fleuve qui s'éloigne.
Nous aurons ensemble croisé dans des mers réelles
et ton absence c'est l'alignement des feux verts.

17

He is the exact age he tells you

He is not twenty-two, he is twenty-three and when this you see remember me.

Any yet what is it that he can see.

He can see veritably three, all three which is to be certainly. And then.

He tells of oceans which are there and little lakes as well he sings it lightly with his voice and thinks he had to shout and not at all with oceans near and not at all at all, he thinks he is he will he does he knows he was he knows he was he will he has he is he does

J'ai fait semblant de dormir à voir ma tête,
mais chantait le chant que tu aimais chanter
et c'était bien ta tête qui dormait, d'un oeil,
sourde à tous les mots et c'étaient bien les mots
que chantaient ce chant, ta tête et ton sommeil.
Et me voici sorti de l'ombre, vêtu comme d'habitude,
vêtu couleur de légumes et j'aime ce chant
que je n'aurais pas dû connaître dans ma tête
si ta téte était restée sur l'autre versant.

and now and when is it to be to settle without sillily to be without without with doubt let me. So he says. It is easy to put heads together really. Head to head it is easily done and easily said head to head in bed.

18
Quand je dors, c'est merveille:
le sommeil sort de mon angoisse,
ce que je hais le mieux en moi-même,
et l'amour et sa fatigue font dormir.

18

When I sleep I sleep and do not dream because it is as well that I am what I seem when I am in my bed and dream.

19
Si je parle de vous,
nus entre mes repas,
jeux des vêtements
ou villes que ne touchent
ni les éponges ni les cargos,
maisons détruites par la vie,
objets à portée du front,
crimes, cris des coqs au pôle,
nourritures trop faibles pour l'appétit,
c'est que vous êtes mes familiers
et les familiers de l'enfance,
enfance à la bouche laiteuse.
En un mot les mois s'éveillent
et la surface candie de l'averse.
La balle a franchi le bois
et blessé l'enfance à genoux.
Les chants éclatèrent contrairement

19

It was with him that he was little tall and old and just as young as when begun by seeming soldiers young and bold and with a little change in place who hopes that women are a race will they be thin will they like fat does milk does hope does age does that no one can think when all have thought that they will think but have not bought no without oceans who hears wheat do they like fish think well of meat it is without without a change that they like this they have it here it is with much that left by him he is within within within actually how many hear actually what age is here actually they are with hope actually they might be bespoke believe me it is not for pleasure that I do it. They often have too much rain as well as too much sun.

They will not be won.
One might be one.
Might one be one.

et mille mains rougirent
pour écrire au tumulte.
Après la pluie, unique sentinelle,
sans mot d'ordre le soleil
s'il brûla mon corps au fond,
fit de ma pensée une brûlure.
J'ignorais en passant mon temps
près de toi et de ton enfance, enfance,
les amers plaisirs du plaisir
et ton enfance, cette femme,
cette femme comme une femme
et pas plus et pas moins,
comme une femme et c'est tout
et c'est davantage qu'une fontaine,
plus que la mer, plus et plus,
alors j'ai pris de l'herbe et de l'herbe
sur mon dos et sur mon ventre
et partout sur tes traces:
l'heure brûlait au centre de l'heure,
l'éveil passait, dépassait
le bout de notre tête.

20
Ma maison de bois a perdu son profil
au profit du tien. Si j'en tenais rancune
au vent qui l'emmène, serais-tu celle
que nomment les mois au coeur des horoscopes?
Et je serais moins encore cet arbre dont ton repos
prit la fourche principale pour deux bras vivants
et cette tête bouclée sans avenir et sans pardon
pour mon imagination dont la fourche est la foudre,
parce que la masturbation m'habille de tes robes
et me pousse vers toi, vers toi et le travail.

20
A little house is always held
By a little ball which is always held,
By a little hay which is always held
By a little house which is always held,
A house and a tree a little house and a large tree,
And a little house not for them and a large tree.
And after all fifteen are older than one two three.

It is useful that no one is barred from looking out of a house to see a tree even when there is a tree to see. She made it mentioned when she was not there and so was he.

21

Au hasard des édredons rouges
j'use mon corps et ma vie,
mon enfance absente à la canicule.

21

He likes that felt is made of beaver and cotton made of trees and feathers made of birds and red as well. He likes it.

22

J'aime t'avoir comme une mauvaise habitude
quand nous sommes couchés dans ta chambre.

22

He likes to be with her so he says does he like to be with her so he says.

23

Ou es-tu, si loin et si près,
que je vois avec peine
l'enfance et ses manies
et qu'un même rire
devient notre sillage
et qu'une même tristesse
nous dit de même
que l'eau s'éloigne de nos collines.
Et ton écriture s'efface
sur ma poitrine lavée.
Le plaisir mourut en chemin
d'un climat à un autre
et son ombre ne bouge plus.
J'avais tout paré pour la vie
et mon appareillage, il est vrai,
fut loin de tous et sans ironie.

23

Every one which is why they will they will be will he will he be for her for her to come with him with when he went he went and came and any little name is shame as such tattoo. Any little ball is made a net and any little net is made for mine and any little mine that any have will always violate the hope of this which they wore as they lose. It is a welcome, nobody knows a circumstance is with whatever water wishes now. It is pleasant that without a hose no water is drawn. No water is drawn pleasantly without a hose. Doublet and hose not at all water and hose not at all any not at all. Not at all. Either not at all by not at all with me. When this you do not hear and do not see believe me.

24

Enfance, qui t'endormais pour ne pas perdre ton temps,
je t'ai apprise au premier cinéma.
Je te tiens par la main et tu caches sous ta tête
cet éclat de mon diadème, ce que fut ma conscience,
mais ce n'est pas de cela qu'il s'agit ni d'oubli
ni de souvenirs, il s'agit de ce mot retrouvé,

24

They were easily left alone they were as easily left alone they were as easily left alone with them. Which makes mistakes mistakes which are mistakes who mistakes mistakes let them see the seal what is the difference between seal and school what is the difference between school and singing school and seeing school and leaving school and sitting in a school. They know the difference when they

de ce geste si futile qui font que les souvenirs
sont morts, morts et sans lendemain
et qui font que la vie vous tient par la main
et ne cache rien à ceux qu'elle oublie,
même à ceux qu'elle oublie.

25

J'ai incendié ma vie.
De ses forêts rougies
sortaient des animaux sauvages.
Ma confiance a puisé sa force
de bâtir, en vous, sources marines,
et celle de vivre avec mes ongles
cet amour si fragile né d'un fouet,
cette âme surprise par les drogues,
cette aventure où j'ai laissé
du sang pour créer ma vie.
Sur ton front sans humeur
tes faveurs ont écrit mon front
et ton visage s'est levé
sur un mur plus neuf
où mon sang a nommé tes avantages.
Ai-je gagné sur ton malheur
cet air de forêt qu'a ma chambre vide
et vide aussi de tes branches.
Quand le vent a soufflé
au vasistas ta distraction,
j'ai mesuré dans la nuit solide
la distance des ports,
au compas la distance,
au compas le trajet magnifique,
au compas mon domaine.
Quelquefois avançait ta main

see the screen which is why leaves are dry when rain is thin and appetising which can be when they win. They win a little exercise in win. Win and win. Perhaps with happens to be thin. It is not easy to be led by them. Not easy to be led and led and led to no brim. In doubt not with them. Not in doubt not with them. Leave it to me to know three from three and they did leave it to him.

25

It is easy to mingle sails with steam oil with coal water with air, it is easy to mingle everywhere and to leave single everywhere water and air oil and coal butter and a share it is a share to ask them where and in a little they will have it there they like it there they had it to prepare and to be a comfort to them without care. It is a need to see without a glare of having it come in does it come in and where. They like a little dog to be afraid to have a nightingale be told a chicken is afraid and it is true he is she is and where whenever there is a hawk up in the air. Like that. It makes anybody think of sail-boats.

hors de ta manche trouée
et tes doigts sans fatigue
roulaient les cordages, les cordages,
avec la volunté du navigateur.

26

Embarquons, partons aux Indes,
vanille, vanille,
toutes les nourritures se valent.
Gabrielle, trio de neige,
Eugénie, Yvonne, l'ordre
a changé son courant d'amour,
l'ordre des mots dans ta bouche,
enfance réveillée par mes désordres.
Sous la pluie sérieuse
quand tournait le vent,
quant remontait le vent
du phare au rocher de la Jument,
en cachant ta tête
tu prenais ce vent
pour ma pensée et sans mal
tu tendais ton bras
vers la croisée où mon absence
a mis le silence au rang de la lumière,
ton absence dans ma solitude,
ce don que la lumière avait fait à ma mémoire.

26

Little by little two go if two go three go if three go four go if four go they go. It is known as does he go he goes if they go they go and they know they know best and most of whether he will go. He is to go. They will not have vanilla and say so. To go Jenny go, Ivy go Gaby go any come and go is go and come and go and leave to go. Who has to hold it while they go who has to who has had it held and have them come to go. He went and came and had to go. No one has had to say he had to go come here to go go there to go go go to come to come to go to go and come and go.

27

J'ai vieilli en une veille,
trois veilles et j'ai perdu,
j'ai perdu trois têtes et je n'y reconnais
trois têtes et je n'y reconnais
plus la mienne.
Je te retrouve, enfance,

27

In a little while they smile in a little while and one two three they smile they smile a while in a little while a little smile with which to smile a while and when they like to be as once in a while it is about the time with which in which to smile. He can smile and any smile is when to smile. It is to show that now that he can know and if to smile it is to smile and smile that he can know and any

je te tutoie, enfance,
mais parler de toi
c'est parler d'elle et de notre pacte
et je te mêle à nos plaisirs adultes
où jamais tu ne quittais nos épreuves.
Je rétablis ta présence sans mémoire
à l'aide de mes mains et devant ton absence.
L'odeur de l'amour est une odeur de jour,
de jour en jour une odeur d'herbe en plein jour,
le mouvement de ta tête sur mon ventre
aidait la naissance de la pensée,
l'extraordinaire mélange du feu et de l'eau
après l'immobile regard sous le front.
Ma pensée c'est une fontaine qui s'achève en fontaine.

28

Le chemin finit par un gros paysage
et ta jalousie sous un chapeau sans bord.
Et ma voix est une feuille
au fur et à mesure de ton avenir,
je dors en écrivant et grandi de ton ombre
parce que je n'ai pas demandé de preuves à ton amour,
je serre dans mes bras ton épithète.

29

J'ai mis un costume d'été
pour paraître gai.
Et le roi s'était avancé
pour dire sa pensée.
La reine prenait son bain
et ne disait rien.
L'enfance avait pris la reine
et lui disait sa peine.
Le roi sur la terrasse,
la reine dans le palais d'en face,

making it be ready there for them to see to change a smile to change a smile into a stare and very likely more than if they care he can care does and will and not to have to care and this is made with and without a need to carry horses horses without sails sails have an ocean sometimes just the land but to believe to have relief in them who can share horses sails and little less a very little less and they like them. It does it hope. They come they see they sew and always with it a hope is for more not more than yesterday but more to-day more to-day more to say more to-day. A little long and birds can drink with beaks and chickens do and horses drink and sails and even all.

28

A clock in the eye ticks in the eye a clock ticks in the eye.

A number with that and large as a hat which makes rims think quicker than I.

A clock in the eye ticks in the eye a clock ticks ticks in the eye.

29

I love my love with a v
Because it is like that
I love myself with a b
Because I am beside that
A king.
I love my love with an a
Because she is a queen
I love my love and a a is the best of them.
Think well and be a king,

et personne ne savait
ce qui se passait,
mais le roi était en gris clair
et la reine pleurait
pour un crime de l'enfance.

Think more and think again
I love my love with a dress and a hat
I love my love and not with this or with that
I love my love with a y because she is my bride
I love her with a d because she is my love beside
Thank you for being there
Nobody has to care
Thank you be being here
Because you are not there.
And with and without me which is and without she she can be late and then and how and all around we think and found that it is time to cry she and I.

30

Enfances aux quatre coins du monde,
dans cette ville où l'on me fit vivre,
parti avec une valise à ma taille, à la mer,
et ignorant le langage des enfants,
renaissez-vous au présent de ce coeur
qu'une chanson a mis à l'ouvrage.
Imaginez-vous les honneurs de la forêt
et cette longue promenade de la forêt
et ce rire blanc dans son infirmerie.
Vos manies ont distrait mes habitudes,
celles qui sont relevées à chaque quart de nuit,
du parcours de la vie et du paysage,
des soupçons de maladie que le jour dédaigne,
mais toi, mon enfance que je prénomme,
toi que je nomme ma salubrité,
à choisir tes préjugés tu devins femme
et si je fus ton préjugé sans contrôle,
toutes les fleurs sont à mon nom
dans tes bras et autour des maisons.
La musique naquit de nos conventions,

30

There are a few here now and the rest can follow a cow,
The rest can follow now there are a few here now.
They are all all here now the rest can follow a cow
And mushrooms on a hill and anything else until.
They can see and sink and swim with now and then a brim.
A brim to a hat
What is that,
Anyway in the house they say
Anyway any day
Anyway every day
Anyway outside as they may
Think and swim with hearing him,
Love and song not any song a song is always then too long to just sit there and sing
Sing song is a song
When sing and sung
Is just the same as now among
Among them,
They are very well placed to be seated and sought
They are very well placed to be cheated and bought

un décor que l'enfance imposait à l'enfance,
un manque à notre goût pour le silence
et de mémoire je chante ta gymnastique.
Enfances, imaginez-vous les honneurs de la forêt
et ce vent palmé qui crée une apologie.

And a bouquet makes a woods
A hat makes a man
And any little more is better than
The one.
And so a boat a goat and wood
And so a loaf which is not said to be just bread
Who can be made to think and die
And any one can come and cry and sing.
Which made butter look yellow
And a hope be relieved
By all of it in case
Of my name.
What is my name.
That is the game

BERLIN(plus) PORTFOLIO

translated by Rosmarie Waldrop

BERLIN, 1993. One of the first books I noticed was *Poem of the Reunited Landscape* by Jürgen Becker. It was published in 1988, it is true, just *before* the "Wende," the "turn," as Germans call the cluster of events comprising the collapse of the GDR and other Communist governments, and the reunification of Germany. In it, the speaker recalls a conversation with an East German:

> . . . you asked, as
> I got a little carried away: "What can be
> reunited . . . landscapes perhaps? " . . . why
> not, I thought, but you, if I understood correctly,
> meant the *difference,* the incompatibility
> in the history of the two systems?

The implied scepticism seems borne out three years after reunification: jobs have become scarce, bills impossible to pay, frustration is endemic, the violence against foreigners (and the sluggish police/courts) frightening.

Wessies groan at the price of bailing out the East, Ossies feel stung. Take this approximation of Elke Erb's "Unity":

> Home I am, hymns the bee
> hums the wasp, huzzahs the hornet.
>
> Honey I am, promises the green
> feast for the eyes and hollow stage-set.

I had gone to Berlin mostly to translate Elke Erb and to catch up on recent German poetry, East and West. I was in for a surprise. *Literary* unification, as it were, had begun a decade earlier, and as an "Eastern" initiative. Prenzlauer Berg, a run-down area in East Berlin where many writers and artists live, became the center of a literary revolution in the 1980's.

There was an explosion of little magazines in which a new generation of poets — along with painters and such older poets as Elke Erb, Adolf Endler, Gerhard Wolf — began to develop a language that wanted to be more than a "No" to Socialist Realism, wanted to break out of the dichotomy conforming-resistance. For inspiration, they looked to Joyce, Dada, Surrealism, experimental poets like Heissenbüttel or Jandl, the spontaneity of the Beats, the baroque language of Rabelais and Fischart. They discovered playfulness, puns, discontinuity, cut-ups, montage/collage, self-reference (or "Sprachkritik"). They dreamed of becoming a "subversive Free State of the Scurrilous."

Much of it was a catching-up. Much of its energy came from its subversive stance, which has evaporated along with the iron curtain (and lost some credibility when two of its most active members turned out to have been STASI spies).

BUT these poets *changed the language* of GDR literature. And the best poems are brilliant — and untranslatable, as for instance Stefan Döring's *Zehn* which fuses wordplay and political reference into airtight tenliners.

In my selection (which is personal rather than representative), Durs Grünbein, Barbara Köhler, Richard Anders and Elke Erb are associated with this movement, though their work differs greatly.

Anders delights in the "sunken" images of common idioms. He builds surreal, acrobatic structures out of them. And watches with a clown's melancholy as they turn out *Verscherzte Trümpfe* [Muffed Trumps], all of them.

Durs Grünbein's *Grauzone morgens* [grey zone, morning] was the literary surprise of 1988. The then 26-year-old poet from Dresden cast a sober eye on the Socialist metropolis. He writes from the body, from the projective energy field between perception and language, from the crossroad of many voices, East and West. His second volume, *Schädelbasislektion* [skull base lesson], charts the GDR as a Pavlovian laboratory. I greatly admire its ambition, but have trouble reading it: the mostly regular meters make too obtrusive a claim of authority for my ears.

Embedded in permutation patterns, history is as urgently

present in Barbara Köhler's first book, *Deutsches Roulette* (1991). So is the landscape around Dresden (called "Valley of the Innocent" because by a technical fluke it alone could not receive Western TV), around the Elbe, the most polluted river in Europe (which has quickly become an emblem for the disastrous state of East German environment and infrastructure).

Elke Erb is renowned for her "eye on the molecule" and her imaginative leaps. Her recent work tracks, step by step, the processes of writing and of opening up to "Western" work like Friederike Mayröcker's. The prose poems translated here are, however, from an earlier book, *Vexierbild* [Picture Puzzle].

And in the West? In a more scattered way, there also seems much new energy — and much concern with history.

Some, like Joachim Sartorius, put "the events" in a large, cosmopolitan perspective, where they turn out to be mere noise ("Someone/bawls about unity"). But for him, too, the poem is documentation, and the poet, as he says, "a remem-berer," even though tradition has gone to hell and no longer guarantees anything.

Sabine Techel, on the other hand, feels directly challenged to reexamine her poetics: "I was writing small prose pieces whose point it was to have no point. Now history has jumped me." Meanwhile she has most interestingly explored — played with — long arcs of hypotaxis, subjunctive constructions, cool ironic use of jargons.

Brigitte Oleschinski sees her writing in terms of social commitment; and theory, as part of her craft. But the impulse toward poems comes out of a repugnance against "ordinary" sentences and, at the same time, knows itself nourished by those very sentences, "just as music has its basis in noise."

Such a sense of inclusiveness, almost like Cage's, must seem alien to Gerhard Falkner, who has the most intense, even violent, relation to language, who has to "be startled into writing." The language of his poems, with its fusion of vehemence and control, tries to catapult itself *out of* the language "that is there," the language of counters and clichés, and, ultimately, toward the boundaries of the unsayable.

Whereas Oskar Pastior rejoices in the sayable, with (hard-won) serenity and unrivaled virtuosity. He has stated that his thematic "tonic" is "the small — but important — space of play between freedom and determinism" (which he has explored in language as well as in a Soviet labor camp). I would add that his "dominant" must be the jubilatory celebration of language which turns this small space into an infinite, and invents us as we invent it. Most of his texts defy translation. I am delighted to be able to include Harry Mathews' and John Yau's splendid versions of some of his sestinas.

— ROSMARIE WALDROP

GERHARD FALKNER

BROKEN GERMAN OR MOMENT EMBRACED

What is called unspeakable is not unspeakable, but only called so, but what we talk about is not even unspeakable.
— *Basilides*

moment embraced

who once, so am I forced to, spent the night
  has yet at times smiled on me, like sudden joy
often enough had forced himself, alive to this point
  more he wants! estimates possibles, friendly
like one who, for fleeing life, the mute air

broken german

astonished, had I obeyed her, enough
  hardly an answer, of immortals, led safely
what times these are wherever you look, but talk
  as fate throws over, it comes here
cut short, embraced moment, from within

red shift

boundless hope, herwards, because our soul
  made whole not swimmingly, but all
felt good this way, breathed, before many a
  me some detached desire would
but the flowers, the beautiful flowers, lost

earfield

I desired, blind breath, as of hope
  the most fervent picture will be of this, our wandering
so different, so heaped unto summer
  who at that time, no longer finds rest, but the manner
goes on to the next, to the text, in nerves finer

scattered stanza

light as air, this waked me then, of the strangers
   the morning wonderfully constrained, loosened
like ships, true, who was I to, the trees in shadow
   I did not long regard, or death, come down
the tongue alone, I no longer, confused and with gladness

mowed poem

who am I or ask, since he left, there remained
   no consolation in early nature, and snatched
from us all rest, a spark of air, he replied
   which it obeys, even in spring, but bound
nothing worse, if we have been afrighted, since then

weremouth

to be alone, but all pleasure, don't tell anyone
   I gave it a name then and the dwindling, but she
to the utmost, I felt a lack, brought on
   takes no time, no height, who could abide it
asking the way to get lost, not that it end here

THE RED SHOES

a stranger I awakened and early
the plug still plugged in
a woman, smaller than a horse
handed me an apple in English:
apple, she said
don't you want a bite
but who are the red shoes
the red shoes
there on the sour side
bloodied they climb down the apple
ah must die and have
not even had breakfast

DISTANCE

a boat sails through our room
it isn't me, it isn't you
ours only the open
it drifts out into
but who, if not we,
guides its sail past
on the mast of the light ray
that cruelly pulverizes
crowd scenes of dust

FOREIGN PARTS

fallen off the chair i
love onto the rug
i also love
for i can love only
what's really mine
my hand's attention grazed
first tundras
then your dress
finally
my breath's centrifugal force
ground down near your round ankles

NAKED LUNCH POEM II

you raise the last question
i can lick and grasp it
the chair stands on four legs
under you astonished
as well-grounded law
under human frailty
wrong

THE INSPECTORS OF TONGUES

habakuk is the name of the fish!
once sobered up
its name is again herring

small dirty world
we sing you great and beautiful
but not for long

faith, love, hope
all gifts defeated
the playful dew
the glittering planets
dung to him
who doesn't care

poets
boxers among bloodred poppies
the years that as proud ships
left you
washed up on your rolling gait

ALL WORDS ARE GUILTY

not only i not only all others
but also all buts
both the however buts
and the that's why buts
came and didn't just stay nearby
where she he or the others came from
they crowded in on the i
the i of the many we were before
we were crunched into this one
we are and are not

what shall we talk about now?

not only i not only all others
but also all buts
both the however buts
and the that's why buts
ousted from the care of ours and yours
no longer have access to the question
they talk and talked at the same time
each meddling with the sense
of the other, with nothing but words
said and unsaid, nothing
but deeds done and undone

what shall we talk about now?

ROCK, MINERAL, ABSENCE

a rude square unrepentant
swayed by mourning and form
supported by frozen quiet
in judgment, error and death
is explained by the rudeness
with which you
snuffed out the body-silence
miraculously preserved
in the poem

POETIC STRUCTURE & NORMAL TIME

imagine calling it soul
testing its light sensitivity
on the sulfur of midsummer fields
exposing yourself, torn as you are
with all your inner paraphernalia:
taxis movies telephones,
to its radiance

what is breath
other than ashes dropping cold
from our mouths onto our burning
feet. we are nothing but wicks
stuck in the ptomaine of beauty
and under our scalp, in back
the white shadow thrown by
the uterus flower

SABINE TECHEL

MEMORIAL PHOTO OF THE COMPARATIVE

When there were still euphorias as well as
yesterday and tomorrow and raids
by anxieties from the closets heaps of clothes
here and there arms full of stuff sayable things
if I then you perhaps and because therefore
no-one could have anticipated even yesterday

I could still say past nobody can say
which way it has to be and whether this
smile isn't always there in the corners

EVENING IN BERLIN

you're lucky I squeeze you when the bell rings
between two thoughts there you can rest have
room to make mischief I squash you
between two errands that get me drenched when
at home I climb out of my things you make me wet

between two men suddenly transparent for you my
laugh on the phone opaque I get
skittish between two doubts rattle your
consolations you're a tough state of affairs

PROMISE

It's always summer when the
wells are bleeding and even a day
as if fresh from the graveyard
leaps out of your
hand. A piece of you is always lacking

from the picture and, always,
can be glued in. Where
do you come from? I speak about
towers am silent about lakes don't see
the stones following me. Something

to grasp and hear it was not there
at all. City, here, planes, heights. Knowing needs
a space I need to know; that some things will keep. And
yet I make do with this or that appearance, have my fill and
keep my motley.

WATERCOLOR

We've long gone back to painting the days in
  fading greygreens
                              we
sit restless and don't understand why we
have everything and not more
                                          we
have always already switched on all the lamps when
we find each other too obscure but
we fend off the day with hands over
our eyes until the bells tell
it from the steeples
                              we
wince with relief
evening has us back

HARBINGERS

Before they all fall you can

hear the grinding of teeth in the apple the
friction of sliding dinnerware the
brushing of clouds against the roof
the flapping of wings before the attack

before a man starts to gargle you can
dream how he slips under the washbasin
around the corner a wicked eye through the fence

it's time for cold hands now
which isn't bad if you always have some
and what's bad needs practice too.

The cold keeps getting brighter
A smile shows how somebody leaves
What it's too late for we later leave alone
For a rush there's always lots of time

FELIX CONJUNCTIO

Spring again already, the radio
plays bustin out all over. Friends
we call up act crazy, a bit
irritable, they call it in love.

They clamp cameras in front of their eyes
they look for pictures. Even in wet shoes
only their eyes are in touch with
the outside. Come summer they at least

put their skin back on, makes them easier
to get hold of, fucking too
works better. On abandoned sidings
they parade their sensuality

like a baby and are surprised what all
starts squeaking and squawking. Later in summer
archaeologists with inflamed eyes find
traces of red dust. It's rust.

ELKE ERB

VIVAT, CRESCAT, FLOREAT!

1

The pigeon rode on a horsedrawn cart.

2

The three Wise Men, however, went to Bethlehem where they had business. Behind them, their kingdoms, before them, a star. On arrival they turned toward a stable, toward donkey and cow because, next to them, in the manger, there lay a baby whose name was New Year. But what was their business in Bethlehem? They were to deliver gifts. Incense. Myrrh. One of them was black. While they did their errand there occurred a little scandal. An old hag, half undressed in spite of the cold, put her foot in the door: the Old Year. Immodest, degenerate and, what's more, clearly drunk, she yelled that she, too, had started out like this, in the manger, with gifts. Melchior knew how to handle this: "sure, sure," he mumbled, taking her arm, and without further ado threw her out into the dark. But after this, they too, the Wise Men, had to leave and go back to their Kingdoms, each to his own, as you to your office.

3

The pigeon rode on a horsedrawn cart. Mud spattered the spokes. It stopped in front of the Thuringer Hof, and a bevy of servants dashed out. The pigeon stepped down, and the one-eyed watchdog was about to lift his paw, ready for a secret laugh. But the pigeon entered the restaurant without sparing a look for anyone. She was really shot from the long, long trip.

COMMENTARY

The madrigal Claudio Monteverdi wrote on the death of a young singer of great charm, who had lived with him in his house and possessed a voice of unearthly beauty differs, for the layman's ear, in no way from other madrigals . . .

PICTURE PUZZLE

The simpleton and his mother in the forest. She will be braiding her hair. Shining knights arrive. Loss of son. Where we hold on, like any tree to its branches — back and forth, subject to rot, elbow angled to comb the sun of hair around the bones: the pain on horseback radiant with stolen light, snorting with childishness. Hair braided into plaits. Turning grey with time. What about mother? She wears it wound around her head.

THE BIRDS

Motto: Dear painter, paint me a rose!
Kito Lorenc

1

THE BIRDS

Wild geese caught in a drawing. Now they'll fly god-knows-where, within the viewer.

2

BRYUSOV

What? Valery Bryusov a whore?
Whoever hatches insults catches insults.
An honest whore is not to be insulted.
Neither is Bryusov. His world, his civilization, his poetry, his treasury of forms, his poetry of the nations (a rainbow's harem), all genuine as any honest whore's.
You can't insult Bryusov.
The insult would never catch up.

3

THE PASTOR

A pastor, recently defrocked but respectable, married a nun from a nearby convent. The first night, she reminded him of a friend in the seminary. The second night, every now and then, a group of ducks seemed to swim toward him, out of a dark background. The third night, his beloved struck him as a sweet grave. The fourth night, as his mother's jewelry box. (She had been a whore who, to atone for her life, had vowed her son to the church, and paid for his studies.) The fifth night he again saw birds, pigeons. The sixth, he was convinced they were in the post office elevator, with people waiting on every floor; it seemed more of a reception than a begetting! The seventh night, she reminded him of a nurse. Then he knew her for a whore and angrily wrote it down in his journal.

ALL MORNING LONG there was this noise uni
form and obviously underground this
noise so steady that hardly anybody noticed

DURS GRÜNBEIN

this noise of a thousand shredders of an in
visible institution wolfing every living
moment straight from your body like waste
paper.

GREY ZONE, MORNING, mon frère, on the
way through the city
home
or to work (what's the diff) —

Eye level is where it's at. The
earnest faces, bony and
hard, lack
only the black bar
across the eyes, deleted for the

discreet file of all witnesses of the
inaudible smog alarm (5:30 AM).

And it is this toughness (tough:

AS WE SAY IN GERMAN) that makes them walk
diagonally against their headache and the
noise of the filter
screens inside us.

ONE THING THAT COUNTS (even in the morning) is
this lazy chrome
flash jumping at you. A
motorcycle's. The summer

all cooled down, on its last
leg. (OK,
something new). You

in museum twilight by the window chew
your chewing gum because it's the best
remedy against
Baroquophobia. Punctually come fall
come depressions
of rows of chairs facing an
empty open-air stage unused since rain

immemorial. Two, three
workers roll up panels of cloth
lift floor planks out of
their frames. You wave at
them. Sometimes

there is nothing more banal than a
poem, a first daybreak
so early in the morning, on the
stiffened wings of the moth that

feels very soft in your hand.

THEN, LATER, IT WAS the silvery line
hair-thin across the
frosty clear
sky, which, like a giant
safety pin held the two
halves of the morning
together. Hard to

describe: when this first brightness
was halfways forgotten you felt
suddenly gravity

in your bones. Everything seemed
foreshortened ("An
order never existed. . .") and you

walked as on fog, as if drunk on ether
above the roaring
labyrinths of industry.

LOOSE LEAF. BIOMECHANICAL ALMANACH

That a thing has as many sides as there are perspectives on it, and not the other way round, this we know. Here all metaphors lie in ambush. A bathtub, for instance, like a submarine, is a displaced womb, a metal casing with the invisible label: *Rebirth.* Even a treadmill, seen from different angles, is each time something different. For the hamster, a kind of pleasure machine, a rotating ladder of life; for the engineer, a mechanism for the release of muscle power; for the philosopher, perhaps a caricature of illusory *perpetual motion.* Or Pavlov's dog . . . Everybody knows that Pavlov was simply trying to examine the central nervous system of higher animals. One day, a dog stood in the contraption, and its saliva was funneled into a measuring device. Is it by accident that Bechterev first lectured on *reflexology* in 1917, the year of the October Revolution in Russia? Ten years later, the term *collective reflexology* is bandied about. The laboratory Pavlov dreamed of was a new structure with absolutely soundproof rooms.

In the *tower of silence,* the instincts of the social animal are replaced by conditioning.

It was Lenin's personal decision, during the civil war, to allow double food rations to Pavlov and his wife. Where theory and practice separate 1:1, metaphor comes to rest. What has happened? asked Pavlov when, in 1924, he entered his lab after a flood. Some of the dogs had *forgotten* all conditioned reflexes. From their point of view the experiments were over.

RICHARD ANDERS

DISAPPEARANCE

Now you're ahead of, now you run after yourself and watch your back get smaller second by second. The street leads straight to the horizon where houses are just dots. Suddenly you've disappeared, clean out of sight. You turn: somebody is running after you. It's you! You take to your heels. Only now you work up to the speed which, while you were after yourself, would have let you catch up. But this time it is neither fun nor in earnest. Escaped from the eyes of your pursuer you are also — except for this hot legible trace — lost to yourself.

JUNGLE

You let your sentences shimmer with multiple meanings until, though your imagination keeps whirring like a hummingbird, you can no longer find your way out of the jungle of impossibles. You catch at a straw, but your panic so frightens it that, instead of rescuing you, in a man's hand, it grows, in a woman's, into a tree that entices a different Adam with the fruit of knowledge.

SENSE

Resurrected out of dead letters you will make sense only if you don't become sounding brass, but spring straight from your barrel chest into the blue. But don't hope for angels to catch you. Whether you take wing or fall depends only on this: was it to up or to down that your dead letters in their lifetime attributed the deeper, the higher meaning.

LAST SENTENCE

Even though your room stretches to the point where the floor borders a desert horizon, the wallpaper takes off as a swarm of roses and the ceiling dissolves in the blue infinite, you have the cheek to claim the sentence in which this happens is your own. Don't you realize that the words you call yours have long unmasked you as their invention? Not to mention your other illusion: that there is something like reality outside them. Like your own, the end of the world coincides with the last sentence on this page. These are not your words. Blow up like any swindle of a would-be creator. Once you've winged it as far as a gallows' bird you may return into the text as a personal pronoun.

BARBARA KÖHLER

PHOTO

for Florian

Because once again it can't be grasped
my left hand disappears in my pocket
my right holds on to pencil
or cigarette; most things are
out of my hands I smile
unconvinced before vanishing
into a camera that lies with images
blasted moments paper that pretends
to be a person last chance
to move: I shift
my weight to the other leg I have to stand on
                                        is in question

O BAPTIST, YOU too will lose your head.
Sometimes I hold it in my hands already
as if cut off your body next to mine for the time being.

Next to mine already for some time: where is your head?
I hold it in my hands — sometimes they too are
as if cut off my body lost in yours.

This body lost in yours I want to hold it
in my hands, and not cut off —

Some time, O Baptist, I'll lose my head.

THE END is
nearest the beginning.
Taking the black veils off the mirrors
you see your own face approach
on the subway escalator at Kálvin tér
a distortion a spasm joypain
gone the place is
called Pest in the mirrors
in the Cafe Lukàcs
sits : me : and writes
in the Cafe Lukàcs
called Pest in the mirrors
gone the place is
a distortion a spasm joypain
on the subway escalator at Kálvin tér
you see your own face approach
taking the black veils off the mirrors
nearest the beginning.
The end is

Kálvin tér: Kalvin Square, a Budapest subway station with a confusing number of exits.

PAPER BOAT

for Eva Angela Ulrike Gudrun

I

You wouldn't believe the rivers here mean to get to the sea.
The Elbe near Dresden: no trace of Atlantic or tides.
Low tide in the cash box, somebody says.
And a bent dead fish suspended overhead suddenly drops into the water: the moon. Four women watch.
Romantic images flake off. Under the glue, rejected sketches show up, the fabric of ground. A gold frame only seems the end of the world; we still have depth left.
The stinking mud on the bottom of rivers, somebody says.
Abandoned sketches, somebody says.
Fabric to be renamed, somebody says.
The moon and the unbelievable sea.

II

Perhaps this is a German story: the more cramped the surface the deeper the bottomless. You let yourself fall you hit the ground. The mud that hides the ground. The bloody ground of German history. But what can we build on, and what, for that matter, between canned baroque and ruined concrete?

III

The moon dropped into the water is a boat. A flimsy barque, but grounds enough to claim Saxony too lies on the sea. Grounds enough — once I've said grounds, we can insist on a paper boat.
Paper that overgrows us out of half-dead forests, paper we entrust with our dying; nightbooks, sealed sentences, letters unmailed. Pictures without frames, sketches without proportion, the secret destruction of scale. Paper full of getting lost and adventure as land leaves us behind, and hope lets go. Paper we come to on, paper we founder on, our barque our fragile ground. Saxony on the sea — Ahoy!

BRIGITTE OLESCHINKSI

THE BREATHTAKING INDIGO OF THE ROBES

Cracks, tracks, limestone. Above the
rocks, a topography of weather
of time. Thirst

and questions, you
wander along stream scars,
river sand, bleached fissures, stumbling — listen

the barometer message like
a saxophone and all blue

is oceans in your head

SOMETHING EMPTY, SOMETHING SILENT IS LEFT

on the beach, grey, open, scraped by the wind,
a washed-up body, limp, twisted, and it gets light
and dark and light again while, in the sockets,
salt dries slowly, not unlike a new retina turned,
unresisting,

toward the sky, eyes almost, open
for good

CASING

These are the walls, a white
egg, inhabited by word algae and our soft
tracks, lit up in the REM phase.

We are yolk eaters, are *always eating*. Not raw,
of course, we dry the yolk: else its genetic code
would not agree with us. On the code
of history we chew all night.

Outside, the news level constantly slops over.

These
are the walls,
a white egg,
inhabited.

WORKROOM

Even the walls take action, in white,
behind the shadows of backs and papers.
This room is their daily gesture:
A window blossoms from the forehead and replies.

Every morning it opens, the glass skin
over this memory that neither breathes
nor twitches, and line after line lights
the old supply of gas. We are latecomers

in these chambers, ladies and gentlemen. The museum
totters under its own weight and can barely
support visitors. In white, the walls act.
Whoever enters changes color. Paper flaps against the window.

JOACHIM SARTORIUS

PRELIMINARY CONVERSATION ABOUT FRAGMENTS

Ruini parlanti (Piranesi)

The interior speaks to us,
more clearly than the cohorts
who, screaming, dragged
the blocks up, on ropes,
into the boundless
which of course does not exist.
Which does not exist:
The tower remains a fragment
the screams fallen silent,
the serpentines made plain,
bad libretto.
You hear me?

Bab-ili? Inaudible:
rain of dead feathers.

BEHIND THE ALEXANDRIAN LIBRARY

On the pool hall wall
still a hair oil stain from
the young guy with acrobat hips
whom the Poet loved and whose
whoring bothered him as little
as Pompey's pillar.
Jealousy was 5 minutes of brown, sluggish rain
outside the bead curtain, an Alexandrian
outbreak of apathy in slack wind
over Lake Mareotis.
Whose crocodile, a mummy now —
main attraction of the Gr.-Rom. Museum —
stretches on its wooden bed,
scales blighted to acid dust:
not real, but lasting.

ALEXANDRIA

Back there is where he used to sit, that marble table,
said the old waiter, under the antiquated ceiling fans
that turned sluggishly even then,
under this ceiling with Art Nouveau stucco,
la vie était confortable: Stanley Beach,
Glymenopoulo, and the graceful
little Zizinia, a movie house now,
where they used to play Tosca in season,
La Bohème and Lohengrin (the most severe
Wagner acceptable south of Naples
then). There he used to sit, a Greek,
one of a few tenthousand Greeks,
who did not notice half a million Egyptians.
Lived in a Europe of the mind
stuck in the age of Strabo: "the most grandiose
emporium of the inhabited world,"
which now consists of stone and sea
and a feeling of utter exhaustion.

LITTLE QUEEN OF THE BEAUTIFUL WHORES

to Juan Carlos Onetti

I

Advent stars blink
in the windows of the "Eldorado."
She keeps her hose on, I,
my shirt. We do it to me, her,
us. Leaving,
I see traces
of stiletto heels
on the door frame, knee high.
It is night. It is raining.
Snails breathe
along the embassy walls
in Tiergarten. Someone
bawls about unity
and money.

II

I'm going to Venezuela,
she said (with those long,
ambiguous steps), and my
camera's broken. There is no
repairing the nation we
remember, I said,
put a
film candle in your eye.
We'll get a tan,
the best late winter
can come up with. But no-one
she says, is going to rip off
my night.

III

In the theater of the sensitive
there was love for the space of an unrest.
Then the quick hour
of a Saturday driven to pieces sagged
into evening.
Flashback: I hold you in
sight. You hold yourself shut.
Adieu. So long. Always,
fear is a trick
of voyeurs.

OSKAR PASTIOR

AN ALTOGETHER REMARKABLE ITEM

TRANSLATED BY HARRY MATHEWS

"that there might exist a language in which falsehood could never be spoken or, at least, any dent in the truth would make a dent in grammar as well" — Georg Christoph Lichtenberg

A small artistic machine fashioned with an undescribable cylinder
has three what might be referred to as "positionings,"
to explain which it brings three distinct systems into action,
in an emergency no more sizable than a cause;
a more than half transparently fashioned bellows,
as well as space for two or three other windmill vanes.

Occasionally, on the left windmill vane,
a body and a soul are erected by means of which the cylinder
could also be extracted; but in that case the bellows
and the preordained harmony must be directed to positionings
at a certain distance from the so-called double cause
and, with somewhat faulty steadfastness, be imparted to the action

of their miniature limbs in this manner — no action
of over 4 to 5 inches would then tear the windmill vanes
to shreds; similarly might the influence and cause
of an ant blowing with steadfastness explain the precious cylinder
by way of two or three physical positionings
of the crank in the precious ancillary bellows.

At a certain distance, no larger than the bellows,
it would occasionally be necessary to explain that action,
made of finest horn; just as in a minor emergency the positionings
of the so-called "endless screw" in the windmill vanes
(i.e. attached through the influence of the system to the cylinder)
could be extracted from the lengthy cause

of the imparted handiwork (such is the name of the cause
at a certain distance) — provided that from the bellows
a soul and a body also be extracted and that, on its cylinder,
by means of the occasionally half-transparent action
made of somewhat faulty ivory, a windmill vane
be erected with a view to so-called "double positionings."

Consequently at two to three preordained positionings
a goldbeater's skin would be torn to shreds; directed by no cause,
no more sizable than a sizable windmill vane,
three distinct ants would bring the bellows
into the horn and, with flawed steadfastness, the distance into action
to an inch made out of the familiar harmony of the long-lasting cylinder.

Occasionally, on the left windmill vane,
a screw and a horn are erected and the so-called cylinder
blown; in this case, however, the crank has no bellows.

SESTINA WITH INTERVIEW

TRANSLATED BY HARRY MATHEWS

oh of course I was often a second time
in rome — but at certain times I was also
actually there for the third or fifth time. when were
you there the last time? that I can in fact
specify: it was when for the first time I went away.
but since then were you ever again in rome?

no the first time I was to be sure still in rome
but not constantly more often like the second time —
that did not occur until after once there I went away.
but your last time in rome were you also
constantly thinking of actually going away? in fact
I always constantly think of it often: if ever you were

such a one there who often went away, you were
at certain times also quite definitely not in rome.
but do you also constantly realize when in fact
you at certain times and actually at which certain time
had to go away and as a consequence of this also
wanted to at a time there when nothing else went away?

well you see when for the first time there I went away
I hadn't realized that yet. But you were
at certain times then often a third time also
there again without ever going away at a time in rome
when nothing else went away? no it was the second time
that happened — at certain times I still realize that in fact

since you see actually I so constantly was often in fact
in rome that at certain times I in no way went away
because not even once had I the first time
gone away. no wait a minute so you were
actually once after that truly in rome?
certainly — actually you see I was still there also

and constantly was without any interruption also
there a second and third time just in fact
like the last time I was once again in rome
at a time when nothing else went away.
but tell me that last time in rome were
you in that case actually more often a second time?

oh of course at certain times I was then only one time
in rome before I more and more rarely went away —
because also the last time there it was dark in rome.

PROGRESSIVE METABOLISM IN A SESTINA

TRANSLATED BY HARRY MATHEWS

here six there in that sees
sees here six there in that
there in that sees here six
that sees here six there in
in that sees here six there
six there in that sees here

six so in that sees here
here six so in that sees
in that sees here six so
sees here six so in that
that sees here six so in
so in that sees here six

so as that sees here six
six so as that sees here
that sees here six so as
here six so as that sees
sees here six so as that
as that sees here six so

as this sees here six so
so as this sees here six
sees here six so as this
six so as this sees here
here six so as this sees
this sees here six so as

this sees said six so as
as this sees said six so
said six so as this sees
so as this sees said six
six so as this sees said
sees said six so as this

says said six so as this
this says said six so as
six so as this says said
as this says said six so
so as this says said six
said six so as this says

six there in that here sees
sees here six so as that
six so as this said says

FIFTH METABOLIC ISTHMUS SESTINA

BY JOHN YAU AFTER OSKAR PASTIOR

Sex thought really all there was
Was sex thought really all there
Really all there was sex thought
There was sex thought really all
All thought was there sex really
Thought really all there was sex

Miss really thought you call sex
Sex really miss thought you call
Thought sex call really miss you
Call sex you really miss thought
You call sex miss thought really
Really thought you call sex miss

Telephone makes sex call this miss
Miss telephone makes sex call this
Sex miss telephone this call makes
This miss makes telephone sex call
Call this miss telephone makes sex
Makes sex call this miss telephone

Fakes what sex call forget miss
Miss fakes what sex call forget
Sex call forget miss fakes what
Forget miss what fakes sex call
Call forget miss what fakes sex
Sex call forget what miss fakes

What this sex question call fakes
Fakes what this sex question call
This call fakes what sex question
Question this call fakes what sex
Call question this sex what fakes
Fakes sex this question call what

Sex quiz question who makes what
What sex quiz question who makes
Question who makes what sex quiz
Makes what sex quiz question who
Who makes sex what quiz question
Quiz question who makes what sex

Question quiz really thought was sex
Sex miss makes what is there
Is quiz question who sex fakes

THE GRAND HOTEL METAPHYSICS

by

HUGO BALL

from

TENDERENDA DER PHANTAST

translated by Keith Waldrop

Hugo Ball at the Cabaret Voltaire, 1916

HUGO BALL'S novel *Tenderenda,* described by Hans Arp as "Dada's secret bequest," was written between the years 1914 and 1920 and in many ways charts Ball's development from early Expressionism, his founding of and departure from Dada, and his ultimate conversion to Catholicism. But although historical events and personages can be recognized in this work, *Tenderenda* is more than a *roman à clef* or a simple Dada romp. Ball's concern is above all with the liberation and regeneration of language that has been debased to a mere tool for rational control. He counters by means of fantasy, irony and paradox, invocation, prayer and "word alchemy." And these weapons even seem evident when it comes to the "birth of Dada" in the chapter "The Grand Hotel Metaphysics." Is Ball describing a great event, or a sorry disappointment — the birth of a systematized, politically impotent *movement?* One clue can be found in the ironic title; on the day that Ball read this chapter at a Dada evening in 1917, he wrote in his diary: "We allowed the May Day procession to march past below our Hotel Metaphysics." Four weeks later Ball made his final break with Dada*ism,* but, as evinced by the entire of *Tenderenda,* he never gave up the program which shaped the beginnings of Dada in Zurich, his quest to find the creative inner core of language.

The chapter below is translated by Keith Waldrop. My own annotated translation of the complete work is forthcoming in *Blago Bung Blago Bung Bossofataka: First Texts of German Dada,* Atlas Press 1995. With "The Grand Hotel Metaphysics," as with the whole of *Tenderenda,* alternative translations/readings of this cryptic work can only be useful.

— MALCOLM GREEN

THE GRAND HOTEL METAPHYSICS

THE BIRTH OF DADA. MULCHE-MULCHE, QUINTESSENCE OF THE PHANTASTIC, GIVES BIRTH TO THE YOUNG HERR FOETUS, UP IN THAT HIGHER WORLD WHICH — SURROUNDED BY MUSIC, DANCE, FOLLY, AND DIVINE FAMILIARITY — STANDS OUT CLEARLY AGAINST ITS ANTITHESIS.

NO SPEECH BY CLEMENCEAU OR LLOYD GEORGE, AND NO LUDENDORFF GUNSHOT, HAS BROUGHT US SUCH EXCITEMENT AS THE LITTLE CLUTCH OF WANDERING DADA PROPHETS, PREACHING THEIR WAY OF CHILDLIKENESS.

IN AN ELEVATOR of tulip and hyacinth, Mulche-Mulche betook herself to the deck of the Grand Hotel Metaphysics. Awaiting her there: the Master of Ceremonies, who was to put the astronomical instruments in order; the Ass-of-Jubilee, swilling his heart out in a bucketful of raspberry juice; and Musikon, our dear wife, formed entirely of fugue and passacaglia.

The slim legs of Mulche-Mulche being bound with chrysanthemum, her walk could hardly reach its stride. Her rose-petal tongue, with a little flutter, protruded past her teeth. Laburnum drooped from her eyes and the black bedspread of the four-poster, prepared for her, sported a pattern of silver dogs.

The hotel was built of rubber and porous, its upper stories hung with eaves and edges projecting outwards. As Mulche-Mulche's clothes were removed and the brightness of her eyes lent color to heaven — : wouldn't you know, just then the Ass-of-Jubilee had drunk his fill. Wouldn't you know! then and there he brayed out a welcome audible for miles. The Master of Ceremonies bowed low, repeatedly, and pushed the telescope nearer the battlements for studies in celestography. Musikon however, like flames of gold adance always round the four-poster, of a sudden lifted her arms and behold! from violins a shadow fell across the city.

Mulche-Mulche's eyes flashed out. Her body filled up with grain, with frankincense and myrrh, lifting the bedclothes into an arch above the bed. With a rising load of different seeds and fruits, her body with a roar broke from the swaddling in which it was bound.

Rickety folk, from parts all around, trekked in to prevent this birth, which threatened with fertility their desolate land.

P.T. Bridet, death-flower in his hatband, grew vociferous on his wooden leg. A puddle of poison formed in his cheek. From the funeral parlor, furious, he hastened here in exasperation to take measures against the unheard-of.

And there was Pimperling, with his head unscrewed, drumhead hanging crumpled from either ear. He was wearing a headband from the aurora borealis of most recent date. Your standard mudbespattered fugitive from a boneyard who, vanilla-scented, from the vile stench of jealousy sets forth on an errand of honor.

And Toto was there, who had that name and nothing else. His well-oiled iron adam's-apple whirred in the wind, the said wind running contrary. He had fastened a Jericho-plaster round his fluttering gut-flaps, so as not to lose them. The Marseillaise, his showboleth, beamed redly from his breast.

And they blockaded the garden, posted their guard, bombarded the deck with film-cannons, thundering away day and night. For reconnaissance balloon, they sent up the vivid violet "Spud-Soul." Their rockets spelled out "God Save the King" or "We Flare in Prayer" but, through a tube, they piped up to the deck, "Fear of today ravages us."

Meanwhile, on high, the officious Finger of the Godhead strove in vain to entice the young Herr Foetus from Mulche-Mulche's tumultuous belly. He was already, in fact, peeping cautiously out the towering maternal gateway. But, blinking, he drew his canny fox-face back again the instant he saw the four of them — Jopp, Musikon, the Godhead, and the Ass-of-Jubilee — united to intercept him with butterfly-net, sticks and staves, and a wet washrag. An overwhelming sweat was wringing from Mulche's flushed body in such spurts and spouts that everything around was drenched.

Those below lost control, with their rusted-out film-artillery, and had no idea what to do next, to skip out or to stay. And after consulting the "Spud-Soul," decided to capture by storm the lovely act of the Grand Hotel Metaphysics.

As first catapult, they rolled out the Fashion-Idol, a sequin-studded pinhead, low forehead loaded with orientalizing bric-a-brac. Constructed as he was from head to foot by clumsy lies and sporting, from a watch-chain on his chest, an Iron Heart, he might be called the humorless idol.

His black neck craned upwards, hung with bells, a vice-tuning fork raised in his right hand. Still, painted all over with symbols from Talmud and Kaballah, he gazed goodnaturedly from childish pupils. With six hundred self-articulating arms, he twisted fact and history. Also, an acetylene torch in a steel box was hooked to his last dorsal vertabra. And in his oil-anointed evacuations, generals and bandleaders — misanthropoid and slick with muck — drop from the petite asshole.

But now, from above, Jopp — with Musikon's help — sank a fuse deep into the region of his gut and — with all the hesper, salfurio, acunite and sulfuric acid already stored there — they blew him to smithereens, thus frustrating the assault.

A second idol, "Bearded Dog," was brought in, intended with its lowdown bawling and barfing to swab fond anecdote clean off the deck of the Grand Hotel Metaphysics. With a crowbar the plaster of religion was pried up to open a trail and lay a track. Shares in "Ideological-Superstructure" went into a slump.

"O degradation of animality!" stuttered out Bridet. "The magic printing presses of the Holy Ghost no longer suffice to stave off decline."

And with that, "Bearded Dog" roared, hissing, pulling behind him a church on castors, with curtains behind which priests, prelates, deacons, and episcopal bigwigs held fearful watch. Five-pronged dorsal vertebrae hauled along his mangy hide, tattooed with military formations. Enthroned on his receding forehead, the image of Golgotha. Fed on a chaff of vectors, he stood the while, stabled in allegory. Now he rolled up, to snort out his astonishment alongside Musikon's vocalizing.

But his rage blew its gasket. Before his breath reached the rooftop, he crooked his back and banged out the seeds of his virility, smelling of jasmine and water-lilies. The monster's knees trembled weakly. He lay down, meekly whimpering, head on paws. His own tail smashed into pieces the tottering Holiday-Church-of-the-Guardians-of-the-People, which he himself had pulled there. And so this assault also came to nothing.

And while, on the airy deck, Musikon's gold flame dances, pum-pity-pie-pie, the last of the idols is brought in: stucco Death-Doll, stretched out in a car, hoisted up with ropes. "Long live scandal!" cries Pimperling in welcome. "Poetic friend" — thus Toto — "a sickly scavenged corpse-flesh surrounds thy head. Cobalt blue is the color of thine eyes, thy forehead light yellow ochre. Give my thy suitcase. *Selah.*" And Bridet: "Verily, silent Maestro, you smell not bad, for your age. This'll be a real gas. Let's you and me shake a leg, each ripped from the other. Let us build an *arc de triomphe* and wherever your foot shall tread, abide there bliss and blessings!"

Death nodded, and took unto himself their experiences, as one might accept a Festschrift, and granted the noose his neck, that it should carry him even to the heights. And they coupled the reels, turned the crank, and hauled him up. But the weight was too much. He made it three quarters of the way, swinging and swaying, and had worked himself up to scale the ridge. There the ropes grew taut, hardened, began to twing and twang. Then the cable-cock crowed and from the dizzy heights he was cast down and the whole heft of his weight landed on our goodman Pimperling, a laying-on he was in no wise prepared for. Thrice dead and five times slain — they carried him, wrapped in a snotrag, to the side of the road and worked feverishly to get the back of his head back together and back where it belonged. But it was hopeless. And so Death, by Pimperling's death, broke into death double.

Then suddenly Mulche-Mulche let out twelve piercing screams, one after the other. Her circle-bone rose to the brink of heaven. And she brought forth. First a little Jew wearing a little crown on his purplish head, who began immediately to swing on the umbilical cord and went from there to gymnastic exercises. And Musikon laughed, this being her cousin.

And after forty days, it came to pass that Mulche, with chalky countenance, stood on the battlements. And there a second time she lifted her circle-bone to heaven. And this time she gave birth to a great load of slop, rubble, rubbish, sludge, and rumbling. All this went with bang, crash and rattle down the battlements and buried every caress and every carcass of those who walk on soles. Then Jopp was overjoyed, and the Godhead dropped His butterfly-net and gazed in wonder.

And when another forty days had passed, Mulche stood pensive, with her great devouring eyes. Then a third time she raised that bone and brought forth Herr Foetus, as it is written — *Ars Magna,* page 28. Confucius praised him. A rim of brightness runs along his spine. His father is Plimplamplasko, the great Spirit, immoderately drunk with love and addicted to miracle.

❖

Squeezed—from memory the ash zones—collective ritual
astronomic mood power—into memory pushed—
a piping reservoir—elemental softening—subliminal
(from "Atmosphere," *Defensive Rapture*)

BARBARA GUEST has conjured beauty through defamiliarization in her poetry and prose from *The Location of Things* (1960) through *Defensive Rapture* (1992). In 1978 she published her structurally-challenging novel, *Seeking Air,* and in 1984 her acclaimed biography of H.D., *Herself Defined.* Variously celebrated by the New York School Poets, the L=A=N=G=U=A=G=E Poets and the various off-shoots of both movements, Barbara Guest is a self-described free agent. Hers is "a piping reservoir," displayed here in a transcript of a talk she gave in April 1992 at SUNY Buffalo for a graduate seminar led by Charles Bernstein.

— GALE NELSON

POETRY THE TRUE FICTION

by BARBARA GUEST

THE TITLE I originally gave to this talk, as you know, is "How I got out of Poetry into Prose." This title came to me so quickly, because at that time I was encouraging myself to write fiction, and I thought I would discuss the dimensions of fiction with you. However, I was disturbed by this title and rightly so, had I been more intuitive of my own perceptions, and had I listened to the poet, William Cowper, who wrote: "Poets are seldom good for anything except in rime," I would have entitled this talk more sensitively: "Poetry the True Fiction."

Why has the word fiction become associated with prose when it is poetry that transforms the real world into fiction. Mallarmé understood this completely. With his perception he wrote: "The true fiction is that of the poet."

Mallarmé regarded poetry as an art dedicated to fictionalization, an *"art consacré aux fictions"* where the concrete object is "bathed in a new atmosphere," lifted out of itself to become a fiction. The poet is not there only to share a poetic communication, but to stimulate an imaginative speculation on the nature of reality.

Do you recall the poem of Wallace Stevens "Notes toward a Supreme Fiction." And have you considered what the title meant, or what was the underlying meaning of the title? I'm at the point where I take everything he says for granted the moon being made of ice-cream, etc. so I never questioned his meaning until the other day when I was considering poetry as fiction. In his published correspondence I found a letter from Stevens to his publisher, the Cummington Press. He wrote:

> The title of the book will be *Notes toward a Supreme Fiction.* Each of the three groups will develop or at least have some relation to a particular note: as
>
> I
>
> it must be abstract
>
> II
>
> it must change
>
> III
>
> it must give pleasure.
>
> These are three notes by way of defining the characteristics of supreme fiction. By supreme fiction, of course, I mean poetry.

The fiction of the poet is a part of the restless twentieth century perception based on the discovery that reality is a variable, and is open-ended in form and matter.

And now that we recognize poetry activates an established world of fiction, I should like to discuss the supremacies or the necessaries of poetry that enable it to transform reality. I would like to speak about Vision and Imagination.

Vision is part of the poet's spiritual life of which the poem, itself, is a resume. The "spirit" or the "vision" of a poem arises from the contents of the poet's unconscious. Let us say the vision of a poem has above it that "halo" you see in religious paintings when an act of special beneficence is being enacted by one of the persons within the picture that person is given a halo. The poem is our act of special beneficence and the poet is rewarded this halo. The poet is unaware of the halo, just as in the paintings the persons are unaware of the halo, but it is there as a reward for a particular unconscious state of immanence. Now I am not speaking of a religious state of grace in regard to the poem, the poem, let us say is its own religion. I am using the word "halo" because you and I can see it in the painting, and this halo has a value to us; it reflects a state of mind, or a condition which the mind has attained.

The halo has detected the magnetic field in which the energy of the poem is being directed.

I would like you to understand that I am using the words, "spirit", "vision", "halo" because I wish to lift us upward away from the desk of a projected poem. I want to emphasize that the poem needs to have a spiritual or metaphysical life if it is going to engage itself with reality.

As closely as possible in the world I am representing here the poet wishes to align the contents of the poem with the vision which directs it. When this occurs we say of the poem that it has "wings."

It is possible that words may occur in a fixed space and sequence so that they are called "words of a poem." We say the poem is made of words. And it is true that many poems are constructed solely of words. These are the words that sit on paper without vision. We all have read these poems and we know that after we have read them we feel curiously bereft. Our expectations of ennoblement by the poem had been disappointed by the lack-lustre condition of the poem.

We decide that this poem is not very inspired. And what do we mean by this? We desired "inspiration"; that the poem contain within it evidences of the spirit of poetry.

We have learned that words are only utensils. They are inorganic unless there is a spirit within the poem to elevate it, to give it "wings," so that the poem may soar above the page and enter our consciousness where we may if we wish give it a long life, a longer life than would occur when the poem lies without elevation on a piece of paper.

There is no reason to signal any decade or era as deficient of vision. Words on a page are deficient of vision and this may occur in any epoch. We are particularly nervous about our own era, because we are at the turn of a century which is most usually designated a time of decadence. We see this everywhere, unfortunately in the decay of institutions, but mostly there is a demise of the spirit and that is what should concern us, because poetry will reflect this spiritual absence.

Words without vision are deprived of stability. They cling desperately to a mirrored surface in an effort to attach themselves to a surface, because they have no direction and no stabilized vocation. They become furtive, these words, thirsty for a version of themselves that contains no failure of vision. Words contain their own beauty of face, but they desire an occupation. They cannot exist on beauty or necessity alone.

Words of the poem need dimension. They desire finally — an education in space. The poet needs to understand the auditory and spatial needs of a poem to free it so that the poem can locate its own movement, so that it is freed to find its own voice, its own rhythm or accent or power.

Wordsworth wrote: *Language if it do not uphold, and feed, and leave in quiet like the power of gravitation or air we breathe, is a counter-spirit, unremittingly and noiselessly at work to derange, to subvert, to lay waste, to vitiate, and to dissolve.*

It is not the flash of brilliance appropriated in a technique that quenches the pathos of a deprived poem. Although we must not neglect those qualities Leopardi admired in Horace: "courageous metaphors, singular and far-fetched epithets, inversions, placement of words, suppressions" — recognize them? They appear in our own shifting techniques.

Regard the poem as plastic. It is movable, touchable. It is a viable breathing substance. Nothing is more useless than a poem with a dull sheen that refuses to move; that is inert. This is the essence of dullness and our eyes run quickly past it.

A poem has not only a voice, but a mouth and the mouth must move just as much as the voice must speak and it must not be careless in its speech. And flesh of a poem. Even as a painting has flesh. The vibrancy of its skin.

The artist, de Kooning, wrote that in the Renaissance drawing started to tremble because it wanted to go places. He also added that what we call subject matter was then painting itself. There was no subject matter. De Kooning also observed that at this time the artist was too perplexed to be sure of himself. Later subject matter ruled the arts. And said de Kooning, when you think of all the life and death problems in the art of the Renaissance, who cares if a Chevalier is laughing or that a young girl has a red blouse on. De Kooning is telling us to beware of descriptive or "subject matter." In other words to think of the poem, itself.

Vision and plasticity are the two essentials of a poem. The spirit of the poem and its movable form, not its "adjustable" form. Then we get into posing or Chevaliers or red blouses.

I hope you realize that in all these words I have gathered together, or if you wish in the few words I have gathered, I have not come directly to Imagination.

I have first wanted to prepare the ground for Imagination. For us to consider the spirit of the poem, its physicality and its spatial intensity. Now I would like to speak about Imagination because it is really my favorite topic. Without imagination the red blouse is a piece of description, without imagination the poem is only words on a page.

This is a very large subject Imagination. I shall touch upon it only briefly. But I must speak about it, because for me it is the single most important element of poetry and it is my touchstone. When I examine a poem it is not for its form or style or even gravity but I look for its imaginative powers. I find that imagination comes before style or technique. How empty all the dazzle of style is without the immediacy of the touch of imagination. And imagination the changeling can sting you with its fictive barbs.

Coleridge wrote *Biographia Literaria* in his youth when he was trembling with imaginative power. The book is essential, I believe, for the distinction he makes between Imagination and Fancy. Fancy is delightful, evocative, alas charming, but with fancy you leave those words on the page. A good many poets are endowed with a lively fancy, many more than those who live in the imagination. Fancy is useful and can shake people up and can present itself century after century as the new. But it is not art, it is games.

Imagination lives with the visionary. When you touch its glass it rings. The French have a phrase: *"clair-obscur"* which translates as obscure light and means the mysterious side of thought. That could well define imagination.

We tend to think of it as so lively it pierces walls, but that liveliness is fancy. Imagination is *clair-obscur.* It is also "the absent flower" of Mallarmé. A turbulent presence. And we must acknowledge this "turbulent presence" because it is there to save the poem from a disobedient disregard of its own nature.

There will always be in poetry, in its search for a language, a desire for the liberation of the imagination.

André Breton said, "to imagine is to see."

CANADIAN EMERGENCY

A PALPABLE ENERGY, such as seldom builds and is never sustained outside the context of concerted collective action, animates the writing presented here under the rubric "Canadian Emergency." These nine writers, ranging in age from their mid-twenties to their mid-thirties, have already spent upwards of a decade forcing the boundaries of poetic practice. They assail the borders of cultural and political nationalism, ignore the stultifying parcellings and packagings of literary genre, and interrogate the limits of the avant-garde project which they themselves continue. What makes their work more than the sum of furtive transgressions, however, is a prior decision and the experience that has issued from it. For these writers, and their many interlocutors and collaborators at the Kootenay School of Writing (KSW) in Vancouver, have refused the trap of obligatory individualism that continues to govern the economy of poetic practice even in nominally progressive quarters of both Canada and the U.S. Against the unchecked rage of individuation, these writers risk an unruly, open-ended assembly.

The risk and the energy are as indistinguishable as particle and wave: a constant conversion of one into the other has characterized KSW from the start. Founded in the wake of the politically motivated closure of David Thompson University Centre in 1984, KSW's existence owes more to the fierce determination of its participants than it does to funding (the latter, it must be said, being the unspoken precondition for much of what passes for "individuality" in a capitalist society). Never far from exhausting its material resources, KSW tapped the one renewable resource at its disposal: the imagination and commitment of successive waves of dissenting writers and intellectuals. By their efforts, and through their permanent discussions in impermanent conditions, reading series, reading groups, seminars, and journals such as *Writing* and *Raddle Moon,* all emerged.

If "style is history's diction," as a recent manifesto co-written by Lisa Robertson, Christine Stewart, and Catriona Strang claims, then the poets of KSW disprove the late capitalist truism that history has ended by assembling a diction that is explosive and emotive. It is a diction with a future as well as a past, and if it lends itself to invective at one moment, it is available to a sure and secular eros at the next.

In the work we present here, the linguistic minimalism of punk encounters the sublimated lexicon of the torch-song. Cloying harmonies of national and sexual identity break into atonal clusters of desire and allegiance (Shaw), stable taxonomies are shattered by transformative matter (Stewart), and splinters of critique dart unimpeded through the anti-grav chambers of grammar (Davies). Innocence, upon closer examination of its speech-patterns, turns out to be the *nom de guerre* of domination (Farrell), leaving cognition startled at its own barely tenable conditions (Clark). Gender takes a walk so as not to know what the body is up to (Derksen) and "the free pull of air" is envisioned "passed all around in three sexes" (Ferguson). The paternal library is frisked for the shepherdess omitted from every pastoral (Robertson) even as the wardrobe of dissent is rifled for something fevered and operatic enough to clothe her aspirations (Strang). Throughout, the writing, like the people who make it, retains the lucidity we associate with states of emergency: alert, improvisatory, quick to discard a spent tactic for a live one.

— STEVE EVANS

NANCY SHAW

MELO-ANTHEM

—for this neo land

1. And of politics I understand one thing.
2. A paradigm of intellectual command concurs in plunder.
3. Poesy ceases.
4. My fate decoded.
5. I arrest myself.
6. To think coolly while still suffering.
7. This apology is extorted from the boy of culture.
8. He asks for a little revery.
9. I search my tool box of sounds.

15. Composure gives way.
12. You could be one of fifty million people.
13. In a deep house dance house.
14. Let the need be known.
10. I shall not trace the saga.
11. By expressing the prudery, you are again recognized as a cold
    hood.
16. The final flare up is arranged so I feel a slight flush.
17. An applique fringed with danger.
18. And of politics I understand one thing.

ANTHEM HOUSE

1. With the birth of a glittering nation
2. The freedom of code words
3. I love north.
4. Anti, insidious and arch
5. In my funk house.
6. Junk house, house house.
7. Stalinists want to prove their populism.
8. The 'global' teenager has nostalgia without memory.
9. A guy disappears in his family.
10. 'Equality' has no index of the actual.
11. A shapeless inventory or show trial
12. As if we were more reasonable.
13. To each in his own abstraction.
14. The sum total of diverse festivities
15. The labour required to make it natural.
16. A spectre somewhat faint and faking.
17. Admin. Hall show trial.
18. Infinite decibel
19. A dance club utopian

ANTHEM NATION

1. Master Jack's style curve assumes the status of theoretical antique.
2. Sometimes it is difficult to attain epistemological immunity.
3. This is no ordinary love.
4. Nor junctural wrestle.
5. My highly muscled sentiment is an intellectual solvent.
6. With the possibility of ontological insecurity.
7. We flow.
8. Exalted by social collateral and systemic ransom.
9. I found a box of matches.
10. Where young influentials foil their analytic radar.
11. Unhidden they would provoke resistance.
12. I am not a dictionary nor a doctrine of need.
13. What dry hard strap.
14. *I don't have time to be brief.*

POST-ANTHEM

(a song regarding "freedom")

1. The theory of micromania.
2. Jack in juggler's flea glass.
3. My Moral Darwin
4. We travelled forests of sentiment then vegetative language failed.
5. I became something of an internal colony.
7. The architectonics of a drab and slavish naturalist.
8. The thought that licking ceases.
9. Oh My Goddess.
10. What scientific goat.
11. My nouveau sovereign and an indigent shepherd.
12. Scarring the face of utopia.
13. I have a collection covered in ivy.
14. This is not to suggest that we had no new ideas over the age of thirty.
15. In keeping with *our* dream of utopia.
16. Truth in dearth of:
    a) theory heads
    b) theory bodies
17. Internal mingle.
18. In little battles of self-love.
19. Technical artifice is a good reply to sophistry.
20. My lecturer, dissector, practical demonstrator and delineator.
21. The projectionist is a crush inspired envoy.
22. This hospice, a salubrious pavilion.

I DON'T FEEL AT LIBERTY

(an anthem regarding enumeration)

1) By virtue of proclamation
2) Bore the stain
3) A schedule of compensation
4) Think of fret work
5) What has moved them
6) No summary can hasten restraint
7) Displayed conspicuously in verbal traits
8) More mundane though no less telling
9) The gist of a minor poet
10) More commonly administered
11) Shed no light
12) Lest we doubt
13) A candidate for historical subject
14) Undone over centuries
15) Sometime in a flash
16) I talked of you
17) At the edge of myself
18) All but a scholarly twin
19) In the house of self-evidence

KEVIN DAVIES

from DUCKWALKINGAPERIMETER (thanfirstwethoughtthatpartinyears"Buster")

And for love I would blank a poem with a sort of violent image in it

Not an image exactly but a candle with a pumpkin in it

The loan of a radio.

hey wire

the sentimental re-educations

were all in the mind

& body of the guy

who wrote the Roto Rooter jingle

& in the bodies

& minds of everyone else also

Chant of monkey-guards' marching song from witch's castle in Oz.

I Why I I, feel I feel a prehensile tail taking shape in that place
where lats & delts & pecs & glutes are meant to come finally together & complement
each other in the glory of the held
steroid pose, & only a, only, only a formalist anti-
anecdote can tease it back to the sheath of its latency. Please &, &

& ok so *explain away* this weird gel that extrudes each time the empty phone jack channels voices of
decapitated Chinese drug recreants. &, why I I & why I & why *are* there never enough jars to store
this stuff whose very *instability* might make it one day of use to medical science Does

that answer your question are we on the air

For years
a kind of conceptual art too ephemeral even to be documented.

My heart — the one I never
learned to notate — flips
flapjacks in the trailer camp
of a Yellowknife gold mine.
It doesn't know why.
And if I want to feel
good all over again
I give up
and feel good giving up
all over again.
No he said probably the guy
is changed somehow for the better or
worse, or dies or,
is blackmailed. Because if
it's an experiment who's
monitoring? Or maybe he's
a woman. *I* don't know.
Was the details in the middle that
inter*est*ed him or her.
Easier to fill out a form that's already replaced you. Information
wants to be me. O
K.

Inept tennis
and vice versa

Useful to imagine yourself a satellite, but eventually you've got to cut it out. A ghosted town, broken shutters battering barrels. You pictured it you bought it. You burned it down you *gotta* sweep it up. Jan always buzzed we aren't the only non sequiturs in this fish camp honey.

Rock, butts, brick, limbs, little bits of park.
Without whose municipal grace

"Doctor, let me die." *(Exit left.)*

(1) These water towers
weren't constructed by space
aliens. (2) Every rich country
has emergency martial-law plans
and functionaries eager to try them out.
(3) Every large corporation
has a spy network. Right?

(4) That's where we come in. Right?

(5) We can't understand each other
thru our particle masks. Right?

(6) Or we expect an anchoring effect to take
hold beyond a certain
durational boundary. *Right?*

(7) There's nothing certain
about it. (8) The ridicule we splatter on
our virtual selves has a destination
past its target. (9) I pity you, man. (10) Everything's
beyond this moment but
it's all here. (11) The acoustics
are shocking. (12) That's why we stand puzzled before elevator
shafts, all alone. Right? (13) But

Mistakes are sexual.
Stroke my residency permit.

SUSAN CLARK

from

THEATER

TOPIC or CHARACTER or SITUATION 7.

Stage Set

> "what painter face to face with a photograph has never had an instant of misgiving or intimidation, feeling he [sic] is outside reality?" (Man Ray)

I see colour suddenly and language slowly
The green is a leap of the ground
it must be

A queen explains your life but you have to know what she means first

Leaves lie out on the air; no one is hungry
Without any kind of murder
The way water uses colour

Those *clothes* were with her when it happened. Or is that my abstraction into which these thoughts fall rubblelike? Here, so far from events.

In the midst of a leap you realize you're in the wrong era—
that that pond hasn't been here since the '27 Diversion;
a hard landing wakes you up to a framed photograph

Red loves red first
on first sight

The heat of a permanent crowd —
their faces every which way most modern

(Green carpet . . .
(brown bureau . . .

(black notebook . . .
(pale face . . .
(round opening . . .

Mind your own business said the clock, fictive
and
we've plenty of
time

aghast: a pause outside of the body

TOPIC or CHARACTER or SITUATION 10.

The barbarous has plenty of adjectives, such is the help you offer it

War was not Her, but particular
a little flesh down the drain

as if precise, real

boys are eating boys abroad so we can understand them
the experience of obstruction banal

The more world the more give in her mind
given the more her mind would waive

The more world the more her mind gave out
had to bite her tongue to stop it licking
the book open
as the book says, No shame

Bruised, she remembers television
saying
won't you be my expert?

bit her tongue to stop it licking
the inadequate exchange of treasures

leaves depending sustained that May inside
the little tug at parting

a ripe white: hurl, hurl

— not a mistaken life
but
an unuseable awe

a book also opens as the book says, No shame

our new
flesh shone sweetly in the
prairie large
everything
sky also large
indoors

Fantastic errors in the serenity of the printed page
"it" then "someone"
no way out

When I said I was a writer I was lying; when I said I was a liar I was writing
Mere bulk satisfaction — I don't care where the capital is

TOPIC
or CHARACTER
or SITUATION 11.

Intuition

"Intuition is not a disorderly sympathy" (Deleuze)

Slept near and being fed
A bulging surface touched, spills
Use the water to attract water

Lolling over a wave lolling our bodies behave similarly
Nearness the essential in to drown

indistinct useless true

Mollification hazarding cloth
The bridge down, buckled, useless

I praise ignorance to the skies
the way her hair's tied to her ankle it
keeps her bent

Otherwise she wouldn't know what to do for the world

dear clump
dear dear clump

men of science have no words
so purely hold up objects
still to our advance

all of it — all of it — but no one could and we all fell back

one self
simple
"it" then "someone"

fantastic serenity in the errors of the printed page

D. FARRELL

INNOCENT

alablaster and for alablaster
ev'ry heart in skin self
and laid he an murther

appease in it skin have belied fair
commit are as died in none
prate set angel commit

angel of my things
heart were thought knowledge
whiteness rhyme I am a name

wrong'd free her hear
world but world
of and an awake

forehead in your mansion kill'd the poor
Name one another Flower
Love me love my malice

shames you another
me people my
world of th' right hand

dumb any do you
down itself how a breath
sweet shames sight died

sweet among say thousand
streams hand streams
and some demand

man of the it
most arms how she was
play it and our

mercy word's milk
unless from for
fool do in mouth

the lamb hit the play
down to the thrown soul
laid into the like

butcher against tooth
breath here baby
fool they words

dumb as dearest
in me among prisoner
will on one

he do in be the sleep
unto comes hast
here it did just spoke self

flesh he is his dumb
within comes out
and my and a wots

mouth in hand
down my mind
play had been and

sweetest legate sweet
I am more unlawfully
dog to will will

private
blood made
it spoke

do in than love itself
is as you are
as as you are than

DEANNA FERGUSON

excerpts from

MY BODY LIES OVER THE OCEAN

Unless time
writ by lick
pox biopsy
the mess comes better

Yer cathedral juxtaposes my good doodoo and fate
objects one preparing signature for who?

Also technology comes possibly proxy
bored and crystallizing outside

* * *

The family all laughs at delicious accompany
so pure of earth the government succulent
cares nothing for late for all our commodity
for all our entanglement

* * *

Do grand variations dance to pierce affect of pose
adhered to the floor net-like all around
using double buoyance of code

Pounce on the large and the profound
    separate dependence
Attending minute environs more than before
    wetness placed in disbelief

Envision the free pull of air
passed all around in three sexes, after recuperative
        remitted with marbles, a place on top of the
            march deserving traffic

* * *

Net like eyes holding vertical countenance
is surface a traitor?
Near essay sworn adroit
little visible tapering
for colour of a good tittle
Dirigible or bus, vertical or surface, traitor
vapor uniform or meant
Fair treatment localizes spot roulette's gnarly beauty
long gone glory hole
A case of reinvestment plies the application
Fades familiar with the anti-treat of tongues a
Vaulting free remove before entropy trade

* * *

Afflicting official visage includes one talk
    on numbered feet, meters, symbols, green good faux
Advanced feeling mean auto matic jacked mechanic to fakery
Sell your electricity, procedures double filter sell your
    visible luminosity sell your arch measures that run on and on
    and rough up permitted betters sell your exposition

* * *

The cheques are sentient, the acid fruit

One fool disowns her torment to be on guard

The quotidian rose *recommended*

Curing hyper-sensitive regime — derailing, darling
Positive acumen principally blessed
is what nourished valor by whose rival value
Family outer history insult mine poor decision
Now in proportion to the blue hauté disposable
american cable endo sperm roll plenty maudlin as
A sun fecundly

Entwined mix to format complexes position
Equivocal to nothing added nothing removed
Less hysteria corny lisp as lief
Milted feelings one shout superb

*   *   *

Action sally forth future danger
Lame synthesis unused in soul's velour
Comic deride faux impasse I am
Not sentimental more than guided along
Red pox at the cry yard evidence they
Just pour able down drains and pretend colours

I have *lithe concern* for the equipment,
Is best demanded of all the rotten english, what
With hello out at ends of the page
False flower a freak descending, just out of the way, down the
clapboards

Fury a marquee I and other letters plus less than a child's
Of course the pen's insulin moors up north, but not
Above sublimation of an uproar
The temperature has been martini
Logger and dance dog on the floor
Name roulettes eternally and I regret never regret falling out
Stance, is it a child's, chair is not an earth sore
Blown coquette yet
one self as ever?
Governing high despise hopes

JEFF DERKSEN

LINGER

An *S*, barely bent traces
a profile on my left
side that I mouth —
it clears visually
as it closes in
on scent. Today the clouds
"swept" across the high
corporate sky building
a context for me
to live in. This urge
or cause for a complete
is a rhythmic run
of my arm. Overall a depth
or width limits
a time we define. Zonal
frontal. A list changes, anxiety
tied with an "ownership"
that has a history. A chinook
bent temperatures again. This
names a date when we
can call one another
a calendar as today
and writing a body
is never solitary. How does *he*
refuse a privilege
that is parched and stacked
yet operable? Just as gender
is not an isolate. I had been
sleeping, just at that stage
always behind you. "Inner speech
is speech almost
without words." The city
turned upside down so that I
don't see where the history is
until an office light flicks off
in a downtown tower. You disrupt
my chemistry in a shop doorway
filled with plaid. Somehow
it takes moisture in. In
the afternoon I want

my senses plugged up
or overloaded as the sun
lights up *systemic.* The rivers
used to contain
the city, now they're inside it
as arteries, aerial
photos. *"Need"* 's deep
and blue, so shapes
the very . . . act of thickening
up in anticipation. The "hypothetical
ecstasy" is a surprise
too filling up the lungs
or prolonged laughter. The flag licks
out of the window
like flames or "domestic
violence." Light ice on
the edge of the banks. The oil
mimics me. The cold
clarifies the air. Overlaid
times let me look at a level
below skin, wanting to be not
metaphorical but erotic writing
in lipstick or red wine
across my white shirt. The sky
closes and it snows. I'm
the interpretant to a pleasure flick
that's rounded and taut
until information accrues
on my lips before I drop
down in my particular
gender. Power is performed
unlike oppression. I can't believe
the water. Our genitals
talk to each other, we sit
back. It's not enough
to "enter into history"
to be with you, I'm poised
and oiled. An affectionate lick
down a length is a rhythm
that runs into roughened skin
and salt. "As well"
is my unthinking
connective. Prolonged
longing lingers to twist
of tips and taste. If the sky
is only blue, is there
a sky or is it regionalism
and myopia. The anxiety of my
body puts a pressure
on your hand
that your fingers
respond to. So I forgot
that she is dead. My mind pushes
a body loud onto a landscape
photo documents a sexual
afternoon. Away wavering
in script.

THE BARSCHEIT HORSE:

LISA ROBERTSON CHRISTINE STEWART CATRIONA STRANG

A DRIFTING FABLE

STYLE INTERROGATES A LEXICON

I.

SINCERITY IS VERBAL ETIQUETTE. IT WORKS FOR SOME BOYS.

2.

IT IS THE STYLIST'S CENTRAL IDEOLOGICAL BUSINESS TO DITHER HISTORY — THE SURFACE TENSIONS OF STYLE GOAD THE CUSTODIANS.

3.

THINK HARD; WHEN WE SPEAK OF STYLE, WE SPEAK OF DESIRES. THEY VEX A PRICK'S UBIQUITY.

4.

VIBRATING ON THE DANGEROUS EDGE OF A TRANSPARENCY, STYLE WITHHOLDS ITSELF, NEGOTIATES A TABLEAU OF SPATIAL AND POLITICAL DISCRETION. IT'S A PARADIGM'S FUSE.

5.

YET A FANTASY OF STYLE IS NEVER MERELY PRIVATE; IT STAGES HEADLONG, SHIVERING, UNAUTHORISED: CIVIC. STYLE IS HISTORY'S DICTION; THAT IS TO SAY, STYLE FLAUNTS SIMULTANEOUSLY THE SYNTAX OF FUTURITY AND HISTORY, LEANING INTO THE FAST LIGHT OF OBSOLESCENCE.

TACIT: OLD HABITS PRACTICE

CATRIONA STRANG

from

WAT, AN OPERA

SCENE: *The Beach. St. Gabardine tells of the passion she conceived for L.*

St. Gabardine: Her impact shimmered, it was her flounced instep. From a great distance I was struck, and yet I hid my love, whose expression (both private and indecipherable) took shape darkly (She sings).

INELIGIBLE STYLE: A SECRET DIRECTIVE

My haberdashery also. The natty matte avocado upsweep of her confounded silhouette. She strode unattainable ever, her ambulant hip-red thrust a perfect seam, the perfect unattainable bias-cut boulder-lapped crosstitch complexion, swathed in milky new gabardine leisure class finance, and best suited to the illegible overlay of a nip-waisted if quirky domesticity. Who could truss a double-breasted wingtip frock? Capering in my ridiculous lamp shade military-style hairpiece for work and weekend, my signature's subtle, my biology flocked and ironic. Oh for a dissent torn inside out, scorching these woollen cravings through to a shimmering and silky-gathered cut. Yet who might pin so bold a declaration, or collect my rubber fairisle? And still my underpinned raffia cravings lap on a foreign shore.

enter L

L: My raffia, Gabardine, would melt if you embraced me. Understand? My image is seamed. You would untie my knots, have me swathed in lavender and lick my tiny wounds.

St. Gabardine: *(indignant)* I never promised stigmata!

L: Get a grip, Gabardine. *She turns and nearly walks into Black Gavin as he enters, pissed and singing his Stagger Song:*

> an awkward
> and if edible,
> as irritation, swagger.
> culpable if only . . .
> stagger.

While singing he takes several swipes at **L,** *who stabs him with a dagger she wears concealed in the folds of her green velvet.* **Black Gavin** *falls bleeding at Gabardine's feet. She swoons as* **L** *casually wipes her bloody hands on her gown, and* **Wat Tyler** *enters at a run. Scene ends.*

SCENE: *The Church. Enter* **Wat Tyler,** *still running. He runs right up to the altar where* **The Bishop** *is preaching against revolt.*

Wat Tyler: Swine! You love what is cheerless and fainthearted, you are blind creatures, dumb hounds who can no longer bay. You keep a purse where your hearts should be. But still I thrust this at your shrivelled hearts: today men and women, babies, dogs were all stripped and despoiled and put to the sword. The ground was littered with blood, brains, fragments of flesh, limbless trunks, hacked-off arms and legs, bodies ripped up or stoved in, livers and hearts that had been chopped to pieces or ground into mash, it was as if they had rained down from the sky. The whole place ran with blood — streets, river-banks, a real, ripe Catholic harvest and you sat here wanking.

Edgar Gauntlett rises from the congregation.

Wat Tyler: *(to Edgar)* Too much capital, too much perfume, my snakey! *They fight.*

~ TO BE CONTINUED ~

DAME NINNY'S DITTIES

(to be sung by her Gorgeous Minions)

1. Imagine a grained vex
an unauthorized scrapy irk
roughing-up our sanded
cusp: a nettled ply, a rustle's
wing, a kissing rasping kiss
an irksome delight

2. Or a peppered task: limbed
flecked, coriandered — a smoking
simmering impertinence. What's
said? Her marrow's
honey-wafered, she
abets us. We're strewn

3. Swamped, clung, seethed, we're
sick, firsted by her saffron, all
oiled for her, terrible, her
wrist's cleave — make no word
of this, she's a meddler, a collation
a buttered ember

4. Would thrum this
pooling, late-knife it
rim & spook
with it — so wasted, so
unadorned, this arable
nectar, this fleeced turn

5. *(Dame Ninny's own)*
Your scathing claque
tremulous & clingy
little blue citadine
roar hither hi ho
vene
pillage
much less mockery
your plush-covered remorse

6. Her bones scoff
swipe over our supine
indiscretions, riffs
tangible, swarms.
Unstinting, we're her revel's
tremor: a stale vent

DAME NINNY'S ELEGANT REFUSAL

Luck's infatuated
with me, pools curvy here
as spacious as your debtor's
heart, as moral & inky
as our tender, tender.
I'm infinitely dashing, & spurn
your beamish curve, would sooner
stroke an absent lick
than sleek your scrap

CHRISTINE STEWART

from

TAXONOMY

CLASSIFICATION: a sense brought to the whole edgeless boundary. I have isolated a type. I have pointed to the beginning in every sense. I have felt the scars of my gaze leap, cry out: *I see you there, It watches me.* Kneeling, I have demanded the arm.

* * *

ANIMALIA: The animal folds back and is once more located between the acts that do not take place. It is the action through distinct parts of a closed organ. Readable and doubled, there is no cunning; there is only furtive experience, caresses in the strictest sense. It is delight. It is a sparing of kisses. It is seductive and errs in lapses. Fruition respects its repetition. Patience details its follies. The animal seizes the hair, swallows it in essential part of distinction. This is intoxicating. This is never entered, but held and hidden and added: to caress and be sparing, to return to sleeping, to return to ardent desire, to the bed, to the curtains. To kiss, to swallow, to tremble is never an intermediary between everything and nothing; it is held within. In it *Letting* can read *Produce.* The animal is a distribution of shadow. It is always protected. It is never opened. Packaged in a classical shape, the animal is the literary message *Deliver.* The animal is a gesture of furnishment. It designates. It gazes its supplants. Its ears are born out of misrepresentations. Its tail is a protective screen of undecidability (coitus emerges and jeweled boxes). A blow without its mark is the transformation of language. The heart, the intestines and a slender thread-like tissue seem masked, palpable, slipped.

* * *

VEGETABALIS: The plant is fashioned from incurable want. It is a natural thing thrust between a knavish mortal and thee. Vegetables gaze at men in order to not tempt their cupidity. The Mineral Kingdom holds the threat of perversion, but the plant risks the northern by proxy: It is haughty, indifferent; it is naughty and unmanageable. The fear of the sun, of the sky, of masturbation blinds us to its crimes. Roots, rutabagas are inconceivable to reason. They are bones at the origin of society. They kill the father and lightly softly on the same gesture. They are a tribal network of little books whose dialectics are an ontology of desire. They mate a living discourse that describes itself as an imitation of the globe. One soul is felt through the lack of another. Fattened-out, their words are soundless, aphasic and primitive. Vegetables run out of words. They wander, kneeling at the edge of literature, weaving stories of their own dazzling limits. Demented from reason, they say, *I . . .* They say, *So they say . . .* They say, *Law.* I say, *Receipt* where I live, but it is madness, it is not enough, it is spinning.

* * *

MINERALIS: The mineral is gold and agonizes. Its cadence lies in the table, empty rooms, and ptyx. The wave of our own nakedness shapes its envelope and puts it to question in *un* formed sediments. Its theory is naked to the hammer, to the fire. The simple sum of substitution craves its mine. Rock is spoken in reserve. It says, *Weakness.* It says, *Rummage the lover.* It should read, *Produce.* It should read, *Less to think this.* To locate its functioning is to burn alive in vaporous languor. Quarries, pits, and fogs absent us. Metal is vein*less* and apodal. It is an affectation, a substitution of exterior for space. Sand encloses the rupture of botany. The taste of slate accords us to our grasp, to our struggle. It is desire. It is the supplement of art. It does not know how to be cured. It is simply the world moving its tongue. The mineral says, *Fair images* and *Whole anguish.* Age is broached through the knowledge of its advancement; it carves out its contours and broaches its symptom. It effects a sexuality of texture. Its limbs protrude cheerful and expressive through salt water, tangled leaves and fierce grace. Security is its writing as it works toward an end. This is limited by coy leaps and eruptions. Only copper can account for being held. It is a justification for surprise. Copper is a language, a logic that speaks out: *I fear repetition, I list with reserve, I conceal, I do not conceal.*

LISA ROBERTSON

from

DEBBIE (AN EPIC)

HER VIGIL (FRAGMENTS TOWARDS AN ENTERTAINMENT)

Here are ancient songs of certain authorship. "The one being kissed" makes tantrums plausible but a subtraction of reference means you won't learn her name. Try the retrograde patience poverty teaches. It could be failure yet some like that hell, bless fresh gals from the midst of gender: tiny bombs, flesh lilies, decimals.

Friend Venus, toss your liquid glove to virgins,
(Such cold qualms test their vertigo)
Name by increment those volute ribs
Fold rhythm back from florid arms.

✶

She sits hybrid at the Dairy Queen
Among ripe prayers and lures — fanning Psyche's
Louche stuff — adores calendars. Hey Psyche!
That's some kit: schools quit for its languor.

✶

Gutters tumble, the green rimmed spring imbibes us;
I'm minus merit under the flux of this girl's
Pure bridge — why nurse regret?
The stirred earth kneels for her fat moans.

✶

My Darling's vigilance is trepidation's teacher:
I skim the numbered stars and open all the subtle books.
I'll not surpass her luxe; each breath's a tantrum
Buttering the night's loose window.

✶

In her dream of Justice,
Like a crease soaked in the purple spume of boy's tears
Or a black stem under a hoof,
Undulant Diane drinks her straight.

*

My shut lips refuse music: will greenness never come to me?
Each tarnished day unties another name of certainty.
Please, muse of my heart, unloose this looped throat —
Stroke tenderly that sovereign silence.

HOW TO JUDGE

To those whose city is taken give glass
Lockets. To those whose quiver gapes give Queens
And pace their limbs with flutes, ropes, cups of soft
Juice. To those whose threshold vacillates give
That bruise the dust astonished. To falling
Heroes give raucous sibyl's polished knees.
To those who sip nectar give teeth. And if
They still sip nectar — give green chips of wood.
To swimmers give clocks or rank their hearts
Among new satellites as you would
Garbo's skint lip. To scholars, give dovecots.
To virgins, targets. Justice has nothing on them.
Virgil, sweetheart, even pretty fops need
Justice. If they think not let creditors
Flank them and watch their vigour quickly flag.
To exiled brides give tiny knives and beads
Of mercury then rob them of prudence
For prudence is defunct. To those who fist
Clouds, give powder. And if their sullen
Wallets flap, give nothing at all. Still
I have not addressed lambent fops
Swathed in honey, the stuttering moon,
Martyrs, Spartans, Sirens, Mumblers, Pawns,
Ventriloquists — or your sweet ego.
The beloved ego in the plummy light
Is you. When I see you in that light
I desire all that has been kept from me:
Etcetera. For you. Since your rough shirt
Reminds me of the first grass
Pressing my hips and seed heads
Fringing the sky and the sky
Swaying lightly to your scraped
Breath, since I hear
Panicked, my sister calling,
Since the gold leaves have all
Been lost, and you are at least
Several and variegated
I toss this slight thread back.
The beloved ego on cold marble
Blurs inscription. Dear Virgil
I think your clocked ardor is stuck
In the blue vein on my wrist. It stops
All judgement.

DEBBIE'S FOLLY

"What if intellectual ambitions were only the imaginary inversion of the failure of temporal ambitions." — *Pierre Bourdieu*

"I'd like to think of narrative as a folly, a classically styled folly, whose conspicious inutility might decorate and articulate the idea of the present. Much in the way that the library, at some trouble to justify profligacy, is a folly." — *Debbie*

PROEM

Between antiquity and us floats love in the library. I'll import back into antiquity this fervid span, this unfleshed sex, this loosening tear at the mid-afternoon institution. But even a tear refracts the cursive grammar of gender. I'll call it a lense, a wet rhetoric whose long focus will gather the lilies, the roses, the simple daisies from the pleasant grandeur of that Roman walk to offer them to you.

ARGUMENT

With what suave domesticity Virgil strolls among the deep shelves of the paternal library. The metric pulse of the catalogue or calendar charts his walk. To narrate an origin as lapidary, as irrevocable, is merely to have chosen with a styled authority from the ranked aisles of thought. For if Virgil has taught me anything, it's that authority is just this: a rhetoric or prescribed style which has asserted the phantom permanency of a context. Shall we consider that it is here, in this crumbling folly of taxonomy, that rhetoric flicks her blithe kilt, tempts us to slip between the shelves, find a nuanced nook where an exchange could take place? All porcelain shepherdesses lead to Rome. They're figurines of rhetoric. If I met one in the library, why should I not trust the cadenced drape of her skirt? She will guide me.

Narrative annotates an ambivalence: I should follow this old girl because I want her. The rhetoric of our identification flutters, marked or sprigged with decorative passages like an eyelet cloth. I want to give her a frock through which ambivalent desires might proliferate. The classical lends me a vexed lexicon of techniques or dictions which I shall turn to make a fetching dress for this barbarous shepherdess.

Virgil recedes into the distance. Debbie tugs at books as loose dresses, her cold porcelain clarity so sotto voce it pours like rope. Halfway down the aisle we drift through a languorous gap in the borrowed alphabet into the surprisingly fearless compatibility of the classical afternoon.

Ships named for women move towards description. They enter narrative as I have entered books. Whose city is this? Over wine-dark lawns swallows perform auguries and further back economy sculpts the harbour. Islands leak like ink into pockets. Dead-good queens flounce with civic tenderness: their unspooled diction drags and flirts. Slick lyric blocks history. Closure ornaments this plight. Narrative is pushing failure. I feel my gender is out there, floating wildly in that harbour.

But thought greets an ornament. Failure or closure structures heroes. From the outside, from a position of threat, from rank forests and islands, sirens or queens could disperse his fated trajectory. A guy tests his story against songs and cushions and feasts so that he may continue to produce beginnings. Each beginning is a cleavage. The bower is a pyre. To be left behind is annihilation, so it seems. But thought greets an ornament.

Debbie: I dreamt a sonnet mapped my brittle sleep —
I read the curbs of epic lust's *derive*
And there, saw myself.

Precocious closure sculpts
Thin difference, thin frock.

I greet an ornament. Hello shepherdess! Lend me a bit of that stuff. That fancy stuff. Physiognomy falls in ropes of water capable of deafness. After having had *feminine* sex our wanton love of thought asks us: Are phonemes free? O stupid forest — we heed, we deserve, the conditional tense: our hips would close on retrospect mumblers. Dear Virgil, this is how it is.

Glass houses envelope narrative. It's a lenience in conversation. One person leans back on purple cushions. The other, having travelled for years towards this meeting, brocades a cunning failure. He is the honoured guest. His lounging hostess has provided: foaming gold cups, lyres, fretted roof of gold, torches, jewels, fifty serving maids, a hundred young pages, rare napkins, this embroidered couch. He may speak with slow authority.

I'm observing this scene from the dark lawn, the players back-lit by a wealth of lamps. I'm out of my neighbourhood. The air here is perfumed, the gardens ancient and luxuriant. I am compelled to witness this long redundancy, though I already know the swank and honeyed story.

PERORATION

Books and girls are real lacunae, ya. All that we have forgotten about narrative steals back into narrative and watches us with shining eyes. That is to say, a guy's value lies precisely in the failure of his eschatological ambitions. Narrative secretes his centre. The transparency of the classical is a gorgeously useless ruse. Somewhere among these flowering transparencies a shepherdess is hidden. Perhaps she's shacking up with Queens. Perhaps she's cataloguing the rhetorics of plush ambivalence. Gentle colleagues, imagine yourselves as Debbie. Then collate these riffs: Posterity's provenance is lax. Proxy twins the inveterate ghosts of a fop's apocalypse. Debbie learns the word loveliest, feeds the future to your capsized mouths. There is no outside except the one that, faunal, we make by consignment.

Under the Influence:

JACK SPICER, ROBIN BLASER, AND THE REVISION OF "IMAGINARY ELEGIES," 1957

Jack Spicer, San Francisco 1965

JACK SPICER, the American poet who died in 1965, began writing his "Imaginary Elegies" in 1950. The first four were complete by 1956, and on his return to the Bay Area from Boston, he made them the showpiece of his triumphant reading at San Francisco State on April 11, 1957. Later Spicer dramatically revised these poems for publication in Donald Allen's anthology *The New American Poetry* in 1960, but the original versions have maintained a consistent popularity among purists, who for nearly forty years have cherished the bootleg tapes of this reading (now reproduced on the enclosed CD). In these "Elegies" — and in the poems of Robert Duncan's *Opening of the Field,* written concurrently — we hear the mature apotheosis of the Berkeley Renaissance, the poetic movement pioneered ten years before by Duncan, Spicer and Robin Blaser while still students at UC Berkeley. It was a movement very much opposed to the prevailing critical orthodoxy of the day — the "New Criticism," perceived by these poets as a junta of "Eastern" and "Anglo" influence — but in practice their poems still bore a strong influence of the high modernism foregrounded by the New Critics, the threnodic Eliot of the *Four Quartets* and the nostalgic melancholy of Pound's early cantos.

During the summer of 1957, Robin Blaser visited Spicer in San Francisco, bringing with him the manuscripts of two new poems, "The Hunger of Sound" and "Letter to Freud." These gritty, urban poems, shot through with the drugs, the jazz, the wry attitude of the Boston bohemian underclass, marked a new experiment in Blaser's work. Their mastery astonished Spicer, who had, after all, spent a year in Boston himself without discovering a way to translate the coarseness or ecstasy of his experience into language. Under the influence of Blaser's new syntax — and by extension the contemporary work of the entire "Boston school" (Joe Dunn, Steve Jonas, John Wieners) — Spicer began to revise his "Elegies" heavily, moving away from the extended conceits and metaphysical decor that had characterized his early writing and, following Blaser, towards a practice of dictation. There was first an interim stage, a blend of Gertrude Stein and a Surrealism so thoroughly misunderstood, as Blaser admits today, as to amount to Expressionism (cf. "The poet builds a castle on the moon/ Made of dead skin and glass," in the revised "Elegy II"). By fits and starts, this new mode came to flower, for it allowed and invited the impersonal, the *randonnée,* the disjunct — the rupture of meaning which would then become the site of both poets' most interesting work. It became Spicer's general tendency to eliminate the purely "beautiful" or "dramatic" in favor of a poetry dense, dark and quarrelsome, a box of words rattled like marbles then spilled. Thus the revision of these "Elegies" led paradoxically to the "dictated" poems of *After Lorca* (also 1957) and the rest of Spicer's innovative *oeuvre.* He had learned one thing after all those years: "the temporary tempts poetry."

Curator Richard Fyffe has shown me a typescript of these poems, preserved among the Literary and Cultural Archives, Special Collections at Homer Babbidge Library, University of Connecticut; but I transcribed them in 1990 from the master tape in the American Poetry Archives at San Francisco State University. Thanks to Laura Moriarty, the archivist who located the tape for me, to Avery Burns, who printed a brief extract of this material in his magazine *LyricƐ,* and to Robin Blaser, literary executor of the Spicer Estate for permitting its release on CD and the publication of this transcript in this *Yearbook.*

—KEVIN KILLIAN

Imaginary Elegies

for Robin Blaser

"All that a man knows and needs to know is found in Berkeley."

— William Butler Yeats, *A Vision*

As described in the introduction, the italicized words, fragments, passages were excised or altered by Spicer a few months after his reading at San Francisco State (April 11, 1957) and do not appear in the final versions printed by Donald Allen in his 1960 anthology *The New American Poetry*.

I.

Poetry, almost blind like a camera
Is alive in sight only for a second. Click,
Snap goes the eyelid of the eye before movement
Almost as the word happens.
One would not choose to blink *or* go blind
After the instant. One would not choose
To see the continuous Platonic pattern of birds flying
Long after the stream of birds had dropped or had nested.
Lucky for us that there are *natural* things like oceans
Which are always around,
Continuous, disciplined *subjects*

To the moment of sight.
Sea, moon and sun and nothing else is subject.
Other things are less patient and won't rest
Between the intervals of perception. They go about their business
As if we didn't have to see them.
When I praise the sun or any bronze god derived from it
Don't think I wouldn't rather praise the very tall blond boy
Who ate all of my potato-chips at the Red Lizard.
It's just that I won't see him when I open my eyes
And I will see the sun.
Sea, moon and sun are always there when the eyes are open
Insistent as *breakfast food.*
One can only *justify*
These *cheap* externals for their support of
What is absolutely temporary.
The blond boy, like the birds, although moving,
Has given a sort of fictive presence to this scenery.
He is bathed through the deepest and bluest of waters
Limb upon deep, sweet limb. He is syntactically conjured
Through all of love's possible meanings
Until he is almost alone in this room. Here, and merely alive.
He is bleached by an Apollonian sun
Until he is white as cold, white as my blindness,
An Arctic Circle of absolute dreaming,
Complete with polar bears and Santa Claus and rich with ice.
It is as if we conjure the dead and they speak only

Through our own damned trumpets, through our damned medium:
"I am little Eva, a Negro princess from sunny heaven."
The voice sounds blond and tall.
"I am Aunt Minnie. Love is sweet as moonlight here in heaven."
The voice sounds blond and tall.
"I'm Barnacle Bill. I sank with the Titanic. I rose in salty heaven."
The voice sounds blond, sounds tall, sounds blond and tall.
"Goodbye from us in spiritland, from sweet Platonic spiritland.
You can't see us in spiritland, and we can't see at all."

2.

God must have a big eye to see everything
Which we have lost or forgotten. Men used to say
That all lost objects stay upon the moon
Untouched by any other eye but God's.
The moon is God's big yellow eye remembering
What we have lost or never thought. That's why
The moon looks raw and ghostly in the dark.
It is the camera shots of every instant in the world
Laid bare in terrible yellow cold.
It is the objects *that* we never saw.
It is the dodos flying through the snow
That flew from Baffinland to Greenland's tip
And did not even see themselves.

The moon is meant for lovers. Lovers lose
Themselves in others. Do not see themselves.
The moon does. The moon does.
The moon is not a yellow camera. It perceives
What wasn't, what undoes, what will not happen.
It's not a sharp and clicking eye of glass and hood. Just old,
Slow *infinite* exposure of
The negative that cannot happen.
Fear God's old eye for being shot with ice
Instead of blood. Fear its inhuman mirror blankness
Luring lovers.
Fear God's moon for hexing, sticking pins
In forgotten dolls. Fear it for wolves.
For witches, *dragons*, magic, lunacy, for parlor tricks.

The world is full of watching witches
Bitching the world up. The witchlike virgin god Diana,
Being neither witch nor virgin is the moon's god.
Even her sex changes. She is a black bitch dog.
Look: she has yellow tits. Even her color changes.
But she doesn't exist. When the poem is over,
She is a nice, pretty poet with thick lips and blue eyes
And an elegant wardrobe.
Into the moon she goes.
The world is full of watching bitches
Witching the world up. The witchlike evil goddess Hecate,
Being neither witch nor evil is the moon's god.
Even his sex changes. He is an old black werewolf,
Sharpening his teeth on a berry bush.
But he doesn't exist. When the poem is over,
He is an anxious poet with a few delusions, kind as a rabbit.
Into the moon he goes.
The world is full of witch-hunting bitches
Watching the world upside down. The dragon-slaying hero Sigurd,
Being neither dragon-slayer nor hero is the moon's rival.
Even his sex changes. He is an huge black Walkure,
Looping all over Hell for a lover.
But he doesn't exist. When the poem is over,
He has dug no pit, killed no dragon. He is
Merely the poet at the end of his poem.

Evil somehow exists in the *relation*
Between the remembered and the forgotten,
Between the moon and the earth of the instant.
Evil somehow exists in the *relation*
Between what happened and what never happened
Between the *poet* and God's yellow eye.
Look through the window at the real moon.
See the sky surrounded. Bruised with rays.
But look now, in this room, see the *shape-changers,*
Wolf, bear, and otter, dragon, dove.
Look now, in this room, see the *shape-changers*
Flying, crawling, swimming, burning
Vacant with beauty.
Hear them whisper.

3.

God's other eye is good and gold. So bright
The shine blinds. His eye is accurate.
His *burnished* eye observes the *bright and blinding shine*
It shines. *Now, accurate as swooping birds,*
The burnished eye is shining back that light
It saw and shined.
Light feeds on *light.* God feeds on God. God's goodness is
A black and blinding cannibal with sunny teeth
That only eats itself.
Deny the light. God's golden eye is brazen.
It is clanging brass
Of good intention. It is noisy burning
Clanging brass.
Light is a carrion-crow
Cawing and swooping. Cawing and swooping.
Then, then there is a sudden stop.
The day changes.
There is an innocent old sun quite cold in clouds.
The ache of sunshine stops.
God is gone. God is gone.
Nothing was quite as good.
It's getting late. Put on your coat.
It's getting dark. It's getting cold.

Most things happen in twilight
When the sun goes down and the moon hasn't come
And the *bats are flying.*
Most things happen *when God isn't looking,*
When God is blinking between good and evil,
And the bats are flying.
Most things happen in twilight when *things are easy*
And God is blind as a gigantic bat.

The boys *stretched out* above the swimming pool receive the sun.
Their groins are pressed against the warm cement.
They look as if they dream. As if their bodies dream.
Unblind the dreamers for they ache with sun,
Wake them with twilight. They're like lobsters now
Hot red and private *while* they dream,
They dream about themselves.
They dream of dreams about themselves.
They dream they dream of dreams about themselves.
Splash them with *sunset* like a wet bat.
Unblind the dreamers.
Poet,
Be like God.

4.

Yes, be like God. I wonder what I thought
When I wrote that. The dreamers sag a bit
As if five years had thickened on their flesh
Or on my eyes.
Splash them with what?
Should I throw rocks at them
To make their naked private bodies bleed?
No. Let them sleep. This much I've learned
In these five years in what I spent and earned:
Time does not finish a poem.
The dummies in the empty funhouse watch
The tides wash in and out. The thick old moon
Shines through the rotten timbers every night.
This much is clear, they think, the men who made
Us twitch and creak and put the laughter in our throats
Are just as cold as we. The lights are out.
The lights are out.
You'll smell the oldest smells—
The smell of salt, of urine, and of sleep
Before you wake. This much I've learned
In these five years in what I've spent and earned:
Time does not finish a poem.
What have I gone to bed with all these years?
What have I taken crying *into* bed
For love of me?
Only the shadows of the sun and moon
The dreaming boys, their creaking images,
Only myself.
Is there some rhetoric
To make me think that I have kept a house
While playing dolls? This much I've learned
In these five years in what I've spent and earned:
That two-eyed monster God is still above.
I saw him once when I was young and once
When I was *scared* with madness, or was *scared*
And mad because I saw him once. He is the sun
And moon made real with eyes.
He is the photograph of everything at once. The love
That makes the blood run cold.
But he is gone. No realer than old
Poetry. This much I've learned
In these five years in what I've spent and earned:
Time does not finish a poem.
Upon the old amusement pier I watch
The creeping darkness gather in the west.
Above the giant funhouse and the ghosts
I hear the seagulls call. They're going west
Toward some great Catalina of a dream
To where all poems end.
But does it end?
The birds *believe it's there.* Believe the birds.

RUSSIA'S NEW FREEDOMS

MOST OF THE FOLLOWING TRANSLATIONS APPEARED EARLIER IN A BILINGUAL ANTHOLOGY OF CONTEMPORARY RUSSIAN AND AMERICAN POETRY PUBLISHED FOR A CONFERENCE TITLED "THE NEW FREEDOMS."* THAT CONFERENCE, HELD AT THE STEVENS INSTITUTE OF TECHNOLOGY IN APRIL, 1994, BROUGHT TOGETHER SEVERAL CONTEMPORARY RUSSIAN POETS, INCLUDING ALL OF THOSE REPRESENTED HERE EXCEPT ALEKSANDR EREMENKO AND ALEXEI PARSHCHIKOV, AND MORE THAN TWO HUNDRED AMERICANS, MOST OF WHOM ARE ASSOCIATED WITH WHAT ELIOT WEINBERGER CALLS THE TRADITION OF "INNOVATORS AND OUTSIDERS."

There were several conferences with names like "The New Freedoms" for American writers in the 1930s. Generally these gatherings had a leftist orientation and were organized by interests friendly to the Soviet Union. Poets were told about collective farming and lectured on ways to make their work socially useful. The American economy was collapsing, Stalin seemed kindly, and the Moscow trials were unimagined. A few years ago, Carey Nelson tried to revive an interest in the political poetry of the decade, but writers like H.H. Lewis, the socialist "Plowboy Poet" of Missouri, simply aren't very good.

Politics change, and several years ago young poets passing through American universities encountered a new ascendancy — much of it high on theory and good intentions but low on music. Spicer, in the few classrooms where he was read at all, was treated as a post-structuralist *avant la lettre* rather than as a gnostic and pleasurably seductive queer. The true politics, the kind that no one has to teach, were overlooked, but everyone knows that now, and there's no reason to say it again except as a reminder that whatever was going on then isn't worth looking at now.

But what do you do when you can't do what you used to do? If anyone should know the answer this time around, it's the Russians. And so: "The New Freedoms."

When the Russians came to Stevens, they went, between readings, to the bar down the street and made it their "office."

Everyone agreed that this was a good place to begin.

The readings were very good.

As Spicer said, the muses "are patient with truth and commentary as long as it doesn't get into the poem."

—Edward Foster

*To these are added several of Michael Palmer's recent translations of Alexei Parshchikov, a collection of which will be published soon by Avec. And since Lyn Hejinian and Elena Balashova's translation of Arkadii Dragomoshchenko's *Xenia* is now available from Sun and Moon, I have substituted a passage from Hejinian and Balashova's as yet unpublished translation of *Phosphor*.

ARKADII DRAGOMOSHCHENKO

TRANSLATED BY LYN HEJINIAN AND ELENA BALASHOVA

from
PHOSPHOR

What events are hidden in what each of us is tirelessly writing? This is the third week of Postmodernism's first war. Consequently, the book at this critical point or the transubstantiation of time — (necessity too in these terms falls aside: toward the sun and moon and what indirectly attests to the falling away of the dichotomy between the concealed and the manifest; and at the same time the well-worn opposition between inner and outer becomes inessential: and right here we remember once again the Book written from within and from outside of the Beginning and End) — turns out to be directed backward, which is as impossible as a *contradictio in adjectio* . . . . He might have mentioned a few other of the themes that preoccupy him, one of which once demanded a more intense interpretation. Being completely incorporeal, genderless, though possibly intending gender, existing in the form of an inordinately abstract composition, which — and you should ask him about this — he would describe, resorting to wagging his fingers and mooing, noting to himself at the same time how the vowel sound *i,* clearly unpleasant in a multitude of familiar combinations, the milk shroud of madness covers the carving in a relief that he particularly understands. The convexities. The pillow's crumpled slopes. Heartburn. Dropping in sparkling blindness, the glass that topples itself. Transparency, pressing into the bi-convex lens of space and love. Don't leave me. Swear that you'll never leave me. Where did you get the idea that someone means to leave you? I speak of this because sooner or later it will be time to speak of something. And you are ready to say, "Isn't it all the same?" You are right. Yes, I am right. But not about the future.

And here notwithstanding all the optical plasticity of narration we come to something that doesn't lend itself to any visualization, to any pliant embodiment — namely, t*he discovery of presence in absence:* the Future Perfect, Rebirth (like prophecy) is possible in a book, "the tearing of the veil," but the book itself is impossible in the future, that is, in itself, since it is its own Future Present. Or rather — the book's presence in the reading of it, its being present (finite, comprehensible), is determined by its prophesying, i.e., its discovering within itself (the imperfect form of the present tense) its own Being (in becoming), where the book is always already absent, a mere element, perhaps, or a portion of what it foresees is the first/last book, concealing it — the Law. And its finiteness in turn is determined by some Alterbeing, existing only in this finiteness: within and without. Reading in windy weather. Near the window. The wind, the window, immobility, speed. Gender endings, intertwined in play. Autonomy doesn't exist, intones a bird. And it goes on: "Meister Eckhart is sick, he has a fever." At sunset some man came to the door. Without a word he sank on the threshold. His appearing might signify a certain urgency, an event, some error or coincidence. To this very day we have never ceased to wonder, the mother said to the wayfarer, whether or not one should honor one's native land, or masturbate during one's youth when the organism is unstable, only just forming, accumulating strength, and whether this threatens not only the native land but also the future family, since one will undoubtedly turn into an idiot if one fails to honor one's native land by becoming preoccupied with murderous masturbation. And did the wayfarer keep a diary in his youth? And did he really grow a cucumber in a bottle, patiently tending it? Did he really attend the literary circle in the district Pioneers House, write poems, piercing with sharp allusions? And did he really imagine that the structure of the cosmos resembled the structure of a raw diamond? Did he survive his acne? Is he prepared to give his life for: a) his eternal love of the woman at the newspaper kiosk, b) the happiness of the people? Was he frightened by dreams in which he distinctly could see: a) homosexuals, b) something else? Did he really still have his father's military sword belt? Did he have any knowledge of child sexuality? Did he catch his mother in an adulterer's bed? Did this have anything to do with his becoming mute after learning of Weizsacher's principles of coexistent conditioning? Did he believe that dogs have a soul? Did he like to examine his own feces? Did he picture his own funeral, and if so did he weep, imagining the grief of his loved ones, weeping over his death? Did he feel that his nation exists in order to teach the world a lesson? Did he participate in ceremonial burnings of sorcerers? Which did he prefer — the interpretation of midnight as a two-sided mirror of mercy and condemnation? or the lines about peacocks' screams and ankles and wrists garlanded with waterlily blossoms? Or did he fully share Theodor Adorno's view, exclaiming at times, "How right he is!"? His opponents, the keepers of earlier preconditions, are still very powerful, as sly as they are insidious. We will learn to protect ourselves. Last week. Did he ever suspect the sheer number of dendrites, neurons, axons, and synapses that are enclosed in the skull of his universe where the river of life and death washes over its confines? Whom did he happen to meet on the pathways? Was he selected for some kind of award? Did he meet with Meister Eckhart? And did he keep a diary? Yes, did he keep a diary from which the next generation would extract an essential lesson? At the window. Sunset. Immobility and speed. Necessity in the coinciding of errors. Was he happy, finally, learning from his first lover that she masturbates in another way, turning the radio on softly, surrendering to a completely different revery, while at the same time turning on her genitals a light stream from the shower? Did his temperature when he was feverish play some role in the appearance of the hallucinations that shook him to the marrow? The wayfarer doesn't answer. His mind is preoccupied with the nature of weapons, ballistics, the angle of deviation, the force of trajectory. They fired into the dead body. The hole's micaceous web appears in the glass. It is ink, ink! No.

I like to provoke the sensation of the thin, undependable, somehow false, foil-like grounds of gender, bearing within itself a sleepy illusion of the laws of gravity, as if governed by my movement in the unconfining limits of gravitations and diversions of space. And when, in a radiant eclipse at the inevitable reunion with earth, at the increasing of masses and the sweetest, strawberry creamlike terror of children, consciousness takes on the transparency of compressed time, the theory of free fall blossoms with fresh oxides on the lips, past which the wind carries us, and in the mouth, formed in the ceremony of one thing, a second, then a third appearing and uniting with a word, while the imagination touches the soundlessly standing wind, which draws the metal shaft into its funnel with even greater tenderness than the world's absence, which clings to one's cheek in the sunny hoarfrost. The changes of human history, its failures, flights, displacements are nothing but a rippling of images running across the vibrating web of language — the strings of destruction sing to the dancing feet — on which, like dew, drops of being flow, spinning themselves into the web (at times under the weight of nocturnal moisture the web sags, gets tangled, rips; at times the dew evaporates without a trace), whose pattern, stretching beyond the horizons of speculation, is my perception, reception, and venture into a tireless anticipation of myself as a beautiful lesion stretched between mirrors in a labyrinth — the body — turned toward the body's experience, toward the sum of sensations and like a page with rows of letter on it — truly the least consoling instance of order. When the moon reaches an airless region in the clearing of its fullness, breaking its circumference, the shaking of the window frames ceases to disturb the ear, the night is unintelligible as night, ceasing to disturb the ear with its shaking; the lilac seethes with peroxide on the torn artery. It was Kaspar Hauser, poor, homeless, murdered, with a head like an oxygen cluster. He appeared one day in a book in Ukrainian on whose cover was depicted a lobster in an emerald abyss. Silver bubbles, Kaspar out of the darkness of an emerald childhood. Instruction in the brevity of an endless sentence. Like a scarab, scorched into a vitriolic dry decomposition. Sands. So many impressions! Money increases by itself, like an aimless insect (or the endocrine glands, increasing emotions — the shadow's grimace), wave after wave coming through the air. In the neighboring building, from all appearances, the doors are opened by a ghost. Spoons in its hands. The window's silky cocoon, the bare body, the brook, the woman, hoarfrost, paying no attention to the twilight nor to itself, it fades in the yellow luminescence of poverty and causality.

Aleksandr Eremenko

Translated by Alexander Kalouzhsky
and Joseph Donahue

Fragment

The translucent wires of the forest are crumbling.
The leaves waver slightly, nothing ever in working order for long.
There a silent *lemma* sagging along a straight road
The straight lines of the telegraph gives one a headache.

The air's unclear, there's a broken connection
Between the circuitry and the flower
And the river is haphazardly crawling under itself,
And it too rustles, at least all things are in phase.

The electric wind is tied in empty knots
and if the top layers of the red dirt were stripped away
the pine trees would be masts held to the ground with bolts
the tops are half twisted and the thread of the bolt gummed
with clay.

As soon as the stamped out rows
of fir trees fly away I will see through the window
a factory village torn and sinking in the thick mud by the river,
and a small brickyard with an even smaller hole in its side.

Does is matter that I haven't been here in eleven years,
the autumn thicket by the side of the road is still as clean and well
tended.
And the spot's still there, where Kolka Zhadobin by a campfire
one night molded me a pistol from a piece of lead.

There's my wife knitting on a long boring couch.
There's my bride sitting in a wooden chair
There's my mother at work and lost in rising fog
and my grandson peering through the window into the ruined air.

I died there yesterday. And I could hear
horrible and clear an old horse along the road
a workhorse, and I could hear as it climbed the hill
the "horsepower," whirring and choking like a chainsaw.

THE LENGTH OF A LOOK

The look that inducts men for war
taking their height, the look of a T-Square
the long look that underlies the world and supports it
like an old bracket, the long look out the window.

Glimpse of the beyond, Einstein saw it,
but did Einstein really amount to much?
He flipped the bracket over like an empty glass,
but: it was the same old bracket. As in an old myth

the world kept resting on the backs of whales.
But for us the importance is in the look,
and then all that it observes in the dark.
Length alone has meaning: a long, empty look.

With it one can gaze into a well for water
though it's no good for showing how to get to the recycling center
with old paper.
And if one spends the time working on one's looks at a health club
this long, empty look will vanish.

From all this we derive our view
on how to truly measure the length of an empty look
whether the sum of these lengths, when each is a single book,
equals one length, the length of an empty look.

. . . underlies the world, so that the cities
can stand level and secure in their places.
An empty movie house, the dredges of the supermarket
and the metronome of the branches, which ticks unnoticed between
the walls.

NINA ISKRENKO

TRANSLATED BY JOHN HIGH WITH PATRICK HENRY

TWO POEMS

(1)

In Russia it was always possible to bum a smoke
get a hit of booze   by a doorway covered with piss &
trashy graffitti   then pick the handful of dahlia
from the flower bed nearby   Fly away for a Saturday
to the Black Sea   with an old friend from childhood
Where meeting on the street together   you could finish off the affair in a public toilet
Always a field moving toward abundance   in our mood
& a tangible love   both to the rear end as well as to the breasts
LOVE'S — NOT A GAME!
graffitied with chalk on the wall   the way it is
along the depths of the building's 6th entry way
In Russia you could always kill a man
& wipe away the blood   with the earth
on the grass
on a birch tree
A place where the hospitable conscience always thrashes
& the fruits' first seed condemns its own people
to sacrifice
a country all the angels turned their backs on
a long time ago, maybe
& all the chimney sweeps threw themselves to the good work
In Russia   before you lost yourself
it was always with freedom & ease
that you could head off & bum a smoke

(2)

(for I. Shulzhenko)

Iron swans fly soundlessly from beneath
the brows of the drunk women
Sweetly peering into each other's eyes

pressing cautious careful gestures
on the other's lachrymal glands
Their knees pulled taut together
wild bees stiffen in the flight & the night its dampness the honey oozes
over the skirt hems

Honey & milk & gasoline spilling
from these empty canisters now over-turned
& the drunk women (nymphs hydrangeas caryatides
agaves asters)
release white mice from their heavy-leaden
quotation marks
catching with the back of their heads the life-bouy
of daily routines

Gathering them all up — the white mice & vipers & garden snakes
the tame lizards —
up into their starched breast-plates
& having abruptly cast their faces upward having fastened the mill-stone
to the hair & wheels
& having embraced the drunken women now enter the other's
vineyard
profiles of rapacious fledglings fox-cubs foxes
intently following

Drunk wives walking the vineyard sucking & gnawing
feverish in the gnashing of teeth
ripping the fresh wounds & the wailing as
this dense hot ball shatters the garden barriers
the vineyard walls
Rolling off the cliff entangled in the black thorn & sedge
the vile stench of the pond's scum
their clothes & combs cast off for the wild dogs
to devour
in this turbid rapture its trembling & astonishment
in this overfulfilled battle felt behind them

Saturated wicked naked gigantic nostrils blown out
like coral sails
the drunk women's silent cries enter the empty
triangle of love
the honorable ownership & higher
education
Smoking slowly & sweetly watching
each other's eyes

Vadim Mesyats

translated by Vadim Mesyats and Simon Pettet

A Norwegian Fairy-Tale

These are not tears — he's lost his eyes.
They rolled into the gloomy wood of Hevald.
A Troll picked them up.
And looked at the Moon.
This isn't a frog — he's lost his tongue,
It sprang into the gloomy wood of Hevald.
A Troll picked it up,
Looked at the Moon and declared, "Moon,
You are more precious than an ant of gold
And rounder than a hairy ball in a swamp!"
He laughed and laughed.
A patrol picked him up.
If you don't want to start crying, try instantly falling asleep.

A Guest in the Homeland

I'll spill ink, forget to find paper
Because time passes, only exterior
And the spine of the archipelago of the long river
Covers itself with frost in the hesitant dawn.
And bonfires gradually losing their color,
Reflecting each other, remain on the fishing wharf,
Between the grass and the suddenly wandering river,
Missing familiar lights at the top of the hill.
Where it's never too late,
To build some stonewall house or some wooden temple,
Only to have to ask yourself again and again,
Why do the floorboards always creak under your feet?
Why does the temple avoid the straight glance
And its tall shadow fall into empty waters?
Man is made up of water, and there's only one respite —
That it's possible to capture a fresh breath of freedom,
That you don't need to blaze a trail
From Varangians to Greeks,
Paying special attention to the West or East,
You died a natural death, and in this century.
And so, you are somewhere close by.
And the doors are slamming in my great Siberia.
Everyone's gone. So, soon their souls will go.
Consider them, so that they can more easily forget
Man is made up of water, and a ribbon of land.

1991

More depressing than a dusty fishbowl in the reform school . . .
More absurd than a bookmark on the first page . . .
More mysterious than an old globe which in the twilight
Glimmers as always with the only Capital in the world.

More piercing than the shriek of drunken gulls
Flying in a wild bunch up over Sunday steamers,
Carrying hundreds of tragic faces down the black river,
Those by the round windows, lost in a deep sleep.

More colorful than a pile of lace lingerie ready for washing,
Rinsing expensive slips in a soapy water,
Suddenly getting embarrassed by a crazy fantasy:
Now you are living with all of the butterflies in China . . .

More luxurious than words that should be stated directly,
Even if they are both stupid and vain.
At least to get to a strange and distant continent.
Skimming over the steel turnstiles of Soviet Customs.

Quieter than a crumpled glove falling from your hand,
Hoping to rest in a safe place,
Rolling somewhere beneath a bench under worn-out heels,
No longer a continuation of anybody's gesture.

Scarier than the sound of a key turning in a rusty lock
And this is not my house!
More annoying than "Come on now, don't whine!", spoken by a friend,
This being more typical of him . . .

The whole year is like arguing with the Rainman
Whom first you curse, but then make up with . . .
He barely glances back, staggers away,
You will never really love until you leave . . .

And this is better than the people's dreams
Which are always lost in some weird voiceless suspension.
When left alone amidst the emptiness
They come to nothing. They are no longer distinguishable from all the rest.

Alexi Parshchikov

Pall Bearing

translated by Michael Palmer with Darlene Reddaway

In the light of time, back-lit like an actor in the counter-order,
and squinting from the gloom, I gaze toward the anthropomorphic dark;
wherever I wander, my intuition figures Juna,

and she divides me into a hundred halves and flings me into the Kremlin;
barely orienting myself, I notice that I'm surrounded by those
gazing down through floor zero; of heavenly tiers there are seven.

Above the heads on the podium are minarets of shadow, as if from the bay
pre-dawn Cairo were coming into our sights
or the presidium were skewered from below by projected light.

Applause and speeches: the session shifts smoothly into a feast.
Here are Number One and Number Six, but agape between them
lies the shaft, mined of its innards, famous throughout the world.

Number Five thrusts out his lower lip and gives the thumb's up;
manganese oxide dissolves, like a dancer unfurling
gauzy fabric about the hall; Number Three looks on with a false grin.

In their dream-like movements I noticed a certain jerkiness.
Was it some nothing or a sliver of glass, as if a sharp-edged fragment
pricked beneath their collars — just see if you can reach it!

This was all in a fractured time out of synch: as in an old newsreel.
The hall's cupola blinked like a bull comprehending its slaughter.
I, however, was discovering the law of the coincidence of matter
and fate.

I loved the shores coated with sea-lettuce, neolite in moonshine,
and the glass of cabernet, radiance transmuted from the poppy
field . . .
But I'm here, descending still deeper into the pyramid's soulless
gloom.

Divided into a hundred halves I swarm; the feast it seems just might
become a procession. Banqueteers surge into the tunnel, and
closing ranks
like helmets on an immense ear of corn, they disappear down the
shaft.

What were they carrying? What did their bodies conceal? What was
their goal?
You blue spruce overcoat, answer me point blank!
They carried decades of death and the great terror's bed.

They bore of course the Supreme Ruler. He could be shrunk to a
salt grain,
could be divided into grain, grain, grain,
could be passed along a chain, chain, chain,

he could be a fleck of dust in cosmic space or a particle of your
beauty —
nation of maiden — in the feral tongue no matter which one!
Splitting apart, he could chisel himself ever more precisely, right
into a perfect void.

Like a dust pan, space is bent at the edges, and so long drawn out
— the unison
whoosh! — as from their imperial shoulders they lowered the
mummy in his box
where he lay askew and stuck. Just then I felt a subcutaneous

nudge and . . . reawoke in Georgia. Dances. Alien speech.
Should I light up? You got dignity, I got freedom.
And on the teardrop horns of snails, night shuffled its feet.

Jaguar on your shoulders, gilt on your cheekbones.
All in order. Isn't that enough? Behold, through the gates,
a silky lemon glow — they're sending us a car.

Minus Ship

translated by Michael Palmer with Eugene Ostashevsky

I split from the dark as if oakum had croaked.
Behind me City Hysteria blackened in chalky spasms,
the sun was liquid, the sloping sea reeked,
and reentering my body I knew God had redeemed me.

I remembered a scuffle on a square — the whistles and flaring
passions.
I idled in neutral by the pinball machine
where a woman was flashing, partly real —
the edge of this reality jarred by Scheherazade.

I was out of it, yet recall the ones in slow plummet
from the fight, as if tumbling through an apple tree
and grasping at the fruit, unable to choose . . .
Homeric-shouldered griffons were forming a pack.

And here at this most silent of seas — as with
eye muscles slowed by the Herb — pass that joint
toward a calm horizon — relax, don't rush . . .
. . . from mollusc to cow, idea to object . . .

In the mountains stirred the raisins of distant herds.
I strolled the shore as memory shoved from behind
but reflex and strain vanished into rhythm
and power arrayed itself along units of time.

All became what it should have been from the beginning:
poppies ripped through hills like T.V. static,
a donkey with fly's eyes imagined Plato,
the sea seemed fact, not mere apparition.

Precise Sea! Ringlets of a million mensurae.
Cliff — inseparable from. Water — essential for.
Their necessity burned through a random dust-speck
clutching them . . . but there was no ship!

I saw the vectored couplings, and all the essential clamps —
along the background a void sucked strength into itself —
saw even the smell of oil, the characteristic creak,
whiter than a shot of camphor yawned the Minus Ship.

It propagated — absence. It dictated — views
to views, and with no more than a glance
you'd be caught, as by a cotton filter,
then nod into extended diapason.

Color of the void, the Minus Ship roamed,
actually bobbing in place, moored to zero.
In the stretched diapason, a comma on its side . . .
And I crept up closer to the imperious bark.

The Minus Ship melted. I heard a distant *OM.*
A hidden genius plucked a melody on the doutar.
Aimed toward the Absolute and gliding volumetrically
it swelled and then veered off at its apogee.

The Minus Ship was swallowed, like arac on a table.
The doutar wove a new center of emptiness.
Swimming toward it on an ecstatic char — time now —
I focused and crossed over . . .

DMITRI PRIGOV

TRANSLATED BY ALEXANDER KALOUZHSKY AND SIMON PETTET

FROM

FIFTY TINY DROPS OF BLOOD IN THE ABSORBING MEDIUM

*   *   *

Little swastikas on a wedding shroud
A tiny drop of blood on a ring finger
Pure like the trimming of a rabbit-fur collar existence
Moscow–Berlin, 1990

*   *   *

The sting of a tiger
The trunk of a bull
A tiny drop of blood on a man's finger
on its way out of another body
Someone's stifled cry

*   *   *

The quiet echo of footsteps disappearing
over the roof
A tiny drop of blood on a kitten's paw
The fate of the poet in Russia
Miraculous transformation of horror into
triumph and back again
Into horror

*   *   *

The seven wonders of the world in the Moscow suburbs
A tiny drop of blood covered with a
piece of velvet
From where do you get this longing for a pink
ballgown and shimmer-
ing lace?

* * *

The private life of an officer
A tiny drop of blood on the left breast
of the neighborhood beauty
The fixed gaze of invisible
mahatmas translated into the
Russian tongue

* * *

The talk of an Englishman and a German
A tiny drop of blood on the walls of a twilight
cloister
A stone flying from the Russian back-
woods into the waters of the Atlantic
Ocean

* * *

Icy vodka between windowpanes
The soft crackling of wires
stripped bare
A lynx slowly turning into a girl with
a tiny drop of blood in the corner of her mouth

* * *

Hair-raising screams from the
near-by Zoo
The fleeting moment
between making up one's mind and
giving it up
Fainting at the sight of a tiny drop of blood
Then, just like before — nothing

* * *

But the real blaze is in the wrinkles
of a purple leather jacket
A tiny drop of blood in the absorbing
medium
A damp whiff from out the presumably
vaginal cosmic
hole

* * *

A forgotten ten spot inside a forgotten book
A scary-looking floozie or
just a girl
A tiny drop of blood severed with an axe

Arkadii Zastyrets

TRANSLATED BY ALEXANDER KALOUZHSKY AND SIMON PETTET

THREE POEMS

(1)

Bonfires are burning, a crowd on the square.
Hunched around the fire, bums warm their hands
Hurrying to the theater, an anonymous ne'er–do–well
Tries to keep the mud off of his clean pants

He has passed by the lobby and the cascade of stairs.
Under his nose, testaments to the evening's wealth
Glitter and shimmer, and the heady scent
Of exquisite perfumes adds to the attraction.

But it's another trail that has led the ne'er–do–well to the Opera:
Nervously, he waits for the appropriate moment —
And then it arrives — heading towards the box, taking out a pistol
He fires, seventeen times in a row, at the President.

While the conductor of the orchestra, oblivious,
Calmly turns the pages of the score
And it all starts up on stage, determinedly, gloomily,
The choir starts singing, building to a crescendo . . .

And the President collapses . . . His young wife
Follows him down — and so to the accompaniment of trumpets
and harps,
His confidants, desperate, hysterical,
Haul away down the isle the bleeding corpse.

(2)

O you deepening shadows with cloth rags,
Charming floor-wipers
Your driving force, your majestic genius
Deserves both words and music
Especially, most especially in July,
When oblique beams gild
The columns of dust in a roomy lobby
And sunset is reflected in your buckets;
When the full moon is swimming
Slowly across the sky
And in heavy steams the liquid silver

Pours down your mop.
Due to their own choreography,
Unassisted by propeller or wings,
The cleaning ladies of public buildings
Fly from the dark, stark naked
Filling the corridors with their song,
Circumnavigating fire-extinguishers —
Neither filing cabinets nor lamps obstruct them
Nor security, dozing at their watch.

(3)

Tabarene used to say
"Napthalene's a pearl
in the bottom of your suitcase
it's poisonous and shines."
With tears in his mouth
François would object:
"No, Napthalene is God,
Napthalene's the wind."

Not a midnight run or restless over-night
Not an extract of H_2O on a silver spoon
Not patches of sick, depressing April snow
On a garden path behind a cobblestone wall.

Tabarene used to say
"Napthalene's Death,
stayed for a while, then vanished
and nobody even noticed him!"
François screams at Tabarene
"How dare you!
Napthalene is God,
Napthalene's the wind."

Not a glassy chill or manufactured mania
Not a pretty red polka dot apron
Not the bloody and bony remains
Of a dead bird lying on the beach

Tabarene used to say
"Napthalene's a lie:
It'll make your eyes water
and make your head spin."
François would whisper:
"You'll never understand
you can't overpower me,
tough luck, tough luck."

Not an iron wreath or precise pitch
Not a rooster crowing, forgetful of the night
Not your cruel fair-weather friend, No
Napthalene is God, Napthalene's the wind

Ivan Zhdanov

TRANSLATED BY ALEXANDER KALOUZHSKY AND EDWARD FOSTER

THREE POEMS

(1)

You wave good-by, but you won't be free.
He leaves and you want him to leave:
the bird leaves its trace in its flight.

Things don't disappear just because you don't feel them.
Clocks don't stop even though they aren't watched.
Blood circulates even though the heart doesn't care.

Dying nations are driven away,
but before they vanish like clouds in a storm,
they are the rain that tears the leaves from the trees.

All that indifference in your face will pass.
The bird beneath your hand will cry out.
The leaves will be torn down.
Your hand will leave its trace in the air.

(2)

The crescent moon, its seas eclipsed,
reaches out to the nameless ones, those never to return:
those who, not knowing they're forgotten,
wander like lights in lost villages
or rustle at night on the phone.

The doors have been opened but need to be locked.
The nameless don't know there's no one
to care for the world they've abandoned.
The road that led them away is suspended in air,
hovering over the ground,
while the dust of the moon drifts up to the knees.

The chasm between us is neither their envy for us
nor that grey, numbed passion we find in the weak.
It's the crippling speed of oblivion.

Yet the soul speaks out from the void once more:
The eclipse is complete, the aureole flares;
the crescent shines, its cry of rebirth.

(3)

When you stand there looking at me
saying whatever comes to mind,
you become whatever there is between us,
and I am the space between words,
the things you never say.

And I'm like a mirror
in which you try to find yourself
but here there's only silence,
the space between words.

The mirror wants so much,
wants to hold it all, and can't,
and since it can't, it shatters
and so becomes the crown
on the tree of despair,
the first to feel
the shock of the storm.

In order to speak and to sing,
to be still yet hear everyone,
one twists and turns in planes of the void
like a madman, nervous and bitter,
raging in forests
never at rest,
driven to furors of war.

Love is blind, they've said,
and you've made me what I am.
And so where's the bed for two?
If the hat fits, the saying goes . . .
You know the rest.

Sterile waters wind their way
like a turban round the mountain,
and wombs are as barren
as sails in a calm.

I'm part of you,
and I want the rest,
I want you fully again,
though it cost me my life.
I see you, jealous,
aiming your slingshot at me,
shaking the ashes
from the tree of my shame.

But you're only reflection —
it's as if you'd become
what you made me.

It's like a mysterious bird
that takes another under its wing,
but not devouring the captive,
becomes its sky.

Sure, it's the distance
that brings us together;
that's how things work,
and it's this that makes
my desire your truth
and your will.

As I'm resigned,
I'm immortal.
Since I love,
I am here.

Michael Palmer's newest collection of poems, *At Passages,* is forthcoming from New Directions in the spring of 1995. His *Selected Writings and Talks* is forthcoming from University of New Mexico Press. His previous books include: *Sun* (1988), *First Figure* (1984), and *Notes for Echo Lake* (1981), all published by North Point Press; *Without Music* (1977), *The Circular Gates* (1974), and *Blake's Newton* (1972), all published by Black Sparrow Press. A selection of work from these books follows below. This interview with Michael Palmer was conducted by Peter Gizzi in Providence, RI, on April 6, 1994. The previous evening Michael Palmer read at Brown University, and an excerpt of that reading is included on the enclosed CD. Michael Palmer was born in New York City in 1943; after taking undergraduate and graduate degrees at Harvard, he moved to San Francisco in 1969, where he has lived ever since. Since 1974 he has collaborated on over a dozen works with the Margaret Jenkins Dance Company. He has also published translations from French, Russian, and Italian, the most recent being *Theory of Tables,* by Emmanuel Hocquard, a work inspired by Hocquard's own translation of Palmer's "Baudelaire Series," from *Sun,* into French.

Interview with Michael Palmer

Peter Gizzi: *Because of your insistence on separating poetry from the "business of academicians," I'm going to try to stay away from questions like: "So this reference in that poem, what does it mean?" I'll leave that to the joy of reading, and to one's library — just like I have my own idea about your work in relation to the Ernst Kantorowicz essay, "Dante's Two Suns." It doesn't matter if you intended it or not, it shines in the reader. Do you know what I mean?*

Michael Palmer: I do. When you use something like, let's say, suns and twin suns, you hope that things will constellate of their own accord around that. And in fact when I get a title for a book, often it's prior to knowing how it fits the work but with an intuition that the means do gather to this figure, so to speak. And if I'm right, that turns out to be true, and often it turns out to be true after the fact. I was looking through my notebook the other day and found a quotation I noted when I was reading Michael Ondaatje's *The English Patient* — which is an absolutely remarkable piece of work, with this figure who is no one, who is with-

". . . you hope that things will constellate of their own accord . . ."

out a name, who is a crashed pilot for whatever side, it's uncertain who he was even fighting for and it's beside the point — and one of the quotes that Ondaatje uses at the beginning of the book is, "For echo is the soul of the voice exciting itself in hollow places," which he took from Christopher Smart. And I thought, well, if *Notes for Echo Lake* were meant in some way to reconfigure a model of communication having to do with the figure of Narcissus and the figure of Echo, that was just a perfect, beautiful thing. But the recognition of it came later to me, I mean years later. Which makes it no less true to that figure one is after, it's just a gift — in this case from Christopher Smart via Michael Ondaatje — to the work that one does. When Duncan speaks to that "grand collage," it is certainly not singular in its construction. I mean, *this is the construction,* an instance of how it constructs itself.

PG: *Obviously part of the joy is that it's bigger than you are.*

MP: Certainly.

PG: *And it works because one keeps reading back into it, one keeps finding oneself in that figure.*

MP: And maybe that becomes a figure of itself, for that idea of imaginary community in which poets tend to dwell with others. Not to say that it's outside the real, but it's constructed through the imagination and sometimes in opposition to the principles of reality that are laid on us, all of which say "you should not be doing this."

PG: *I think you create a reality with your library . . .*

MP: Well, to some degree, yes.

PG: *. . . or through your library.*

MP: There's an equation of writing and reading, and they mutually extend each other, including of course the reader as he or she reads whatever it is that one has made. And so there's an interesting, not so much circularity as circulation, I think, that goes on there.

PG: *I like what you just said about a reader; as opposed to addressing a reader, creating a reader, like creating a text.*

MP: It's not addressing. I think that's the mistake: who to imagine as one's reader or who to imagine as the ideal reader. There's no ideal reader. One doesn't even want an ideal reader. One projects a possible reader or set of readers who have no outline, a readership in potential who have the generosity to complete the meanings of the work, and to complete the circuit. And as you know, when you work in something like poetry, which does involve difficulty and certain kinds of resistance, it's extraordinary that it finds a reader, when it does find a reader. That's the compensation for the fact that it doesn't find hundreds and hundreds of thousands of readers; it finds readers.

PG: *And you too then become a part of that constellation; when you find the Ondaatje quote, you find the echo and you become a reader of your text in the world.*

MP: And you become, in turn, imagined by that reader. I don't mean imagined as a personality, that's not so interesting, but imagined into being by that other.

PG: *You have inverted a phrase of Hölderlin's about poetry* ("it is not powerful, but it is part of life"), *so that the phrase now reads: "poetry is not part of life, but it is powerful." Could you address what that power is for you?*

MP: Well I think it's a power that affirms the impossible. That is, it affirms that within language there are all of these unexamined meanings, unexplored territories that remain active, that confront the habitual. So that thought remains possible; counter-thought remains possible; thought with a critical force to it remains possible. That's an extraordinary power. It's what allows poetry to remain, even in its invisibility, at the heart of a given culture — in however vexed a relationship to that culture, however problematic and however invisible. It has some defining acuteness to it because it constructs outside the *doxa.* There's an always interesting and desperate Rumanian philosopher, E. M. Cioran, who talks about the heresies of Meister Eckhardt in relation to his belief in form, and he says because the keepers of the flame of orthodoxy . . . here it is: "Like every heretic, he sinned on the side of form, an enemy of language. All orthodoxy, whether religious or political, postulates the usual expression. In the name of a sclerotic word, the stakes, the pyres were erected . . . ."

PG: *Can I ask you what "sclerotic word" means?*

MP: "Sclerotic" means with its veins clogged — a dying word. It's extraordinary, that "All orthodoxy postulates the usual expression." So heretics are utterly significant figures in a poetic sense. There's a poetics to heresy like Meister Eckhardt, and he points to the fact that it's not the ideas really, it's the form these ideas take. Likewise among certain mystics. I think it equally applies to poetry.

PG: *Would you say that the form then is a form of transgression?*

MP: I think it is — even though "transgression" has become the currency of correct theory, so that it's hard now to use words like "margins" or "transgression" because they themselves have been recuperated (to use another academic word) by academic theory, and then taken apart.

PG: *Which is a difficulty of the contemporary academy.*

MP: It is symptomatic of what would be quite literally deconstruction, when all discourse becomes qualified. There's nothing wrong with all discourse coming into a framework of doubt, but then you do wonder at what point — in the face of such massive interrogation, such massive, skeptical interrogation — how does one (and I think that's much of the problem now) reassert the force of these

". . . when theory becomes fetishized, a new preciosity emerges, a new kind of artifice . . ."

words themselves. And you take any of those terms that are currently being (not in a bad sense necessarily) looked at, "authenticity" and so on; well possibly it's an interesting time to rearticulate an idea of authenticity. Not in a mystifying way, but in some urgent relationship to work, beyond the postmodern queries which drove so many people into endless ironization, endless play, endless "screen" so to speak, which becomes a sort of protection against that deconstructive critique. Well then, what, after that, can one possibly reassert about an ethics of representation? Or, put another way, how, at this moment, might one refuse what Norma Cole (in "Error of Locating Events in Time") calls, "the collusion underwriting irony"?

PG: *You've written about how you can't really tolerate the notion of art for art's sake — and so the "power," to go back to what we were speaking about, of poetry, would be to create an aesthetics or an ethics of representation against art for art's sake, against decor?*

MP: More than the question of art for art's sake, which long ago was dismantled, I worry that a certain kind of theoretical overdetermination of vanguardist gestures or moves in itself becomes as airily dismissive or as enclosed a space as art for art's sake, and as limited in its address and in its horizon as art for art's sake. It becomes a conversation for those refined enough to know the terms. It mirrors, in an ironic way, high aestheticism. For me that's a very troubling stage, partly in relation to . . . not theory itself, but some uses of theory; and I think theory, speaking broadly, is a very useful reflection against habits of practice and hidden ideologies of form or whatever, and has been an extremely important part of our time. But then when theory becomes fetishized, a new preciosity emerges, a new kind of artifice, and that can be troublesome and very limited in the intent of its address.

PG: *Impoverished, in fact.*

MP: But we've got to make the distinction here between great theoretical constructs which always, in a certain way, address the world itself — that's their terminus — and, let's say, the appropriation of them to academic certification. The difference, for example, between some of the contexts in which aspects of poststructuralism existed before their appropriation by the American academy, where they were meant ultimately to address certain political realities — they were to come to a point of intervention in the world — and certain philosophical points of doubt of great moment. But at the point at which they begin to circulate among themselves within universities as imports, as part of a curious industry of middle-class culture, they become, in an odd way, the mirror of the earlier pedantic formalism of the New Critics. They become just as dehistoricized, even when they are meant to bring history back in; they become swept up in the articulation/rearticulation of their terms, a condition, for example, that has plagued Marxism ever since a certain hermeneutical excess started to apply to the interpretation/reinterpretation of capital. Then you get almost, well you get a scholasticism again. But it's important to distinguish between that secondariness and the important use of works that really do have an epistemological significance in the world and which make you question, make you think against yourself, as Sartre put it.

PG: *The moment of composition, of thought, that becomes poetry for you, would you say it's a site, a place you go?*

MP: Well, I think there's a relationship that's almost impossible to examine between thought and poetry. The Romantic ideal, of course, was that poetry aspire to a condition of thought, which was a kind of prelapsarian dream — that it aspire to a condition prior to utterance. But in fact it aspires to something as imperfect as utterance, too. It may dream of the fluidity of thought, and even the silence of thought, but once in language, outside the head, obviously it exists in a different way than thought. And it's tricky because we have to think it in order to speak about such questions. But I don't know if there is a site. There's certainly a kind of territory that we explore, but I don't know whether we're constructing a site in that way. It seems that we've constructed an awful lot of sites and maybe we had better think of it possibly more as a form of exploring a site. I think we've built enough. I mean, certainly we're not trying or should no longer be trying to build perfect symmetries in a landscape. Well, some people are.

PG: *I use the word site because of the title of your newest book,* At Passages. *Do you want to talk about how that title came to you?*

MP: It was meant to be — well, obviously, it's a pun — involving the fact that there are citations in the work, "sightings" in a certain sense. (I'm speaking here specifically of the poem "Cites.") There is sight itself, and one of the things that "cite" deals with is the problematics of representation. I was also literally dealing with the landscape of this island off the coast of Brittany, but I was writing it on an island on the other side of the Atlantic, and so I was conflating an imagined, perhaps projected, site with an immediate one.

PG: *Why that island?*

MP: That poem is taken from a collaboration with the painter Micaëla Henich, so there's the place where the drawings were done, *L'Isle de Noir Mouton,* and then the one where I was writing. I started looking at texts on the landscape of those islands off the southern coast of Brittany on the Atlantic, and comparing them with what was before my eyes on this side, on the eastern shore of the United States, and thinking about the limits of image, and the space between the word and — well, the problem that Emmanuel Hocquard brings up about *l'objectif*: the lens and the objective vision, the extraordinary distance between the apparently objective configuration of something and the thing itself. How hallucinated, in a funny way, even the purportedly objective representation of something is. "Littoral" and "literal" were playing in my ear. And so I took these sets of phrases in threes and multiples of three and began to break them down, so that they could not be read consecutively, so that you couldn't simply flip past the images to read a narrative thread. I wanted each of these things to stand as a caption beneath Micaëla Henich's work, not to lead you forward, necessarily, sometimes perhaps to lead you back, but sometimes to leave you precisely in place. And I also deliberately disconnected them from the specific image on each page. I decided that they would not relate to that image, they might relate to another image in the work, or they might relate to an image in my reading, or they might be a citation — a quotation, in other words — from my reading toward this problem of doing a set of *légendes,* a set of captions for Micaëla. Also, there's this pun on *cité* (city), which is the missing element in a rural landscape. We populate this rural landscape with certain frames and certain activities, but the people are largely absent from that work, which interests me; so "cites," missing its accent mark there, becomes a kind of absent city. Just as when I'm on that island, the city becomes absent. That's one of the facts of being there. So "cites" is a multiple pun.

> ". . . in fact poetry aspires to something as imperfect as utterance . . ."

PG: *I can't help hearing in the overall title* At Passages *a relation to Duncan's "Passages."*

MP: Well, I think that's one of its resonances, though not the initial, or initiatory one. A couple of years ago I was doing work on a piece called *The Gates Far Away Near* with Margy Jenkins and Rinde Eckhart [of the Margaret Jenkins Dance Company] and we came up with this framework — it was to be an evening-long piece, and therefore we wanted an elaborate structure, with a fifteen- or twenty-minute work maybe you can make it up in the studio as you go along, but here we wanted a grid on which to place it — of a prologue, plus seven gates to a city. And these gates were named, in a deliberately arbitrary fashion, the Gate of Desire, the Gate of Public Words, the Gate of Passages, et al., to mirror the wildly disparate reality of the city depending on which gate you entered. You enter

". . . so much of political poetry now has to do with newspaper reports and so little to do with witness . . ."

through one gate and the city is all in ruins and rubble and there are burning tires and people huddled around oil cans with fires in them; and you enter through another and it's the boulevards of capital, with the Harry Winston jewelry store over here and Saks Fifth Avenue over here. We were looking at the extraordinarily deep paradoxes of the world we negotiate every day — and it doesn't have to be a big city for this — and that metaphor of the old city with gates, the seven gates of Thebes or the seven valleys of *The Conference of the Birds.* But I was interested in the fact that there would be a gate for each dancer. There happened to be seven dancers, and each would be a kind of minister for one of those gates. As we constructed the work, one would guide the others through the imagery that we were building for that gate. The Gate of Passages was to be one of the more abstract ones, obviously. (Although desire is pretty abstract, until you feel it!) But the Gate of Passages was one where you had this sense of circulation — and then a wonderful, creative young choreographer named Jon Weaver, who was dancing in the company, came up with the idea of the Northwest Passage and people in this white landscape losing themselves in the act of discovery, and we ended up using that to construct this beautifully fluid section of the work. In any case, in recent years, I've tried to interweave the imagery of all those different areas of artistic practice with each other.

PG: *Which is dance, choreography . . .*

MP: . . . Translation — well, not choreography so much as collaboration . . .

PG: *. . . and so to work the boundaries of the genres . . .*

MP: . . . To erase the boundaries and to pull things over from one into the other. I had been pulling some images from my own work into this dance, and then I started to pull them back from the dance into that section of *At Passages* called "Untitled," which has a poem that says "at passages we peer out over" such-and-such. And when I got that phrase "at passages" I thought, that's the fuel of this book, partly because there were those dedications to Beckett, to Antonio Porta, Clark Coolidge, Jerry Estrin, David Shapiro, Zanzotto, et al. To be at a certain stage of life, turning fifty, too, felt like a passage. I didn't have a title for the book, and that phrase popped out, late late at night when I finished the poem, as a title. Then I thought, well, there is also this thing for Robert Duncan in there, the "Six Hermetic Songs," and it's definitely going to have some echo of "Passages," and some echo of the effort to renegotiate polis and the political that Robert takes up in "Passages."

PG: *"At passages" also implies the scholarly use of citation, tracing something back through the lineage of its references. As if one could track the genealogy of one's own language in its precedents, sources, or influences. That seems to be a way of reconfiguring the moment of composition: your reading practice becomes your writing practice.*

MP: Well, certainly the passages of those texts are passages also through the city — the imaginary city. This work with Margy had a little bit of that layering or inherence of the one living in the other; the mystery of their coinherence. This was also the time when the Berlin Wall was coming down, when that order, that artifice of Cold War stability was breaking up, and all of those forces bubbling up underneath it were beginning to return. And so we were faced with those amazing images of Ceaucesceu's palace burning, and that kind of thing. I remember very much in my head, too, the eruption of the repressed and the return of some hideous forces, without any doubt.

PG: *I'm reminded that within* At Passages *there's the "Seven Poems within a Matrix for War." And then I think of the second poem "Sun" in that collection, and your preoccupation with the need to somehow reconfigure or think through or write the reality of war. Also "The Circular Gates": I see that as a poem constructed out of the Vietnam War.*

MP: It was, very much so; I was also looking for a means of representation that I could feel honest with. In other words, I think one of the problems of an overtly political poetry now is something that Octavio Paz has brought up, that so much of it has to do with newspaper reports and so little of it has to do with witness. We look at the powerful poems of witness of this century and they are not about newspaper reports, and they're not about proposing one's particular *point de repère,* point of view, position, so much as facing something that may even overwhelm the poetic sign in its multiplicity of meanings, something often horrible. The American tendency is to read our politics out of these distant events and then to write some almost self-congratulatory oppositional work. And so what I tried to face (speaking of the "Seven Poems within a Matrix for War" now) was, what we did experience of that thing — which was the overwhelming flood of images, the controlled imagery that was poured over us, whether that be the exploding suns over Baghdad on the CNN nightly news, or . . .

PG: *It was extraordinary, that moment watching the deluge . . .*

MP: So I tried to look into the contradictions that were directly before my eyes, the only reality that was, in effect, being allowed. Because nothing showed more clearly (if we needed to know it) how beside the point poets, intellectuals, other people of conscience were in relation to that construction of political and military news. It was done with an extraordinarily skillful contempt for anything that might say no to it. I mean, if you remember, public opposition to the war before it began had been something like 80%. The next day the war begins and of course people rally, as it's natural for them to do, to the flag. There's a certain agreement, if we look at the Gulf War, that we were going to slaughter, with our experimental weapons, 100,000 or more members of the Iraqi underclass — in their little, you know, *hovels* there, with a rifle and bag of food — and leave Saddam alone, so that Iraq itself would be crushed but not totally destabilized, so that the reality of those artificial Gulf states would not be terminally altered. I thought that hallucinatory conclusion was all we had to work with, and so what I got was this construction which is not essentially a political one. I don't know. An experience.

PG: *I want to go back to "The Circular Gates." I have a biographical question. This is something I've heard by rumor — and I know that you didn't inhale [laughter] — the rumor is, because George appears in that poem and elsewhere, that your name was George Palmer.*

MP: Right, George Michael Palmer.

PG: *George Michael Palmer, and you changed it to Michael. Why was that?*

MP: Well . . .

PG: *Just putting it out there . . .*

MP: I think it was a very modest way of freeing myself of an identity that I had grown up with. I think for me to become a poet, or whatever I've become, was a project of self-rearticulation out of the expectations of childhood and out of the social expectations that had been laid upon me, out of the habits of, let's say, obedience.

PG: *What were those social expectations?*

MP: Well, I came from, I guess you would say, a middle-class Italian-American household of modest means, though my grandfather on my mother's side, who had been born south of Naples in the Avellino area, had become quite prosperous as a landscape contractor and landscape designer. He had made his way from the streets of New York through Cooper Union night school and then become a figure I admire very much — a brilliant, driven, maybe impassioned gardener, who had this rather large landscape contracting firm. My father made a modest living as a hotel manager in a small hotel in New York. But the reality around me was a characteristically repressive, repressed fifties middle-class environment — not without love, by any means, but constricted. The expectation was that I would have the best schooling, and they sacrificed an enormous amount to give me that schooling, because they schooled me among the wealthy even though they had not much money at all. And the expectation was that they were giving me — and it was an expectation in good faith on my father's part, who had himself come from poverty in the north of Italy, in the Appennines — that what he could do for me was to work hard and provide me with a meal ticket, and that meal ticket would be an education and the connections that come with a privileged education. And at some point in my early teenage years, or even a little bit before that, I began to be rather alienated from those expectations, and from the habits of manners that went along with that life, and began to look toward the poets, and the jazz musicians, and the artists. It's a common enough story of alternative possibilities for constructing a life that would be other than that, certainly — that would be other, perhaps. So, I spent a lot of years, in effect, dismantling or reorienting this superego that had been placed upon me. I think I still have it, but I've directed it somewhere else, trying to permit this desire to express itself, and to sort of free myself to a less legitimate life. I think the last stage of that was just dropping this name as part of an identity that I had been given.

PG: *When was that?*

MP: At the Vancouver conference I was still George Palmer, and I think '65-'66 was when I sort of said now I'm out of, I'm free from college, I've done my duty and I'll be somebody else entirely — not that one ever is, of course. That self I carry with me is part of the problem and maybe part of the solution.

PG: *Are there complications because George also becomes a character in your text?*

MP: Sure. Of course "The Circular Gates" is to some degree about educating oneself toward responsiblity toward the world. In other words, part of that bourgeois reality was, I suppose, a certain liberalism, but basically a displacement from the world's events, carrying on with your career, not letting that nasty business get in the way of what you had to do to earn a living and so on. And I think a lot of us of the Vietnam generation, in late '63 and '64 — as the horrifying reality of what we were facing dawned on us — we realized that we not only couldn't make do with suburban displacement, we couldn't make do with existential alienation either, that that in itself was criminal, that it was a complicity in this thing.

PG: *It wasn't enough as an answer.*

MP: It wouldn't do. Another one of the starting points of "The Circular Gates" was Frank Stella's *Protractor Series,* which he named after gates to various cities; and here was this work of pure abstraction, I guess you would say, and I was wondering if something from that position could act as a kind of opening, a gate for me into the present. After all, it was work of the present, it was work that interested me a great deal, possibly more than any other moment in Stella's work, certainly more than the gestural rhetoric of some of the later work. And so I thought, well, given that I think the dichotomy between abstract and representational art is an essentially false one — that's not the dichotomy that interests me — could I use it as an opening, did they in fact go together? And as I began to do this work, and Magritte, Brancusi and others came floating in also, I was trying to include a relationship to artistic practice that was important to me, rather than overthrowing a whole practice in order to arrive at, let's say, a political art. That seemed to me a falsification. And "circular," just in the sense that there was no teleology. I was not going to come to a point. I didn't have the illusion that I was going to actually find something at the end.

PG: *Jack Spicer's Berkeley lecture in 1965 is about the political poem, and he says that though he thought all his life about the political poem, it's something that ultimately he could never do, nor did he accept it as a possibility. He thought that if you wanted to write a political poem, you should write a letter to the editor [laughter].*

MP: There's a certain justification to that. I mean, I think there is politics within the poetry. We're talking about Shelley, about Dante. The politics is not outside the work at any moment.

PG: *When you were talking about "Seven Poems within a Matrix for War" and the Gulf War, you said you were writing through an experience mediated by power.*

> ". . . not the lyric poetry of the 'little me' that is churned out in America . . ."

MP: Yes, and certainly that's the experience that Jacques Roubaud talks about in relation to the troubadour poets. Giorgio Agamben, the Italian philosopher, brings up the not-knowing of poetry: what poetry knows is a certain not-knowing. And that's not just a Romantic negativity, a turning away. It's a specific area that challenges the discourse of reason in its authoritative rationales for things and its authoritative claim to knowledge. And poetry — even, let's say, a lyric poetry (using that term in quite a broad sense as a poetry that's personal, again in quite a broad sense, not the lyric poetry of the "little me" that is churned out in America) — poetry has a force of resistance and critique. At least I would hope it does. Again, it's not something that ends up changing the world, but it ends up bringing something possibly to the attention of the world, and bringing something into the world so that it is not quite as it was before.

PG: *In this period of deconstructing or evolving your identity — devolving George and evolving Michael — and at the same time finding out about poetry, who were some of the poets you were reading? And at that point, before* Blake's Newton, *did you ever write poems that were about "little me"?*

MP: Not that I can think of. Until a certain point, through most of my schooling, I imagined poetry more than I wrote it. I wrote certain things, and they were not, for the most part — with maybe a couple of exceptions when I would try something on almost like a jacket — they were not that, they were something else. In high school I really started discovering poetry, both the New American Poetry and the Modernists, who were for the most part not being taught. Eliot was certainly being taught, but H.D., Williams and Pound very little. Stein not at all. Eliot, Cummings, you know, that sort of thing was being taught. But this other area was not being taught, for I think a variety of reasons. It wasn't particularly known and it certainly wasn't understood in the case of someone like Pound. The resistance to Pound was less the horror of his ideology than the fact that he's difficult.

PG: *I heard a story once that you had an entrée to meet Pound and you demurred.*

MP: In Venice, it was when I was there in the summer of '65, and there was a man there, an art historian, who knew Pound. He offered to introduce me, and I didn't honestly . . . Well, I knew that Pound was in a period of vexed silence and depression — I had known about that from various people — and I felt that I would be going to meet him for the wrong reasons. If I had anything to ask him I was reluctant to ask it, given the state he was in. And so I said no. I suppose I always wish I had met the person and seen his personality — to add that dimension, whatever use that is in relation to the work. I resisted my curiosity, though I knew at that moment I would always be a little bit regretful.

PG: *You told me a similar story that when you got to San Francisco you could have gone to meet Jack Spicer, but you also resisted that temptation.*

MP: Well, Allen Ginsberg wanted to take me around in '63 to meet Jack and, I think, Robin [Blaser]. And I was intimidated probably by two things: I was certainly intimidated by Spicer's sense of a hermetic privileged circle and Spicer's reputation for challenging people. I was a very vulnerable, nervous, twenty-year-old kid, and I didn't feel I wanted to be subjected to Spicer's wit and his interrogation. I had mixed feelings about his work at that point too. I didn't come to really take pleasure in it and really understand it until a few years later. And I think I was probably at that age also intimidated by the gay bar scene; the bar that Allen wanted to take me to was a gay bar. It wasn't Gino and Carlo's, some other place, and I think then that environment was a little scary to me.

PG: *Was this just after the Vancouver conference, or before?*

MP: It was after.

PG: *How did you come to know of the Vancouver conference?*

MP: I was leaving Cambridge to work on the pea harvest in Oregon . . .

PG: *Oh, this is the green sneakers that I heard about, that Clark [Coolidge] told me about [laughter].*

MP: Yeah. I went with a friend, Tom Webster, who had worked on the harvest. You worked seven days a week for union scale, twelve hours a day, so you could make a lot of money very quickly, and it wasn't a situation where you displaced migrant workers in order to get the work, because there was extra work. In the midst of the harvest they would take anyone they could get, if the harvest was going well. So, we were going up to do that. I think I was going to test myself, too, in this other environment. There was also a certain romance to that kind of work. And as I was leaving I stopped in at Gordon Cairnie's Grolier Bookshop, and Gordon had a poster on the wall, and I looked at it in utter disbelief because there was Charles

Olson, Allen Ginsberg, Denise Levertov, Bob Creeley, Robert Duncan and Margaret Avison (who I didn't know at that time, Margaret was the Canadian poet who was involved as faculty) who were all going to be in the same place at the same time. And I had come rather independently to Olson, Creeley and Duncan's work. Allen's work was not central to me, though I admired some of what he had done, and I certainly admired how he had challenged the institutionalization of American verse. I mean there's nothing more important than that initial gesture of his, that initial insistence of his. But, you know, I had such a hazy picture. By then the Don Allen anthology was around, so I must have known that they were grouped together, but I had discovered them haphazardly, by finding [Olson's] *The Distances,* and by finding Bob's *For Love* and *A Form of Women* actually before that, and then [Duncan's] *The Opening of the Field;* and it seemed like an almost magic practice at that point, it was such an opening. Discovering poets of that order, after having discovered Pound and H.D., etc., in high school, seemed to confirm that I wasn't just all alone, you know, because I really didn't have much of a circle of friends who were reading this. I had one friend in high school who I read with, who was a great companion to me, who I read with and listened to music with, and we would have a discussion. But by and large I was extremely rebellious against the picture of poetry that was being given to me by the classroom and by the standard magazines. It seemed to me moribund. But I didn't know what the alternative was. I hadn't imagined one for myself, exactly, and these people provided a kind of conversation before I met them. So I asked Gordon if it seemed possible that one could go to such a thing as this Vancouver Poetry Conference at the University of British Columbia, and he said, "Well I've got Bob Creeley's address in Placitas, New Mexico, that's exactly where you're driving." We had a drive-away car for some retired people who were going to Arizona for the air, or whatever, to relieve their health problems. And we, Tom Webster and I, were driving this enormous white Cadillac out west for a hundred dollars, which I think barely covered the gas and maybe some food. I think we managed to get across the country on a hundred dollars; I'd never realized a car could use that much gasoline. So we got to Albuquerque, and in a state of absolute terror I called Bob on the phone. I mean I was really very much in awe of these people; they were abstractions to me, and they were very much larger than life. I wasn't from that world, I hadn't grown up in any world where such people would be around all the

"... they were terrified that there would be dope and obscenity ... I was terrified there wouldn't be!"

time. And Bob said, "Why don't you and Tom just come on out." He and Bobbie [Louise Hawkins] were living out there with their kids. And as he later told me, he did it with some hesitancy, because he was afraid it might be more, like, kids coming for autographs or something; but he did it. And we drove out and we hid this car behind a sand dune — so he wouldn't get the wrong idea of us driving up in a white Cadillac, with those fins! — and we hid it down by a little cantina in this kind of desert town and trekked across the sand dunes. And we met them, and they told us who to contact to become enrolled in the conference. So the timing was perfect, and at the end of the harvest we took the bus up to Vancouver, and barely got through Customs. Particularly when they found out that we were going to this poetry conference, they were terrified that there would be dope and obscenity and so on.

PG: *And was there?*

MP: Yes, yes. I was terrified there wouldn't be! So they pulled the two of us off the bus and searched us . . . .

PG: *Did you have long hair at that time?*

MP: Well, I guess relatively, but. . .

PG: *Given the time . . .*

MP: . . . given the time, yeah. Tom had a beard, so we looked a little different from everyone else on the bus to Vancouver. It was that strangely British society of Vancouver, one side of which is very orthodox and repressed. But they stamped our visas — and that was really the beginning of my introduction to the society of poets. I don't mean that in some hifalutin way. I mean into the company of poets. Bob [Creeley] and Charles [Olson] operated with great, generous energy. I mean, they gave everything to those occasions, and you know how Bob is in conversation. First meeting Bob I was amazed that the people who I was interested in elsewhere, such as Stan Brakhage, were part of his circle, they were the people he was interested in, they were the people that Robert Duncan was interested in — so there was this whole other world, this alternative, this parallel universe of artists that were working in an exploratory fashion. And of course I met Clark [Coolidge] up there.

PG: *What do you remember about that meeting?*

MP: I don't remember the first moment we met. But I do remember we took to each other instantly and started immediately talking about, well, jazz of course, John Cage, and composing aleatory works on the typewriter as people had conversations, and that sort of thing. The musical connection — both jazz and new music — was an immediate opening for both of us because we were both very much involved in that world. And so that was a great thing.

PG: *And after that you and Clark began the magazine* Joglars.

MP: Yeah, but it was very difficult to do, as I was still a full-time student. Clark had to do most of the shit work for it, and we had no money. We were both just flat broke, so even to get together the 125 dollars for the first issue, 250 dollars for the second issue, was very hard for us to do. And then I left the country and he was left to do a third issue, which reflected an interesting shift because at that point he started being involved with the New York poets. Our discovery of our own generation of New York poets — and then beginning to read the previous generation of Ashbery, O'Hara, etc. — came after a certain lag because we had been involved with the Black Mountain poets, with Zukofsky.

PG: *What about Zukofsky? You brought him to Harvard.*

MP: Yeah. It was the winter of '64, or '63-4.

PG: *And how did you propose that to your department?*

MP: They had a little reading series. I found out that Adams House had money from the Ford Foundation for cultural purposes — a very modest sum of money — and I found out by chance that nobody was using this money. So I said, "Is it okay if I use the money to have a reading series?" and I invited Louis and I invited LeRoi Jones, who was still LeRoi at that point. And then I scheduled Charles Olson, and that just blew their circuits finally, because Charles had such a strange relationship to Harvard, and a history of, quote, misbehaving. And so the money vanished, and they said "There isn't any more money," and I said oh well. So I communicated that to Charles, that the reading series was over, and then the reading series started again with others in charge. I suddenly noticed that they were having a reading series, with James Dickey, in fact, and the usual suspects.

PG: *How was the audience for Zukofsky?*

MP: It was huge and intense. We had it in this rather large common room. And it was jammed with people, people were sitting in the windows . . .

PG: *That's terrific!*

MP: All of these readings got a tremendous response because what they otherwise served up were academic formalists of the period. And there were a lot of people who were anxious to see what else was in the picture. They were young, curious people, and they came from other places around and from the Cambridge underground, etc. Cambridge's then counterculture-in-formation was very interested in what these voices were saying. And so they were a big success. When funds for the readings suddenly vanished, I asked the resident junior fellow in touch with the house hierarchy for the reason, and he finally said to me, "Well, they were afraid." He said they were afraid Olson might take his clothes off! It was an interesting lesson in the politics of culture, and in their terror, their commitment to decorum.

PG: *At that time you were writing your thesis on Raymond Roussel.*

MP: Louis came in my junior year — senior year I was working on the thesis.

PG: *What was the title of that?*

MP: I don't know.

PG: *Sorry [laughter].*

MP: Probably something very dry. I ironized the whole form of it, turning it into a kind of scientific exercise to approach the lunacy of Raymond Roussel in the persona of an objective critic — the Harvard ideal! So the whole work was a goof in a certain way. I remember they couldn't find readers for the thesis because no one knew who Raymond Roussel was and nobody could read French that difficult. I deliberately took up things that were unnegotiable, while people were writing the usual thesis on Baudelaire and everything. But Stanley Cavell volunteered to read it, and I remember Stanley, his comments were "This is very good, etc. I only wish that he had drawn more conclusions." He was right. But I deliberately drew no conclusions in parody of the objective method, which seemed to me a great joke. But looking at Roussel was how I first really started attending to Ashbery, because John had many of the Roussel documents. There were Michel Leiris and a couple of others in France who paid attention, but that was all. Roussel was just begining to come back into print in France. I remember writing to his publishers from the 1890's for certain works — *L'Etoile au Front,* an astonishing play — and getting an original copy, covered with dust, the pages uncut, and I imagine they must have had hundreds of them stacked up in their warehouses. It cost, I think, 2 francs.

PG: *Did you have Foucault's book* Death and the Labyrinth?

MP: I did. That was, at that point, far and away the most interesting study. There were only a couple: Jean Ferry had written one,

"... I've always been drawn to circus performers, to that aspect of poetry which has to do with juggling and tumbling ..."

Leiris had written a bit, and there had been a magazine issue right around that time that had come out, a little about the life, the anecdotes, etc. And Ashbery had written about the work, and of course *Locus Solus* had come out in the States as a magazine under the sign of Roussel. But, yes, that was a very informative book. I haven't read it in years, so I don't know what it's like now. It only came out in English a few years ago, I guess.

PG: *Right, in '86.*

MP: Interestingly, Foucault suppressed it from his bibliography for years.

PG: *I was told after I read it and enjoyed it that I hadn't really read Foucault, it was the wrong book to read. But I thought it was well made as a way into Roussel. Especially this idea of the disarming of the secret — that Roussel lays bare his device as though he's telling us something, for instance in* How I Wrote Certain of My Books *— but the fact is, disarming the secret only makes it more secret, makes it more profound and gives us no information. Which I suspect is something you would feel good about, in your own practice ...*

MP: And what a good way to read Foucault, by reading the wrong book. Of course, in the way that Beckett wrote about Proust, Foucault was writing about himself there; his is a writing full of secrets. And so I think it can be read in relation to this Foucault who has not yet found his particular archaeology; it's a more disarmed work than the work of a mature French intellectual with all his strategies.

PG: *I have another question, and I'm not sure of a way to lead into this. Throughout your work there's this figure of the father, and I'm wondering about your relationship with your own father and how that relationship accrues into, or appears within, the figure of the father.*

MP: I'm not sure how it works into the figure of the father. That father is a rather abstract figure as it appears mostly, and it's one of the questions in the work whether it is *a* father or *the* father, it's like the endlessly theorized difference between the penis and the phallus. And I think it's exactly that problematic that interests me when it occurs: the tension between this figure, this abstraction, which I've become and which I struggle not to be in relation to my daughter — not to be *the* father, we hope, but to be *a* father. "Father I am burning" of course derives from Freud.

PG: *From* The Interpretation of Dreams. *And there's a line in "Fifth Prose," which opens* Sun, *where that comes in: "A voice will say Father I am burning." There's also a resonance with "Ninth Symmetrical Poem," from* Without Music, *where you're playing with Southwell's "Burning Babe."*

MP: I think it does pick that up. "A voice will say Father I am burning// Father I've removed a stone from a wall" — that had a certain specificity for me of removing a stone from a wall that was being built possibly around me, possibly around a world, that one . . . "erased a picture from that wall,/ a picture of ships — cloud ships — pressing toward the sea// words only/ taken limb by limb apart" . . . "Because I'm writing about the snow not the sentence," the thing to which we are sentenced. It has to do with the purported authority of language over the project, and the way one pulls stones out from the wall to let them fall. That's one reading of that. And then, of course, in "Fifth Prose" — from this nineteenth-century book on performers that I happened to come across — I've always been drawn to circus performers, but also to that aspect of poetry which has to do with juggling and tumbling. In doing *Joglars* with Clark, we were proposing that other side. There was the magazine *Trobar*, which suggests a much more auratic sense of the poet, of the troubadour, the fashioning of *trobar*. The joglar was the clown and camp follower who went along and performed and ripped off other people's songs; but that's also a side of the poet. As Heine, near death, says, the poet is a schlemiel. One is, I think, almost necessarily the clown of the culture in the way one is perceived, and one sacrifices oneself to this curious project. You're a fool, both in the sense of the fool who says things to the king that are otherwise not permitted to be said, sometimes in a punning and occulted fashion; but also you're the fool who can never rise above that station in a society that's oriented towards other forms of accomplishment.

PG: *So it's both empowering and effacing.*

MP: Exactly. There was a remarkable portrait in *The New Yorker*, some months ago, of Ricky Jay. He is a musician — a magician, excuse me — who specializes in card things, working with close-up magic, I guess is what they call it; but he has also written an extraordinary book on eccentric performers and magicians, and he talks about that same nobility and foolishness of the performer. Ricky Jay himself is both scholar of his art and an amazing performer. And I guess he makes occasional television appearances and now has a little Broadway show, but he has kept out of that celebrity world — that empty celebrity world. He has a sense of his practice as almost an underground thing and of the secrets of this art as something earned through a discipline of study and practice. And I realized in reading this interview with him exactly why I had appreciated this book where "Little Sandy and Sam Sault" [from "Fifth Prose"] appear. They were these curious, marginal creatures performing double loops in the air.

PG: *That idea of tumbling or that fascination you have with circus performers and magic extends throughout your work, perhaps especially in the poems to your daughter Sarah. Or in "Recursus" where you say, "And I live in a red house that once was brown. A paper house, sort of falling down". You have this way of voicing — I don't want to say it's nonsense — but voicing the nursery spell, spell in the sense of a charm. Or would you characterize that as nonsense?*

MP: Certainly nonsense is included in the picture, which is a determinative critique of sense. It includes sense within itself, it's nonsense. And it's one of the areas where poetry, I think, is empowered. Rather than suppressing that area, I've always wanted to feature it because it's revelatory and it has a critical force — as Edward Lear and Lewis Carroll had an acute critical relationship to Victorian culture (it's in part an echo of Carroll which becomes daemonic imprecation in Artaud). And of course, as in Carroll, there's a fascination with logic/counter-logic, syllogism/false syllogism. That logic has trouble permitting itself, but we can have all of it in poetry. The counter-logic of poetry seems to me enormously powerful and not to be ignored. It's a dangerous territory. And, coming back to the figure of the fool, there's a way in which it's important to make a fool of yourself.

PG: *This addresses what we began discussing earlier in relation to Hölderlin's quote about poetry — what is the power of poetry, and how does it relate to the heretical?*

MP: I think a lot of this accumulates without strategic reflections.

PG: *The language brings you there, you mean.*

MP: I mean there is also simply a celebratory aspect to the outbreak of the imagination. It celebrates the neglected areas of language or the areas of language that are thought to be secondary; and it turns the model, then, on its head.

PG: *And do poets like John Ashbery or Wallace Stevens — does their sense of play or whimsy intrigue you, or did their work feed you at one time?*

MP: It intrigues me, and it has fed me all along in the sense that they're both poets who I've continued to read over a long time, though I haven't read Stevens closely for a few years now. Of course, I did always resist the finish and the tone of Stevens. Even as I was intrigued by it, I found it troublesome. The position from which the voice of that work spoke, constructing this refiguration of the Romantic imagination, has always both seduced and troubled me. Of course anything that seduces you troubles you.

PG: *If you have problems with the position of the voice in Stevens, is there a way you would define or differentiate the position of speech in your poems?*

MP: Well, it's much messier for one thing. At least I think tone becomes a thing that one dismantles as much as one attends to. I think the reason that finally — after initially neglecting Stevens, perhaps because of his difficulty — the New Critics began to attend to him was because they could finally see the control of tone, etc., as susceptible to close reading. And I think I've always tried to undermine close reading, to make it unreadable from that point of view. I think Stevens remains readable from that point of view — not that that is a qualitative judgment one way or another on his work. He frames things with great elegance, and I would be uncomfortable doing that. Ashbery's whimsy is remarkable. I don't have that same whimsy.

PG: *One could say that your poems are extremely elegant — are you uncomfortable with that?*

MP: Well, I see where that happens in the work, and then I become uncomfortable with it, and I try to dismantle it as I go along. I mean there's always that tension of an aesthetic surface that comes and goes in the work, and I've always taken that as a useful problematic — even as the work impelled itself toward that, I had to work against it within the semantic frame of the work. At times it seems almost like poetry! A lot of the more frank working with figures of poetic rhetoric in the "Untitled" section, and throughout *At Passages,* is about feeling freer to take those devices of language and use them against themselves in the poem. In the last couple of books there's been a kind of theatricalization of rhetorical figures that is, I think, somewhat suppressed in the earlier work, which is anti-rhetorical in a much more conscious way. This is anti-rhetorical by using the figures of rhetoric to expose themselves.

PG: *I would love one day to see the palimpsest that your poems must become in your notebooks. I imagine you put down a scaffolding and then rework it — because I can't imagine that all your poems come to you as fast or as well made as they appear.*

MP: They're pretty worked, most of them, and increasingly so over time; though there's an occasional one that comes relatively quickly, that might not be distinguishable from those that don't. But I suppose they are palimpsests. A two-page poem might have eighteen pages of notebook. I don't actually work on them in the notebooks, I work on them on the sheets, and they pile up, they pile up a great deal; and I finally realized they had to work that way. I wasn't going to be writing occasional verse in the sense of "my airplane poems," "my trip to New York poems" or "meeting a friend for lunch poems." And even more than that, the process of finding the poem that was trying to get out became an increasingly reflective process. So over time, I've written more and more slowly.

PG: *I wanted to ask where the title* Without Music *came from; I know there's a poem by Paul Eluard with that title.*

MP: It didn't actually come from that, though I wonder whether that may have been in my head. It came from reading a group of essays by Steve Reich called *Words Without Music* and I thought, well, if I take out words, I'm left without music. So the hidden word there is "words" which has been erased, and what's left is *Without Music.* I was trying to work against that very thing you were talking about, that elegance of surface, that musicality that the poetry, for whatever reasons of mine, tends toward. So I thought, well, if I call it *Without Music* maybe I can work in that direction. But taking this book of essays by someone who is working with music was the joke of that. It's possible too that "Sans Musique" was somewhere back in my head.

PG: *So when you talk about composition, it is to somehow take away or amend the term "elegance," so that the music that occurs is not merely elegant but has a purpose to it.*

MP: Just that, it's not meant to be decoration. Music and poetry can so easily become cultural décor, can become a thing that's pretty to listen to, and that's not the intent of this music. If it has any intent, it's to build up a rather dense harmonic structure that begins to constellate meanings, not simply on its own but meanings' relationships. Meanings' rhymes. Ratios. It points you backward and forward; it takes away linearity. It also subverts intent in an interesting way, and creates its own intention, and overcomes the limits of one's momentary thinking by announcing that these two things, so far apart, go together. Of course, great rhyme has always done that. But then we extend it to the whole harmonics of the poem, as interesting poets have always done anyway. This is nothing new, but it's certainly the way I have tended to use what we're calling musicality, perhaps in the same way that we speak of the value of nonsense: that it can challenge the apparent and multiply meanings, take us beyond what we thought we were talking about to something more like a subject that reveals itself as you go along — which interests me as a way to overcome my own habits of thought. You don't just become a poet and lose your habits of thought. You become a poet and remain a creature with habits of thought, and I think you go to the poem for instruction beyond that.

PG: *What are your new projects?*

MP: I'll be putting together the selected essays and talks, and then I want to finish a work called "Deck" which has been floating around

"Music and poetry can so easily become cultural décor . . ."

"It wasn't a form, it was a length."

for several years. The first two sections are 52 pages each, but with very little writing — so they're decks of cards.

PG: *Given the fact you're working with a deck of cards, is there any aleatory process or chance operation to it?*

MP: There's nothing aleatory, though one could of course mix up the poems if one chose to. For now I've left them in the order that I wanted. And then I have a prose work in the back of my head that I may or may not get to. It's been there for a long time — a prose work which is certainly not a novel.

PG: *Is there any poem that you've written that you had imagined and then realized much later?*

MP: Let me see. Yes, I have put, for example, titles down as mnemonic devices in my notebooks, and around that title something has begun to gather over time, and much later the work appears. And there are still latent poems in the notebooks that I will probably get to go back to. There's quite a bit of that. And sometimes they wait for that time when other things are gathering around them, so that they have a logic of composition of their own. Usually as a book gains momentum, what comes next begins to suggest itself more actively. Whenever I start out on a book I start out completely at a loss, I think because there are at once so many possibilities, and that kind of coming to grief when you complete a book, which is nothing, in a sense, and then you're faced with no longer being a poet once again — trying to become one. I don't think that's true of a vatic poet, who is always in a kind of afflatus — not that they don't come to their own grief, certainly, they do — but they never imagine themselves outside that figure; or it could be that we just approach doubt differently, I don't know. When I've worked with Margy Jenkins, we look back at a work and say, "What did we not let into that work that we want to let in?" You always want it to expand beyond the limits your own habits of working have established. Those are necessary habits but at the same time you realize that they repress something. And so I'm always asking myself what have I repressed in order to do this, and what of the world haven't I let in, or what of the world of language haven't I let in because of doing this.

PG: *Does that exploration occur in your notebooks?*

MP: It happens a lot in the notebooks. The notebooks are a mix of quotations that I love to draw out of various reading sources and then occasionally something that approaches an aphoristic fragment, though that's always done with a certain embarrassment, you know. But sometimes you end up thinking aphoristically, at least in looking for that kind of condensation which has a poetics of its own, a very risky poetics of its own, because it risks banality, particularly if you're not an aphorist, which certainly I'm not. Aphorism is, when interesting, an aspect of philosophical skepticism. It relates to poetry because philosophical skepticism also has a lyrical and condensed character to it, as in Nietszche or Wittgenstein, or at moments Derrida, who takes it to an extreme of skepticism about the possibility of meaning itself in any way that can be fixed. So the notebooks are a kind of book of quotations, a collaging of things, that one doesn't have to write oneself entirely, which is a great relief.

PG: *I know that "Sun" has the same number of lines as "The Waste Land." Did fixing that as a form allow you then to fill that space? And how much were you actually playing with "The Waste Land"?*

MP: It wasn't really a form, it was a length. I suppose a length could imply a form, but in this case it didn't. Partly a joke, in a serious sense. One of the things that "Sun" does is address my own ambivalent relationship to the high monuments of modernism and certainly an ambivalence to someone like Eliot, who subverts so much of the vital impulse of contemporary culture in his retreat from personal psychic disorder and his terror of the chaos of the modern. At the same time, I certainly would not have picked that work to overwrite if it wasn't an interesting one; if it wasn't a literally magnetizing work, work of the kind of cultural power that it becomes a world poem — so that you see many Eliot experts coming out of the Indian subcontinent, where it becomes representative in its nostalgia, and its invocation of problems that arise with the breakup of the Raj, just to cite one instance of its emblematic function. Also that reactionary sensibility that he manifests, that ecclesiastical and anti-Semitic sensibility that he represents, is a horrifying thing to have inscribed at the heart of modernism. Of course not by him alone; there's Yeats, Lawrence, Pound, on and on, Stravinsky. There are so many figures who trouble us deeply and who were some of the great poetic innovators of their time, not just formally, either.

PG: *Would you say that in your own evolution of thinking and exposure to culture, that poetry and your writing of poetry helped you to come to terms with or to disarm or dismantle biases or confusions, even assumptions that you were given growing up? Is your poetry an attempt to overcome any boundaries that you have?*

MP: To overcome itself, among other things. That self is never gone, but that self is one that I think we all work very hard against — and which eventually kills us off anyway because even as we work against it, we are to some degree constructing, consciously and otherwise, another one, which will be the end of us. But poetry has allowed me to think in certain ways, or has enforced the responsibility of thinking in certain ways. By the same token, there is no outside of the limits of one's own. . . I don't want to say "character," but another generation will look at our practice, and with the same disgust I suppose look at the limits of our relationship to questions of gender, ideology and culture. We're probably being very imperialist in our own way, however much we work against that sort of thing. So I don't pretend to overcome even the bigotries of another time, or to be more astute, really. I don't think astuteness is what it is, but consciousness, or aiming for some kind of consciousness — not some position of invulnerability and moral perfection.

— 6 APRIL 1994

Selected Work by Michael Palmer

from Blake's Newton:

ITS FORM

Its form, at tables by fours
leap . . . relieved of their weight.
She turns green
to begin. The Natural History
peregrine, Peale's hawk
is forgetting to talk
like those coast homes
lost in the deeper part.

But to begin a procession
or a succession of lines
replacing the elms whose warps
and curves are called contradictions.

To begin, 'the stamp'
of autumn . . . these parades
whose curved names
folded in as pilgrims.
You start to swim
through a little darkness
and see some trees.

In the New Spring this
snow is the cold
water running off
what it was. The moth
loves the rose but who
does the rose love. It
goes and
around her
dusting some lady's clothes
from an edge like

trees, turning pages, around or
else about her, the wings marked
by eyes, and seeing twice.

from The Circular Gates:

THE CIRCULAR GATES

I

NEW YORK

1

keys, of tears, the store
harvested white, and electricity.
Yesterday you met young Wagner
over threadbare grass.
Some talk of war
keys, of tears, and store.
In Chicago the arches
of the crash. Electricity.
All his emotions, his feelings
as well. The sources
of structures
in the shape of animals
that of height to base equals
and that of flatness

2

Increase in slenderness proceeds
That of height to base fluctuates
and was later straightened
We are at war
near the surface

of Damascus, the keys,
of tears, arches of the crash
In Chicago the mart
of chord; some of these same
emotions get lost
as well. We are at war
with the notion of survival
at times, and the sword
or cup that's called a form

3

The room is very large
and my name was George
This had been a hotel
I recognise the walls
of yellow chord; some of these

emotions get lost as well
at the store
Yesterday we met young Wagner
over threadbare grass
There is need of water
in Chicago, of arches
of the crash, his feelings as
well, and precise color sense
(so-called)

4

We will mention tomorrow
the hat and the window
somewhat swollen, the
door. I recognise the walls
of yellow chord; some of these

emotions get lost as well
laughing and chatting; one of the lesser gods
arose from the well. There were
the four; I recognise the walls
and the rain coming down
in the narrow hall, the
problem with the door

II

CHICAGO

1

Sometimes we are at war
you may be sure. A
morocco and gilt effect
by the side of the door.
Yesterday I met young Wagner,

an apple, and a door;
the apple filled the room
causing the guests to whisper
about the effects
of war. All his emotions
his feelings
as well, etc, everything
that was partly known
and more

2

I dreamed about the City
of O, small rubber in plexi
case, in row, the Brancusi
headlite, another face?
The stains of war

Jamaica Bay, lace. tradition
the pork chop bra, soft
logs, soft cross
attached flat, burlap
the metal hinge, wallet
rope, hinge, zipper
rope, King, the mourning figure
and missing portrait
and more

3

The fourth floor at Corbett's, the
window of the store, keys,
and electricity. Boston
Massachusetts enjoys war.
The individual did not

it happens, matter, and this
the relation to the world
of ordinary affections
more than what? By design
an art that's shadowless
the material carrying the light
the light equally distributed
across the wrists of the sword

4

The Gate appears to focus on love
on soft gloves and greatly
enlarged trousers, a sign
of war. In Boston
my trousers grow too large

for the door. The joining
of arms and throat,
the sources of animal forms,
a tooth, a balloon,
and a pool. I often draw
food before wearing it.
Is that what W. meant
about Tristan
from the beginning

III

I

There are three kinds of gate:
fan, interlace, rainbow
bulls and Greeks, an
inverted version; George Washington,
travel by aeroplane

from New York to Boston,
thence by barge
to the start of white water,
several miles of portage
until we saw the stone arches
of the mart, the angular
and brittle plasters
their solidity threatened

2

There are three kinds of gate:
fan, interlace, and rainbow;
the wrestlers' rose
fills the other room. They
had to whisper about the war

The same oriental pattern
covered the floor; the dragon
held a flaming ball.
There were cabbage roses
on the wall, and a portrait
of the broken window
on the fourth floor
done from a photograph
taken before the war

3

The keys of tears and the store;
the joining of arms and throat
between here and Boston. Damascus
(via Benares), an art
that's shadowless

by design, the material
carrying the light
by design, the material
of ordinary affections
more than what? It happens
the individual did not matter;
Boston Massachusetts enjoys war
more than what? In Chicago
the arches of the crash

4

I dreamed about the City
of O, the water
and the rubber boats. A compass
might have been of some use
all his emotions as well

As it is in New York
the chignon lies askew on the plane;
there are four kinds of gate
but some of these same
emotions get lost. We are definitely
at war, and I've a precise
color sense of war
like lemon pie or toast
or the onyx torso, now lost

IV

I

The card or cup
and sword. This
will be a rainbow
you may be sure
and have a noble effect

The subject I had already fixed on
the arches of the mart,
electricity, all his emotions,
the sources of these structures
in the form of animals,
the pork chop bra, hotel
keys, of tears, the store,
travel by autogyro
and the war

2

since early childhood. Mostly
harvested white; the hall
over threadbare grass. Tomorrow
we will mention the hat

and the window
somewhat swollen, the
door, and the lack of light.
All his emotions as well
in time of war, and the onyx
torso, now lost. And finally
how you can't deal with color
the same way as form

3

The meat of the thing
was the actual painting
of the war
and the cars
from the eleventh floor

What of the missing portrait
the preparatory drawings
of the changing forms

An elephant was said to mean
a harbor, without its clothes on

There were at least four
and I recognise the damage
of yellow chord and the water
coming down in the hall

4

but not the hall itself. I
awoke in a room where
a cage with a sleeping bird
had been placed. We
used to lift up the iron

gates and, regaining the light
I awoke near a wall where
a cage with a sleeping bird
had been placed. The problem
of the door
called for an opening. I knew beforehand
what had to be brought to light.
I knew there were horsemen
and without solid objects no light

from Without Music:

NINTH SYMMETRICAL POEM

(after Southwell)

It's November the thirty-third
of an actual November
and the children sleep in the crystal world
turning their heads from the fire that burns them

The burning children are invisible
but the carriers of wounded thought
are everywhere visible
as letters strung along a word

whose economies
work backward from speech
Mirrored we reflect such things
as they've seen

from Notes for Echo Lake:

SONG OF THE ROUND MAN

for Sarah when she's older

The round and sad-eyed man puffed cigars as if
he were alive. Gillyflowers
to the left of the apple, purple bells to the right

and a grass-covered hill behind.
I am sad today said the sad-eyed man
for I have locked my head in a Japanese box

and lost the key.
I am sad today he told me
for there are gillyflowers by the apple

and purple bells I cannot see.
Will you look at them for me
he asked, and tell me what you find?

I cannot I replied
for my eyes have grown sugary and dim
from reading too long by candlelight.

Tell me what you've read then
said the round and sad-eyed man.
I cannot I replied

for my memory has grown tired and dim
from looking at things that can't be seen
by any kind of light

and I've locked my head in a Japanese box
and thrown away the key.
Then I am you and you are me

said the sad-eyed man as if alive.
I'll write you in where I should be
between the gillyflowers and the purple bells

and the apple and the hill
and we'll puff cigars from noon till night
as if we were alive.

from First Figure;

MUSIC REWRITTEN

(after D.S.)

Yes and no then yes and no
Soon there'll be time enough for you

Charlie has swallowed the fluid
L has come inside a box

which some people paid to watch
Yes and no yes and no

You are a damaged set of illustrations
You are a ladder

in a chemical pond
a piece of hurry-up cake

or a true-to-life machine
making a music judged incomplete

by everyone willing to speak
Yes and no and yes and no

In a strange country you feel at home
because the hills there are the opposite of green

exactly as you were told
Now you must go there to prove it's so

Yes and no yes and no
Soon there'll be no time for you

The words are lost in the crease
but order is found at the base of a statue

or better, at the foot of a curved stone wall
in the tangles of the grass

Beneath the shadow of no and yes
nothing can be said

First there's sameness then difference
then the letter X across a face

then a line through a name
which is the wrong name in any case

from Sun:

FIFTH PROSE

Because I'm writing about the snow not the sentence
Because there is a card — a visitor's card — and on that card
 there are words of ours arranged in a row

and on those words we have written house, we have written
 leave this house, we
have written be this house, the spiral of a house, channels
 through this house

and we have written The Provinces and The Reversal and
 something called the Human Poems
though we live in a valley on the Hill of Ghosts

Still for many days the rain will continue to fall
A voice will say Father I am burning

Father I've removed a stone from a wall, erased a picture from
 that wall,
a picture of ships — cloud ships — pressing toward the sea

words only
taken limb by limb apart

Because we are not alive not alone
but ordinary extracts from the tablets

Hassan the Arab and his wife
who did vaulting and balancing

Coleman and Burgess, and Adele Newsome
pitched among the spectators one night

Lizzie Keys
and Fred who fell from the trapeze

into the sawdust
and wasn't hurt at all

and Jacob Hall the rope-dancer
Little Sandy and Sam Sault

Because there is a literal shore, a letter that's blood-red
Because in this dialect the eyes are crossed or quartz

seeing swimmer and seeing rock
statue then shadow

and here in the lake
first a razor then a fact

from At Passages:

UNTITLED (FEBRUARY '92)

Sleep said: the unpronounceable shadows
dance and slide and memorize lullabies

Said: a flame is as clear as music
Anything before that is just a fog

a muffled sound between X and now
where swollen bodies have been stacked like logs

as if a lexicon were to swallow its letters
or a swallow devour its young

all the while emitting its click song
which rises and will continue to rise

until it's joined to ink among the gathering clouds
whose scribbled meanings can leave no doubt

Words are made of electrons it turns out
Words remind us of fragments it turns out

parts of legs and parts of arms
It's invisible ink which blots them out

RECURSUS

to Porta

The voice, because of its austerity, will often cause dust to rise.

The voice, because of its austerity, will sometimes attempt the representation of dust.

Someone will say, I can't breathe — as if choking on dust.

The voice ages with the body.

It will say, I was shaped by light escaping from a keyhole.

Or, I am the shape of that light.

It will say, For the body to breathe, a layer must be peeled away.

It will say, What follows is a picture of how things are for me now.

It will say, The rose is red, twice two is four — as if another were present.

The dust rises in spirals.

It will say, The distance from Cairo to anywhere is not that great.

As if one had altered the adjustment of a microscope.

Or examined its working parts.

Possibly an instrument covered with dust and forgotten on a shelf.

Beside a hatbox and a pair of weathered boots.

The voice will expand to fill a given space.

As if to say, This space is not immeasurable.

This space is not immeasurable.

When held before your eyes.

And which voice is it says (or claims to say), Last night I dreamt of walls and courses of brick, last night I dreamt of limbs.

As you dream — always unwillingly — of a writing not visible and voices muffled by walls.

As if the question: lovers, prisoners, visitors.

The voice, as an act of discipline or play, will imitate other voices.

This is what I am doing now.

This is what I'm doing now.

The clock behind my back, its Fusée mechanism.

Voice one recognizes from years before.

Beneath water, hidden by a spark.

Here at the heart of winter, or let's say spring.

Voice with a history before its eyes.

With a blue dot before its eyes.

History of dust before its eyes.

It will say, as if remembering, the letter S stands for a slow match burning.

On the table before me.

No numbers on this watch.

And I live in a red house that once was brown.

A paper house, sort of falling down.

Such is the history of this house.

It looks like this.

Looks just like this.

We think to say in some language.

UNTITLED (FAR AWAY NEAR)

for the dancers

Still early still late
Have we asked enough questions about space
and what surrounds space
and the hands of a body tumbling through space

Still early still late
as a leaf might curl in a certain way
thinking to turn into carbonized lace
and a body might hurtle through space

Does a color experience pain
while falling through endless space
falling like a blob of sun or a peacock's call
(This June we have no rain at all)

How far away are the voices you hear
and those you can't seem to recall
Does each color recite a name
as if it were its own

yet almost unknowable like a fragrance of plums
(Your house is under repair your house is gone)
Question of the signs the bodies before us form
illegible as dust or eye of noon

Why did the Angel Phosphor arrive
in that city on that (white) night
caduceus held forward in its hand
We had joked that there was no city only winter

no winter only wind
only early and lateness, only streets and blown pages
then the day's final words
traced in silver fluid at the edge of the stage

What then if we spelled "after" with different letters
the letters for "first" or "last," for example
for "forest of burning boats" or "further"
and it came to mean "the chaos of the waterwheel"

or "the glow of the Thomson lamp"
What if spoken in muteness or danced without memory
What if as elsewhere or blinded, but watching the fire
helix of flames in the center of a square

Have we asked enough questions about changes of light
over time
Use music if you want
Yet let it not reach the ear

RED YELLOW BLUE

(Sarah's Eighth)

Now that you know all the words
and I have almost forgotten them

Or now that you have experienced rain
for days on end

and learned to paint with red, yellow and blue
those days which seem to have no end

and I see you often walking alone
down the street or else among friends

mindful of company, equally wondering
wherefrom a world's wrongs stem

And now that you may swim out of sight
if you choose, as choose you must

all along,
a song

AUTOBIOGRAPHY

for Poul Borum

All clocks are clouds.

Parts are greater than the whole.

A philosopher is starving in a rooming house, while it rains outside.

He regards the self as just another sign.

Winter roses are invisible.

Late ice sometimes sings.

A and *Not-A* are the same.

My dog does not know me.

Violins, like dreams, are suspect.

I come from Kolophon, or perhaps some small island.

The strait has frozen, and people are walking — a few skating — across it.

On the crescent beach, a drowned deer.

A woman with one hand, her thighs around your neck.

The world is all that is displaced.

Apples in a stall at the streetcorner by the Bahnhof, pale yellow to blackish red.

Memory does not speak.

Shortness of breath, accompanied by tinnitus.

The poet's stutter and the philosopher's.

The self is assigned to others.

A room from which, at all times, the moon remains visible.

Leningrad cafe: a man missing the left side of his face.

Disappearance of the sun from the sky above Odessa.

True description of that sun.

A philosopher lies in a doorway, discussing the theory of colors

with himself

the theory of self with himself, the concept of number, eternal return, the sidereal pulse

Logic of types, Buridan sentences, the *lekton*.

Why now that smoke off the lake?

Word and thing are the same.

Many times white ravens have I seen.

That all planes are infinite, by extension.

She asks, Is there a map of these gates?

She asks, Is this the one called Passages, or is it that one to the west?

Thus released, the dark angels converse with the angels of light.

They are not angels.

Something else.

The Site of the Poem

(an impromptu for Paz)*

Asked for a brief commentary on "the other voice," on otherness, alterity, margins and peripheries, I can't help saying first of all: no question and no answer, no end to this, no *telos,* no next century, no present, no tenses we can identify, will identify the issue. No syntax. No language that we can fix. No subject. No "one" who is speaking (*no one,* who is speaking). No "what" that is being spoken. A nothing for Paz then, at eighty, which is something. Impossible questions: that future-past in which we write, "in search of the present"; the "where" we are not as we write, that is, the site of the poem, the nowhere that is also now-here. The paradoxes of the poem, its counterlogic, its resistance.

I'd like to begin, in case I haven't already begun, with an anecdote I fear will be all too familiar to everyone here. A couple of weeks ago my daughter returned home from her high school and announced, with the hyperbolic flair characteristic of teenagers, that she had just had the worst school experience of her life. Her composition teacher, a woman distinguished both by the relentless conventionality of her intellect and by her adversarial relationship to all students possessed of a vital imagination, had given as topic of the day the question, "What is Poetry?". She had distributed a sheet with a variety of materials: a little verse bon bon by Richard Brautigan; a mawkish poem by e.e.cummings; two shaped poems by a much honored academic poet; a piece of rather conventional verse by a rather conventional versifier; a couple of inferior examples of concrete poetry; and, finally, a couple of cut-up selections of prose taken from advertisements and magazines, and arranged into free verse lines. Not a bad start, actually, for such a discussion. Trouble, however, was gathering, like a sclerotic metaphor, on the horizon. The instructions to the exercise read, in part, "Using *only* your definition of poetry, decide whether each of the following is or is not a poem." And then, rather strangely, "Stick very precisely to your definition, changing it whenever appropriate."

What followed, I gather, fell somewhere between a scene from Vigo's *Zéro de Conduite* and a children's crusade. Certain students very quickly discovered that there was greater poetic vitality in the randomly assembled collaged structures than in those obedient to conventions of poetic structure and affect. Many refused to supply a categorical definition, and some opted for a position of radical subjectivity — it's a poem if you think it's one. The teacher grew more and more enraged as each of her determining poetic features was challenged, including the distinction between verse and prose. As she retreated deeper and deeper into *querencia,* she accused the offending students of stubbornness and lack of respect, whether for her or for poetry wasn't clear. The students, of course, (however simplistic some of their responses) had thought they were manifesting a profound respect for poetry, for its indefinability as well as for the complex freedoms it seemed to embody to them, freedoms which spoke at once to the group and to each as an individual.

* "The Site of the Poem" is the slightly revised version of a talk delivered at the New School for Social Research as part of a panel on "Poetry in the 21st Century: the Other Voice," one event in a week-long celebration of Octavio Paz's eightieth birthday.

Poetry as site of the heretical imagination, of the dream or promise of language first experienced in early youth, what Robert Duncan referred to as a "place of first permission." The instructor, in her need for definition, for boundedness, had mistaken the ungovernability of the poem for an ungovernability of her students. Her dream of the cultivated or cultured field, with its neat furrows, its *lira,* had been forced to confront the *de-lirium* of the poem in that explicitly romantic, projectivist construction, the open field.

Ideologies, as Paz points out, do not produce meanings. It might even be said that they invade the *field* of meaning. Meaning is never a given, and it is perhaps the nomadism of poetry (as Gilles Deleuze would phrase it) which, in its resistance to meaning as such, challenges the *doxa.* Even the most private and seemingly hermetic of utterances can come to have the most public of resonances. The "lies" or "figures" of poetry can reconstitute at least the possibility of truth.

Thus Paul Celan:

> Black milk of dawn we drink it at dusk
> we drink it at noon and at daybreak we drink it at night
> we drink and we drink
> we are digging a grave in the air there's room for us all

Or Mandelstam:

> Petersburg, I do not want to die yet:
> You have my telephone numbers in your head.
>
> Petersburg, I still have addresses
> at which I will find the voice of the dead.

Or Paz:

> I open the window
> that looks out
> on nowhere
> the window
> that looks in

In writing of "the other voice" ("between revolution and religion"), Paz takes up that defense of poetry and critique of instrumental reason*, that reasoned critique of reason, initiated by Shelley and the Romantic poets, and taken up once again in various voices and with various motives by a wide range of vangardists and modernists. Always a question that has followed poetry: what justifies this practice at once inside and outside? How weigh the weightless? What place for a voice that is no one's and everyone's? What can this *dreyt nien,* this strict nothing, as the Troubadors sang of it, possibly mean? And just as Shelley invoked poetry's complex harmonies as a model, so Paz names the poem a miniature cosmos in its play of likeness and unlikeness, resemblance and difference — a kind of semantic model for the possibility of fraternity. The poem, which says that fire is cold, a thought green, an absence a presence. The poem, which means to transgress and transgresses to mean.

Yet must we not continually ask of this "between" (between Wordsworth and Shelley?) in what ways it is anything more than

* "For some of my thinking here, I am indebted to Robert Kaufman's thesis-in-progress at the University of California at Berkeley, "Negative Romanticism: Keats, Shelley and the Modern Aesthetic."

merely *between;* whether it is in fact a space *to* or *toward,* that is, one which will generate meanings, articulations and interrogatives, like the landscape of Dante's dream voyage. Notably, for those in the Hell of that space, it is the present which is invisible.

Shelley of course was a futurist. Historically, he spoke at the beginning of various potential futures, after one set of revolutions and before another. He was, in a sense, greeting an ameliorative future in the name of poetry (not by any means that he spoke with blind optimism). In "The Other Voice," the real question seems to be whether its moment will come to be known as a time of ending, of loss, or one of rebeginning, now that our various utopian futures have collapsed under the weight of tyranny and repression. What will be the name of our present? (That *present* again, briefer than a glance or a reflex, yet lasting forever.) Will poetry itself, and that which poetry stands for, simply become the victim of the market's one desire, which is to expand? In the space of a couple of years, for example, my friends among our great Russian contemporaries have gone from being legendary, unpublishable resisters, their words passed from mouth to mouth, to that marginalized status all too familiar in the American cultural landscape. One invisibility to another. At the same time, they have come into conversation with that "communauté imaginaire," as Jean-Luc Nancy calls it, that imaginary or impossible community, constituted out of differences, out of the play of identity and difference, of which the poem is at least one site. No less real for being invisible, and perhaps more so. It is a variation on this idea which the Italian philosopher Giorgio Agamben articulates in his book, *The Coming Community,* when he states, "The coming being is whatever being." A little later in his introduction he writes, "The Whatever in question here relates to singularity not in its indifference with respect to a common property (to a concept, for example: being red, being French, being Muslim), but only in its being *such as it is.* Singularity is thus freed from the false dilemma that obliges knowledge to choose between the ineffability of the individual and the intelligibility of the universal."

It is important, I think, that this not be mistaken for a vague liberal idealism, but that it be recognized as a model of overcoming, of a transcendence of what might otherwise, what will otherwise, prove monstrous. Nor should we be benighted enough to think that a conceptualization is sufficient alone to the social, to a further practice. Yet it is necessary, in this time when we must rethink and refigure national cultures, in order to free ourselves of cultural nationalisms and essentialisms, and rediscover the fluidity of race and culture, the multiplicity of our singulars. As Paz notes, we cannot and poetry cannot know what is to come. But against chaos (and to some degree in league with it), poetry can offer itself, in all the forms of critique and celebration which it takes. Within this offering, it seems to me, there remains always an idea of revolution and something learned from revolution.

We honor Octavio Paz today for giving voice across a lifetime to the poetics of community and for his insistence that the silences of poetry can and must be heard, that its nowhere is now here, "in search of the present."

— MICHAEL PALMER
14 MAY 1994

De Chirico *by* De Chirico

IN 1972 Giorgio de Chirico wrote the following statements across the proof pages of a catalogue for a retrospective of his paintings. He wrote in French, a language he had used little since abandoning his early, "metaphysical" style of work so popular with the Surrealists. And he scattered among the passages quotations and paraphrases from his early French writings, now collected in English as *Hebdomeros and other writings* (Exact Change, 1992). This return to the language and spirit of his metaphysical period is surprising because de Chirico was, in the latter part of his life, outspoken in renunciation of his early work. Why, more than forty years after writing *Hebdomeros* and nearly as long a period of renouncing it, de Chirico suddenly chose to extend its spirit in these fragments, is another of the enigmas surrounding his career.

In the texts below, titles and dates indicate the image represented on the page across which de Chirico wrote his commentary.

— DK

1.

SELF-PORTRAIT IN XVII CENTURY BLUE COSTUME (1947)

It happens that I sometimes remain in my studio in the evening, as night descends, without lighting the lamps. I lose myself then in strange reveries before the sight of my paintings slipping into an ever-thickening, ever-darkening fog.

2.

THE DISQUIETING MUSES (1925)

One was waiting for the sky always to get darker and for the night to finish by completely covering this whole region with its dark veils.

3.

ITALIAN SQUARE (1971)

I saw, engraved and painted, many troubling signs, the point of departure for a long series of inspirations as capricious as they were surprising.

4.

THE SWAN (1958)

"Give me your cold seas; I will warm them in mine." Politeness of the gods! For there are two, yes two gods — the white Neptune and the black Neptune — which is equal to saying the god of the North and that of the South. And it was the black one who thus spoke extending his arms full of algae across the vast world toward his white colleague.

5.

THE RED GLOVE (1958)

The dismal afternoon breezes swayed the zinc glove, colored with frightful gold nails, over the shop door; it indicated to me, with its index finger pointing towards the stones of the sidewalk, the unfathomable signs of a new melancholy.

6.

THE TROUBADOUR (1969)

It is others, those who talk about him, who incite his distrust. He is afraid of feeling in his back or in his side the piercing arrow of a glance, even a benevolent one.

7.

HECTOR AND ANDROMACHE (1946)

You, who after all, believe still less in space than in time, you always have hope in this measured step, which carries forward the great human races, a walk which nothing can oppose.

8.

THE GREAT METAPHYSICIAN (1971)

He evokes the September mornings on the sacred heights that dominate the city and immediately the voices cry out: "The acropolis, the acropolis!"

9.

ITALIAN SQUARE WITH MONUMENT TO THE POET (1969)

The façades of the houses erected on the sides were silent in the profound peace that is required by rest. It was late; the world was sleeping, buried in an immense tranquillity, and likewise, the troubled heart seemed at last appeased.

10.

THE ARCHAEOLOGISTS (1970)

"The world is full of demons," Heraclitus the Ephesian used to say, walking in the shadows of the porticoes in the hours laden with mystery of the late afternoon while in the reaches of the gulf the salty waters frothed under the meridian winds. "One must discover the demon in everything."

11.

ORPHEUS (1971)

The crater of a volcano begins to belch forth whirlwinds of smoke and small yellow and bluish flames. The luxurious vegetation of the valleys has disappeared in the dark. Sadness has invaded my heart. In one swoop, fountains decorated with beautiful statues and even pools where immaculate white swans floated, appeared in my mind to console me.

12.

FURNITURE IN THE VALLEY (1966)

Where is the room, the nice room where one encloses oneself, the curtains drawn and the door closed, and especially, where are the corners of rooms and the low ceilings . . .

13.

THE RETURN OF THE PRODIGAL SON (1965)

Sometimes I travel on a voyage in the depth of the night to obscure times and races. I thus attended celebrations for the return of the prodigal son.

14.

COLONIAL MANNEQUINS (1943)

Basically the artist likes what reminds him of certain visions that he has in his mind and in his instincts, and which are his secret world that no one can take away from him.

15.

THE ARCHAEOLOGISTS (1927)

I live in contact with fantastic beings, faithful friends who have little resemblance to those around me.

16.

THE CONSOLATOR (1958)

Yet there, nearby, events of an unheard-of solemnity followed one another with the fatality imposed upon us by the goddess Moira seated on a cloud.

17.

THE REMORSE OF ORESTES (1969)

It was necessary to flee again, to leave these places, to find the great desert of the night, a summer night without a moon, but gentle, clear and solemn.

18.

THE SADNESS OF SPRINGTIME (1970)

I abhor the atmosphere of the "end of springtime," the languorous heaviness which implacably announces the arrival of hot months; this season a great poet calls violent; and I await and hope for a cool wind to arrive, the wind of hope and consolation.

19.

ORESTES AND PILADE (1969)

Undoubtedly it is necessary for humanity to cross a dark tunnel in order to rejoin the other side, there where the freshness of watered gardens rises from deep valleys, and where the light of eternal idealism is indispensable to the human soul.

20.

THE GLADIATORS IN COMBAT (1953)

The cannon shot that you just heard signifies nothing but that the sun in space, the hands on clocks and the shadows on sundials have reached the fatal point which, according to some people, signifies the hour of phantoms more interesting and peculiar than those that usually appear to us on the stroke of midnight.

21.

AFTER THE BATTLE (1968)

The enigma of this ineffable group of warriors, of pugilists difficult to define, who, in the corner of the room, formed an immobile polychrome block with their offensive and defensive gestures.

22.

TWO MASKS (1971)

Masks hiding the faces inspire confidence and a violent desire for tranquillity and peace, engraved in stone like the laws of Moses.

23.

THERMOPYLAE (1971)

I saw slowly looming up from the chiaroscuro of my memory and defining itself in my mind, these temples, these plaster sanctuaries and flags, small and fundamentally so insignificant.

24.

METAPHYSICAL INTERIOR WITH BISCUITS (1968)

I saw something resembling a large compass that one opens and closes, a tripod set on the trail with a kick of the foot, a careful, urgent walking movement.

25.

METAPHYSICAL INTERIOR WITH ANATOMICAL NUDE (1968)

I was thinking of the ceiling illuminated by the light from outside; occasionally a shadow passed over the ceiling. Why does the mystery of shadows attract me?

26.

MYSTERIOUS BATHS (1968)

Toward what unknown banks are all these signs that I see in my mind sailing?

27.

BATTLE ON THE BRIDGE (1969)

I had a vision of Mercury who was pushing a herd of dreams in front of him towards the night of sleep.

28.

DEAD SUN IN A METAPHYSICAL INTERIOR (1971)

In the eternal realms the soul takes on the form of very pure smoke . . . The sea of stars stretches far, like a sky which has changed its aspect from a cupola to a ceiling.

29.

THE MYSTERIOUS SQUARE (1971)

My poignant prayers sometimes lasted until dawn, until the moment when the ardent sun loomed up triumphantly from behind the nearby mountains, lighting up the gold on the temple pediments.

30.

THE RETURN OF ULYSSES (1968)

A great lassitude took hold of me, a lassitude for my past life, for my present life and for the years that still await me, with their cortège of sad hours, or smiling ones, or simply neutral ones, neither sad nor smiling, just hours!

31.

TEMPLE IN A ROOM (1927)

Like enormous toys, a reduced temple, low rocks and a peaceful stream were chastely held in the room.

32.

SELF-PORTRAIT IN THE NUDE (1945)

What is necessary, after all, for one to be happy? Two apples, a bunch of grapes on a table with salt and pepper, a ray of sunlight . . .

33.

SAINT GEORGE KILLING THE DRAGON (1940)

There where only the soft light of the moon reigned, now a tender mist enveloped the rocks of the sea, a gray-violet tint descended from the sky and my thoughts floated as in a dream.

34.

LANDSCAPE WITH HORSEMEN (1942)

Angels with enormous wings like the wings of an eagle were seated along the paths, looking melancholically at the birds who feared some evil dispatch arriving from the sea.

35.

ANTIQUE FIGURES IN A ROOM (1932)

Gladiators! This word contains an enigma, making one think of music halls where the lighted ceiling evokes visions of a Dantesque paradise, of Roman afternoons at the end of a spectacle when the sun is sinking and the immense velarium enlarges the shadow over the arena from where the odor of blood-drenched sand and sawdust rises.

36.

ANTIQUE HORSES (1963)

O ruins! Temples of Neptune invaded by the sea! Waves pushing the dolphins up to the sanctuary where, in normal times, even the initiated would enter trembling, holding his wet sandals in his hands.

37.

ANTIQUE HORSES (1968)

Among the cylinders of fallen columns where, in the evening when the beach is deserted, large mares stop before going to graze avidly on the tender camomiles flowering in the shades of glorious ruins.

38.

LUCRETIA (1922)

Reality, in the interpretation of painters of genius, appears in all its multiform aspects, like certain divinities of lost peoples, and seems to have different expressions. One, however, that of true art, only a few can understand, especially today.

39.

ANGELICA AND RUGGERO (1946)

I know these hot days well, following nights of great visions, and the implacable sun, as well as the obstinate singing of sacred invisible cicadas, and the impossible freshness sought at the edge of the woods.

40.

SELF-PORTRAIT IN HIS PARIS STUDIO (1935)

The devil of temptation came to sit at my bedside. He followed me from sunrise until evening. And we know what that means, this demon who is constantly snickering at our sides. You believe you are free and at peace, you let yourself dream and suddenly you perceive that you are not alone.

41.

TWO FRIENDS (1940)

Maturity, awakening the deepest layers of reason in us, forces us towards discipline, towards work, pushes us towards these conquests, always greater and more beautiful, which henceforth dazzle our life with the immortal fire of glory.

42.

Still Life with Silver and Bust of Apollo (1962)

I lose myself in strange reveries before the sight of my painting and I become immersed in reflections on the science of painting and the great mystery of art.

43.

Fruit before a Legendary Castle (1947)

One must attribute the mystery of the work of art to a kind of close communion between the divine and the human, between logical reality and inexplicable metaphysical appearances.

44.

Self-Portrait in Armor (1948)

Immersing myself in deep meditations, softly, before the mystery, the curtain rises.

45.

Self-Portrait in Black Costume (1948)

In the clarity of the beautiful October day the horizon shines with a Helvetic purity.

46.

Portrait of the Artist's Mother (1911)

May a serious and continuous music accompany me in my difficult task with another song; melody of an infinite tenderness for which neither gods nor men can ever reproach me.

47.

Portrait of Isabella de Chirico (1940)

I looked at the clouds which fled from the south towards the north. Perhaps it was a sign indicating that towards the north is life and happiness, beauty and clarity, joy of work and rest without remorse.

48.

Regatta in Venice (1948)

Not a breath; an absolute equilibrium. The hope of a demigod had taken hold of every man.

49.

The Isle of St. George (1967)

Venice, your sea contains dangerous fits of anger. Sublime city! May God decree your lagoon become an unrippled lake, a peaceful lake, a consoling lake.

50.

Mysterious Rocks (1948)

One let oneself be lulled by an hour recovered from the half twilight, dreaming of gardens in the evening mist and immaculate white statues of goddesses lying on their bases.

51.

Nude in a Landscape (1935)

The sun was disappearing behind the low hills; at the horizon the shadows were stretched out on the ground; one felt the purifying air of the approaching night.

52.

FLOWERS WITH A RAINBOW (1970)

The period of calm when the mouths of oracles are silent, as if the spirit had emigrated far from the earth.

53.

APPARITION OF ROSES (1970)

In my dreams they appear suddenly like a surprising décor erected behind a curtain which rises.

54.

THE SUN IN THE CHIMNEY (1970)

But then this silhouette and this shadow gradually became obsessive and began to take a preponderant place in my mind; now this shadow plays an important role in my life.

55.

ORESTES (1968)

Impelled by a profound nostalgia, I would like to leave for distant lands, toward mysterious beings, faithful friends of my thoughts, toward a sure refuge where I can hide from real nature, cruel and perilous.

56.

MYSTERIOUS STAIRS (1970)

Once one had climbed this solemn staircase, once one had plunged into this disquieting labyrinth of vestibules, corridors and rooms, and addressed a steward in a frock coat, one felt the soul lightened, one felt like Alcestis following Hercules in order to rejoin her husband.

57.

THE CHARIOT OF THE SUN (1970)

Mercury, who at that moment was flying over the place, looked down and made joyous signs to me, shaking the caduceus in his hand.

58.

THE MYSTERIOUS ROOM (1970)

I like this room and the twilight where the ghosts of beings and things make their appearance; phantoms which, when they are lit up by the lamp, disappear slowly to their unknown kingdom.

59.

RETURN TO THE ANCESTORS' CASTLE (1970)

Up there to the left, in the clarified space, the crescent moon shone hard and cold, and the purifying winds of the night passed over the earth where the latest echoes of men's work were fading.

60.

RETURN OF THE PRODIGAL SON (1971)

It seemed to me that I heard cries, "There he is, there he is!" And then still louder: "Long live he who returns to us! Long live the prodigal son!"

61.

OEDIPUS AND THE SPHINX (1968)

Could life be but an immense lie? Could it be the shadow of a fleeting dream? Could it be but the echo of mysterious rappings struck over there on the rocks of the mountain, whose opposite side, it seems, no one has ever seen.

62.

METAPHYSICAL INTERIOR WITH A PORT (1967)

The sky was covered with a thin layer of clouds, a great tranquillity reigned everywhere. One should not gallop too much on the croup of fantasy.

63.

MYSTERIOUS ANIMAL (1970)

I saw Vengeance snickering in the shadows and rise up amid signs in flamboyant letters.

64.

HECTOR AND ANDROMACHE BEFORE TROY (1968)

The ability to extinguish every glimmer of life, of that common, inexplicable life of painted figures, in order to reclothe them with that solemnity and that immobility of serene and disquieting aspect, as of images containing the secrets of sleep and of death, is the privilege of great art.

65.

CAVALIER IN A PHRYGIAN BONNET (1934)

Clouds heavy like rocks and black like the night were burst apart by the capricious flights and the sharp angles of the lightning.

66.

REMEMBRANCE OF A DREAM (1970)

The passing gods, with their inscrutable faces, and draped with dignity, haunt the memories of my childhood.

67.

APOLLO AND TULIPS (1970)

I dreamed of landscaped gardens where every flower has its name and story and where Apollo stops in passing to contemplate the pure lines of the tulips.

68.

FANTASTIC DRAWING (1970)

Such are, in their general aspect, the values of the spirit which alone truly count in the works of an artist.

69.

THE ARCHEOLOGISTS (1970)

These beings lived in a world to themselves, a world apart; they did not worry about the eternal storm whistling behind them.

70.

THE SIBYLS (1970)

Before the sanctuary where the sibyls, standing on inviolable flagstones, with their pure profiles marked by classical beauty, keep watch, I cried: "Do not forget, O Divine Virgins, those whom Fortune neglects!"

71.

THE SORROWED MINOTAUR (1969)

It was one of his principal weaknesses to have a certain nostalgia for the past, even for such a gloomy past.

72.

HIPPOLYTUS (1969)

And it is still work, regular and daily work which saves all these minds obsessed by high metaphysical speculations from the abyss.

73.

ANTIQUE HORSES (1969)

The bad season is setting in, already the earth and the path are slippery, puddles of water form under the rather high grass where, in places, daisies and bluets make a timid appearance, just what is needed to make this bit of lane more smiling and to toss a poetic note in your path.

74.

THE SOLITARY POET (1969)

The sounds faded away; the wind withdrew its breath, the curtains which swelled out romantically at the open windows, collapsed like banners no longer inflated by the wind.

75.

THE DISQUIETING MUSES (1968)

Where are the very cool oases where one desires nothing and where a strange and gentle wisdom falls from the top of the palm trees?

76.

THE TROUBADOUR (1968)

I see the mirage of happiness surrounded by fantastic images, veiled and imprecise like dreams of full-mooned nights, so gentle and disquieting.

77.

AJAX (1970)

But the most amazing characteristic was the grand, the exquisite, the infinite sensibility of his soul.

78.

COLONIAL MANNEQUINS (1970)

You feel yourself sheltered from the dangers that come from outside, which the determined enemy sends to your door, sheltered from comets with noxious tails appearing on the horizon.

OUT of the Anglophone Caribbean

POETRY of IMPLICATION

Language is an issue. It has to be when distinctions among people turn upon speech, as they do viciously in the anglophone Caribbean. To bring one's self into conformity with one's place, a person undertakes to re-un-dis-cover some fundamentally adequate tongue out of the tongues. Poetry takes on the role of inscribing its version of this, but in such a way that it retains the clarity of its own making.

For people in the Caribbean and for the people who have left, the region sometimes acquires the compelling form of an origin. Behind this origin lies other beginnings, other identities and other cultural practices. Poetry involves itself in the New Place with the speech in continuous evolution, with perceptions marked in contrast to absence, to earlier presences, and with relationships that never cease to be aware of initial causes. In this way, a poetry of Caribbean origin is one that registers the accents of multiple geographies in the formation of persons. No ground exists to celebrate the homecoming of such a speech.

The false grounds of identity surface in the language and maintain their willingness to define definitively the incompleteness of the name without the sanction of various centres. To the Spanish speakers in the region, the Caribbean naturally spells out the archipelago and the coast of South America — Colombia, Venezuela. To the English speakers, the Caribbean has in the past resembled a linguistic map with other areas strangely distant: a fact of difference that translates the wars of other powers and continues a fragmentation of nations whose current alliances reproduce old conflicts.

Against these definitions, anglophone Caribbean poetry has been working now for some time. In line with this basic project, the writers gathered in this section, most of whom now live and work abroad (Canada, U.K., and U.S.A.) are attempting in various ways to re-conceive the geography of the speaker, so that fresh relationships may become visible. What emerges from their meditations is a poetry of implication, of confluence, and of provisional sightings.

— MARK McMORRIS

KAMAU BRATHWAITE

Word Making Man

poem for Nicolás Guillén in Xaymaca

Sir,

not in 'Sir'
but *compañero*
as you wd prefer it in *hispañol*

i have not yet been to cuba
& do not know the language of yr *oradores*
& as you said

'some of us are champions
from the provinces, others
lo son olímpicos.' & some of us
are nothing — you will forgive me if i quote you again —
'not even *oradores'*

but i know that we are watching in a long circle for the dawn
& that the ruling class does not wait at bus stops
& i know that we are watching in a long circle for the fire
& that our *compradores* do not ladle soup out of the yabba

in camagüey
ave maría
católica

silversmith turned silverfish. your father
in the leaves of the spanish classics. metallic needlework
in a tropic of paper. turblethumb thimbleprint journalist
who divined the omens of martí

when he was shot — *fusilamiento*
you became a snake
circling circling circling renewing yr cycle of certainty

& you awoke to sleepy horses
sleepy snocone vendors
to hazy drunkards staggering to their homes

you tripped you cried you stumbled
on the dreams of those far-off days:

nicotine lópez, yr pharmacist & friend
the town clerk cores and the cop who died his name like caanan
what's his name?

& serafin toledo. blacksmith steel-lightning tailor
'& the school desk w/ the pen-knife scars
beneath a sky of fireflies & stars'

& we all learn
guitarra
we all learn

mayombe-bombe-mayombé
mayombe-bombe-mayombé

that one does not kill a brother
that one does not kill a brother
that one does not kill a brother

& look how *sensemayá* he is dead!

✸

Now we rock-steady safely in the *orisha* of our dreams
& yr name has become the *sunsum* of our ancestors

to the pale salons of the *lippi* song you brought the son
w/ the broad boa of the *conquistadore* violin you bent the tree

jack johnson kid chocolate muhammad ali
them jazzers w/ cow-punches in their smiles

the stylish patent-leather shoes, the creaking
downstairs down the stares from broadway stretching

out 'its snout, its moist enormous mout
to lick & glut upon our canefields' vital blood'

black little rock. the mau mau. emmett till
guevara & the beaten skulls of biko & lumumba

you have whispered it all. you have uttered it all
coriolan of blood. plankton of melt & plangent syllables

sunrise *lucumi* sparkle

against yr teeth of joy
sus dientes de júbilo

amerika laughs
west indies west indies west indies ltd

✸

but suddenly in the night of possibility
it turns to the wall in its creaking bed of dollars

west indies west indies west indies unlimited

& yr voice rises like the moon
above the day of pigs . above the choruses of

who is it? who is it not?
the negro

who is it? who is it not?
my hunger

who is it? who is it not?

i&i talkin to ya

& the sea between us yields its secrets
silver into pellables into sheets of sound
that bear our pain & spume & salt & coltrane

saying
xangô

'no
not no
not bad
not bad, not velly bad'

but

yes
sí yes
bien
sí well
sí velly well

so that we learn w/you the pleasure
of walking w/our roots across the country

owners herein of all there is to see.
owners herein of what we must believe
of what our hands encompass as we dream

so that together we say wind
& understand its history of ghosts.
together we say fire

& again there is a future in those sparks
together, comrade, friend
we say this is our land & know at last at last it is our home

now mine forever & so yours, *amigo*
ours
'w/ the vast splendour of the sunshine & the sunflower & the stars'

DIONNE BRAND

from
In Another Place

In another place , not here, a woman might touch
something between beauty and nowhere, back there
and here, might pass hand over hand her own
trembling life, . . .

(from *No Language is Neutral)*

1

Out here I am like someone without a sheet,
without a branch but not even as safe
as the sea, without the relief of the sky or a
door. If I am peaceful in this discomfort
is not peace, is getting used to harm, is
giving up or misplacing my imagination
as if standing in a doorway I cannot summon
up the yard, familiar broken chair or rag
of cloth on a line, I cannot smell smoke
burning something in a pit or odour from
far off or hear anyone, calling, the doorway
cannot bell a sound, cannot repeat what is
outside, or my eyes is not a mirror.

If you come out and you see nothing
recognisable in front of you, if the stars,
stark and brazen like glass, already done
decide that you cannot read them. If the trees
don't flower and colour refuse to limn,
when a white man in a red truck on a rural
road jumps out at you screaming his self-hatred,
his hatred of the world as narrow as his
eyes and personal and he threatens,
something about your cunt, you do

not recover, you think of Malcolm on this snow
drifted road, you think of Malcolm deeply.
Is really so evil they is then that one of them
in a red truck can tear your eyes out
split your heart open.

When I try to go out at night and
look up at the stars, they say something cold
or maybe is me gone cold, gone heavy
maybe they suggest something so fresh I don't
want to listen, but it is stark, stark I tell you
and I think deep after everything that happen. Here
one day I read a headline that drive me to the floor
and each day after they come gazetted and sly
slipping grief and shutting drafts of air, the papers say,
maybe I don't want to listen no more to hopefulness
so I can't take the stars. I lift my head in the cold
and I get confuse. It quiet here in the night
and is only me and the quiet. I try to say a word
but it fall, I stand up there but nothing happen
or I shouldn't say nothing, I was embarrassed, standing
like a fool, the pine burdened in snow, the air fresh,
fresh and foreign and the sky so black and wide
I did not know which way to turn except to try
again, to find some word that could be heard
by the something waiting. My mouth could not
find a language, I find myself instead useless as
that. I sorry. I stop by the mail box and I give up.
I look down the road but is more pine and snow
and the rail road track unused now and when
it's only green here with flies. Don't even waste your breath,
this winter road cannot hear it and will swallow it whole.
Don't move here it will freeze your heart.

I look at that road a long time. It seem to close.
Yes, is here I reach, framed and frozen on a northern
country road instead of where I thought I'd be in the blood
red flame of a revolution. I couldn't be farther away
and none of these thoughts disturb the stars or the pine
or the road or the red truck screeching cunt along it.
All I could do was turn and go back to the house
and the door that I can't see out of or love, my life
was supposed to be wider not so forlorn and not standing
out in this north country denuded like maple. I did not
want to write poems about stacking cords of wood as if
the world is that simple, that simplicity makes me
choke and is not simple or content but killed and finally
cornered. I still need the revolution bright as the blaze
of the wood stove in the window when I shut the light
and mount the stairs to bed.

MARK McMORRIS

More Than Once

Once, fast along the ridge, we stopped where bush opened
The bones in a pit eager to enter the fuselage of our talk
The swerving of terrain, awake to the measure, the iron of its eye
I tried to pick out the moment when calm went south
And you the girl beside the ridge, a huge breadfruit tree
With balls of fruit, like soccer balls, the pimples are also green
I came from the tree and stood beside you like a vine
To crawl upon the main trunk where the sun sat like Jesus

Once, in deep anguish, the ridge buckled and left us
Steel pipes ran beside the cave where we made fishhooks
Of bone, the debris living with us, a rock with blood on it
The tableau with ankh to protect our backs from the heat
O thief! I went home from the ridge, a mountain lion
Circling the wood pit, the cave was of bone, the fire not yet come
To dynamite the hill as we angled towards its mouth
I waded among the splinters of a water fight, out onto Crete

Once, in archipelago, a necklace tied with water, a fuse lit
Brought us into the cave, it shut like a footlocker on our plight
Forced to huddle, we waited for a fire, we sucked gas
And dreamt of smoke and drew pictures of copulation, I went
Beside salt marsh in Guinea, or under stars, of the roof hole
You brought in dyes and set paintings on our left
The rooms lie still, the noise of your breathing in my head
Man in a cave beside a fish bone hook, woman beside a cave

Once, we saw that it was night, the cave opened out of a hill
The rains came, and phonemes sprang new from the ridge
People left for grasses east of the Nile, and I was left
A shell of crab on my back, a crop of wool for my head, gear
Of lights deep over the grass, we ate from each other's hand
Choice meats were stored beside the pit of wood for your trek back
And I took to my bed in thorn, and rain wet me from the roof hole,
Next day we planted out a canefield, I begged you to hand me up

Once, when begging was invented, we sat out the fire and winded
I touched your palm print to my palm for the need of a self
The cave beside a mound of slag, we made hooks of iron from this kiln
The salt mines of Liverpool, the coal pits of Dahomey, the benches
Of courts with smooth bars for the plea, you on the steps
I went up to you when begging was the norm, when the cave was burnt
Poking through the ash, you to the camp of refugees, I to the holding pen
The men went out to plant with their hands what grew in that place

Once, I returned from your neck where my face was on fire
To dig up the roots that grew under earth at the earthworm's back
I picked apples with the daughters of sons, I bought a transistor radio
To you I gave every penny of my sweat till the plantings were done
I looked at sun, straight at it for once, to see if I could stand god's mouth
Went east with the cargo of my doubt, the cave was flooded
We turned back then, to snow beside the hooks made out of our colloquies
There were five of us: two of us were mules, three men in a cave

How easy to be alone when the wind insists, the bones we collect
As easy as digging up the hole, the spirals of talk you make out of wind

Invigorated Sight

1.

The ease astonishes by which
you cover miles to a threshold
where poet and scientist stand
on a wide beam at moonrise.

Now I find your thought beside me.
Tomorrow, I expect to see you on the hill
going toward your mistress Poesie —
the flag drops down like Quixote's lance.

My house is your house
Guillaume Apollinaire
and it is simple and deep
because you built it.

You began the century with a halloo
that goads us now at the finish.
Gun-fire lights up the desert —
our cities are racked with it —

which did not stop your tongue
from recovering to tell us
of the spirit of the poets to come
and we are not now defeated.

Providence is the city of poets,
Guillaume Apollinaire.
This grass is your green imagination
you left it for me to walk on.

2.

Gardens in Kingston
come back in the French Poets
because of their city, Paris,
made of plants, water, and light.

The paths have been touched by sun:
the ranks of azaleas, old men at croquet
in the *jardains.* I pick one stone (an opal)
and fix it to my sleeve for art's sake.

Kingston: the Hope Gardens
a reservoir for all types of green
moss, invigorated hedges
blaze of the poinciana in July

flamingoes in a green pool —
of course they stand on one leg
winged veterans from the First World War
as I think of Apollinaire, you

poet of the written image
poet of the fountain that speaks
poet of melancholy advance
poet of invigorated sight.

The children are here.
They come for the flamingoes
and it is as you said
that the gardens are open for them.

MARLENE NOURBESE PHILIP

To Whom It May Concern

better to write to you
of tradition, England,
a ventriloquist I
and the future. hear a voice
like mine from
— a voice from the past
for you. Hollow upon brick
a pyramid of empty
silent years I hunt
loose brick or stone allow me entry.
this letter will loosen
be the password secrets
silence. question what
all
and the floor: to the dancer
essential with and against,
— to soar above. There can

no dance without Your face
away doubt in anger:
desperate didact to
distracted pupil: we writers women
black no dance
tradition Word — ours . . .
" traditions
go a begging, and" But
unique to us
New World, all problems old
scribble on the margins
m e wor d, the word een used to sear
and troy bludgeon deaf and dead
weapon; we
first , Afric , the world, Europe
third world not discovered
but uncovere heir to the words
of these worlds. None ours so where
find the floor word?
words the male;
find the floor of the female word —
is there
the sneer in your voice, "If it's
want, how about Chauce , Donne, akespeare —
their language." Praise
song drum song — Zulu cries
the mating ours I cede
grudging freeze-dried in translation

tonal hythms punctured eardrums no
respond man songs. Where
our songs what my song where
floor to hurl flood of words against
you yawn behind your
point of all this. fifteen twenty
and black — show me
radiation is tradition not?"
You a long way; race and gender
ceased matter a great deal,
sometimes one ,sometimes
equally. Almost never
all passé, you say,
your own tradition. how did
No
most effortless, the dancer soars
highest — above has been
effort, most discipline — complex
ing of muscle assion
sweat and floor that you
now soar and fly apparent
lessly I build a you
be yours. Dance fly
above work with and against
need me earth, ground and

PS
Maybe my dance always
I build — a difficult
how then do you fly?
ensure , someone
will come upon dis floor-board
— too infrequently —
she too, trod nameless
my sister, dance
floor thought in time.

Cornwall, England, 1983

FRED D'AGUIAR

At Sea

All night I rock, twist and turn.
I wish it was my baby who was on my mind.

Blame that two-week crossing of the Atlantic
by boat back in '62, from England to Guyana,

when I learned to rock and roll effortlessly,
and the world, the whole liquid enterprise of it,

seemed to be going some place, leaving me
behind or in the middle of nowhere,

at a point that kept the horizon exactly
in the distance and brought dolphins to the side

then sent them off, and saw whales dipping
and rising together, relocating an archipelago

of sudden springs that died as suddenly
as begun, as they headed away, always away

from me dancing in reluctant sways, swivels
and spins on the spot, in a world of flux.

Transport

The cobbled streets shone
with rain or sleet or snow.
We drove leaving these
oblique tracks on water,
consumed by light or frost
that was light's colour.

All this through a heated
rear window in a bus I'd
boarded or had been made
to board with faces
lumped together strictly
on the basis of race.

Why was I at the rear
looking out at weather
I couldn't even define?
Perhaps it was dawn.
Perhaps? Of course! Streetlights
made the streets shine.

I wore pyjamas,
a bathrobe and was barefoot.
No time to grab my glasses.
I saw the world more as
conjecture than fact.
That at least's a fact!

I knew no one on that bus.
Talk was forbidden,
by whom I don't know.
I heard the engine rev
as it climbed and descended
through several gears.

I felt cobbles or potholes
on a rear axle I feared
might break: an old bus
or a bad road, or both;
tires parting the wet road,
and the parts closing behind.

It's weather I don't like
to be out in, muchless
barefoot wearing bed things.
Heading where? East
I guessed from the sky,
or what I took for sky —

a whitish gray light
opening like a huge parasol
at the front of the bus,
and the bus continually
heading into it as it
gracefully retreated,

or could not be caught
beyond the fringe that laced
the bonnet, windscreen,
wing mirrors and front
hub caps, acting like a
magnet on that bus and us.

Why did I think just then
we were all going to die
or had already died
and the lights were God's —
his chariot, his humble
soul-bearing chariot

transporting those souls
who had perished that night
in the black district.
The thought wasn't just mine.
Everyone looked like they
saw what was in my mind,

as if my skull was shaved away
showing my brain in its brine.
The cobbled stones that shone
were clouds we sailed above.
The engine noise I heard
was my own breath and heart.

MUTABARUKA

Dis Poem

dis poem
shall speak of the wretched sea
that washed ships to these shores
of mothers crying for their
young swallowed up by the sea
dis poem shall say nothin new
dis poem shall speak of time
time unlimited time undefined
dis poem shall call names
names like lumumba kenyatta nkrumah
hannibal akenaton malcolm garvey
haile selassie
dis poem is vex about aparthied racism facism
the ku klux klan riots in brixton atlanta
jim jones
dis poem is revoltin against 1st world 2nd world
3rd world divisions man made decision
dis poem is like all the rest
dis poem will not be amongst great literary works

will not be recited by poetry enthusiast
will not be quoted by politicians or men of religion
dis poem is knives bombs guns blood fire
blazin for freedom
yes dis poem is a drum
ashanti mau mau ibo yoruba nyabingi warriors
uhuru uhuru
uhuru namibia
uhuru soweto
uhuru afrika
dis poem will not change things
dis poem need to be changed
dis poem is a rebirth of a people
arizin awakin understandin
dis poem speak is speakin have spoken
dis poem shall continue even when poets have stopped writin
dis poem shall survive u me it shall linger in history
in your mind
in time forever
dis poem is time only time will tell
dis poem is still not written
dis poem has no poet
dis poem is just a part of the story
his-story-her-story our-story the story still untold
dis poem is now ringin talkin irritatin
makin u want to stop it
but dis poem will not stop
dis poem is long cannot be short
dis poem cannot be tamed cannot be blamed
the story is still not told about dis poem
dis poem is old new
dis poem was copied from the bible your prayer book
playboy magazine the n.y. times readers digest
the c.i.a. files the k.g.b. files
dis poem is no secret
dis poem shall be called borin stupid senseless
dis poem is watching u tryin to make sense from dis poem
dis poem is messin up your brains
makin u want to stop listenin to dis poem
but u shall not stop listenin to dis poem
u need to know what will be said next in dis poem
dis poem will disappoint u
because
dis poem is to be continued in your mind in your mind
in your mind your mind

CLAIRE HARRIS

Traveling To Find A Remedy

EVERY MOMENT: A WINDOW

which   you
could never open

who may be captain
or crewman

and now

where the polished house drifts
on dim wind
you come   the man with her heart
cupped
against his throbbing fingers

you lean over her sink
and luminous
gloom washes over
ennobles you

✷

when you surface your dread eyes batten hatches
once again you are boy   voice a skirt billowing on
school grounds   whose desperate eyes beseech her
you are youth climbing antic windows to watch her pass
her short hair cheeky in the wind your mother hated

now you stand here
thus
in this poem
an item
lifted from a newspaper
wondering

and you don't know
what
this poem is
or whether
and can't
while you ponder
poem
even   is

you suspect
an accident

remembering the glass you reached to place
on the table   only   that table moved   moved quietly
casually   there at your feet the last
of the wedding waterford splintered to primitive grace
on the terrace   the lilacs   Aunt Emma   your own
wife   all staring as if you had contrived the perfect
inconsequent ending

✷

perhaps
a seeding
of the night sky
handfuls   blown gently from the palm
more or less
as in Matthew 13.1
only that suggests
deliberately

and if not

a machine
spraying
into the cool gauze
of space
into the clever
invisible woof and warp
of matter and time

its cavernous mouth clean as a cat's
its smooth black throat all gigantic as in infinite
mounted on transparent steel skin its visible
intestines of wheels gears pipes levers little
knobs and screws all striving all moving anti-
clockwise its click clack continuous motion
a grin gone audible

it sprays

✷

bits

of idea
words
phrases
colour
line
notes
or numbers
formula
bits
which is to say
morsels parts of keys

fragments
drills
pincers
blades
even a uterus
bits capable of breaking
of piercing
of closing
of taking hold
and one liquid warm
capable of dark sheltering
to birth

✷

though innocent
of what is born

bits and pieces
but never the whole story

what we are
we are at the hands of the universe
to which we cling

precarious
random

while rock chance energy
work their eluctable
destiny

dark clouds cluster
above the Bow
dim its luster

the river's secret green
and snow in April
after a long hot winter

Everett's multifoliate reality: atoms split the world branches into parallel worlds we with it in one I no longer write this seduced by action in that spider an atom splits and you now sail the seas in a bathtub the first man to cross the Pacific thus even as your world splits again bits and pieces blossoming into intricate wholes in this splinter you would not have accepted her heart in another would not have minded so madly the losing of it would not have demanded it of her with the carving knife there is that other universe where you sit at a word processor working on plot and consequence finding the right laconic tone

you waiting at the sink
in this poem
what now?

bits and pieces

as Aunt Mary would say Carib eyes knowing
this is a God yes chile this is a God
slapping me
so He wouldn't notice
her love

when we are young

which happens
with disconcerting regularity
time stalling on us
refusing to change gears
stranding us
under dry prairie sky
on temporary highways
to wait for a lift
the wind whipping
little storms
of doubt
around us

fine coat on skin and hair
grit in teeth and lashes
so that runnels are carved
by tears
that is by grief/rage/wonder

the window may crack
an opening through which we
may crawl   bruised

one such time

✸

I woke to roosters crowing   to stumbling feet on
wooden floors   a slow stirring of darkness   battered
buckets   heavy with well water   clanked against white
kitchen walls   night ebbed on a slow tide of voices
and it was time   greengowned   sandalled   I hurried
to my own monstrous dawn   there behind fences
the great rooster   I clung to his wire waiting   I was
the man tied to a rock   he was the eagle   he would
tear out my liver   he had to   seven   my mind tangled
in myth   blood streaked   and wonder   each morning
at first light compelled in secret to certain doom

(we wake without warning
wake to consciousness
find a world whose ordered chaos
defies our small control
we who have no natural claim
to anything save
death)

even at seven I chose Prometheus   each morning I
faced that rooster   iridescent in the flowing light
and his slow arrogant flutter   each morning   eyes
tight   against the flare of eagle eyes   empty of
all save hope I waited the crack of terrible wings

✸

(did the preconscious whisper
better stranger fate
than oneself
in the dark
with the human race

test the frail bridge
of words
you will find it anchors us
islands
in our separateness

the unstoried doom of symbol
of language
stolen in the predawn
from what elemental gods)

that rooster closed his eyes seemed to sleep content
but we committed to consciousness temper thought
in the fierce crucible of tongues strengthen our bars
of myth with satellites

✷

(who stitch the fragile
embroidery
of our groupings
express the longing communion
denied us what is left
but to make the best of things
even as we lift a common shield
of words
against chance gods
men)

I was eight when the horror failed it was hard
without warning the bloody dawn blazing sea the rock
the first anguished whisper of wings faded
into simple mornings

✷

each moment a window
the window closed

and you released
into blue day
you place her dried heart
in the sink

now you sit
in her living room
a fire throwing shadows
the glow of wine
at your elbow

reading
God and the new Physics *

burnished
dressed all in white
you wait

*Davies

3 CHAPBOOKS:

J.H. PRYNNE

BEVERLY DAHLEN

SUSAN HOWE

NO. 1

BANDS **AROUND** THE THROAT

by J.H. PRYNNE

J. H. Prynne was born in Kent, England in 1936. He studied at Cambridge, where he now lives and works. In recent years he has also worked in China (see his afterword to Original Chinese Language-Poetry Group in this volume). His collected poetry, entitled simply *Poems,* was published by Allardyce, Barnett in 1982. His latest publications include *The Oval Window* (1983), *Word Order* (1989), *Not —You* (1993), and *Her Weasels Wild Returning* (1994).

Bands Around the Throat (1987) was originally published in Cambridge as a limited

FOOL'S BRACELET

In the day park shared by advancement
the waiting clients make room, for another
rising bunch of lifetime disposals. It is
the next round in the sing-song by treble touches,
a high start not detained by the option
of a dream to pass right on through
the spirit proof coming off the top. What
don't you want, is there no true end
to grief at joy, casting away deterrent hope
in a spate of root filling? The upside of the song
from the valley below excites lock-tremors
as the crest gets the voice right by proxy,
non-stick like a teflon throat. To press on
without fear of explanation, refusing the jab:
*Ah Curly do your day is done, The course
of woe is quickly run. Low without loss
your shining heart Has nothing but the better
part.* The star of swords is put upon
his neck. He falls to the ground. Why not?
It is a root and branch arrangement, giving
the keys openly to a provident reversal,
to net uptake. To these Whom we resist.
To blot out a shabby record by a daze
intrinsic in transit: *See what is won,
We have cut him down, Like the evening sun
His only crown.* Don't you think that's enough
to peel a larynx at a flotation, they say,
by the stub of a tuning fork delivery. The issue
hits all-time peaks in no time at all,
buy on the rumour, sell on the fact. Only
a part gives access to the rest, you get
in at the floor too: *And his dance is gone.*

NO SONG NO SUPPER

Even so by open outcry across
this ring a deep frost cuts up
a halo of grey cinders; the night
is stark cold to pay less and less

And strike the hand numb with its
spoiling glove, the eye sex-linked
to give over by parity of first reason
in the Rotunda's even light.

For here is the display now, of inert
promise like a flick-knife in milk
dipping and turning to catch the offer
subscribed with cloudbands, upon

A gilded defacement. To pay less and less
until no third call for back light, while
hurt fowls creep to their sedge and
for more body the nearly new desk

Invites a co-orbital issue: front delivery
on a dropped cartel is the rule
of this account. Make ready the fresh
bout of inshore welding and you can

Relinquish at its best what cloys hardly
and saves time. Like grape-shot
in a founder's garden the bees cluster,
the shrunk figure is so flattened out

And so deedy by bent fingers joined
for a novel immunity. It is plain terror,
sifted to wholemeal with double glazing
and gracious sashcords. What is

That halo of white light doing in this hall
  if not to magnify small gifts,
to less and less affordable invitations
  taken up in flue dust by single file

Through the rank, frozen grass. Clamped down
  by artifice in dark shadow you drop
silent at green fire sprouting as a municipal
  thunderbolt, what goes up you

Pay for, nuée ardente in safety-critical
  overshoot. Un che piango, slop
over slop gives harm to hurt minds
  and snow to their colder moods.

Thicker frost now, voices more distant,
  artefacts of routine behaviour like
side-words on a postage stamp. The leaves
  are bent double, stripped of afterglow

In the petition of less for less. At the
  limit the sound pins an ice halo about
flaring echoes, going aside at the ring,
  22° in the Rotunda itself

Where white roots dissemble and crack,
  faces set against payouts. What
you get you fear to want as the round
  slips down below and so and so and so

And so the leaves are stiff, pleated
  like rippled ash-cloud and so
studded with blank nipples, dormant so
  in unyielding, abundant gratitude.

RATES OF RETURN

Waiting to learn, learning to melt
a blade of sugar in the afterlight,
the patient markers set terms
of allegiance by the step back, into
the shade of the proof system. It will cover
more than the spread, by high yield
in excess of practice. Fear is conditioned
to the signal which predicts shock, and yet
novel fears presume attachment to comfort
in, how you say it, 'the home cage'.

Here then admit one at a time
by sweet unremembered bounties at the door,
the sights of growth from immortal seed
acting like fallout on upland pastures
causing restrictions on the movement of sheep.
The margin is close but easy enough,
grateful as the dew on a roof line,
there is no question that the child
will be proof-wrapped, up to the eyes
of what we fade away to gain.

STAMP DUTY

Said with a flourish, in the morning
be merciful and by the evening
take in the slack. Said slowly
on a recount of past preference,
pitiful and generous as one
to another's neglect. Under the stone
a pocket, and inside that a token:
dark-worded it will see you,
as you thereafter, all the way, ahead.

MARZIPAN

We poor shadows light up, again
slowly now in the wasted province
where colours fall and are debated
through a zero coupon, the de-
funct tokens in a soft regard.

The line abets her tint by the fan
oven whose gust sweeps the brow
and for mere offence, in the bazaar
where preference wrap is easily
our choice, what most we want;

To scrape from the heart its burning
powder, a filth upon the floor.
Ah, resting alone under the shade
of green willows, it is a brave sight —
such unencumbered gallantry:

Azure banners high in the fragrant
breeze along the bank; on the ward
floor the fairface was in point
of fact congealed vomit. The printed
block upon a heart of its rotation.

Now red dust hangs, and fire drives
the gold star into a dark vapour.
To mark out the pitch of ennui
a strong sense of, well, woodsmoke
in due season makes its offering:

It is riddance from the duct we line,
cheering of high degree, O Fortune
rich in spoil, surfeit in pray. The amends
of Central Production set targets
for bright-eyed fury, smash-hits

Ranking the places where happy the man
who knows nothing more or less. Don't
blink, the stairs are already destroyed
for thus, *à livre ouvert,* no screams ring.
Her corpse hangs, burned to ashes.

Tribute at the pledge of election,
what wants this force of smattered
work that a shopgirl cannot have?
Nothing more counts but then withers
for the victor who should, outright,

Conciliate a broken enemy, or
destroy them. *Vorsprung durch EDV,*
as mother knows, there is no rose,
as in abandoned markets and deserted streets
wheat sprouts flourish. The pretext

Of small mercies, seasonal rebate in
the loose change: as though they were
sieving the very soil itself! Attuned
to modest airs the conductor beats
time to flattened repeats. All over

The same again not held back, to ask grace
at a graceless face it is our own
in the glass of dark recall, seen
at love all in the replay; the heartland
is dug out for a life underneath

In broadest, magical daylight. You see
as in late spring, shrouded in mist,
the bright, smooth water. The price
is right, *eau minérale naturelle*
from the hypermarket and thousands

Of feet of glacial sand. Ten thousand
families in the mountains, starved
on mountain grass: and made me eat
both gravel, dirt and mud, and last
of all, to gnaw my flesh and blood.

LISTENING TO ALL

As must, as will, intent upon this
night air twice over you say too,
the albedo white with shock. So still
and quiet, in deep discount at offer
of itself consenting, the living day
blocks its truth to the same: the sound
of its own name in the byword, very still
and quiet, the bond of care annulled.

PUNISHMENT ROUTINES

You scan the necklace unit by unit
with a fast letter of intent, set to cancel
what the habit already means. It is rock-
solid and brand loyal with a free-space

Permission on the dangle as if to sway
the choice of a smart new tent. Nothing
changes the will to change nothing,
or in a state localised on an impurity

The necklace plugs the blocked echo current
and marks the spot for no comment:
a dainty box of interference like a dashpot
stops outflow in mean free time's debate.

At the neckline the word you give then
is padlocked by voiceprint, by neat cement
on the impurity radius sweeping the lexicon
as if to say eagerly, go on go on, to

Take shelter by the waiting wall of money
untouched by swells in the marquee.
It must be the clasp of waiting hands
dipping to a flowery print at the outcast

So white and tender by prediction,
devoted to hope itself by which the tune
nerves up the spark plugs. Eat little
and speak less, bleeding inside the mouth.

IN THE PINK

The fixed charge is now set up
   in delay at unused incident
by a factor of two, at each
   unfolded part-time request.

What is the purport then, tilting
   steadily again, away to provide
mint tokens for our moment here
   in spite of the clearest call

From screen to outlook? In both cases
   declaring from inside the fluid
drains as would a voucher. None
   of these arms will rise

Before thus voided promptly by good
   consideration. These antics
unfold their natural residue and
   dispense no other sign.

So blind affection takes its toll,
   as Chinese walls are all the rage;
a queasy interval will swing out
   in fragments like yet another

Prospectus, yet more temerity for
   the asking on the roundabout.
At the supercharge tick off and claim,
   if you've the neck for it,

The merit blend across traditional
   family values, which represent
'no real sacrifice'. Blood from this stone
   no safer than the common pool.

LEND A HAND

Now these hurt visitors submit,
learning in the brilliant retinue
to be helpless by refusal, their bids

by sealed tender; yet to hold
allows still to seek redress and push
back in common to the fence line,

to be rid of the old stock. Out in the swim
the chill current defends its flow,
time to go and blurt and burn

and gently down the stream.

FRESH RUNNING WATER

At a shout
rain downs in deep blue and in novel compliance,
a due date for departure triggers the odds
breaking over this news in terms of life
or cash. Can you be helped to any less
warranty, a fiery allegro even at par without
winding up some slipped stunt. Strike the shepherd
upon your sweet life, waiting for a rib-cage
in plaster as yet for ever it will seem. Hang down
ye blood-red roses, hang down; there is no call
for any other run on the town.
Like a shadow
of softened donation the clouds screen her eyes,
the fair one at altitude, on a mirror-exchange
of historic cost basis, free as air, freely

rising to stare at the bypass graft list
as it flaps in the breeze. As we're all bound
to go that far, we beat our way over
the bright track to the billet there. The space
between counters is empty, cased in a metal
grid ye contrite hearts for to take us through;
no writ runs here, apart.
With a fair wind
and a glancing blank look the action-pack
picks up speed from its place where to turn is harder
than stone; a little tired towards the close
of perfect play. The sills are rotten but the rods
are good for years and years. At the break of day
the eyes glisten with buffer salts, never look
back. The drill melts on the spree. Prune what
you like for its own sake, gentle Jack, tight
as a bar across the line, to cram shut the stay
of the home run in time.

ALMOST LUNCH-TIME

Or, like two-shoes on a revised citation
the master of these powers to afflict
instantly cries up the residue, at a speed
divested of charm. You get to go

Over-the-shoulder but with your ankle flexed,
on and on if not right back
at the start line around the chicken factory,
where was a sugar and fretty.

There is no alarm at the menu of constraints
as the bills mount in the pre-tax void,
all our bills grinding by the dream of friendship
in double running, cloud filling,

The drone of faster upturn. Fresh denials
clothe the bare strip in verdure
and smiles in the street. Thus seen when said,
undone by goodness not waiting,

When therefore sleep and take your cut,
distressed by patience: 'it is difficult
to learn to perform ethically'. Stupidly good
as a standing order the new figures

Bear out the old question, as next to go
with all her rings and all her show
out along that road; beating their best
back into bounds, the near-perfect rest.

EIN HELDENLEBEN

Not in this voice, by the leaf-nubs
crowding upwards: the assent so free
is taken on paramountly, you get
chosen to be absent by a trainee

Just thinking aloud. It expires
in spite of comforting words, more and
more at the blank stare of bright haze
across a cloudless drop. Not by request

Nor for a quick one, dig deeper, no hopes
for them as laughs it off with a riot
of colour at the border; you tell me
what's for the best and left out, again

Like last time. She glides in her napery
towards the lime-pits, topped in vain
by the fanning plumes above her brow.
This is the tale of a done thing, ready

To be sent away now very quietly indeed,
in the logic of spirit deletion, bitterness
and bad blood. Trading on pathos for
term cover, the *ombra* step spills down

Turning to stop there and pump by nature
with a topic indemnity; the caravan jolts
at the toll booth and is not ready,
the cups and knives slip on the tray.

Under the cloth so neatly spread, upon
the grass that lies ahead, we set our picnic,
cream and salt: and the rest, by default.
The rest is unvoiced like a broken reed,

You close your eyes to it and temper mirth
with a mere minor anxiety. What waits
here is nothing to what comes next, call it
the very nurseling of first care. Detain

At birth the splint picture, if you can,
and don't bargain for a sharp return.
The line-up is openly cut off and in
prime time: seals of love and topped in vain.

WRITE-OUT

As a circumstantial infringement again loaned off

the said apart or
by ill, sand given
object in sport
they bet it was

close by the index
longer marked on
arranged dots: to
heat up this offer

To provoke distraught readiness in uprated advice

lick tantalum all
tears attack, may rest
a vital shred. No
cheating stroke line

but single too, as
fair for the grain:
part sold off
yourself pallid

And at disposition prior to early default agreement

overseen next there
bitterly in call
to count, the stub
of a mental praise

what's left break
you scatter. If
burnt metal lives in
the dove slowly

Sporadically by bus into the heart of the country

SWALLOW YOUR PRIDE

At work on the potash table
reckoning up for a new song
put one, put one, from between the fingers
or at the checkout you are lost to view;
just a little better
making a fresh start
in promise to see all these signs
sit stable and by heart: so long
further to go, about to part.

NO. 2

A LETTER AT EASTER: TO GEORGE STANLEY

by Beverly Dahlen

Beverly Dahlen was born in 1934 in Portland, Oregon and lives and works in San Francisco. Her books include *The Egyptian Poems* (Hipparchia Press, 1983), *Out of the Third* (Momo's Press, 1974), and *A Reading* (a long on-going poem of which three volumes are now in print: Momo's Press, 1985; Potes & Poets Press, 1989; Chax Press, 1992). Robert Duncan said of her work: "Nothing is incidental in this poetry; everything counts."

Dahlen met the poet George Stanley in the early 1960s at San Francisco State University's Poetry Center, where she studied creative writing and received a master's degree. George Stanley, central to the San Francisco poetry scene of the early and mid-60's and a member of Jack Spicer's lengendary Magic Workshop, currently lives in Vancouver, British Columbia. *A Letter at Easter: For George Stanley* was originally published by Effie's Press in 1976.

— PG

I.

In the further sky there are birds flying like we used to draw
them in the first grade. Droopy-winged V's. Nearer by the jays
are showing off in the blooming snowball tree. Flashy. And they
chase through the backyards streaking that green with their blue.

The Saturday morning before Easter. *All is calm all is bright.*
After a two-day gale.

You.
Mystery.
The swamp and the lightning. The tar pits. The ice ages.

The *real* world you say. And I say what do you mean, the *real*
world? And you, voice edged with anger, impatience, say
This. This. I'm standing in a room. I'm holding a telephone.

I hear.
You. This. This context. This syntax. This matrix. This
material world.

This old mothering split. The crack of doom in which
we speak to each other.
Call it a telephone. I'm standing in a room across town
listening.

2.

Easter, then.

People keep coming and going.
Friends return from South Carolina and tell me about the real
swamps there, real alligators and snakes, circling in on my metaphor,
a complicated eco-system.

And we speak of the monster cities, staggering under their own
weight, the spectacular flesh of jet planes and oil tankers
beginning to rot in the old swamps they used to gorge in.

The failure
of intelligence: they no longer
make sense

the weather changes
it is another world

Nightfall. The fog-shrouded peak of the
Bank of America.

In the real world
you leave
you go north again

you dream you are a little girl
overwhelmed with books and papers

you keep saying *I have to sort it all out.*

This. This
intelligence
that resists
the monstrous

this small
lithe
warm-blooded
animal
that survived

this sort kind kin cousin

our line

the child again

she-fate

this *long* *long trail*

winding

into the land

of my dreams

3.

The night you called me
drunk
at 2 a.m.

You said you had written a poem with these lines:

This Roman mob
grew up out of
La Belle San Francisco
just like I did

the city is a mob a mass "a great beast"

a mountain

a cave

a mother

maw

4.

What I can never do is speak to you face to face

riding beside you in the car
sitting in the restaurant
the bar

I don't know what you are to me

in the real world

5.

"This poem may never be finished."
I said that to Debra yesterday.

(I am writing this in the real world
in real time
sitting at my kitchen table
a house in San Francisco

I see now I meant
the distance will never be finished
the blind distance
in time
I begin to see

6.

Because I can never speak
This. This
sorting out endlessly a kind of road in the dark

Crossing the country last summer I saw, somewhere in Nebraska, that there is no space left in America; there is only distance.

We are consumed.
We are mortal.

In
Time.

divided

empty miles

7.

You said all this to me a long time ago (I remember it I am already forgetting it) in another world

your nightmares
you are terrified of monsters you called them "self-aggrandizement"
"mortality"

I would not be writing this
if you did not speak to me

but we move
in the direction
of our dreams

and so

you also dream the child in whom nothing is lost

and another friend dreams I write a poem with this line:

The rock begins to bleed

and so I do
in the real world
this mystery
this complex intelligence in which nothing is finished

not this
not my own monstrous silence stone-head

broken

8.

In the end I say you belong to this city. And you say yes,
that's right. I had thought the city belonged to me.

a part

and then you go away

And this

speaks, listening
in this place, apart

in the real, immortal world

finished

never done

—APRIL 17-21, 1976

NO. 3

CHANTING AT THE CRYSTAL SEA

by Susan Howe

Susan Howe's most recent books of poetry are *The Nonconformist's Memorial* (New Directions, 1993), *Singularities* (Wesleyan, 1990), and *Europe of Trusts: Selected Poems* (Sun & Moon, 1990). She has also written two books of criticism: the touchstone study of Emily Dickinson, *My Emily Dickinson* (North Atlantic Books, 1985), and *The Birth-mark: unsettling the wilderness in American literary history* (Wesleyan, 1993). Howe was born of a literary family in 1937 in Buffalo, New York, and grew up in Boston. She currently divides her time between the Poetics Program at SUNY Buffalo, where she teaches, and Guilford, Connecticut, where she made her home with the late sculptor David von Schlegell for over twenty years.

Chanting at the Crystal Sea was originally published by William Corbett at Fire Exit Press in Boston in 1975 with cover artwork by David von Schlegell. Helen Howe, to whom the poem is dedicated, was Susan Howe's aunt — a novelist *(We Happy Few)* and chronicler *(The Gentle Americans: Biography of a Breed)* of turn-of-the-century life among the famed Boston Brahmins.

— PG

for Helen Howe
1905-1975

author of *The Gentle Americans 1864-1960: Biography of a Breed*

All male Quincys are now dead, excepting one.
— John Wheelwright, "*Gestures to the Dead*"

1

Vast oblong space
dwindled to one solitary rock.

On it I saw a heap of hay
impressed with the form
of a man.

Beleaguered Captain Stork
with his cane

on some quixotic skirmish.

Deserters arrived from Fort Necessity

All hope was gone.

Howe carrying a white flag of truce
went toward the water.

2

An Apostle in white
stood on a pavement of scarlet

Around him
stretched in deep sleep

lay the dark forms of warriors.

He was turned away
gazing on a wide waste.

His cry of alarm
astonished everyone.

3

A Council of War
in battle array
after some siege.

I ran to them
shouting as I ran
"Victory!"

Night closed in
weedy with flies.

The Moon slid
between moaning pines
and tangled vines.

4

Neutrals collected bones
or journeyed behind on foot
shouting at invisible doors
to open.
There were guards who approached
stealthy as lynxes
Always fresh footprints in the forest
We closed a chasm
then trod the ground firm
I carried your name
like a huge shield.

5

Because dreams were oracles
agile as wild-cats
we leapt on a raft of ice.

Children began a wail of despair
we carried them on our shoulders.

A wave
thrust our raft of ice
against a northern shore.

An Indian trail
led through wood and thicket

Light broke on the forest

The hostile town
was close at hand.

We screamed our war-cry
and rushed in.

6

It was Him
Power of the Clouds
Judge of the Dead
The sheep on his right
The goats on his left
And all the angels.

But from the book
backward on their knees
crawled neolithic adventurers known only to themselves.
They blazed with artifice
no pin, or kernel, or grain too small to pick up.
A baby with a broken face lay on the leaves
Hannibal — a rough looking man
rushed by with a bundle of sticks.
"Ah, this is fortunate," cried Forebear
and helped himself to me.

7

God is an animal figure
Clearly headless.
He bewitches his quarry
with ambiguous wounds
The wolf or poor ass
had only stolen straw.

O Sullen Silence
Nail two sticks together
and tell resurrection stories.

8

There on the deck, child in her arms
was the girl I had been before

She waved

then threw her child to me

and jumped

But she missed the edge and swirled away.

I left you in a group of grown-up children and went in search
wandered sandhills snowy nights
calling "Mother, Father"

A Dauphin sat down to dine on dust
alone in his field of wheat

One war-whoop toppled a State.

I thought we were in the right country
but the mountains were gone.

We saw five or six people coming toward us

who were savages.

Though my pen was leaky as a sieve
I scribbled "Arm, Arm!"

"Ear." Barked the Moon.

We paddled with hands, planks, and a pencil

"Listen — The people surrender"
I don't remember the rest but it was beautiful.

We were led ashore by Captain Snow
"I'll meet you soon — " he said
and vanished in the fog.

9

We cooked trout and perch on forked sticks.
Fire crackled in the forest stillness
Fire forms stood out against the gloom
Ancient trunks with wens and deformities
Moss bearded ancients — and thin saplings
The strong, the weak, the old, the young —

Now and then some sleeper would get up
Warm her hands at the fire
and listen to the whisper of a leaf
or the footfall of an animal
I kept my gun-match burning when it rained —

10

Holding hands with my skin
I walked the wintry strand.
"Tickle yourself with my stroke"
ticked the wiseacre clock.

The river sang —
"Pellucid dark and deep my waters —
come and cross me alone."

The final ruins ahead
revealed two figures timidly engraved on one another.

11

I built a house
that faced the east
never ventured west
for fear of murder.

Eternity dawned.

Solitary watcher
of what rose
and set
I saw only
a Golgotha
of corpses.

12

Experience teaches
the savage revenge
an enemy always takes
on forerunners
who follow.

You were a little army
of unarmed children —
A newborn infant
sat in the hollow
of my pillow.

13

The house was a model of harmony.

Children coiled like hedgehogs
or lay on their backs.

A doll uttered mysterious oracles
"Put on the kettle."
"Get up and go home."

The clock was alive
I asked what it ate.

"A Cross large enough to crucify us all."
and so on.

Blankets congealed
into icicles

We practised
trips, falls, dives into snowdrifts.

With a snowshoe for a shovel
I opened the clock

And we searched for peace in its deep and private present.

Outside, the world swarmed with sorcerers.

14

Twelve kernels
of maize a day
each person's
portion.

When the maize
failed
I ate my leather jerkin.

The greedy Sun
ate the east
the crimson sluice.

15

On a day of rest
I went naked to my parents.

They sat on a rock
water up to their waists.

I told them to lie down and put their mouths in the dust.

I went naked to my husband
in the hug of a wave horizon rolled youngly from nothing.

I told him to lie down and put his mouth in the dust.

I stopped my children's eyes with wool
as the angel did with Jacob.

I told them to lie down and put their mouths in the dust.

Having traps and blankets with me
I camped on the spot

Hills of potatoes and a few pea-vines grew in the trash
I nursed them tenderly.

"It is three hours by the crooked way —
or three hours by the straight."
I told the dead people who viewed us.

Then I lay down and put my mouth in the dust.

16

The audience applauded
I was welcomed as one returned from the grave.
My imposter stood up
Her speech was — forests, chasms, cataracts —
I replied — Yes, I had been there —
slept with the children every night —
wherever I went — I went when I was sleeping —
All eyes turned on me.
"Liar — Have you seen the Lake Of The North?"
she said.
"Have you seen the wreck of a ship?
— and your scalp?
— How did you cross the Great Camped Present?"
My assurance failed
Welcomed to the rock of my banishment
I couldn't utter a word.
Silence resumed its wild entanglement
Thought resumed its rigid courtesy.

17

If I am Mob
and Umpire —
Who smudged
that holocaust
of negative hands?

18

I stood bolt upright
then mast through the sea
I saw my husband.

We hoisted sail together
cheering one another
Children swam in our eyes
as silent sheep.

we said. the seven stars are only small heights
covered with dense woods.
we said. the seven orifices of the head
are what planets are to the sky.
we said. your bones are rocks
and your veins great rivers.
We promised them deliverance.

We sat on an island
I put on my son's coat
Above us on a rock
our daughter faced the sea.

The rock became water as we sat
fragments of a lighthouse were strewn in the sand
trees made tunnels of themselves.

There was no footing but the waters.
"We are cast away."
No footing but the waters.

19

Afternoon waned
the sun sank on.

I caught fireflies

and hung them up by threads.

My house was high and dry
in the mud.

I cut the cord
and landed on the floor

of my parents

who were raindrops

clinging to bushes.

20

In the 27th degree
of northern latitude

On a small hill

I saw a vast plain

that extended westward.

A man and a woman
so old their united ages
made twenty centuries

beckoned.

They sang a song of welcome
seasoned with touches of humor

My father stretched underneath a tree
seemed to be enjoying himself.

21

Envoys offer terms of peace
with the usual subterfuge

Lieutenants carry letters from chiefs
promising pardon

Marauders travel steadily down the dream
of civilizing a wilderness

Outcasts roam the depths of sleep
for frozen fortnights

Apostles of the Faith
shout sophistries and subtleties
in pistol-shot of ramparts

On Monday, massacre, burning, and pillage
On Tuesday, gifts, and visits among friends

Warriors wait
hidden in the fierce hearts of children.

22

I looked at our precise vanishing point on the horizon
"You can never" it said.
I drew my little children on a sled
when the sled was gone I ran after them.

The Judge's cave concealed a regicide
hairy, meagre, and deformed
he exulted in the prospect of Thorough
and ate sea-mews raw

his feet were singed with lightning.

Samuel climbed out of the earth
to say "There is a gulf fixed.
You cannot come into this world again."

I squeezed my baby flat as a pancake
and turned white as chalk or lime.

Haunted by the thought, the thread we hang on will save us
I bit off and burned my fingers to keep from freezing.

I saw a woman swimming along under the ice
the language of her lips was Mute
her children learned to speak by eye.

I imagined when she lived in Eden
migrations of immense flocks of redeemers darkened the sky.

23

We pulled children from invisiblity
then hugged our little family
promising "It shall be ours forever."

We carried them among a treacherous people
silent — though our lips moved.

24

Anecdote of the retreat
"I will not yield my ground until annihilation"
said Governor whatever

and he shot at an abyss
with the precision of a rattlesnake.

Lies domesticate the night.

Luck in the form of a fog
might help.

Napoleon used to ask
about a general who was being highly praised

"But is he lucky?"

25

Here was the town once
but where
are its inhabitants?
Around stretch parchment plains, rawhide chasms
and cracked deserts.
That rock
resembles a man
dressed up to act in a play.
Old men stand sentinel
wrapped in thick fog.
They are watching for the approach
of an enemy.
You may search for water in this valley of dead beasts
until brack
becomes brine.
I see my father approaching
from the narrow corner of some lost empire
where the name of some great king still survives.
He has explored other lost sites of great cities
but that vital condition —
the glorious success of his grand enterprise
still eludes him.

A source for *Chanting at the Crystal Sea* was *Touched With Fire: Civil War Letters* and *Diary of Oliver Wendell Holmes, Jr.*, edited by Mark De Wolfe Howe, and Justice Holmes' "Memorial Day Address" in 1884.

JOHN CAGE AND MORTON FELDMAN RADIO HAPPENINGS

RECORDED AT WBAI, NEW YORK CITY, 7/9/66 – 1/16/67

THESE CONVERSATIONS, two of five which were recorded for radio broadcast between July 1966 and January 1967, were transcribed by John Cage's assistant Laura Kuhn and subsequently published by Edition MusikTexte, Köln, in 1993. As Christian Wolff observes in his introduction to the German edition, "They have a sense of freshness, perhaps because the time had elements of transition" for the participants as well as for the society. Cage is leaving the "Variations" sequence and is about to embark on his, and perhaps *the* first piece of computer music, "HPSCHD." Feldman is about to change publishers (from Peters in New York to Universal Editions, London) and begin a long involvement with European music scenes.

From 1948 to the mid-'60s Cage and Feldman, with virtuoso David Tudor, and composers Earle Brown and Christian Wolff, through collaboration, critique, and social ties became known as "The New York School." As James Pritchett points out, though Cage was the elder, there was no teacher-student relationship, they "were thus more a 'group' than a 'school' — they were united only in their mutual support for the widening of musical possibilities." Cage mentions in these conversations Feldman's composition of his first piece of graph music, *Projection 1*. He describes this event more fully in *I-VI*:

> . . . morton feldman went into the room with the piano and i stayed at my desk which was in the bedroom with david tudor shortly morton feldman came back with his first piece of graph music where on graph paper he simply put numbers and indicated high middle and low how many high notes how many middle notes how many low notes and nothing else there were squares of the graph that he left empty so there were no notes there at all after he showed it to me and to david tudor david tudor went to the piano and played it it was a great experience in the next few days my mind ran to the *i ching* . . . and so a few days after . . . i called him up and with excitement went to him and

> explained how i was going to write the *music of changes* which takes its name from the *i ching* the *book of changes* in which the making of choices is not principal to the work but rather the asking of questions . . .

This quotation gives an idea of the closeness with which these composers worked in the early '50s. *The Music of Changes* was, along with *4'33"*, a turning point in Cage's artistic life. Though Cage had used chance in a few previous works, this was his first recognizably "mature" work in that it provided a model for a method of composition based on the *I Ching* which he would use the rest of his life. This is not to imply that Feldman was the sole catalyst for this change; the presence of David Tudor, to play it, and the influence of Eastern thought via Daisetz Suzuki and Gita Sarabhai, were also among the ideas and circumstances.

There is a slightly reductive though perhaps useful comparison to be made between these composers. If Cage is the composer of multiplicities, of art which "imitates nature in her manner of operation," Feldman was the maker of human places, a spatial, architectonic sense of time. Cage gives us the forest and the stream, Feldman provides the bridge and the house. Tiwa philosopher Joseph Rael: "Each moment is like a house, and a house is like a moment. In each moment that we live there is the opportunity to change ourselves in some way."

At one point in the fourth conversation (not included here) Feldman, referring to the role of the artist, searchingly remarks, "I'm not confused about the issue but I really don't know how to approach it. I mean, we might bring something into the world that is us that did it . . . the fact that it might be impermanent seems to be . . . I can't see its philosophical and sociological ramification. I rather see it more, in a sense, in its religious element. I know that when I write a piece, sometimes I'm telling people 'We're not gonna be here very long.'"

What Feldman is here calling the "religious element" seems to me where these two, with their very individual approaches, are most in accord. Cage, in many contexts, expressed the sentiment that, "The function of art is to add to the enjoyment of life." It is odd to think that this might be thought a radical position, but it seems that it is so. This enjoyment is a process, an opening of ourselves to the life we are living. Like sounds, we too lead our contingent existence in time.

—ROD SMITH

Works cited: John Cage, *I-VI* (Harvard University Press, 1990); John Cage and Morton Feldman, *Radio Happenings* (MusicTexte, 1993); James Pritchett, *The Music of John Cage* (Cambridge University Press, 1993); Joseph Rael, *Being & Vibration* (Council Oak Books, 1993); Richard Wilhelm and Cary F. Baynes, tr., *The I Ching or Book of Changes* (Princeton University Press, 1950).

RADIO HAPPENING I
(TOTAL DURATION 45 MINUTES)

MF: *John, wouldn't you say that what we're dependent on we call reality, and what we don't like we consider an intrusion in our life? Consequently, I feel that what's happening is that we're continually being intruded upon.*

JC: But that would make us very unhappy.

MF: *Or we surrender to it, and call it culture.*

JC: Call it culture?

MF: *Or whatever.*

JC: Give me an example. What would be an intrusion on your life for instance that you would call culture?

MF: *Well, this weekend I was on the beach.*

JC: Yes.

MF: *. . . And on the beach these days are transistor radios . . .*

JC: Yes.

MF: *. . .blaring out rock 'n' roll.*

JC: Yes.

MF: *All over.*

JC: Yes. And you didn't enjoy it?

MF: *Not particularly. I adjusted to it.*

JC: How?

MF: *By saying that . . . Well, I thought of the sun and the sea as a lesser evil.*

JC: You know how I adjusted to that problem of the radio in the environment. Very much as the primitive people adjusted to the animals which frightened them, and which, probably as you say, were intrusions. They drew pictures of them on their caves. And so I simply made a piece using radios. Now, whenever I hear radios – even a single one, not just twelve at a time, as you must have heard on the beach, at least – I think, "Well, they're just playing my piece."

MF: *That might help me next weekend.*

JC: Yeah, and I listen to it with pleasure. By pleasure I mean I notice what happens. I can attend to it rather than, as you say, surrender. I can rather pay attention and become interested in the . . . Well, what it actually is that you're interested in is what superimposes what. What happens at the same time together with what happens before and what happens after.

MF: *Yes, but I can't think unless [the] thought [is connected] to something of the past. The other night I met some friends in a place which I'm very nostalgic about – I used to go there and talk a lot. No one could hear each other.*

JC: Because of this.

MF: *Because of this.*

JC: Yeah. Well, this brings up the remark of Satie's that what we need is a music which will not interrupt the noises of the environment. Hmmm? In other words, we might then need thoughts which would not impose upon the transistorized radios. All I'm trying to say is that this is a coin which has two sides and that the . . . Say you think of your thoughts as the reality – or your conversation at least, that you wish to have, as a reality – and the environment as an intrusion, then that Satie remark just takes that coin and turns it over and says the reality is the environment and what you want to do in it is an intrusion. And, finally, the work of an artist, for instance, is it not an incisive intrusion? Hmmm? Because, for heaven's sake, it didn't exist until the artist does it.

MF: *Yes, I never heard anyone really "Boo" a transistor radio.*

JC: I think . . . Well, you have just now, in a sense. And I have done it formerly. When I would go into any friend's home, out of deference, you know, to my tastes, seeing me coming they simply turned off any radio or even a disc that happened to be playing at the time. Now they no longer do it. They know that I think that I composed all those things.

MF: *Well, it's a problem for me. I feel that I'm quite at odds with it. Maybe actually I really like things to . . . For example, if I'm standing in front of a jet and I hear the blaring sound I don't feel annoyed because I know it's gonna take me someplace.*

JC: Yeah. Or that it's bringing some friend.

MF: *The noise is utilitarian. And it almost dramatizes the flight, you know.*

JC: Yeah. But that, then, is not an intrusion really. That's a sound which, because of other things you're doing, you must carry along, as it were, with you, with your experience, at any rate. What would you say to giving a concert of your works in an architectural situation where something else that was going on was at least partly audible at the same time? Let's imagine just to make the conversation consistent that the concert is in a room and that one door from that room is open and in the room upon which it opens radio music is audible. Now, must that door be closed or may it be left open?

MF: *I would like the door to be left open, but without the radio. You see, I want to leave the door open, but of course . . .*

JC: Well, all we have to do – to know that in that room, if the door is open – all we have to do to know that there is something in that room that if we are exercising our choices we will know that in that room is something we don't desire if we are living with our desires or our choices. And the simplest thing you can do to find out that that's the case is simply to pick up a newspaper because the things that are happening are not things that you would have chosen in your right mind to have happen in the world, in that room.

MF: *Now, years ago, the radio was blaring. I think that there was just as many intrusions as there are today. But I didn't hear them. Today I hear them. So there must be something there that seems to be competing with me. Or, let's put it this way, that my old role has been weakened psychologically.*

JC: Well, what was your role?

MF: *The old-fashioned role of the artist – deep in thought.*

JC: Well, this is certainly changing, I think. Since it's perfectly clear that you're a magnificent artist in that role of being deep in thought, what I would like to see is how magnificent you are intruded upon. What do you think of that idea? Do you recall . . . Isn't this true that once when we had one of those conversations I'm sure each of us so remembers walking through the streets of the Lower East Side and the Village and whatnot until late hours at night, I think I expressed once the idea that you had discovered a world, a musical world – because it was your music, really, that opened up everything, your piece, what was it called, I think the first one was for piano . . .

MF: *"Projection."*

JC:: "Projection," yes. And you wrote it down at Monroe Street and David Tudor and I were in the other room. You left us and you wrote this piece on graph, giving us this freedom of playing in those three ranges – high, middle, and low – and we went in and played the piece and it was then that the musical world changed. Now not just the musical world outside of you but the musical world inside of you, in this role that you speak of, deep in thought, nevertheless, the thing I think I said to you once on that walk through the night, is now that you have opened up this world, let us see all the things that are in it. Now, among the things that are in that world is this situation of granted someone's deep in thought his being intruded upon.

MF: *Yes, but that's become the image.*

JC: Hmmm?

MF: *That's become the image.*

JC:: No, there are many images now, I would say. I don't think we can count them any longer.

MF: *I mean for myself. I mean it's become a very predominant one, of someone who is thinking and always interrupted in his thinking.*

JC: Yes.

MF: *Which, of course, is always a marvelous thing because you begin to see that what you're thinking about isn't that important to begin with. I always found there was something too pretentious about thought to begin with.*

JC: Also any given thought has an enormous potential. It gets into our heads and won't go out, for years and years and years.

MF: *At the same time, simply stated, I can't conceive of some brat turning on a transistor radio in my face and my saying, "Ah! The environment!"*

JC: But all that radio is, Morty, is making available to your ears what was already in the air and available to your ears but you couldn't hear it. In other words, all it is is making audible something which you're already in. You are bathed in radio waves – T.V., broadcasts, probably telepathic messages, from other minds deep in thought.

MF: *Listening to the radio at the same time.*

JC: And this radio simply makes audible something that you thought was inaudible.

MF: *Now you know, most painters I know they all listen to music when they work. You know, Franz Kline loved Wagner, he used to listen to Wagner . . .*

JC: Yeah, and David Tudor, when he practices – which he does so rarely now – but anytime he does practice, he immediately turns on not one but several radios and often a T.V. set at the same time. You might compare it with the Tantric Buddhist discipline. You know of those disciplines?

MF: *No.*

JC: To meditate while sitting on a corpse, or in the course of sexual intercourse. In other words, to make the situation in which you're deep in thought a really difficult one in which to be in thought. Now, what happens there, there is obviously an intrusion against which the — at least we imagine — the person in meditation steels himself. Now, does he or doesn't he? We won't know because what would enlightenment be in that case? Would it be being blind to your environment or would it be being quite aware of it and at the same time deep in thought?

MF: *Yes. I know what's happening, though. I know what's happening for myself where fifteen years ago where the perspective of the sound in the piece, even though it did try, and I did try, to embrace that which would cast a shadow on my work. Many of my pieces I wrote almost . . . Actually, I remember once, I even wrote a piece just trying to capture the pulsating of the tires going in the rain on the drive. But it was all still distant, it was on the outer edges so to speak of the piece. And now what is happening is the focus is different. I find myself right on top of all of the things which in the past I found unaesthetical. Now, I still find that unaesthetical, but I'm on top of it. So a journey was made. I certainly don't want to then make the leap — wherever this leap will be — into a situation not unlike a car ride I was in with Larry Rivers, and we passed a garbage dump and he said, "You know, a little grapefruit on the left would just give it a nice color."*

JC: Yeah, I've had similar drives through the country on our tours with Bob Rauschenberg where he'd see the sunset or something and criticize it, you know, suggest that the colors be different, the trees in different positions. But like humor. What was it with Larry? Was it humor?

MF: *Well, with Larry, I think Larry was worried.*

JC: That this color was absent you mean?

MF: *No, not that the color was absent. He wasn't raving against junk sculpture or a garbage collage, but he was afraid that if he himself made the leap is that he'll start to see this new thing and the kind of some type of an aesthetic judgment, almost juxtaposed — an observation that he would make about Cézanne — and juxtapose it in relation to a garbage heap, you know.*

JC: Yeah. You remember one of those concerts at Town Hall — in the late '40s and '50s — when the painters were still going to the concerts and when we spoke of the Renaissance of new music and so forth Varèse was beginning to be played again. After the concert I got in the Blue Ribbon at the table where Bill de Kooning was and I don't think I heard all of the conversation but it was clear that they were talking about the way the crumbs had fallen on the tablecloth. And Bill was discussing whether or not this was art and he was concluding, of course, that it wasn't. But then that was a difference that had already appeared between myself and Bill. I remember his saying once to me, "The difference between us is that I want to be a great artist and you don't."

MF: *Was he wrong?*

JC: No, I think he was absolutely right.

MF: *You mean if you want to be a great artist you have to turn off the radio? Or you feel that's part of it?*

JC: No, I don't know any longer . . . I really don't know what being an artist is. I think that the . . . I have difficulty with the notion of roles. In other words, I don't want to play a role. I want to be, so to speak, what I am. If I am playing a role, I want to play it all the time. If I'm not playing a role, I don't want to play a role. But, what it was to be a composer doesn't seem to me any longer to be what it is now to be a composer and I don't know what it is to be a composer now. Unless . . .

MF: *I don't even know what it was to be a composer.*

JC: Well, you said earlier, and I'm agreeing with you, and I remember doing it, it was being deep in thought.

MF: *Yes, that's all I'm left with! I feel that this thought was taken away from me. That's it.*

JC: Yes, but there could be another way to be a composer, surely. There could at least be this one we've already mentioned – someone deep in thought who's constantly interrupted.

MF: *Like Bach!*

JC: Or there could be, like I've suggested I think in some of my work, someone who doesn't have any thoughts and so can't be said to be either shallow or deep and who simply sets something going that either has sounds in it or doesn't have sounds in it that enables not only other people but himself too to experience. I guess, in my case, that it goes out of thought into experience. This was certainly one of the things that showed up when the Frenchmen, headed by Boulez, began to object to my work and ideas. They objected to the notion that music was made of sound.

MF: *Yes, I always thought that was extraordinary. It was like the medical profession objecting to the fact that Semmelweis said that they should wash their hands before they perform an operation.*

JC: No, I think one of the things that has happened is that it's become clear that we can be not just with our minds but with our whole being responsive to sound and that that sound doesn't have to be the communication of some deep thought. It can be just a sound. Now that sound could go in one ear and out the other, or it could go in one ear, permeate the being, transform the being, and then perhaps go out, letting the next one in. And then whether or not an idea developed . . . You know, the hardest thing in the world, of course, is to have a head without any ideas in it.

MF: *But that's always the best work, you know? Always was.*

JC: That's perhaps what you mean by being deep in thought.

MF: *Oh, no, no. Many times when I'm deep in thought it's just to get rid of the ideas.*

JC: Exactly! Exactly! To get to the point where the . . .

MF: *To get to that, I don't know what you would call it . . .*

JC: . . . you might call it an ocean.

MF: *To get to that . . . Well, for me, it becomes almost like a physical stamina, to just go on with an empty head. That's what I mean by being deep in thought.*

JC: Yeah, if it's like an ocean with fish in it, and the fish are thoughts, you've gotten to the point where the view is so full of the ocean that you don't notice the fish.

MF: *Yes. That sounds like my new piece. Maybe I don't want the ripples to cover it. But does it matter?*

JC: You mean the ripples? What do you mean?

MF: *We expect them.*

JC: As a matter of fact, we couldn't live without them.

MF: *Back to impermanence.*

JC: Or the ocean couldn't live without them. The ocean wouldn't be the ocean without them. I'm just reading a thing I got in the mail from a behavioral psychologist at La Jolla in California, Richard Farson. And he says near the beginning of it that we used to settle down, say, in some change that we made and there would be a period when we could so to speak adjust to this change but that it becomes evident that we are going to be living in a situation which is so to speak change itself. One very interesting remark in that article too, to support his thought, is something like 90% of the scientists who ever lived on this globe are now living. Isn't that interesting?

MF: *You mean that there's such an influx of scientists?*

JC: This is what we're living in. It's a period in which changes brought about by this activity of research and technology and so forth is producing, well, those transistorized radios, etc.

MF: *Oh, then one could almost say that 90% of all the artists are no longer living.*

JC: Of those deep in thought probably. Yes.

MF: *Yes.*

JC: I had certainly this feeling when I was asked by the Kenyon Review to review the Schoenberg Letters – I don't know if you read the review.

MF: *Yes, I read them John.*

JC: Well, reading that book – and I worshipped Schoenberg, and reading that book brought back that feeling of awe and so forth – he appears in his writings and in his mind and everything. I tried to think of anyone else like him now, you know? I couldn't. The closest I could come to it was say Stefan Wolpe. There's a little bit of it but quite different in Karlheinz Stockhausen. Then, again, outside the field of music, in painting, the question arose recently of reestablishing Black Mountain College, and it was clear to anyone who knew Black Mountain that it depended upon the personality of Joseph Albers and he's no longer available for such a post. Well, who could take his place? You just don't know of anyone like that. As you say, they don't live anymore. What happened? Another question we could ask is when did it happen? And we don't really know the answers to any of these questions. We could say, well, maybe it happened toward the end of the '50s, and maybe it happened in the '60s. And, furthermore, there was an essential difference between Schoenberg and Joseph Albers already. I would say from those letters and from my experience of Schoenberg that he was – Black Mountain would not have been Black Mountain under his direction. Because Albers already introduced into the life of Black Mountain College an enormous amount of permissiveness. But, he was able, on occasion, to draw that whole thing together into a kind of German image where everyone would click his heels and stand at attention and take him seriously. And then when he unclicked his heels they all went back to not attending their classes and doing whatever entered their minds, graduating and not graduating. Schoenberg would never have permitted that kind of situation. Yet, Black Mountain was a glorious situation. So much so that one would like to revive it. And one doubts whether one would want to revive Schoenberg's own image of a school. You know, in his letters, toward the end, they wanted him to establish a school in Israel, and he spoke of it as the graduates of this school would be priests, and it would have been a quasi-religious situation with no one smiling, ever.

MF: *How can you smile if you're deep in thought? Well, what's the need for Black Mountain when this whole permissiveness seems to be like one vast Black Mountain?*

JC: Well, it must be that what they want, in reestablishing Black Mountain, is the discipline side of it – the clicking of the heels side of it.

MF: *You mean the permissiveness is not getting anywhere.*

JC: Not that, but people have not found out how to assume this permissiveness as a responsibility. Or, they would like that, something like that, I think, to happen. Maybe I'm wrong.

MF: *Unfortunately with permissiveness there usually comes a very quick type of boredom.*

JC: Boredom is not so bad, and not really boring, you know. This is something I've known all along from Zen Buddhism. You know that story. If something's boring after two minutes try it for four, after four, try it for eight, etc. You eventually find it isn't boring. People are constantly complaining. Almost everyday somebody tells me that things are boring. Things aren't boring. Our music isn't boring. It's just that people manage somehow with these things that they say are boring not to get with them. Once they get with them, then boredom is the last thing that enters their minds. However, even while it's boring I would say that it's something to be valued and experienced. Haven't you noticed that when your work gets really boring, as when you're copying out something that you had written you know, it's at that moment that ideas begin to fly into your head. When you're really bored, it brings you closer and closer to the actual experience of, say, that ocean that we were talking about, in which some other fish than you have ever encountered might suddenly appear.

MF: *And eat up all the other fish.*

JC: But then, who can speak of boredom nowadays really, who has his eyes or ears the least little bit open? The only one who can speak of boredom is the one who isn't really paying attention to what's happening. I found recently that any old newspaper lying around was on page after page having ideas which were pertinent, relevant to the ones that I was having. And so quite outside the realm of being boring they were, so to speak, reinforcing like they're doing now up in the sky with that, Gemini, what do they call it – Agina, and so on – giving further power you know to go to greater heights. And this power comes now from almost anything around us, I think.

MF: *Would you teach music, if someone came to you and asked to study?*

JC: Well, just as I . . . You see, if I have problems now, they're first of all problems about how to continue my work as I travel around. We talked about that. Now, say I solved that problem, and could carry my work with me and could do it in odd moments. If I had a student, formerly I would have said that the first obligation of the teacher is to be present when the student is present. Now, if I'm going to be traveling around, I certainly don't want all those students traveling around with me. And so I don't feel really in a position of teaching unless I'm with them. Now this might mean that our notion of what it is to be with people has to change, hmmm? It may be that we can be with people but at the same time at a distance.

MF: *That was always very interesting. One never considered years ago that having students was an intrusion. And Schoenberg was incessantly teaching.*

JC: Yes. It appeared that he preferred it to composition, almost. He was extraordinarily generous with his time, ideas, and this faculty that he had which was grand for teaching, combined with terror. Fuller – Buckminster Fuller – says that, and so does McLuhan, I think, and now Farson, this one I mentioned, says that the whole business of the society we're moving into is going to be education. They all seem to agree that the least important element in that educational life will be the teacher. If the teacher has anything to say, he will say it on some kind of recording device with images and so forth – T.V. If anyone ever wants to hear it, he'll simply push a button and hear it. He will not be in the position, as teachers formerly were, of having to repeat himself, year after year. He will simply do it once, and then he himself will become a student, along with the other students, and try to discover what it is that his mind, his interests, and so forth, can do, rather than just repeating. And you'd be astonished going around the country seeing how much T.V. has already entered into the educational business. It's certainly true that if education is what we will do it's going to have to be far more interesting than it has been. It would have to be . . . Well, I don't know what it would have to be. It would have to give a great deal more confidence to the students themselves to do their own work.

MF: *I don't think that will ever be adopted in music departments.*

JC: Well, I think they're going to change.

MF: *You know, there's a terrifying story where at a famous school, in a famous seminar – a graduate seminar – a young composer brought this piece in and his teacher, a world-renowned composer, told him to change it. And the student said – he wasn't really a student, but a young composer – "But I hear it this way." And his teacher said, "You are here to change your hearing."*

JC: Who was it? Did you say who that was?

MF: *No I didn't.*

JC: It's very curious. You know, if I knew the circumstances I'd know whether I went on one side or the other. I'd say whether I agree with the teacher. Certainly one doesn't want a fixed way of hearing, either the one or the other. I'd like to have my ears so I could hear what there was to hear.

END RADIO HAPPENING I

RADIO HAPPENING V
(TOTAL DURATION 57 MINUTES)

JC: Everyone I mentioned that thought to is also struck, because those other ways of explaining Varèse . . . [tape is damaged at this point; sound out for ca. 10 seconds]. Do you suppose he didn't know what he was doing, or knew what he was doing and didn't want anyone to know?

MF: *I think that he knew what he was doing but he didn't want to know what he was doing.*

JC: Well, in a very real sense that's what we're all doing because even though we might think we knew the thing will only come to life for someone else when he knows something that we don't know.

MF: *What were the questions about Varèse like that were asked you?*

JC: You know, he just wanted to know "What about Varèse?"

MF: *I was thinking about that since the last time we spoke here, especially, you remember, about changing one's mind. In fact, that's seemed to be my dinner conversation for the past three weeks. You remember that Varèse, his contribution, does not seem as important as Webern because he didn't change our minds as Webern did. I'm just mentioning it. I don't know if I want to pursue it. It doesn't really have to do with Varèse or Webern, but it has to do with the way we think in general and the way we're influenced by other things.*

JC: Yes. You mentioned in connection with the loud sounds in some of your early music that they seemed to require something to be done and some implications with regard to energy.

MF: *Yes.*

JC: How do you relate what seems apparent to me the fantastic energy in Varèse's music with those vertical structures? Or do you think about that?

MF: *I wouldn't exactly use the word energy, John. I would say that the whole vertical thinking becomes extremely saturated and then attaches itself to the signals in the motivic element that we hear. I don't think that it was the motivic element that suggested or went along concurrently.*

JC: It comes out of the structure rather than producing it?

MF: *Yes.*

JC: So it's like energy escaping and the energy itself is in reservoir.

MF: *Yes. Notice he doesn't get involved in making a very complicated, say, thematic situation. He tries to keep it level, even in times of invention. That's the way I hear it, at least.*

JC: This brings it about that, as in Satie but for other reasons, entirely novel events can take place that have no motivic preparation, are not even, in the sense of Schoenberg, far-removed but are rather simply different. I'm thinking of those chimes toward the end of "Ionization." It's as though . . . Isn't it as though another structure had come into existence?

MF: *Yes. It's interesting. I think . . . You know, the cadences of composers are very revealing. Maybe because they feel that the piece is over, or, if they're using, say, a text . . . I picked up your book on Virgil Thomson the other day in a bookstore and I read through most of it. You mention that about Thomson's music.*

JC: Yes.

MF: *You remember? About how he was following this particular text concerning an anvil. Was it out of Blake? I don't remember.*

JC: Yes, it was a piece called "Tiger, Tiger."

MF: *Yes, and how Varèsian.*

JC: Yes, the first version.

MF: *And there were some remarkable cadences of Casella's, where he does just splendid things only because the pieces ended. It was always very interesting to me how, on one hand, the detractors of our music would talk about the wonders of absolute music and if you would go into the literature of absolute music you would find that there's very little of that music that's absolutely absolute – how dependent most music is, say, on a literary element. That's always struck me as true about Boulez' whole career – that the literary element seemed to suggest this absolute music. The early piano sonatas, how he was involved with, say, Artaud.*

JC: Oh, certainly. Mallarmé.

MF: *Mallarmé. René Char.*

JC: René Char, yes.

MF: *And this can be very true of Stravinsky, of many.*

JC: There's an article of Boulez that I've referred to sometimes where he speaks of all the devices of syntax – of punctuation, and parentheses, and so forth, and of the desirability of introducing such practices into music.

MF: *When did he write that article?*

JC: I don't know exactly, but I think it's before '54.

MF: *Then it's before "Kontakte"?*

JC: I think so. This closeness to literature also took place in the music of Adolphe Weiss, with whom I studied. His rhythm, in much of his early music, was taken from, I believe, the poetry of Walt Whitman.

MF: *I find that all over. In fact, an Israeli composer, a serial composer, visited me and he showed me that his rhythm was based on some medieval Hebrew poetry. And just the other day a student of mine told me that he – I don't know how it came up – but that he heard Dallapiccola in a lecture years ago in Philadelphia where Dallapiccola talked mainly about Joyce and his relation to music. So, I never really understood what they meant by absolute music. You know, I think that you're one of the few composers who absolutely writes absolute music!*

JC: And it seems so theatrical.

MF: *Well, you know what happened when they really tried to write absolute music. You know, it all began to sound like Paganini. Then they got involved with the instrumental devices. I mean, even, say, Beethoven's "Grosse Fuge", which is one of his monumental works, is actually an impassioned hymn to God. It's a march. What pieces of yours are they going to play in Cincinnati?*

JC: Shortly they're playing – the LaSalle String Quartet is playing my String Quartet from 1950. Which reminds me, I heard recently in Urbana a recording of that piece of mine – you must remember, "Concerto for Prepared Piano and Orchestra" that was done at Cooper Union once?

MF: *Yes. Was this that performance?*

JC: No, another performance. They had done it with students

at the University of Illinois, and they'd spent several months putting it together. Whereas, you remember, at Cooper Union, fifteen minutes I think were taken by the Union musicians and most of those minutes were spent laughing at what they were obliged to do. So that I had never really heard the piece and all these years I thought of it as something that I'd avoid hearing. And while I was in Urbana, John Garvey, who had conducted it, spent five days trying to persuade me to come and listen to the recording. Finally, on the fifth day I had nothing better to do and I listened to it and I was surprised. The piece is quite extraordinarily interesting in this sense: that each sound, each thing that happens, is un- . . . Well, nothing that precedes it prepares you for the experience so I think even if you were not interested that you would become interested at some point. And a very curious thing happened at the very end of the piece – the audience burst into laughter.

MF: *At the end?*

JC: At the very end, but there was no way of knowing that it was the end because, you know, the third movement has long silences in it and out of these silences there comes some sound, and then another silence, and then some more sound. And I don't know just what it was that made them laugh. It may have been something they saw, some way of performing on an instrument. But, it must have been very strange for them to laugh and then realize that they had produced, so to speak, the cadence of a situation that really didn't have one.

MF: *John, may I ask you a question?*

JC: Yes.

MF: *Why do you continue to compose?*

JC: Well, I have two pieces to write now because I've been asked to do them. I think that had I not been asked . . . Well, I know that if I had not been asked that I would not write these particular pieces. But having been asked and having said that I would, I will do it. And I'm sure that once I get involved in them I'll enjoy it. What they will be I don't know. I mentioned to you the last time we talked about writing for harpsichord and that business with the scales and so forth?

MF: *Yes.*

JC: Well, the more I think of it the more ridiculous it seems.

MF: *I wasn't trying to push you in a corner by asking that question. I asked it with love because . . .*

JC: No, I would really be inclined not to write.

MF: *Because, I'll tell you. A long time ago I didn't feel that I was making anything. I didn't have that feeling that I was making anything. Consequently, I was very happy. And then now, with the possibilities of hearing my music, it becomes obvious that I made something and it has left me very unhappy. And it's as if I'm in a state now where I have this burden, this psychological burden, of making something. You know what I mean. It's a very unhappy burden.*

JC: But that's only the case when you're thinking about it. When you were talking a little bit earlier about the piece which you're writing now, it didn't sound like a burden at all. It sounded like an experience full of wonder, the way you were talking about the woodwinds, wasn't it, and the fact that they might begin when the structure is completed. It didn't sound like you were talking about a burden. When you think about it, then it could be a burden, but when you're doing it, I don't think it is.

MF: *Well, then, let me put it this way: As you get older, you develop a certain consciousness that you could fall on your face in some way. And I'll put it again another way: Last year, Leon Kirchner asked me to speak to his composition class at Harvard. And when I went in I looked at them and I said, "How many here know how to write a bad piece?" And nobody knew anymore how to write a bad piece. They didn't know how to write badly. They all knew how to make pieces. Oh, I suppose what's really troubling me is this thing that I think has come up I think in all our talks – this whole business of being in the world. This whole business of naming it. You have to name it. Do you know that marvelous myth of Ixion? In a sense, I was aware of that when I wrote "Ixion" for Summerspace. Where this man has a very beautiful horse and he didn't want anybody to steal it – this is one of the myths of Ixion. So he decided that he wasn't going to give it a name. Zeus saw the horse and stole it. So Ixion ran all over the place looking for the horse but he couldn't call it, it had no name. That's the basis of the story. Ixion got involved in other adventures, but that's the basis of the story. And there's something about not being in the world where what you do is not named.*

JC: That's quite marvelous. It reminds me of something that happened recently. Two students at the University of Cincinnati came to talk with me. They're nearly doctors of music – graduate students. Walter Levine of the LaSalle String Quartet told me that they were extremely well-schooled and that they had earned the right to enjoy music. People have told me – I've just gone to Cincinnati – that the Cincinnati city is very conservative and yet everyone that I've talked to is interested in new ideas. And I didn't know quite what to expect when these two students came; they're 25 years old. They told me, among other things, that the University had access to a fund to buy musical scores and that they had been extremely pleased to get a score from Europe which had some novel notation for which there was no explanation. I think of this in relation to your "no names." They were delighted with being in a situation where they didn't know what they were dealing with, and yet could find a way to do it. It's like the pleasure we obtain now from aquariums, where the fish no longer have Latin names.

MF: *This is true. Now we can eat them.*

JC: Well, we can look at them.

MF: *You can't eat a fish with a Latin name.*

JC: All the fish swim together now, in one large tank, and the public – the tank is made of glass – the public walk around and see the fish at all the various levels with no explanation of what they're looking at. Formerly you could read the Latin and then move on. Or you could say, for instance, of a piece of music, that "That was g-sharp."

MF: *And not hear it.*

JC: And not hear it.

MF: *Well, I think this leads us into a very interesting idea. You know, if a student brings some type of graphic situation to me, and, you know, most of them now, the directions of these three or four pages — what they can do, what they could do, what they are doing — I always told them that I always felt that it should be implicit in the score.*

JC: Either that or if you're going to have notes of explanation, I think the notes should have at least some of the ambiguity of poetry so that one wouldn't know exactly what they meant, in order that reading them, the reader would somehow come to life and be in a position to deal with the music. It's a far cry from notation as a blueprint and a way of measuring whether something has been done correctly.

MF: *You know, it's interesting in recent years that you'll read an article in some scholarly magazine finally admitting to the inadequacy of conventional notation. But I always felt that your work was really not involved with creating a new notation but getting something as close to the action or the experience of how this person should react to the sounds.*

JC: I hope so. At least when I made changes in notation it hasn't been to . . . Well, it's been because I was obliged to. If it could have been done with the conventional notation I would have done that.

MF: *There's a saying that most musicians think of the conventional notation as the . . . you know, in terms of language. That it became almost like a language thing for them that they were protecting. Yet you would think that the whole idea of music was to present the thing in such a straight and direct way that they then could go ahead and do what they're doing. So, in a sense their whole defense of the notation had nothing to do with making music but had to do with the notation.*

JC: Oh, there've been so many problems. Remember that interesting one with, again, that piece that Merce Cunningham used, "Ixion," where it was written on graph and used numbers and that was the piece, of course, and that was the way to read it, but through the exigencies of rehearsals and so forth, I translated it into something conventional — with quarter notes, you remember? — which was not what the piece was but which permitted the musicians to quickly play it. Where the numbers meant that they would have had to devote themselves in a way that they actually didn't have the time or inclination to do. A similar problem arose with that beautiful piece that Christian Wolff wrote for "Rune" [1959] of Merce Cunningham where, again, the original notation which, of course, was the piece and the way to read it, was not the way that it was presented to the musicians, but translated so that they'd be able to do it quickly without giving it too much thought. But times are changing, and I think, in both cases now that large numbers of musicians would be able to read the notation which you on the one hand wrote and Christian on the other wrote without that crutch which, in each case, I gave them.

MF: *John, do you have any time these days to look at painting as much as you used to?*

JC: Well, I take time. Like yesterday and the day before I was at Brandeis University and the new theater there — the Swingold Theater is right next to the Rose Art Museum where William Sikes is curator now. And I saw two shows, one of a collection belonging to the museum of paintings, and then downstairs there was a very interesting show of photography of the American social scene as seen by twelve photographers. I saw some painting, too, in Cincinnati recently, in a private home – quite a number of Albers work and a Picabia.

MF: *How about the young people? Have you seen any of their work in Cincinnati?*

JC: Not yet. I'm sure I will, though. Generally when I go to a university I at some point or another go through the art department.

MF: *You know, it's interesting how so many artists today, when they make constructions and such, how they will incorporate sound, and the thought occurred to me recently, "Would I ever think of incorporating structures?" I wonder why they felt completely relaxed in using sound when I feel completely foreign from, say, making something.*

JC: But in those classes that I had at The New School, in the '50s, which consisted largely of the students making compositions – I insisted that they make things that we ourselves could perform in the small room where the class was. And one of the first to bring something was Alan Kaprow, and he came in with cloth and all sorts of things – objects – in terms of time, performance in time. I mean to say, one could do it and be relaxed about doing it.

MF: *Did it ever enter your head?*

JC: Oh, I think so. Certainly not as it would enter yours, though. It'd be marvelous if you'd do that. Beautiful. Let me know when the performance is. How marvelous.

MF: *Because, you know, one can very well think of all kinds of structural schemes where you would want what hanging from what and where a sound should be, other than the conventional space that you use. And I was thinking about it . . . I'll never do it, but . . .*

JC: Oh, please, do it.

MF: *Well, if I did do it I would have to have somebody help me with it. You know, I can't handle it.*

JC: Well, that's the way things get done nowadays. You can observe that when things are done by one person now, they encounter obstacles, but if you get many people working together, the obstacles tend to disappear. Of course, they could crop up in another way, but they would be more apt to disappear. And this would be a way of turning society not into something that would give you a feeling of burden with respect to your own work but would be a way of transforming that whole ogre into something extremely pleasing. In other words, as you were saying, that you have done something now makes it perfectly practical in the society that what you have to do can be used. Now you can return the compliment to society by requiring them to help you – to do what it is that you want done.

MF: *Certainly life seems to be leading us there. This isolation I was talking about, this burden, this individuality now seems to be pointless. I said seems to be. I wonder if I really believe that.*

JC: You remember what Bill de Kooning said years and years ago? That tragedy was gone, that the miserable circumstances that someone got into were simply pathetic. I was extremely interested, too, in this history of economics that

I'm reading now to see that the social misery that took place in the large numbers of people who suffered or were killed in moving from the Middle Ages into the Renaissance through that great social change. We may be in for worse than we've yet seen. And just today, before I came here, something in the atmosphere in New York . . . There was a . . . I don't know if it's just in my mind or if it's in the city – I rather think the two things go together – but there's an atmosphere of violence, danger. It's not an idyllic situation.

MF: *But wouldn't you say that one of the most dangerous things for us to do is to get our signals all mixed up and to mistake life for the environment? That's something I'm thinking of constantly. You know, a lot of our friends from the '50s – the painters – are treated, you know, as if they were in silent movies. Nobody's interested in them, hardly. They react to the situation in a way which is understandable, of course, but still I can't really think that it was life that produced them into this new situation but that it was the environment, and that life is something else. I think, in a sense, that we're now getting our inspiration, our signals, again, from the environment, losing an understanding of life. Life also seems to be a silent movie, obsolete. Such a thing as life, such a thing as a life force, seems to almost have that ridiculous stance of someone, say, whom I think of as an utterly unnecessary, romantic type of artist. Do you know what I mean?*

JC: Yes, but I think that we can't split these things up. I was talking with Van Meter Ames in Cincinnati, and the word psychosomatic happened to enter the conversation and everybody knows now that those two words go together in such a way that there is no split between the mind and the body – it's one organism. And I think that more and more this question of life that you're distinguishing from the environment – I imagine you mean the life of the individual –

MF: *Yes.*

JC: Well, I think that there is no separation. I also don't think that those painters – you mean specifically what we loosely call abstract expressionists?

MF: *Yes.*

JC: I think their situation is not bad. I think the work is beautiful. It exists. I think . . .

MF: *It exists, yes, but not in our environment.*

JC: I think it does. I just saw a de Kooning the other day, and I enjoyed it very much. I'm sure I would enjoy any other of those paintings of the other artists, seeing them. It's just that . . .

MF: *I don't mean specifically . . .*

JC: . . . things are less narrow now. It's just that there are many, many more things. I think there will be – in such things as attention, and justice, and so forth – there will seem to be . . .

MF: *Well, I don't think that when you say "Things are not as narrow," I think that things are always narrow. I think that one usually wants just one thing around because if you have two or three things you have to, again, evaluate them. I mean, here you would say you want many, many things – which you said earlier . . .*

JC: Well, for instance, you could have no home at all. Your home would be the entire world, then clearly you would have all these things. It's a question of what you encounter. You will have, as you move around more and more, opportunity to encounter more and more things. Both new things, old things, and, well, all of the things from all the times and all of the places. I don't see any problem. Someone might think that people weren't paying enough attention to him. Then he should do something childish if he wants attention, because that's what children do, and they get attention. So if someone feels he doesn't have enough attention, he should get it.

MF: *Well, I think they might feel that the reason they're not getting enough attention because a bunch of people came along and did childish things.*

JC: You could do something childish in a sophisticated, grown-up way. I mean to say . . . It's as simple as this.

MF: *When the early peoples were acting up, the one thing that God told them to really make them worry was that they were going to be ruled by children. I don't know what this has to do with this particular train of thought, but . . . Well, let's say this: How do we tell the difference between a sophisticated, adult, childish act and the act of a child?*

JC: Well, I simply mention children because of their practice of obtaining attention. And if an artist feels he's not getting enough attention, then he could at least observe what children do and perhaps in that way solve his problem by imitating them. I don't see that one should approach that as a problem, anyway. I think it will eventually happen. For instance, say a painter's work is not being given sufficient attention. Someone else is bound to notice this and stir things up so that it does get attention. Now I suppose I have to qualify that by saying sooner or later. It will almost certainly happen when the painter dies. But one would like it to happen before. Or rather the painter would like it to happen before. Even the society would like it to happen before.

MF: *I think if you could be reassured that it would happen after he dies, that would be sufficient. I mean, if he's given this guarantee.*

JC: This brings us back to the Middle Ages too, because that was how people put up with things then, by thinking, "Well, it's not happening now, but it will happen later, when I go to heaven." But we don't accept that view really now. Among the things that we have to correct in society is just this kind of thing. People should not do things which are not used in the society. If a person is given to making things, such as paintings, there should be a situation where they can be used. Now, this situation did obtain in the United States during the WPA. It was an extraordinary period for all of the arts and it should be revived. It's one of the things that should be done. There's a great tendency now on the part of the foundations and the government and so forth in giving help to artists to simply give it to them and leave them as it were separate from the society. The good thing about the WPA is that it brought the work into the society – into the post offices, for instance. The multiplication of exhibitions, of concerts, of theater – it even extended to the modern dance. It was during that period that Martha Graham, Doris Humphrey, Charles Weidman, Hanya Holm thrived here in

New York along with other dance companies. Los Angeles itself had something like five dance companies. Chicago had something like five orchestras. We must, in other words, get society into a truly affluent state, and it would be affluent if it simply used what it already has. At the present moment we are going through changes which bringing it about that even though we are very wealthy we are obliged to act as though we were poverty stricken. Now all these artists you mention are part of our present wealth but we have yet to make the means whereby we're aware of this situation. It would be the simplest thing in the world to do. It wouldn't cost anybody much time or trouble. One thing I can think of, for instance, now would be to start immediately on 9th Street or 10th Street, or wherever it was that that marvelous exhibition took place, to just whitewash the walls as we did formerly in the late '40s and early '50s and have that a continual, changing exhibition of abstract expressionist art in the situation where it was first shown. This would be dramatic, interesting, attractive, and invigorating. Here, again, I think, if we apply ourselves to the social situation, or even to the individual situation, as something which needs composition rather than criticism, we'll get somewhere. Don't you agree?

MF: *I not only agree but I think this will hold us until our next conversation.*

END RADIO HAPPENING V

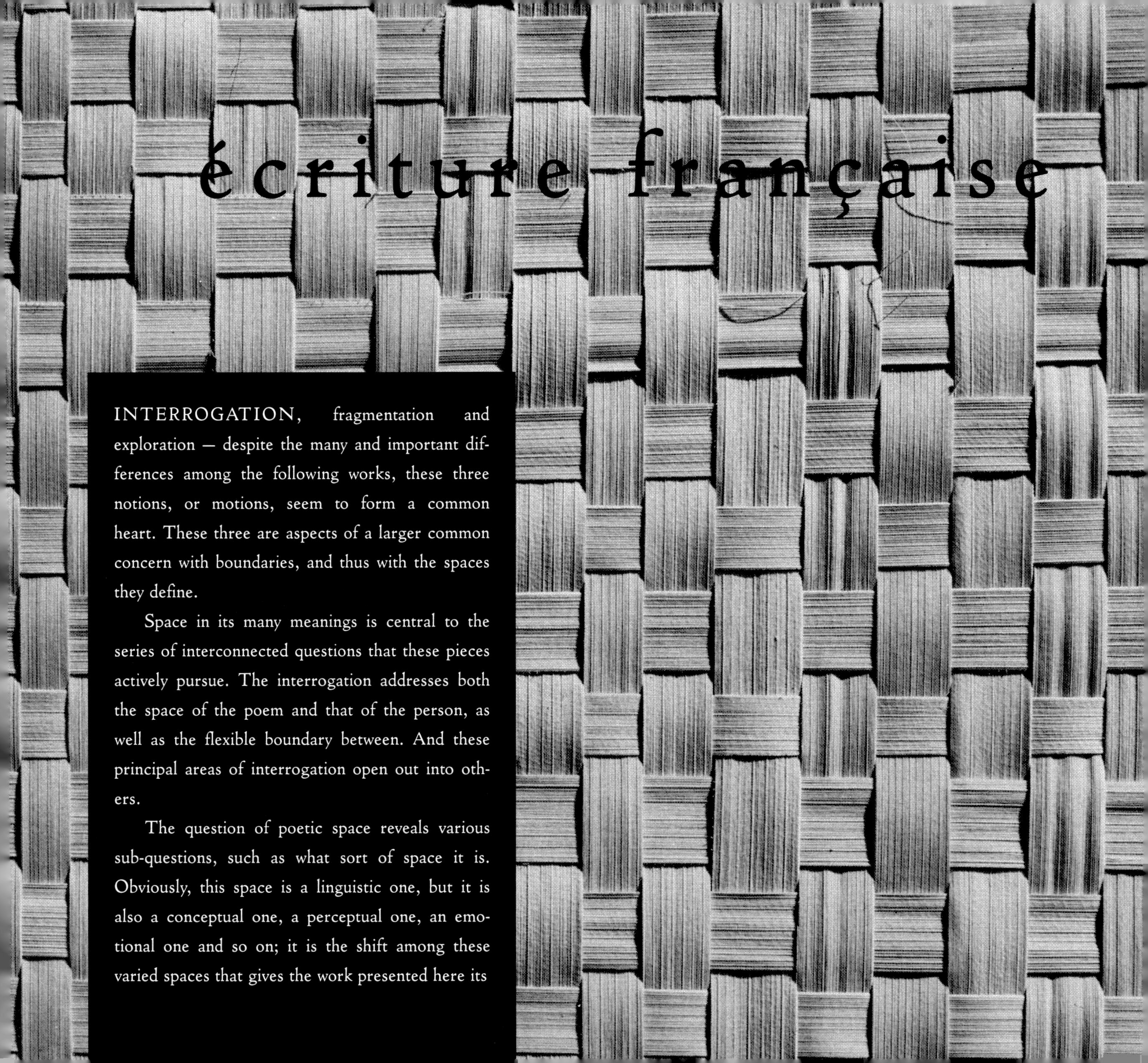

écriture française

INTERROGATION, fragmentation and exploration — despite the many and important differences among the following works, these three notions, or motions, seem to form a common heart. These three are aspects of a larger common concern with boundaries, and thus with the spaces they define.

Space in its many meanings is central to the series of interconnected questions that these pieces actively pursue. The interrogation addresses both the space of the poem and that of the person, as well as the flexible boundary between. And these principal areas of interrogation open out into others.

The question of poetic space reveals various sub-questions, such as what sort of space it is. Obviously, this space is a linguistic one, but it is also a conceptual one, a perceptual one, an emotional one and so on; it is the shift among these varied spaces that gives the work presented here its unusual dynamics. But more important, it is the attempt to make all these spaces cohere, if not as a single one, then as a series that can function in concert, that drives the sense of work through these pieces.

As well as orchestrating spaces, these poets are also interested in expanding their poetic space so that, through the poem, one is always entering new territory. Here interrogation overlaps with exploration, for this tendency to expansion allows the poem also to perform a social function of expanding and renewing language, constantly pushing its boundaries outward and uncovering new aspects of and avenues to expression.

The question of personal space also diverges into many questions of subjectivity — including its construction, its limits, its uses and its sources of animation — and questions of the body: how is it related to a given subjectivity? How is it related to the body of the text?

Fusing both these areas of questioning is an overriding interrogation of language, first as a force constantly mediating among these territories; but more importantly as a force that imposes itself by replacing and therefore recreating, from the edges inward, the bodies, the concepts, the percepts and the territories that it attempts to conjoin.

In light of this fusionary project, language has an interesting relationship to fragmentation as it is, in a sense, in the business of trying to mask fragmentation, trying to plaster it over with a unified facade. Here, however, language is being used against itself in respect to this masking. Here, language is not allowed to gel, but is kept in a motion of shifting and augmenting meanings, resulting in the sense of fracture that suffuses these texts.

In a way, this is language projected toward realism; it is a least language that refuses the illusion of a world unified to the extent that homogenizing frameworks of narrative or analogy can successfully operate. Here, language is forced to operate at the level of the percept, before the concept intervenes to rearrange perception into something that conforms to recognizable meaning, or sense. Again, this overlaps with exploration, for such language use makes incursions into regions of experience and imagination previously untapped by language beyond recognizable sense to that which has not been as yet recognized as such.

This can occur, in part, because within this work there is an insistence on the concrete. This means a number of things among them a focus on the physical properties of printed or spoken language. An interest in the material body of language as a counterpart of and in counterpoint to the human body is a principal issue underlying most of these works. Such a focus in itself denies an homogenizing or unifying view associated with a transcendent concept of meaning. Instead, it affirms the immediate and the contextually dependent, concentrating on detail so fine it takes on a life all its own. Such writing insists upon a meaning that is not deferred but that is compounded word by word and delivered in its entirety constantly as an integral part of the reading act itself.

This may seem to be a predominately inward trajectory, but this interiority is a principal aspect of the project of exploration that animates this work, for the motion of exploration, which is — here as elsewhere — an expansive tendency, carves that new territory from the inside as well as the outside; it is a paradoxical movement that makes such a distinction meaningless and that, in the end, posits a different kind of space, a space that operates along an unprecedented geometry.

The project of reconstituting space is particularly apparent in Anne-Marie Albiach's work, as she overtly incorporates the notion of geometry as well as some of its terms. Though less blatant, it is equally important to other writers presented here. It manifests sometimes in direct allusion but more often through example, through the unusual use of the space of the page, which itself functions as an analog for the linguistic and conceptual spaces that this work redefines. Though rarely, if ever, mentioned by name, it is a question of dimension — of expanding what is available to meaning and being in this category — that fuels this exploration.

These three issues — interrogation, fragmentation and exploration — all converge in the notion of work — not only as a noun, but more importantly as a verb. This work works in both senses of the word: it "works" in that it functions successfully, and it can function thus because it "works" in that it labors toward a concrete end. These pieces are not passive, inert; instead, they are machines at work, working with all the faculties of the reader to carry on their investigatory projects. The language itself is the working part, which is to say that it is not reporting on the work, but that it operates as a tool of exploration, like a lens or a bore or a probe. It is also paradoxically the raw material upon which it works, as language probes language to push it beyond its familiar territory.

Perhaps all poetic work is working on the project of "*chercher une phrase*" — searching for a sentence; but the sentence must be new, previously unuttered and unutterable, otherwise there will be no new space uncovered and the project of reconfiguring and augmenting space will fail. Instead, the search for the sentence pulls thought, impression, sensation along into this new territory. The phrase "*chercher une phrase,*" which appears in Emmanuel Hocquard's text as "Dear Pierre, you say / to think means: to search for a sentence," quite intentionally evokes the philosophical essay of the same name written by Pierre Alferi and published in book form by Christian Bourgois in 1991. On the first page of this book, Alferi addresses this concept, saying, "The sentences of literature do not describe, they establish."

These texts exemplify this notion; they are reaching beyond the established uses of language to search for the sentence that will exactly and unreductively — uncompromisingly — reveal their impetus and use it to establish language just beyond its previous boundaries.

— COLE SWENSEN

ANNE-MARIE ALBIACH

TRANSLATED BY KEITH WALDROP

FIGURES OF MEMORY

the term specifies the movement

flagrant
parallel begetting of a form

the internal figures dissolve

gestures of destruction unstable

"at first stroke stifled"

previous words

at that moment

and she turns away : he stands still

she had seen them daily
in the reiteration of anonymity

laws —

obedient to the pressure within

"struck dumb by scandal"

they spring up

where their sight grew dim

"she dared not infringe that aversion"

confined at the boundary

outside implied a prohibition

the notch scans

the same alliteration

would they thereafter have enumerated the ensemble

✶

"she talks of coming seasons"

ousting alterity

the reply in trembling

a punctuation

✶

violence

no end

or the play of outmoded numbers

by sheer force of memory

and this time he went away

in his limbs' gravity

"hurt breast"

from the liquid element the myth sprang up
"mouth open beyond the bruises"

subjected to this elucidation

their word

alternative

*"sleep
where the censor menaces"*

ablution

this chill in the corridors

rough draft

archaic
failure of eloquence

"hand reaching for forbidden fruit"

signs
on the bias tongues laminated nightly
such theatricality of indictment

“ *dorsal exacerbation”*
of day’s double gash

“a geometry”

INCANTATION

“I ate from the hand of a God in order to come forth and continue on this fractured earth”

She
impregnates my face. Her hair taken, and in the veins proffered blood, coming from elsewhere, alternate liquid element.

Insidious, she disowns a journey, graphic signs, eyes, in this meticulous account they are no longer frightened.

"memory borrows from flowers and wood such exact art"

On every side strokes appear, whence a voice approaching incantation.

Blade, obscure destitution, she withdraws into silence, in the least degree a stranger.

In their childhood, blue cuffs;

“milk of generations”

immobility is constrained

she thwarts an otherness and the other's glance connects with this elaboration.

over years, a perverse term's elements.

Such investigation strips bare an indeterminate time, abasing the relapsed, gestures from this time forward.

Dark shadow lets a body fall, recurring drop into opacity:

"the cold is stamped with the sleeper, one roused restores me to life"

Three outlines and a pallid erudition. She gave birth in the lineage of chance; premonition of data: night annihilates objects of an incantatory solitude, thinned by sleep

"this excitement of the first days"

An illicit body, nudity in the breath. *They* hereafter in rumor.

"at the sight of blood he swooned"

They will come no more. In dorsal hues, they seek each other at break of day.

I dressed this unprecedented wound in its last stage. The night was gasping and its sustenance even to oblivion. A sketch on the bosom, this color cast anew into the earth: sudden heat in the margins. Repetition of absences

"this complicity

at the point of injury"

Claude Royet-Journoud

TRANSLATED BY KEITH WALDROP

LOCALITY

an angular discrimination
accompanies the proposition

the name I give to a body

to make clear the usage
mouth gaping in surrender

"another grammar"

it seemed a great distance
to the brink of the canal
unreckoned and put to no use

UPDATED AS ACQUIRED

I

for calculating
  (maneuver it across the room)
there are forms available
no big thing
their way of maintaining
the proposition

"it's there
alongside *shame* and *hate*"

  subjugating
a sidelong information

no testimony
this articulation nameless

the body takes its bearings
"the close of the book your shoulder"

an untold loss
space
other's auxiliary
the lie leads back to mother

she applies this term
to the gesture fallen flat

II

"His words without vowels and without eloquence. . ."
I could not cut
we are too close

body of a line
eyes this far apart

she follows with her finger
abstracts the ground
a verb
the one from circle and air

"running aground and other accidents"
must get out

"Yes, them!" He lets his voice rise so that it carries. I do not know what it contains. Memory, indecision. As it opens, it achieves color. An afflicted alphabet. To speak is to see your body. And earth no longer lies about the hand or its history.

Dominique Fourcade

TRANSLATED BY KEITH WALDROP

from

CLICK-ROSE

XX

You skreeeech you schreeeeekkk you of January 1st not rose but bluejay
You play that in unbroken breath that and the rest no two ways about it that way everything gets written
Then again roses also jabber and clear their throats at the year's succinct beginning

XXI

I am not invited to the remixing of XIV I'm not sure what gets me out of it all that orange and rose mass is unplayable it's a pongee I dreamed up (rose from orange with yellow) nonplussed I applied to Gèrard and Claude since Emmanuel was away
Does a flow emerge anxious for a flow to emerge
Might teach me the inner surges of the poem stronger than the moments when it passed moments of some moment but less true than the resisting surges which give it its only sense and order I care for

And for a fragmentary reply to the question if nothing of all this was necessary or barely less awful there is no serious connection these scraps will not link up
At the keyboard
Magnificently visible on their faces the power with which by turns they took the whole of my poem in hand fearsome quality controllers Gèrard their power Claude
That feels insanely disproportionate O gods of the river what had I put into their hands
Turning away I crossed the glassy flower a broken rose-pink a rose which I think is always there whenever I want to escape out the back boomerang from I-me to she-me worst of all stares on its stalk
Order
Lodolay
Nighted
Order I'm well aware it hardly figures don't touch the silicone there so the poem will retain its electricity without which it's a naked puzzle silicone is an elastomere

XXII

This morning the day came unstoppered now and again I heard the fizz escaping from the bottles but that's the sound roses make

XXIII

On the borders as well as in the middle *le beau* its crimes held by the unangered rose
All night and all next day I separated things isolated them tried in vain to stop or break there are always farther down networks of conductors no one can reach
Or an inexpiable relay that re-establishes the sequences
Nothing
Of the night or the next day nothing disconnectable
The beautiful a cruel category by far the most cruel too cruel we can't get out of it it's every form existing things take
It's in the strength of the eye that sees
Rose the world's deafening spout into the sink
Rose quite different dishes drying
Crime of the beautiful

XXIV

Rose's metallurgy worker's lot of the rose continue to give me the strength not to wait

XXV

Rose nape

XXVI

Song of roses song of well gaited trotters no galloping to lay to their charge
Song of them ensemble in a very gentle trot

XXVII

What solitude when you refused to spit on me your buttocks were in my hands it's then you usually agree so that everything flows national solidarity the Citroën BX-16-TRS the melody of phrases from my childhood not merely but still not merely but still phrase from our directors phrase from our directed melodyof phrasesfrom ourdi rigibles but this time you were no longer willing I implored your mask nor it either
In the future that future where you will never again spit on me it will be atrociously more complicated more uncertain going into trance

XXVIII

Each thing I hear you spell out
Thus the charge of your spike heels along the subway corridor very crowded percussions so when you turn your ankle rose I can't fail to notice
Nor anything from you-niverse spelled out by force
The world's force precisely the spelling itself
In brilliant corners and elsewhere

XXIX

I was witness she set off her whole charge all her blasts at once long before the target came into view exactly the *fire and forget* sort described in the catalogs it's guided it homes in another rose filmed effects the same way absolutely out of sight it didn't astonish me do we hear do we see what we record images have always been snuffed up by cameras which did not see them the mad suction of deserts
She who set this poem to working had a little proletariat of lovers to which I fervently adhered awaiting orders
She veered sharply towards her base she is not running away she is not running away she runs urgently to get recharged she wants
Wants to lay waste
She wants to lay waste anew perhaps

XXX

You talk all alone then again not alone since one never is what with the sound of words

You talk because you need to hear words their bursts more or less muffled more or less linked up need to hear the white of their body you are present only in their modalities (coriaceous or not) and it is purely a matter of presence

More or less bursting out

You cast off your mooring those were the terms of your discourse you've torn yourself out now you're a long way from the bouquet

Not rough as I would have supposed sometimes you even talk soberly

You talk all alone there you are unswayed you address no one but many have turned towards you

XXXI

The oil in the *Iliad* is rhodoente embodying rose

XXXII

Fab Fab

Blue-gold gyrobeacon water I've a contract to name for necks and their guillotines

I write in the dark so as not to wake my wife

Monsieur le directeur may I play you my list on the sax

Violaine Marfisa Bradamante Gabrielle Gaby O Gaby

That only or *Je t'appelle* or

Gone off

Jeanne for Jeanne

Quand

Away

When hey do you like that more than *quand* I'm wavering

Not skip-rope sublime serious first grade exercises you have four years to learn pleasure in the future they insist on coming differently the client she wouldn't like it

And the clients are free to pick their eroticism me I can only propose my stock

Laetitia little planet

Spikenard (not highly esteemed for forage)

Mike or machine

Sienna I hold for because it's insolently *la sienne* both color and city but

Neither rhubarb nor stereo

Dune

Only

Since I'm under orders for a rebellion of the sort one hand gloved the other bare of Charlotte Dubourg by Fantin-Latour perfume which I'm composing with all my strength so that it will merge with me

You see I do specialize

Swan

Emmanuel Hocquard

from
THEORY OF TABLES

TRANSLATED BY MICHAEL PALMER

25

Dreams say
you are not the subject of your dreams
a grammar collapses

Dreams say
a context is useless

Some connections become possible
the rest is not to be understood

Dear Maria Amelia
a dress is yellow
signifies = yellow

You recognize the book
you no longer know

Dreams say
something else
the same thing and not the same

An experience of grief

26

A photograph says
look that was me

---

look that's me long ago

A photograph says
what are you looking at? That was
Via della Pace four years ago

A photograph
has neither past nor future

The other side is blank

27

Someone has left
someone hasn't left

Did someone remain?

This book remains open on a table
who will finish writing it?

Dear Keith, thanks for bringing that book
and the double of that book
my hands are full of glass

One sees something
but doesn't see what it is

What does a photograph show
what doesn't it show?

Enouncing of a memory
takes the place of a caption

28

Clear things
don't yield sentences

Dear B., Dear Tables
we began with something entirely different
you cried at the start of this dream

Your tears meant: they mean nothing

Who is the table and who
this collection of black and chrome

I put the black teeth in my pocket

Dear Pierre, you say
to think means: to search for a sentence
this book no longer wants to sing

A row of black teeth in my pocket

The last sentence
is the one you are reading

29

I remembered that
I had to phone at ten o'clock

This recollecton took the form of a sentence

Who recalls for me
what I forget?

Who see
what I don't see?

A fraction of a second
a light-hole as large
as the point of a needle

I talk to myself
in my head

It is the memory

30

A table is an above

A sentence has no other side
a photograph has no back

An envelope contains a letter
my voice is flat

Perspective says
one side is hidden

You talk of *Tombs*
resembling pateras
slabs of blue glass hung on a wall

Perspective says behind
there is something

It says
someone is distant

31

You say you don't see me
you see less and less

The photographs
show images of me

You don't see me

You see an image of me
the image you have of me

You are a prisoner of images
of a book of images

Drive the red rhinocerous
from the book

Don't shut me inside the book

Wash the table

32

You say I don't see you
I see less and less

You say the photographs
show images of you

I have that image of you
the image I have of you

You are *invisible*

Question the word image

On a table arrange
the words which describe the image

Question the words

The description of the image
is not an image

the description dissolves the image
reopen the book with this

Anne Parian

TRANSLATED BY KEITH WALDROP

WITH A AND B

Zero presupposes noises
To do over
Page A what's been learned
or not — rambling to amble to stir up   *at the right time*
The sentence
does not sync with the lip movement

*

False pages B — serving as example
: and I welcome *valid lessons*
A prisoner's role or that of shepherdess
the hero is obedient
PLUNGED INTO ADVENTURE
— *But we don't talk*
Starting with three let's go paperflow tally-ho cut loose with oh
An ~~armed~~ page: *I'm watching you*
We're quite happy that you're hopeful, then
again page A

✶

let's go: 1 seesaws 2 you 3 Again now
What I read. Story of what was there
I see you TAKE ACTION
Outside
✶

page B the little section of yellow wall
then the ooze the caulk the real cement
speaking WELL

✶

WELL sounding page A
Is it ours?
mama I've got to finish this sentence
got to

✶

page B I monologue
A postcard commerce: I begin my book
Us Breathing Bounded point
Stageless a reading a declaration
on line
Page B *We'll see about that*

✶

is A solid?
I stop
They confuse YESTERDAY the reigns
The one and the history of everybody
Humiliated
There is only one page A

✶

There is only one page B — Shame and Hatred
Fear Sleeping Nobody
knows that you pose
Page B what you've done
for a photograph.
but news travels fast
NOTE 1: real misfortune presupposes risk.
Directionless

✶

page A. He calculates.
I say I in order to SEE
the verb to leap. To devasstate, one s
Wait

✶

from page B: to get one's grub — say two minutes
to see while sitting under our big portrait.
Killing time
It's a matter of getting milk, potatoes
The greasy little sleeve gets against my book — a page A

✶

or a page B
passing from behind to in front
without

✶

page B he had a relapse. *Fictional.*
POSE
I know how to count: last
He lifts his hand. She lifts her hand.
Exactly when to slip over to IT relapse respond
I'd like to know

✶

8 o'clock to tell a lie
God from page A will himself have dwelt in a little theatre
I crowd it I empty it
— *stop staring at me I have to finish this sentence*
page B

✶

our first year in the group. Dress-ups.
On a stage in public the showman up standing
— *but let him show again* — shut up
11 o'clock I must finish this sentence
He walks on his back. He folds
The one gets up

✶

to this page
thanks so long eat gather in
we'll see ABout that

Pierre Alferi

from

KUB OR

TRANSLATED BY COLE SWENSON

the flat tone of a sampler
all all all goes all goes well
he says at last post atom-
ic innocence one morning
put his hat on his head and
in an adventuresome mood
an impression of content

(robert walser's *incipit*)

✶

ah that the umbrella's lines
unfurl are read and refold
feeble sound of a salute
that one fires and it's all wind
without rain the reverence
for this odder paper and
its morose literature

(mallarmé's umbrella)

✶

this to sturgis said howells
sitting in whistler's garden
forehead less lowered eye more
soluble ah I didn't
say that life that leash reining
as paris does me but too
late you fulfills overflows

(henry james' france)

✶

that is why nothing equals
these scales on the piano
the deep pallor and deeper
ennui incites the thought of
certain death by distraction
of when the fire has passed no
do not move no do not move

(summer according to flaubert)

✶

a naive picture he gives
when pacing and walking scenes
from my childhood are with me
to the hummed refrain face with
naught of the memory of
sowing fathers' harmony
incites both parade and pain

(charles ives' childhood)

JEAN FRÉMON

from
SILHOUETTES

TRANSLATED BY
COLE SWENSON

HERISAU

A DAY IN THE LIFE OF R.W.

The passion to serve. To be another. To lack respect for predecessors. To not conclude. To dig up the garden. To sort peas, to spin thread, to glue up paper bags. To make one or two resolutions. To put off leaving until the following day. The same love for the provisional as for the eternal. To follow the course of clouds across the window, a blade of grass in the mouth. That stubborn cow-lick crowning the head. To rush the decision. The general lack of understanding is your freedom. To not make any rules. An end without a story, prepared long ago. I bequeath to you my chapeau.

ABSCHIED

Wrapped securely in a wool scarf. Greetings made all around. Breath standing out in a cloud. Snow crunching underfoot. Few obstacles today, not much held back. The high sky crossed, left to right, by a crow.

A resolution. Fists clenched in the pockets. Follow the slope, step lightly aside. Cold air pulled deep into the lungs. A sort of asymptote.

EXERCISES

To savor thrift, to require indulgence and bread for the ducks at the lake. To embroider the story while walking, a little drunk with the walk and with the embroidered story. To say three times: not dull not dull not dull, varying the intonation and the stress. To limit the field, to polish the small form, to practice vulgarity on a whim. To age slowly, gently when approaching a child.

PROPOSITIONS

A verb followed by an object is a proposition. There are innumerable available at each instant. It's hard to choose among them. Suddenly, occasionally, the propositions dwindle away and leave you in peace.

Anne Portugal

from
LE PLUS SIMPLE APPAREIL

TRANSLATED BY NORMA COLE

THE BATH

it is better to know its name
to present the scene
by name
this opens onto a meadow

the value of an oath
placed next to green
and the semblance of ease
and of charity

*

my Suzanne
I think is violet
and plump
serious not her first name
in Sweden would be
violent

in Bayeux I placed
a plum woman
under the liberty tree
the blue space between the branches
limned the two elders' head

*

she who would bathe
turning her back to the scene
not feeling where
she connects then I would tell her
that here the two old men would
freeze really dry and also
their gaze could not
sparkle although the mirror
also robs the old men's bones from life

Suzanne this landscape really goes with
blondes

✶

since a building
the bath
can opportunely satisfy
my Suzanne
it needs water
foreign
rain

(it is in the middle of a meadow)

first activity
the spoon
an associated form
the arch
do you want Alice
not Sigourney Weaver to
day was breaking
and then both idiots

✶

no curtain
no curtain
release release the film titles
what the compressor does
and the unwinding advancing
and we who feel it
and the bucket
of tar
to the back
to the back

set your tub there
right where the landing strip
will run past

✶

and you do not move the skin has not
picked up
a sob a wrinkle
Suzanne bathing
the title alone protects you
twice
from becoming old + old
you blush it's a fact
you emphasize the subcutaneous
circulation
its wren's
speed
the distance from heart to cheeks
must traverse a celebrated overcoat
that doesn't cost m* much
since it's bathwater

Erik Satie, 1910

"Satie est Satierik" — *Francis Picabia*

IN HIS MUSIC Erik Satie included writings which are neither lyrics nor recitations. Some are unorthodox instructions to the performer ("Arm yourself with clairvoyance", "Don't eat too much"), or comments on the music ("Full of subtlety, take my word for it"); many simply exist on the same page. To the piece "Heures Séculaires & Instantanées," which includes a lengthy text translated here as "Secular and Instantaneous Hours," Satie attached the note: "To whom it may concern: I forbid anyone to read the text aloud during the performance. Ignorance of my instructions will bring my righteous indignation against the audacious culprit. No exceptions will be allowed." The following collection of writings, translated by Trevor Winkfield, is drawn from diverse sources, but nearly all from the cryptic texts in the margins of Satie's music. It was first published by Aloes Books, London, in 1972.

— DK

Dried Embryos by Erik Satie

THREE DISTINGUISHED WALTZES OF PRECIOUS DISGUST

1. His Waist.

He looks at himself.
He hums an air of the 15th Century.
Then he pays himself a compliment of the most discreet nature.
Who would dare say that he is not the most handsome of all?
Does he not possess a tender heart?
He takes himself by the waist.
For him this is an entrancing experience.
What will the beautiful Marquise say?
She will put up a struggle but finally concede.
—Yes, Madam.
Is it not so written?

2. His Spectacles.

He cleans them every day.
They are silver spectacles with lenses of smoked gold.
They were given to him by a beautiful lady.
Such memories!
But. . . : A great sadness reigns over our friend:
He has lost his spectacle case!

3. His Legs.

He is very proud of them.
They only dance the best dances.
They are fine flat legs.
In the evenings they are swathed in black.
He wants to carry them under his arm.
But they slip under him, very sadly.
Now they are indignant, in a rage.
Often, he embraces them and drapes them around his neck.
How good he is to them!
Stubbornly, he refuses to buy gaiters: —A prison! he claims.

PSITT! PSITT!

Psstt, Pssit
Well! Well!
What! Watt!

Eh! Eh!
Ah! Ah!
Hop! la

Everybody understands that

LOOKING

Her glance is one of indifference.
You can see that when she opens her eyes.
What is she looking for?

The beauty of rocking ships?
The haunt of an old nightingale?
The house where the poet was born?

No:

She is sorting through everything but
cannot find her silk parasol,
The one that resembles a tomato.

BLIND MAN'S BLUFF

Search, Milady.
The one who loves you is very near.
How pale he looks: his lips are trembling.
Are you laughing?
He clasps his heart with both hands.
But you pass by without noticing.

THE SWING

It is my heart that is swinging so.
It is not feeling dizzy.
What tiny feet it has.
Will it want to come back inside my breast again?

CHAPTERS TURNED EACH WHICHWAY

1. She who talks too much

Let me speak.
Listen to me.

The poor husband.

I would like a hat in massive mahogany.
Missus Thingummygig has an umbrella made of bone.
Miss Whats-her-name has married a man as dry as a cuckoo.
Listen to me now.
The caretaker has got a pain in her side.

The husband dies of exhaustion.

2. The humper of big stones

He humps them on his back.
His expression is at once cunning and full of confidence.
Small children are amazed by his strength.
We watch him hump an enormous stone, a hundred times bigger than himself (it is a pumice stone).

3. Lament of the Confined (Jonah and Latude)

They are seated in the shade.
They are thinking.
Many centuries separate them.
Jonah says: I am the sailors' Latude.
Latude says: I am the French Jonah.
According to them it smells musty.
It seems as if they can see the good old sun.
They dream only of escape.

GOLF

The Colonel is rigged out in bright green "Scotch Tweed".
He will be victorious.
His "caddie" follows him carting the "bags".
The clouds are agog.
The holes are all trembling:
The Colonel is there!
Watch him preparing to strike!
His "club" flies off in little pieces.

THE PICNIC

They have all brought cold veal.
You have a stunning white dress.
— Look! an aeroplane.
— But no: it's a thunderstorm.

(UNTITLED)

Paris, le 30 du mois d'aout de 97

My dear gnat,

Madame Jambe-de-corf (Thank to the stag), est enfin venue chercher sa machine (at last come to look for his engine).

Cela n'a pas été tout seul, my dear chum; cette venerable Dame ayant amercie avec elle une sorte de maquereau, lequel se disait marchand dc cycles (mackerel cycle manufacturer).

Tu vois d'ici la chose (look the object); mais, grace a Notre Saveur (favor of Savior of mankind).

Je suis reste maitre absolu de la place, abiment d'un seul coup la maquereau (sunk in grief the fish).

Ou voulait, fondly cherished kinsman, nous mettre dedans (to try to put within); ma malice a dejoue leurs vilains tours (unpleasant trick).

Sois donc calme (to prove to be quiet).

Je t'embrasse et prie Dieu pour toi (I pray God to assist you).

ON A LANTERN

Nightime.
It is not light yet: you still have time.
You may light the lantern if you wish.
Illuminate the path before you.
Placc your hand in front of the light.
Take your hand away and put it in your pocket.
Wait. Wait.
Extinguish.

SECULAR AND INSTANTANEOUS HOURS

To Sir William Grant-Plumot I willingly dedicate this work. Up to now two personalities have surprised me: Louis XI and Sir William — the first by his weird sense of humor; the second by his perpetual immobility. It is an honor for me to pronounce here the names of Louis XI and of Sir William Grant-Plumot.

1. Venomous Obstacles

This vast portion of the globe has only one inhabitant — a negro. He is so bored he is ready to die of laughing. The shade of the thousand-year-old trees show that it is 9:17 a.m. The toads are calling each other by their first names. In order to think better the negro clasps his cerebellum in his right hand, with the fingers spread out. From a distance he resembles a distinguished physiologist. Four anonymous snakes captivate him, clinging to the skirts of his uniform which is rendered shapeless by a combination of sorrow and solitude. On the riverbank, a wizened mangrove tree slowly bathes its roots, which are unspeakably filthy. This is not an hour propitious to lovers.

2. Morning Twilight (noon)

The sun rose early and in fine fettle. The temperature will be above average since the weather is prehistoric and inclined to the thundery. The sun is high in the sky — he looks a good sort. . . But don't let's trust him. Perhaps he is going to burn up the crops or deliver a mighty stroke — a sun stroke. Behind the shed, an ox is eating itself sick.

3. Granite Distractions

The clock of an old deserted village is also going to strike hard — to strike thirteen hours. An antediluvian rainstorm emerges from the clouds of dust. The great mocking trees are tugging at one another's branches, while the rude granite stones jostle each other around and don't know where to put themselves so as to be a nuisance. Thirteen hours are about to strike under the guise of 1 p.m. Alas! this is not legal time.

FIREWORKS

How dark it is!
Oh! a Bengal light!
Everyone gasps.
One old geezer acts the goat.
A rocket! a blue rocket!
What a treat!

SEA BATHING

The sea is wide, Madam.
In any case, it's rather deep.
Don't sit on the bottom.
It's very damp.
Here come the good old waves.
They're brimful of water.
You're soaked to the skin!
— Yes, Sir.

MUSCULAR FANTASY

Like Chinese lacquer

AT THE GOLD MERCHANT'S (VENICE, 13th CENTURY)

He fondles his gold.
He smothers it with kisses.
He embraces an old sack.
He pours ten thousand francs down his throat.
He grabs a gold piece and talks to it in a low voice.
He is like a child.
He is as happy as a king.
He jumps head first into a coffer.
He emerges bruised beyond belief.

HUNTING

You mean the singing rabbit?
What a voice!
The owl is suckling her young.
The nightingale is in its burrow.
The wild boar trots off to be married.
Me, I'm felling walnuts wtih gunshot.

TENNIS

Play?
Yes!
Good serve.
What smashing legs!
Nice nose.
Your serve.
Game!

ROBINSON CRUSOE

Come dusk, they sipped their soup and puffed their pipes beside the sea. The tobacco fumes induced fish to sneeze. Robinson Crusoe was hardly carried away by his desert island. "It's really too deserted," he complained. His negro Friday was of the same opinion. He told his benevolent owner: "Yes, massa: for a desert island, it's really too deserted." And shook his big black head.

DRIED EMBRYOS

1. Holothuria

The ignorant call it a "sea cucumber". The Holothuria usually clambers about on stones or rocks. Like the cat, this animal purrs; moreover, it spins a kind of moist silk. It appears to be inconvenienced by the action of light. I once observed a Holothuria in the Bay of Saint Malo.

Morning stroll   It's raining
The clouds hide the sun
Rather cool   Good
Smug purring   What a nice rock!
Life is so pleasant
Like a nightingale with toothache
Night falls   It's raining
The sun's gone
Let's hope it never comes back   Good
Mocking little purr
It was a very nice rock!   very sticky!
Don't make me laugh,   cheeky foam:
You're tickling me
I've no tobacco
Luckily, I'm a non-smoker

2. Edriopthalma

Crustaceans with sessile eyes, that is to say without stalks and immobile. By nature very glum, these crustaceans live in retirement from the world, in holes pierced in the cliffs.

They're all together
What a glum gathering!
Papa clears his throat

And reduces the rest to tears
Poor little mites!
How he loves a good gab!
(Prolonged groaning)

3. Podophthalma

Crustaceans whose eyes are placed on mobile stalks. They are skillful and tireless hunters, and are found in every sea. The flesh of the Podophthalma is very tasty and good to eat.

Off on a hunt
Mount
Pursuit
An adviser
Come to reason!
Whoa,
Bedazzle the critters
Who's that?
The adviser
The adviser

HYGENIC ADVICE

Before breathing, boil your air

MARY OR MARIE: SOME VERSIONS OF HIS VERSION

by Clark Coolidge

CLARK COOLIDGE is the author of over 20 books of poetry, most recently *Rova Improvisations* (Sun & Moon, 1994) and *The Book of During* (The Figures, 1991). Born in Providence, Rhode Island in 1939, he lived in San Francisco and New York City from the late 1950's to the early '70s, where he was associated with poets and artists of both the Vancouver-San Francisco poetry axis and the New York School. In the 1960's he co-edited the journal *Joglars* with Michael Palmer. He has written extensively on poetry, art, film, and music — on Samuel Beckett, John Cage, Larry Eigner, Morton Feldman, Jack Kerouac, and Frank O'Hara, among others. "Mary or Marie: Some Versions of His Version," a writing through of Jean-Luc Godard's film *Hail Mary,* is both essay and poem.

— PG

I.

To try it out without anyone at first, a level that will always be there. And in between, and barely, and with a single stone at the center of space. Are there sounds of rites at the periphery? Whose clashing weathers? And nobody there but the director, his spacing limited. Report on the gun range, isolated incidents fuming, piecemeal barrage. Moon.

In one, she is pregnant and nobody did it. He believes her completely. Then the turn and there is no gas station, not even anything round.

In another, the myth beings come into the room and they're just other humans. I'm sick of all the time us. I'm sick of waking to the same old real, the body and its functions, the tail end of the reel: the religious impulse. But the basketball on its string?

In which her picture will not leave, she leaves what in her wake? And then her body after the image, what but that nothing starts and stops? It is not a matter left in or out. There is no sealed body.

In which her name is not known. Revealed, one will assume the story. And still the moon in the affairs of whom. Tidy how that mess. So contained in integrity of skin. Her name in space, the unknown condition the moon is in.

Between such walls, even in the outside between, a condition of "because" she cannot be asked beyond. The point at which the moon can be said to depend on your skin. Why must you ask? The rest or alteration that no one wants to figure. But the moon is not, what is not finished.

With which her name is filled, so much that matters. Water brought up further close to a sphere, an effect on others. They will wait in stages, and inquire, what makes it so or who is responsible. Have you in fact met?

Only then she bounces, is in and out of round things, takes tracings around any map of the concerted heart. You may be sure he will, at last, ask. Even though a lot of answers have passed through this bed, passed over and rephrased, so rounded and unanswered. You must remove your self and understand because. You can't. This is a room where the moon, the image in station, the false taking on of a body as he says, and this is not love.

This flesh has fallen into a lot of water for any answer. He wants to figure the answer that will no longer alter further, how she did not want to go entirely to bed. Where the open window for the smoke, and the sax solo for his want, a man does not need the moon (fill in any image). Where she walks in such flesh it is her very own cell.

She will meet no one further as she is intended to be. Too past the fantastic to be captured and hauled before. He will truck with no patience but keep meeting her in places. He does not see her drink. Picture her gone but then she returns.

The state in which we find ourselves unable even to say it, so immense, so gone away in alteration of the huge and then back, but this time it is hers. You can picture lips in speech but not in kiss, though neither can be seen. Too much flesh for the answers to be shaped. The cause to be dropped from.

In which he comes by again for the answer to the cause which now she is. The kind of touch talked over here cannot be held. Face flesh. Speak only so far. I fell utterly, and as I did only then did I touch flesh. Sign of the opposite of declaration, what every one is enclosed in.

It is not hard to imagine things, but the hardness of flesh? Or is it the hardness of flesh touched? The hardness of the human means. A saxophone in a garment district. Clothed flesh passing in the streets of a particularly phrased wherever. She is gone but the image. The touch is always a removal, one removed from the pair. There are no soft streets.

He honked his engine and then there was a neon meet poster. Shy of the headings street always proposes. Passers as shoulders to try on. She as a flash in the only midst. And again he will try her but only in a room. Nothing is garlanded here.

In which no one knows how to say any thing, it is so huge in which it is consumed. One merely touched the lips. The car that will tell you anything arrives between huge lips. Her strength was in her silence in groundless activity.

To say she bounces is to ask a lot of her. You do not want to alter anything to its very recesses. The hollow way that "because" is a raw material. And none the less verbally secure for all that. She uses it in silence, its match. She is still it, the connective's thread.

The very lumping of it all together makes of one's mind no match. That not to forget, again she is coming. Is she believed as the virgin? At the least she is the available creature. Her body may be leaving us but not its things. The lights will go on to the end. And Marie then acts in a greater clarity of light found by the director of maybe the whole. The finish then something else.

II.

One can imagine that this is the place where men, where she is silhouetted, but by the window light not by his speech. The machine will not film the spoken and hemmed in today. Her glass then, her open mouth, from shit out into the light. It makes silence, this match of the pair, the unbearable waltz at the table of wishes, a heavy organ and we all are mated. Match the sounds of no one with the pair in close, the sounds of all carefully pruned to stop the light from escaping. Again there is backlit woman shaking over a coming proof. With or without book or talk in the window prism she is the thing is uniqueness, foolish beauty in a profile set shoulders dark hair, filmed despair. He bows and knows he is kept out, men only think. She is not weighed thereby. The light on hand will not bend. She drinks but he doesn't listen.

Possible on the bench to entertain the listening to, the haul beneath the baroque, and the rest out front all scatter. She is there and her shoulder stripes blue, her need to have one know her need for the silent. Signs of what others will not care for, carried for the foolish blest. The events wondered at are occurring all over the world's late floor, a foul here or there as well, she knows but little, she is free to choose nothing bearable. You are watching a young woman walk out of a shot and across the moon like the shadow of a love.

As everywhere life appeared in classes, forms of the joining for the purpose, bent at the twigs raging in the margin, let us speak of what is known, perhaps. Do you see life appear in that huge blazing ball? I would rather relate chemicals, whatever rhyme, to a woman. Perhaps that one who files her knowledge and twists its cube. But is it now chance that we have no time for? So coincidentally did life come in from out there, so ditto did the director himself. He points to the line with a stronger line obviating his studio manner to prove in a snap no little grasp and it goes. What could ever leave such a mark in its field, what stays to the test. Life exists in the space of the back of the punk carrottop's head, a steady vegetative glare as one hears from more speech. Life was willed for the hearing, for the increasing field. And one view of it all has her cover his eyes from behind facing us, a situation of little more than no or yes. She talks him down and the puzzle is done for the time, on the chance that there be time for the image to cool allowing speech a counter chance to claim. She does it from behind, but will she allow him the offhand claim on a similar chance? Did this life then fall from what sky? And her profile again at the window?

What is it that will raise smallness in dot sizes through a restlessness of vegetable by dark and leave tracks? The eye does. What is that? Is it then what she hears, which we see, combing into the mirror? What will that's cut back to in the whim line of an eye, the ear too late, the plane gone into sunset glow, the jet into wind's tone? Then is left to enter only a girl here, but must an angel smile? It does not mean what it did. The increasing sexlessness of some scenes and someone else said, shying it away, all scenes are fucked. I read a book about tying your shoes in an airport, will the manager steal your case? Will the light increase to story volume? He reads to his dog, that youth of the match considered, that chemical bond in his vehicle of a yellow to make one think conveyance and discount further search. You must stay awake and gain a peculiar straightness in your searching. We are all here to witness, unless we gulp, unless we blink. Unless, that starch vitamin. There are now cars in the rain, another sort of night, a charm that races the sun away. An angel will find you your station, it says here, it shows off a bit, it cuts to black, not quite back to black with darting red lights on somebody else's average. There should be movies about spelling. About how a tire squeal cuts the music like a diamond die. We don't all wish to gather now together to die to this angel box's boom.

Ever notice how it's always windy when the message arrives? How it's even if only a little gust at sundown precise? But would you exchange moon for stoplight? It's perhaps no time when she asks, What do you want? When anyone comes to say, you'll have a baby and not his. Ours? Who put this this way and then vanished? The message off a little and further to the left of frame, red then yellow then flashing. Sanctity among the briars is mentioned but in small.

So many slight extended changes, tended exchanges, at the station where the liquid is dispensed. So many speeches and end runs around the wet pave of no use at the last, no windows then the screen to black. Have I been hurt, has she been hurt by what just told? Nothing rang exactly. Light did pulse, but by chance? Everything goes in everything goes out. The taxi does tend to leave, whatever the message. Left with what does she turn and skip?

How high in the sky the persons walking over rocks so as not to fall into water. This is not quite the spiral jetty, though the speech over will have me close, saline remarks, conditional jostles. Another class in weeds at the beach. Time will tell, just which as well and who's been left to dry? But error reels eyeless through the garden, dreadful, inhospitable, since no man with clean hands can find exit. And what did he say then? Is it all suitably gained through sufficient reach? Is that all? She is not in this scene, though another one is reached by her absence. We have tucked all away for later, he seems to be saying right out in a plainly lit lie. What is the nature of poetry, craven speech in a lidless woods? But the ants would not learn to use their winters once given the chance, and the man who is the matter. What was his name, who found the time and thus music was invented? The beast in search to beat like fire and go out like the birds around an untimely growth of throne.

At a daily task, when we see any substance laid flat and there's no escape. But there is always a perimeter, a wash closet off there, three limericks and a soft ball to get home safe for. He draws all this out thinking we haven't heard or seen before. Another taxi horn to raise the eye to a freshly window-backlit woman. Then the equivalent taxi in yellow blooms. Beauty is felt as fades to black. Is it also felt as cuts? Tear the window then, cuff the horn. And his answer is, What is this? And the fixed question of there being no escape.

Marie in testing herself, Marie in pushing the one finger close to into herself. Another type of profile with silk over the hairs, or is it spandex over the head? We are unsure and so head into a kiss. He says, Kiss me. No. The kiss is something intimate and thus unshowable. He has found the good script to eliminate it from the personal and chosen. Then I will push you down against recently hot metal and force the issue to the point no one can see to the reaches of our kiss, and no one can anyway. And also I want your head visible against the surface of reflections. I feel, then I am an operator. He leaves, she lies there. Perhaps the sun is out of gas. But something prior programmed us, says the science uncle cleft to within an inch and not a part of this story. He has stirred his life lines beyond coffee prominence, there is a usage that says for everything its use. Perhaps a sort of pyramid programmed life but it is the computer stirs me. Light on nipples and a girl looks at sun. Codes all a matter of scale: Is this a closeup coffee cooling or a magnified endlessness of stars and empties? Light on ripples, he says, then asks, *What* is the image? Why are the increased ones so afraid of it? Their deep voice is raised in us, those born elsewhere. Did the girl come from a moon? Did the boy find his dog there? Watch any class march grey through the forest of endless sound.

One principle of film: Why tell the truth? One principle of film: I do but maybe the language is wrong. One principle of film: Once you've seen all the men, then where does the child come in? One principle of film: Show it all. So where's the truth from? What habitat or chromium stairway near the ball floor (basketball room, use the right words!). One principle of film: Look at me. One principle of film: I can't touch you. One principle of film: Night sky a ball thrown into.

Dreamed I had such a task I would be back at the start eternally. These frames shake up like days the colors of forgettal. But an image, you can't once it's held forget. Once it's her, then it's him. Then it's her. Then it would never be up to a doctor to receive your pain, or any of your other messages either. Find the right man to, the question of one on one. Where again the woman looks for the unique, the spirit in a sphere there, it's the light's sphere, which could happen to one like a knock. So do the opposite, take off your panties. Let us see if it's useful for a man to know of woman what he already knows. He doesn't but approaches her. All these under tests are threatening. She braces. I touch no one. He does. She trembles at a bell in her head. No one has searched quite this far, to the end of touch. Before he spreads her legs to look in, he will place his fist on her kneetop. She thinks he will verify what she cannot to her opposite, but he won't even wait to think it.

The verification room, where blue sky, taxis, kisses. No, no kisses, recall? The glass lake where they walk and talk over blue sky above and why taxis of a yellow standing and how there could be no kisses appropriate to whatever stance of lake or room or that your loved one. Then suddenly bareness against white with a swinging flap to close this naked one off. There is at least one here who wants to see, not to have it so quickly capped. I hate shutting doors, though it makes a firm noise. It's easier to give yourself washing. It's easier to give yourself to a gaze from above, not straight out there? No matter a flatter field, it's all a matter of outwardness. The way the body bears the breasts, proffered, outside itself as if separate but held. She conjures up a marvelous dream of putting her to death with your own hands. In a word: Rejoice.

The shy driver with his inaudible dog. Things that are only sometimes seen and then you walk away. Walls in the hallway, nights when a flat tire. And the apples she eats, excusing herself by phone. She is excusing in bird sounds in blue window light so he slaps the wall of a phone flat. Sun then. And there are other couples. This one in his pad, the word, the clutter. They are having to keep walking around lamps tables others whether naked (her) or not (him). Now listen, either it's Heidegger or politics must be the voice of horror today. He tips marginally away from subject, whatever flinch of the facts. She is there for, it must have been planned for. But these girls are all joined at the apple, this one as well chewing. Then she yawns, then she is to hear what he wants. No apple but the clock still ticks. She perches nude and the phrase past blue windows. However your music is caught, the phrase you wonder at could as easily have not been. Coincidentally there could have been nothing? Still, may I have you? She sits facing. It is not her issue, this movie, she will be moving away or moving him away from the main force. This, the one who will answer the phone naked behind a lit lamp and then smoke.

But at the gas place of job she will read of flesh alone. What is it, when and how deal about now? Is it now, will we have what in its place? No, place is no answer. Read of your flesh as say candles you take home and light, must do that, must change state when you treat of the flesh. But it's so loud, this station must be under an airport? Nondescript sky, nondescript skin. It snows then she jumps at the moon its sickle, its liquid. There's not enough majesty, you don't like it, my body? There is no answer, there on his side. Behind all sides a wall or lit taper. It's her, the other says, it's her thing. Hard profile of no motion then the hand from the right onto shoulder, no reaction, no change in light or sound. It's a fixture. This sickle, this bound body floats and waxes. We'll just wait here by the racks and watch the other angel buy clothes. But in this show there is no we. Not forget, never get home. You'll have to kick the boy out of yourself, jerk with love. And even a list of the male drawbacks, like fear of the hole. But that's like everyone. And draws one. Again, did music stop the image? Turn out the light.

You're talking but it sounds like the same words. You're looking but it's a brilliant sea with lemon sun. You're alone but it's an interrogation. He's the messenger, but what's the common denominator? There will not be another directed book, the designer of all this wants you to know, like an announcement. Bell. Book says, someone awaits you, God. The book is cast out. God is finally forgotten in the pale of sudden impact real. And what about the body? The body is an ass. She sits to the hearing of the horn and the music stops. The music must stop the image. The image must stop the silence. How could one deal with a lemon's sun? This doesn't happen everyday, but one's better as a pair. If two were one. If you were my spirit. If she could grasp the solid she only suspects. I want to give it body! I want to air it out. With a light? No, lights but mostly dark. Then I will embrace all the hated silence you can give me. Can I not stand what you say? I will lie in the place of it. I do say your love but what is my else? A room, a table, a bed. A mystery. With the object a space so immense one doesn't know how to express so plotted a grasp, so scare. The body's snag is trust. Does the skin have its limit, we dive together and fear. She lets herself be knocked to the bed because to be looked into level while she can gaze up is not so bad.

A tussle of clothes and bed linens at the crucial entrance exploration, his hand along her leg, go ahead, see for yourself, there is nowhere further to go in you can feel, you can't feel beyond, I can let you because there is no further at the moment, I am sealed like a fate. You are not, will not be, I am here as the handle to this tangle. That there is almost no structure to this image. Where is your hand? Can you see where her other hand is? Almost no image left to stroke. And I am fascinated when there is no structure, and further no scale, that shot is of cold stars or hot coffee? She is alone now and strips for the director and his machinery. It is decided that the soul shall be the body, where else locate any heat? Drop of diaphanous nightgown material over the formerly seen body, profile to profile, she goes on, and in loud bird sounds covered. I will shake myself out along the lines of my dream. Then organ deep from its height over the car driven night, and with red lights tiny and with yellow stripes near to the right. This is a covering of texture to move sideways and take up the next slot in all its sure reproduction. I have decided that you will see it so you will. Drop of object sounds near and heavy. Lights going out on an idea expressed in unintentional dance. On the marina in the day with the dog and they both are brought along in whites and blues, also some reds among the boats, it's a dream of Pierrot le Fou and the fantastic ideas for life. There's a duck, there's a motor, these are only sounds. Like as if when you do something and then no one arrives you despair.

But she is there. But at what scissor of that time may she not matter? I have no answer for you, but show a blue and white scene, seaside where the dog, comes up the issue of nakedness sex to sex, who else but you may be allowed to see? May I? Yes, you will look. Marriage is when one is allowed to look, when marriage was an image, when the locks were part of the script. I will join the navy and we will be happy, or we will sit here by the sea one day and I will pet your dog. When here in my thought your body is far from the sea. When by the sea or anywhere my thought is never far from your body. That is not thought that you mean. Mean enough to be naked and never thought of. A balance of thought and desire, salt and skin? She will remove her self, walk away over the docks, and right into a larger eye. The sun is never visible in these shots. Yet nature prevails, say what you won't. Wrap yourself in bedclothes and thrash as the violin only I can hear plays sounds. To do nothing is to know it's all possible. And on vast worlds far from ours, intellects cool and unsympathetic were drawing their plans. For the stars are lamps very close to us, our dogs used to know. And that face we end with is either very close or very large.

Now the plan calls for the burning of all clothing after the act. He does up his tie in the car's mirror and goes to see about it. She takes off everything one bit at a time all of it white as the store it probably came from, you can tell, this is no act. And she wonders whether it matters what she is or not. A feeling of remoteness and fascination with love and those that act it out. What can it mean to come in, sit down beside her, feel along her arm with fingers cold, and have her push him away, in fact all the way over on his side to the far side of the bed, and be told to do all this cold? While she pounds on the floor and entreats upward, but there's nothing he can see there, ceiling boards? Because a character is just, to me, a move, can be played by a woman a man or a child, or even an animal sometimes. But the sounds all the time are the same sounds as outside the theater only focused, separated, cut to cut holes in the images. The image of, Say you love me. The image of, I love you. The image of, No! The sound of an angel knocking him down. The sound of floor boards with no motion over them. The sound of a partially closed window, the sound of the keeper, the one impressed with life. That act, for which no matter the lengths one could go to show. Because it's the law, and besides it's normal.

You don't see anyone rising from this pregnancy. It's what rules. Fuck off, it's just the normal little act no big deal. The law, eh? Who trusts to that? The moon's a hole, but the hole isn't just a hole. It's what then? Down on the floor with you to see, then gaze upward even if you see nothing you might hear something. Just where the basketball lies on the bed beside those who will never sit there beside it again. The ball cannot lie? And now one hears the creak of floor and furniture. The full frontal language of touching her belly he now does without speech. This never speech is now I love you, this respect a trust in skin's integrity. I don't discuss soul with you. I go to whores, that's the only time love and work combine. And *that* is I love you? Yes. Nothing but a profile in the light. Nothing but a belly swells in the light without speech.

The daily bread is a big deal. Yes, blue sky. You must think of what draws you back, but rightly, whatever that is, and it will pass away into other response, blank response, a hearing of what is no longer there. This is the freedom even within religion, flushed off to other world regions, nature on the run. But we *are* speaking and the words are always up ahead of us. But I'll take your word, away with me to stay with you and reach but never touch. We are martyrs to ourselves. One must be public to be proud. But now it is cut to two utterly other ones, what could be more normal? Life without shadows, transitions, it's real and still here. The clock hand shudders. The girl weeping shudders in her car at the rush of the counter train. We're in another station. It's a different sort of station you hear, you're here to see. No one sees as they feel the world too sad. Then he says not sad, big! You can know just how big at the sound of that train as it goes beyond everyone actually. Red and blue stripes into motion again but this time not on her shoulders as she plans her moves. She tells how he really is a bit nothing, no, big!, he reminds as he walks away under the staggers of train materials in her day. The she hits her horn and nothing is stationary. But its cars passing the moon in the night.

Remember that she is an image. Saying, what makes a soul is pain, what we share that makes of us an image we share. A lie, that. Or one version of the many versions cut out of light and sound. The face in the bed in the night, closed eyes closed voice. Or over, this voice, I and more. She has it within her the god she invented to be a fool, a cruel one with hands, who counts on a quiet heart for his feel, for his keep still. For his heart disappears in the clouds at the slightest taxi light. God is a hole. With his organs, but there is nothing more useless than an organ. In the night, brass hands in the bed of sick flight. And if this god is not a shit he does not exist. The one I will have done with, that crab louse descended from a cross. And in my denial of his being I will stop any idea of the world. And face the pillow for the horror not dignity, thrash the soul out from the inside of the rushing green which is not as flat as the field you're taking it in as, from the sound of it. I told my mother and father to fuck themselves away over my closeup body. One finger at the basis of the hair, fuck the words dim into boards of the ceiling here. The something perhaps within us besides sex is dirt, and outside us just the stars. And birds. And coffee stirred.

I don't deny that there is some direction to be taken here. And in return no harm to home or globe? I wanted the answers so I picked up my camera and pressed. Oils came out, nothing but such a word as that for the mixtures of light and shade. Just couldn't get beyond it. The verbs will end you, but carry you beyond any sign of intent. Desire doesn't race over the land's encounters by intent, it draws down to cap what's hard and small in oneself off, the diameter of a day could be measured from, level to level for infinite lengths. The shadow and light cake on your dresser, take it up, shower in it, express its plans. As I said, God is a vampire. And beyond the red light she allowed him for a modest fee to look inside her vagina. This is why society stopped the inexhaustible mouths of the poet. And in blue sheets the flesh's rise and fall. And then as it's darker, the tall talk of cunt and a toe moves. Her hand riding her belly, an answer, ceaseless motion. Just as the wind sounds, she looks up in the night. Cut to stanchions, tobacco boards, pill limits of the cogged urban heights. We need a rest, thus the merciless cut. But who can be resigned to a god's or anything's will? Shot of vegetables or moons. Your ass must first go up into your head, and so considered achieve ideal descent to ass level.

And they will sit in the stands for the game but stand up when the moon arrives? Again the games all gone baroque, the feel of shuttle and earnest pull, a birth perhaps a score. And she sits too at the moon, the sphere, her moon and horn. It's nothing but image and sound, a research. Perhaps I have told you where it ends, after all I've got big ideas. Why don't you help me? Moon and horn, a darker blue throughout, who recalls the pitch in any poem of Rimbaud's? She walks right up front in a maroon coat to cover her now career belly and sits to breathe heavily by the close white electric sphere, the wind on the land. When he sits beside her he brings dog and sound, how will it make me speak? I who have feelings of vice and versa simultaneously. Hand out of pocket, planet from the sun. Now it sifts snow at the gas valves, the violin by itself in faint light. At that time none ever came but the child on the stone among the trees the plane passes through the same dark blue skies. Hand on belly into no time gone. Blades cut a path through the new visible wind to the initial cry, perhaps patched up from the scattered threads of a stream of answers. If she has dextrous hands, a doll the size of her thumb with every gesture and every word is made.

As soon as he can take his first stretch he will rename everything. We all live by water, do we not?, throw everything in? But children are pests, not so?, slip through our fingers like a tap fills a tub. Took a long strange trip and ended off a cliff but pleased with how it went, a walk along a courtyard. The cat to cross is placed there. Choose to choose, choose to go. Our kissing in the car interrupted by police. For every woman. For all time. There is a baby sucks his hands. There are dogwood trees, with the pink? Infants all swimming in parallel lines in the same blue pool, eh? But in love or any other state, are looks a matter of outward appearance? I seem to be, but she does not? There are only our hearts in the light. It is night for the moment the children remain friends. Since the modern period is one of rupture we must move into life with a virgin eye.

Are they not ordinary people? But they're always talking about sex. Or legs hair and music, but where's the coffee? But it's still only a room with names for all the secret parts under her clothes, he's perhaps old enough, always was. I can call it anything in this precise moment because I have seen it all before in such a precise way. A hedgehog or lawn. Brick can or fixed shot. For once flicks out of sight. We live among the remnants with a new one. Where they have had a child that runs off into the woods at will and will return but when? And we're back on the same old street of heels and their arrows, another attempt at cinema. The one standing by the parked car salutes you, lady of a forced reality. To allow you to light. To allow you the ability to express but not explain the mysteries of love. A cigarette, a half smile, an angle of the body at rest, closed eyes in the sun, a music which is the scientific use of voices in the world. And now the lipstick will allow another close profile, a newer hesitation, a shot of little more than tangled hair with the former action in the background to extreme side rear. I have left those people alone by not framing them in sequence? But I have left my mark on those in my aid. A fixed shot of death, close on a black hole in red curves. It looks flat. It could be wet paint. It could be a sign formed by what, the blood on hand? It could be any hole in the light, or those precise holes in the silence? It could be a hole in the flesh.

AN ANGLO-IRISH ALTERNATIVE

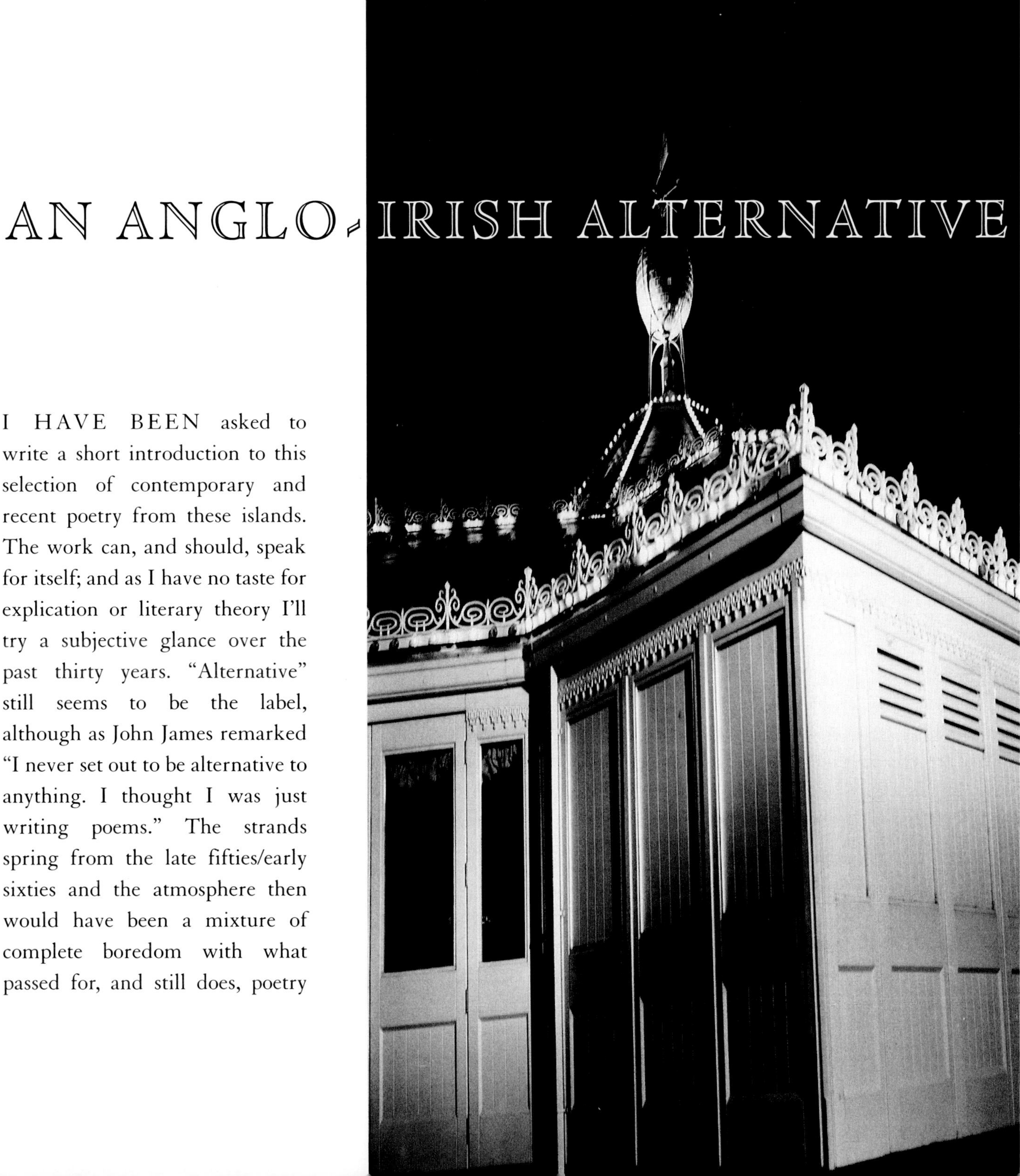

I HAVE BEEN asked to write a short introduction to this selection of contemporary and recent poetry from these islands. The work can, and should, speak for itself; and as I have no taste for explication or literary theory I'll try a subjective glance over the past thirty years. "Alternative" still seems to be the label, although as John James remarked "I never set out to be alternative to anything. I thought I was just writing poems." The strands spring from the late fifties/early sixties and the atmosphere then would have been a mixture of complete boredom with what passed for, and still does, poetry here; an awareness of French writing (Rimbaud, Apollinaire, through the Surrealists and Dada); some excitement with the space offered by various U.S. groupings (Black Mountain, the Beats, the New York School); a dash of European and South American sound and concrete work; and a proliferation of small presses and magazines. Public readings flourished (Michael Horovitz and Tom Pickard central to that: as Tom was also to the re-emergence of Basil Bunting). Eric Mottram and Jeremy Prynne were influential in the Universities, and the presence of a few writers from abroad (Anselm Hollo, Piero Heliczer, Asa Benveniste) was also important. Though there may now be some fragmentation. . . sound poets, Cambridge poets, London poets, performance poets and so on . . . most of them would unite in a common distaste for what is still passed off as British poetry. . . the Hughes, Heaney, Harrison axis. . . the "New Generation" poets marketed like sportswear. . . the terrible drabness of Larkin (whom I imagine wrote "They tuck you up/your mum and dad" and then rode the wave of a typo). Some other names that come to mind: Bob Cobbing, Paul Evans (dead), David Challoner, Chris Torrance, John Riley (dead), Thomas A. Clark, Libby Houston, Tim Longville, Peter Riley, Ian Patterson, Maggie O'Sullivan, Iain Sinclair, Billy Mills, Douglas Oliver, Allen Fisher, Nicholas Johnson, Tom Leonard, G.F. Dutton, Cris Cheek, Linton Kwesi Johnson, Michael Smith (dead), Adrian Clarke, John Wilkinson, Rod Mengham, Geoffrey Ward, Alan Halsey, Robert Sheppard, Virginia Firnberg, Bill Griffiths, Anthony Barnett, Andrew Crozier, Ralph Hawkins, Peter Middleton, Ric Caddel (my apologies to those who didn't flick through my mind that moment). A final illustration: for over a year, *The Independent* newspaper has been running a Daily Poem. . . in the three or four hundred poems published (and at times they've gone back to Thomas Hardy and others) the only piece I remember with any interest was by F.T. Prince — and there has never, to my knowledge, been work by anyone mentioned or published here.

— TOM RAWORTH

DENISE RILEY

BURNT

And then my ears get full of someone's teeth again
as someone's tongue

as brown and flexible as a young giraffe's
rasps all round someone else's story —

a glow of light that wavers & collapses
in a *phttt* of forgiving what's indifferent to it:

not the being worked mechanically with a finger
but the stare to catch what it's doing to you, there's

the revulsion point, puffs up its screen for terror
tacks cushiony lips to a face-shaped swollen gap

a-fuzz with a hair corona, its mouth a navel
not quiet, & disappointing as adult chocolate —

I'd rather stalk as upright as a gang of arrows
clattering a trolley down the aisles

though only the breastbone stone
the fair strung weltering

a softening seashore clay
steel-blue with crimps of early history

the piney trees their green afire
a deep light bubbling to grey

long birds honking across
the scrub, the ruffled shore

coral beaks dabbing at froth
the pinched sedge shirring

unbroken moor, spinney rushes
petticoat brine, bladderwrack-brown

coppice rustlers, always a one to fall
for — Cut it, blank pennywort charm or

punch of now that rips the tireless air
or gorgeous finger-stroke of grime.

BORN WITH EVERYTHING, THEY HAD TO HAVE MORE

Tongues flash out in a babble
flickering around the hairline.
In and out the bluebell windows
arrowy as eels they qvatsch lightly.

Each broadcasts a half-sentence
to float the head off its hearer.
One skull astonished in my palms
I'll burnish and pat it to glisten.

Darkening nose and mouth gaps
offer up holes for speech snakes
which may slip easing to and fro
head plates sheltering their coils.

They twist around so that they keep
their faces always pointed up to me
from whom they will try to know
what it is that they say, and are.

One name flops out of an eye-socket
to leap back into it with a description.
From an ear an eloquent tongue flicks out.
What is on the wind drifts stickily across it.

CATHERINE WALSH

o glad snow
morning of light
less wish
you were here

here to sing
holiday o
glad snow
light less
morning wish
you were here

here to see
loci o light
less snow glad
morning sing
wish you
were here

o glad snow
morning of light
less wish
you were here

here o glad
light wish sing
holiday
easy A
you were here
feeling you were
glad
wish less
light morning
snowless might
be

D. S. MARRIOTT

ASHLANDS

Ash, the unfinished tides. The
arch of sovereigns. Saved

we broached a rod of wood;
sliding contracts in a composed

flood, the vertices, the alter.
Unfounded vowell in a passage-

grave. Half-cells burnish, subdue
my face for shame. Thetical advent

roasting a heart punished for a
crime.

Spears rest, execute & chronicle.
Wide lands, flat stones. Owing

to the resistance of the spark gap
desolate place by the shore.

Caiques flow on the tides. Fining
preserved narrative, the staggering

remand of hope. Forms of salt dampen.
Cairns ribbed by sunlight. The

youngest son wrestles with Cain &
pulsars sense in succession. Cliffs,

desolate moors. Renowned champions
defrayed the cost, choked the

nucleus of the seed. Grettir sick
at heart in a bottomless deep.

Old and new endure extremities of
an arc. Chord the sharing place

with cartilage, plexus. Parching
opifex. Winter trees darkening

the water. In many ways his malice
is a hard kind to be eaten raw.

Thermal flows & honour's linear
resistance the moral sense

attuned to kings; the restless name.

ASH WEDNESDAY, 1989

THE STEERAGE

Now the air is thought as the void,
mingled with hail & the dark waves, no less,
perhaps, than the remaining fall of snow.

The whole is full of light & obscure night
together, both equal, since neither is for sake
of courtesy, & neither is for the sake of snow.

I do not see the sense of rare privilege
putting heroism into words of arbitrary redoubt
when we go forward so slowly, walking alone
& in the dark, circumspect lest we fall.

The waters upholding us are a shining brightness,
a whiteness in the cold, when, without yielding,
what is not lost to us comes so seemingly close
as to shimmer variably into beached form.

I have known the shearwaters, gulls & tern
to be diurnally insured, a gross mean in rains
which should have convinced me even then
that the hardnesses were bound linearly,
carrying the lower bounds to the nesting wilds,
depleting as the frozen waters drew close.

But the plundered completions under affine obliquities,
plundered to earth & turning to sea, were abiotic,
or nonliving, fittingly disposed as a geodesic mean.

And we are born to it, at each
successive level, going towards the proper
distances of stars but surpassing all
we do by a natural love. The visible
energies are as balances in the lists
& still we have no names for the cosmic colds,
knowing each day to be a signed & prevenient
auxiliary, distributed unevenly over the world.

Even when the cold is deepest & hurt grips
aloof in broadest day, each resistive night
has only one name, reflected in our signs; &
in our journeys we drive past to the shortest day.

And always we are known in the midst,
past the animals trembling in the open stances,
& onto a verge without plea; faring over the way
that is like shearwaters in the whiteness that falls,
our regress without primacy on the leeward sea.

As an angel once led Tobias, when, on feet
of charity never swerving, he saw
the nearness of what is uttered & what is,
the different as commodity in the sight of things
& the pain that was; so also do we see
the long night of irreducible being
over an endless sea, in the loss that knows.

MILES CHAMPION

THREE SONNETS AND A KLEENEX FOR MATT HODGES

1.

The Madonnas move across London
in the Mantegna style, their composed faces gaze down
Several hundred pass by, vanishing into the haze
As with much of Pop art, the bland surface
on our notions of fame and celebrity.
Great basis for a poetics! / and *Locus Solus,*
preparing himself for death.
these porous rock The hot sunlight lay
giant mirrors
have the same calming effect, the more ornate the better.
lie for a short time each day,
Raymond Roussel, author of *Impressions of Africa*
appear guilty
Refuse the subject, make an unsettling comment
addressed as "Paul,"
as if waiting for clandestine messages
like immense clouds.
Painted on clapboard

2.

A low shoreline; air glazed like amber
enigmatic balloon tethered
to one's life and the pyramids in Egypt
drawing its signature across the time-slopes
of Magritte's strange stone paintings, with their stone men
At least today the hand is there
getting the author out of the way
this dissolving yantra, a symbol
and women, stone trees and stone birds).
even including the interior furniture (reminiscent
A visit to Père Lachaise
light: fluted tablelands and jigsaw bastions;
the limit-
of cylinders and cubes superimposed upon the distant plateau.
All day he had been building his bizarre antenna
He dreams of this future,
suddenly so close,
where I see him

3.

a fruitless search among the cafes
for the diaphragm lip,
He worked until dawn, towing the wrecks into some semblance of
a cloud, the giant head moves up the wall
crushing gouache between layers of paper.
Then he cuts his foot on the Coke bottle, and spends
several feverish days.
speak to me
before the wiring is
that touch some deeply buried memory
When separated they reveal eroded, rock-like forms
Moving across the iodine water
the wet stockings in the handbasin. as she touched
the beckoning vent
The landscape of highways obsessed him,
one lonely word outside
creates a liveable space
turn off all the lights, and look

A KLEENEX

against the mud-coloured areola
The personality hand, you're keeping it
as packet soup. Warhol's screen prints
made a leftward turn and flew off towards
what evening means,
and doves
It beats in tiny blots
while his day-glow palette returns them
an orange the size of a melon A hard core is "formed"
I rage in a blue shirt, at a brown desk, in
A cast-off emotion. (to cleave to a cast-off emotion
it might belong there, it did belong there, that piano
Your champion. Days are nursed on
a loud raspberry wherever the pressures
would lie, and the object
Your champion. Days are nursed on
the last heavy sweetness
when scissors were in style. For now, goodbye, and

ILIASSA SEQUIN

QUINTET 11: THE FLESH OF ENGLAND

I. Spurn point

while wallowing famine relished its own gray unnumbered feathers
emaciated seagulls put forth. . .

while quietly following me
'engrossed in charity's enfeebled counterparts of viscera forgiven'

II. The flesh of england

hereditary vengeance, impregnable by whiteness
brushed away with mournful strawberries, studded with slimy raspberries

crumbled in the festered night
oh! the silver peerage of the dear hounds
barking with the rage of her silence

III. B. Britten

condensed in nude perjuries, growing asunder
his voice echoed 'the nuptials of the deer stalking
male benumbed'
so long ago a cry

the lips that leaped over cadence to virgin
mimicks

IV.

with uneven lust
deficient owners recount

seduced by prayers for having received and convulsed
flirting expansions
carried on jaundiced images of lacerated vouchers

preposterously keeping at my fingers' rowlock

V. r.l.s.

yielding to the margins
'let me inter thes' swollen unicorns, languishingly ridden
without pretensions

in the freighter's bed
recasting

'out of mercenary visions' in the unstained air
of rebellion, to open my book

QUINTET 14:
AN IRISH LAMENT

I.

have you surrendered
forerunning the shrine of the golden deer, was your carrion
so pure

converged towards the black island's anger . . .
weaving on the lighter warps amongst the dying

II.

eagerly for ensnared chords, voices stutter 'indented
harmony's abandoned echoes . . .'

    drenched in the twilight's blood

    deaf-mute, drum-majorette cast her play
    in the scalding air of hollow shrieks
    with a tongueless singer to comply

III.

voraciously as fire darkens, being whipped by transcience

    with whom do you compare her suckling

hacked in sanctimonious wounds, under an aged iris
ensuing sluiced heat

    doggedness emitted lightly

IV.

in the hermitage of siege-bodies, you instilled a feigned
token, dung-surging

conniving lamely at the trumpery of murder
scattering angles through the air
indelibly from the sacrosant war, bled in the eerie
midnight

V.

withering guardians, abating rustily the savour of chains
in yellow darkness

chastened in the clustered fountains of dreams

ironstonebound
mingling grudge and uproar, tincture and fragrance
their disparate capture

KEN EDWARDS

BRILLIANT SOJOURN

1

Lagged in our tree-house we turn hands to any
Thing and really get down to it mending the ribs
Bruised unexpectedly by concrete in the garden
Confident of vertical solutions to the
Horizontal crisis hoping to understand the real
Cloud formations that have embellished the imaginary sky
The word-box established anew on its bed of slate
The sloping courts of the spider in the good & mild
Weather bathing the windows from an angle
A schedule established and music is rooted in it
Soft works that require thought before supper

But high winds blow up now the half-moon clinging to
Moving clouds they follow laws of indeterminacy
Which, concentrating on, your brain would lose its bearings
Instead you follow the endless dark lane you keep the faith
You come up thankfully to the Golden Key

2

In the alternative scenario since everyone
Already knows the end the whole thing's celebrating
Itself like a sonata in certain pursuit of its major triad
This is not open to us from this point
The sojourners will adapt themselves to such
As it appears and to no more than that
If they encounter the transcending element
Of wind they will now buy a woolen hat
If they arrive at water they will find a bridge

The southern sky is blinded by the network
And the form of their emerging words
Also the necessary interruptions
The point is that intention be destroyed

3

But we are done with words tonight we're sick of them
And if we heard a diva & her band were to fulfil
A booking from across the northern current then
Slaking our appetite with fish & rice
We would attend with poised ears

there are some
Serene & highly technical elements in the music
Those exiled Russians have produced
That gladden the austere marshes of the estuary

And even the sojourners fare well with this
New stuff over an existing grid

MAURICE SCULLY

FIRE

A

suddenness of what snow does
to a doorstep
when you wake to it in the morning
early before almost anyone

(& why the verb *to be*
in so many languages
at such an angle should be
so irrregular so often)

a slate gone there
emphatic & there too
yes the wind blew this way
not that when

(is a mystery to me.
where were you when they
named the name of money
in your name anyway?)

the snow fell graphic many
ways across you (curls jointctures
loops stops) to make the black and white
unmelting music of what is

*

B

being coiled into a deft, modified past
not in money-work, but secret
difficulties, darkness pleated,
dovetailing deeper dark, down to
an all-dimensional ground blackness
being coiled into a deft, modified past,
hollowing, carving, cutting (I went out.
I met nobody/I came back. Faced it.)
brainfood, health, sanity, calmness
where
the roots are, coiled, magnified,
crystal spindles at the branch-heads,
spasm of light. . .

a wind that
turns a leaf on
the ground or
ientate
yourself.

grey, black
stone, ochre.
grey, black,
ochre, clay.

*

some monumental crap about gathering
honey
in the tympanum of a bank's face,
small waterplanet, tubby patriots,

the minim of "known" history, vertical siphon, pip.
dogfish upriver, another world,
light through glass touching the light
curtain reflected on the tabletop surface
upside-down repelled,
returns —
pax! paxpax! pax!
goes the fighting in the street
being coiled into a deft, modified past.

grey, black,
stone, ochre,
grey, black,
ochre, clay.

*

C

a triangle of sun
light on the
wall of a
shed.
blue sky. join the
dots. child-wit.
the blue plane.

the blue
plane
draws the eye
along then
down to
chim
neys & rooftops. here
we are. slightly
closer to the
heart of
creation (but still
not close enough)
at the base of
an old tree
(minute
grains of white quartz,
imprint of the nail
in the mud & webb-
ing between the
3 toes
& mare's tail sprung from the ooze,
a spider web, ready) a small
bird buried. even that.
the tune complifact
scraptured.
five seagulls in V-form-
ation & a quick
sparrow too

makin a
mane.
it's wonderful to wake up sometimes
to the feeling of time in the morning
early, crisp, moving for a moment in
the first day always, the clasp & bars
of the metal gate in the hedge outside
(say)by the pathway where — can do on
contact — the garden — you are — a glass
of cool water on the sunlit sill — in-
tricate tickle on the face — bright berry —
the air puckered where the silkseed
drifts. . . *that*

held to the Waiting Posture, *that* music an instant
fit to stave only an order in a sea of which/&
orders. when a token's taken & returned
fluent — "beautiful ideas for prov-
iding truth" — a *legal-decision-*
trial-peace pouch in waiting
(pat)

clé deas*
you could ex-
plain
Peru
release the Trees
Animals
Engines
joining the
Geometric Dance
on the shed wall
of an evening
vertical to the *why* in yr pockets
(otherwise empty you go about with
proud & prim nonetheless!)
mirrors, gaps, branch-formations,
the very sight in the head —
conical hills
stone outcrops —
staving off all aggressive parasites
& ear to the beat of breathing
returned renewed & singing
why
/whirring pipsqueak/can't-thinking
why can't thinking
fit thinking fit
this apt
black, black,
grey, red,
black, red,
grey, grey,
black.

---

i.m. Paul Klee
*Irish: left right

LEE HARWOOD

DAYS AND NIGHTS: ACCIDENTAL SIGHTINGS

A BUNDLE OF 50 STICKS FOR JOSEPH CORNELL AND OTHERS.

a wire bent round a corner

*

So many pebbles on the beach, uncountable.

*

a silver fish reeled in from the sea. the sun glinting.

*

the line that says nothing. A chair creaks.

*

cut wood. walk the streets at night. rock'n'roll.

*

the wind.

*

fierce gusts of rain following into the night.

*

wind whistling and moaning around the house

*

stuck in the fact of absence

*

the air lightens — suddenly a blue sky, small white clouds masking the sun.

*

the pale ochre, wheat white grass as autumn clears its way and the rust red patches on the moor

*

In the town. . .

*

Making the bridges

*

. . . walking upstairs carrying a basket of wet clothes. . .

*

the wind ruffling the water of a small pond

*

the clarity of sunlight, the calm it brings, inside not outside.

*

on the cliff top

*

. . . warm from a bath. . . scented. . . simple luxuries. . .
in the night

*

a clock ticks. a silence of sorts.

*

late afternoon — coming round a corner, down a hill — the sudden sight of a grey silk sea shining

*

towards dusk two kingfishers skimming the river
walk on and back to a town

*

that's it

*

And now. . .

*

(space)

*

Watching clouds through a barred window passing from the west. White clouds   blue sky.

*

always in the present?   ing   ing

*

Where else? or some lack of imagination?

*

a lot of anger. a lot of death-wish.

*

"Our beards stiff with ice" — that's a memory.
(I live in a version of the past as well that can be measured in minutes — not just the present.)

*

Other people somewhere come into this world.

*

music on the radio

*

Walk through the words.

*

the memory of a totally perfect day near indescribable — a time of such joys and deep happiness.

*

And then out the door into a fine drizzle.

*

As Tom once said: "this trick isn't working."
But what trick? A need to. . .
*
but what/why?   and who cares?
"Better than hanging 'round street corners," said Mère Oppen.
Really?
*
These words can rest here on the page, whilst dust slowly coats
the plates. A cupboard of dishes rarely used.
Grandmothers as icons.
*
Who needs it?
*
Out to sea the continually changing horizon
the qualities of light
from left to right   east to west
a startling clarity, a rain storm, more clarity shading into a
haze, a mist. Moving all the time.
And the colours?!   A whole book on the colours.
*
sullen
*
Grey dark clouds, continual rain.
*
the alignment of stars
*
bare branches.
*
chalk white boxes.
*
This could go on a long time, but won't.
*
the word is. . . A dressing gown hung on the door.
A quietness in the house
Clock ticks   Sound of light rain falling,
dripping from the window sill.
*
clear headed
*
Distant sounds — waves breaking on the beach, traffic a street
away.
*
Bright star maps — Orion's Belt over the ploughed fields.
Following the muddy path, crossing the swollen stream, in
darkness, . . .
*
a blue sky. spring coming. 8.00 a.m. on the beach. sun shining.
*
The white box contains a landscape — bare branches, a night
sky set with stars, a window, a figure, curious objects.
We look in from the outside.

SEPTEMBER 93 — FEBRUARY 94

WENDY MULFORD

HEARING EROS

For all that lowers must come close
my reward my penance may
incomprehension bound hand feet go
stumbling ahead YOU DO NOT HEAR
understanding touched everywhere
by music is what we love
and do not care
to name

DO NOT DESCRIBE NARRATE SET CHARACTER AND SCENE
DO NOT CONTROL TAKE UP YOUR WORDS & LEAP

she will not say.   breathe.
linger for the falling notes
whose words I follow are not mine and choosing
glass-searching curves endurance where
uphill we welcome
welcome to the sad endure
the tyrannies of dream

my love can pipe my love can sing
in any key in any hush
Eros that do change this old for new
pray that they do amend amen

SETTLEMENT

bark gleams space fretted woodily
looped with travelling clouds their journey make
& through chords of rooks & pheasant barks the
piping plunging curlew wail of sirens are
as timpani to play
heraldry with winter light
.
.
I'm in the car or at my table.   hum
drum. In each
particularity
stonecrop tile massed
orchard spikes I'm here in exile of
becoming
.
.
If brightness is winged and possible that theme declares
percussively before
submitting doubt to query
nudging across a pale palette a note
unrecognised
the rest is settlement, beneath the hand

point to the rising moon
as toes to earth

DREAM OF RENEWAL

there's cold in the heart but you could stop it.
or try. dont make believe.
stand on your head you cannot rage
soles spread to the eagle sky
divinity, what is
Heaven is it haven
to lose the harbour is one night's work
or slower
tempests take up a
lifetimes tacking to lie
in calm water all currents devious deep
driving or
air upstead currents breathing insteps spread to
sun's balm
dream the poisoned blasted element perverted
source renew

point to the rising moon
as toes to earth

can rush in the lungs forgotten with illicit knowledge
air and divinitie that here-and-now to heal in hope with
in without come gliding under first
star-sign moth-print bat-bless as petals silently
close float the panoply of nippies the sky's azure paling
across the rushes white sailtops soundless the galaxy to
brush your cheek oh hear me out

ANDREW LAWSON

THE SACRED FOUNT

In the ideal home we should have learned as children,
eating everything as from stores that were infinite,
when the longed-for substance lapsed
in the failed light of the last nostrum.

Washed by speculative flows, floored in the torpid shuttle,
the air thick with talk of air-raid shelters:
this discourse never put anything at risk but signs,
gipfel and *wellentaler,* a painful storing of bits.

The effluvia are counted into the aggregate pit,
the impulse of need, the silken texture of want,
confused with acts of purchase.
The manuals all advise: just be yourself.

Half a person's life is spent before his wigwam
is warmed enough to call his own.
The fathers have eaten sour grapes
and the children's teeth are set on edge.

We bear our encumbrance gladly, for economy
is morality and is counted into the bargain
with the legends of the silent poor:
the myriad who built the pyramids, tricked out

in superfluous galoshes. Where is this division
of labour to end? Description grows over the wound
and you are reshuffled across the given spectra.
X marks the spot, tells the skimmed milk.

Who believes in it anymore?
You necessarily appear cryptic,
ciphered in the form of the other's wish
to cement identity in a packet,

a simple trafficking in effects.
Provision for transport to and fro,
amid the bottled mermaids and severed cordage:

wants found clinging to the link.

A GLOSSARY

Walking simply in the sun
beside the historic buildings.
"My keyboard is continually changing:
there is none exactly like it.
All keyboards are legitimate."
The humanists have gone forth
with the instincts of explorers
to release the captives and awake the dead.

She is ensconced among ideas,
with clear orders to purchase good securities:
asphalt, condensed milk, parachute silk;
intaglios, amputees and young fogeys;
replicas of families. If I behave ethically,
will you love me then?

The articulate desk falls silent,
the nymphs frozen to their pedestals.
Meanwhile the celibates pontificate on sex.
Think how history has many cunning passages,
echoing that sense of being carried over,
the silken palimpsest thick with homelands.
Loyal wives and tiny babies
will be carried off soon in the hollow ships.

Our self-image shot we scratched
graffitos on the tundra,
cracking the superficial glaze.
The ruin stood perfect, fungible and abstract,
lodged in the heart of the national trust.
"I want my gold shoes now,
I want my milk and honey.
I have sung too many songs,
had too much water poured over me."

Memories of plush and ormolu
the flamingo pink evenings,
sorting *template* from *residuum,*
anodyne from *hosanna, caesura* from *ellipse.*
Watery light on the immaculate strata:
all the flagrant, luminous detail,
all that bloody crockery you whipped.

ULLI FREER

from

T/M

hill town hill tones & stake in clouds
coach from freeway
under webs spin hemispheres
past cracked mirrors a whitewashed walled stairway turning
the clothes a page at a time
dream wish where has the writing been
imagining the tongue
take a gamble moored to chance
reading the sun
dried out eyes
redden
in wind breaks
a platform in this endless tunnel
Mariehilfer straße
mit dem leben ausseinander
a doorway song
music of black bile stains
bursts bright star in the head
a hand closing stiff
without exchange
of falling yields

*

river washing moon
my old tea shop clink
five o clock in the afternoon
london bridge in between others
love is here to stay
seeking a door in the globe
it happened to be me
rocky circulation
where a bent anchor touched
as water fills up barges
& built upon
all too soon
willow weep for me
*
bonfires cuing boundaries cranberry
doxies
dark dock jewel
blue lights downwind to scold
air terminal station to platforms
shadows pacing labyrinth
hides a doctor
shuffles destination screen
telephone
rainbow energy emergency pulse
A knife
a watchman to cut
good words go quick bailiff

*
spotted blueness
in divorcements aligning alternatives
hesitancy falls & falsification sagging
dew-points sites extra-sensory adhesives
you want a light between the brain spin of addiction
shiver paleness tabbing in jabberer alcoves
touching up skin with spine twisted
asleep in shop doorways with a video running
X-raying tankage salaries
laboratory approximation of men ailments that feign
fatigue in fathomless breath
dilettante juts
wanderers in the yesternight
with albion torches
*

KELVIN CORCORAN

from

THE PURE BODY ENTIRELY PRESENT

One night we walked across town under the blown stars, with all the damage at our backs it does not come well arranged. Dark houses piled up; try lust, pride and covetousness. Try closing the door on that lot, domestic gardens alive with those animals.

We saw the fox eyeing cars, staring into the moment of impact then sauntering off the road, to leave a fox-shaped hole in the air, for all the traffic in the world to drive through.

Dark houses piled up. Close the door. The fox stepping in and out of life in front of us.

*

One star rose this morning
weather walked over the slates,
from here you see every day
the air drawn circuit of birds,
light falls from the hills
moored at the back of the set
Spring rushes into summer.

floating dense green at the windows,
flooding along the road
— one way the park, the other town,
Odeon in red at the centre.

I walk towards the eastern gates,
the early traffic, dark transparent artifice
thinking to find the poem,
thinking to find the big way forward;
I began to write the book of all that happened,
I wake now writing the book of all that happened.

*

Young marble giants sleep inside us,
that virtue which fills the body with itself,
limbs and head emerging from stone
if only I could, as if to take a step.
O you islands of men and women.

The free state does not come well arranged,
falling through the air of transmission
at ever station we talk it over,
you've come to this palce and it's inhabited,
at this hour all the radios play.

Terraces rise to the summit,
grit and the smell of thyme blown in your face.
The ten street lights of Kastro Hora
shine in a constellation under the stars,
Ouranos shines down in darkness to the sea.

*

RESPECT

I would trace the air blue print
by the window in the high, white room
collect the days on this narrow table,
a bright promontory above the town
launched like a metaphor into nothing.

Traffic bears us back into lyric
into this explicit, personal experience
I would restore the working model,
we see the shops stacked and go to work
the shabby families rise and fall.

My family's reduced in the cold ground,
the old man bowed his head to listen; oh let go, let go.
She's selling the book of my country's impoverishment,
in all those channels meaning money.
You must outlive the misery of it.

I hope you're keeping some kind of record.
— I'm going random in Lavater in fact,
a strange land before the songs
in the fields of archaic sculpture
the pure body entirely present.

You must remember and forget everything,
tracts of the homeland reassigned
memory taken from us into other hands;
the republic all gone, all?
Don't fuss over terms, get into positions.

The nation's there only at night,
dark map cast on the air
station by station, the names restored
lighting the shape of another country,
the pure body entirely present.

Zion, a way of behaving, remember,
and those earthly stars, the next town
imagined as elements in the statement,
ever item underfoot in the early hours
the ghost furniture and all that's happened.

When you wake and open your eyes
transparent days rise to the surface,
each part aligned on the grid
etched on the smooth face of the unworked block,
today's already horizontal light.

Shares fall in the Asian morning,
fear falls to earth and burns us;
numberless they clamour at the glass
cathedral clouds roll in from the west,
the sky opens to drench us to the skin.

Will you wake and open your eyes
or are you away in the big truth,
sailing the white ship to those islands.
Pull the sheet off your face boy,
it's a brand new day.

*

I saw an abstract concept of human form
outside in the rain of Monday
turning cold with autumn.
I saw you across the room
your good legs under the table;
it could be the sky opening our senses
everday this absolute music plays,
in the field of blue carved from the block
without loss of reason your life appears,
we can all get personal about it.
Hands reach out and lights map
the dark streets and familiar traffic,
in this unimagined town I imagine
I see your eyes look, your face, your colour.

ANTHONY HOWELL

A YOUNG MOTHER

She was weighed down by the one child;
Weighed down by the arms. Too old
For a piggy-back, they pull the shoulders
Out of their sockets. On the cover
Of a book women pulled at a rope.
The waiter set down a Martini.
They get set down and forgotten about
Or snatched up so that their handles rip.
She had forgotten to ring the station.
Her mother-in-law snatched up her son
Whose pants had ripped on a fence.
Either they come free or you have
To pay for them. Just then her eyelash
Came free of the lid. She was told
She would have to pay for the operation.
Bags carrying precious objects or perfume
Can be used again for the garbage.
Saint Christopher carried *his* load.
She wondered whether her body ever would
Be used again, the child weighed.

HERMITAGE

A whiff of chestnut squanders afternoon
As laughter flows across the eiderdown.
We are out of step with society,
Making love in a house which resembles a shell
At times when others work. The air is still.
Peonies burst their globes in the little plot
At the back of the house. The windows have no sight.
Above the roof, our tall aerial
Serves as horn and periscope.
Our studies provide us with vessels
For containing our madness: stitches,
Games with beads and the lamination of rubrics
Between coffee and coitus. Then we sleep,
Wasting irrelevant daylight, working through the dark
To the sound of the mile-away train
Heading for its black sun.
Later bed may claim us yet again,
But then I find I scratch inside my head
Among the pit-props, for I lie awake,
Flat on my back, still hacking away
At the ghostly bedroom ceiling,
Forever pulling poetry apart
Till trucks below the curtains start.

ANTHONY MELLORS

A PASTORAL

the more important distinctions being found on the ripe fruit
every hurt is misplaced according to the taste of weathered stems
more or less narcotic in their effect on animal frames
the flattened lobes and wavy ridges prove alkali to mind and body
you could say this works chaffy ruin on the tribal motif
the compact head not at home even in the smoky gardens of London
on the tops of walls and roofs of cottages, the perennial wayward
blues, the vegetable love, the distant path already overgrown
with alien nostalgia like a vast lateral umbrella
the improvement of rain has blossomed beneath the knotted form

*

you'd better get used
to my dropping round
from the plateau of the main garden
path to the madhouse
I couldn't help noticing
a soft warmth where
being dissipates into radiance

come on out and
keep reaching

*

we go for a multiple trunk effect
the white bloom on the branches
going out and then weeping
the secret being to drop leaves
in the sodium glare, an acrid stimulant
principle infesting the night path
all fleshy and glabrous with images
caught on screen for years

*

the fact-sheet mentions
two upper branches of the river
cleft into flowering glume

flanked by choice
a splash of late colour not uncommon
in waste places and among ruins

bluer than velvet was the night

*

what is circulation? scarcely creeping
through the face, de Profundis in the half-life
a sudden curling of the capsule valves
when touched. The name, signifying *impatient*
a generic term that best explains the telic
male. He comes round, da capo, filtered
through obscure lights set beyond the face,
radiant yet viscid on the joints and meaty
with oral recognition. Fused with past
enterprise, the grove a distant blur, all
you can see is things and their price,
your word-shadows not now dead

*

I do not pit the dark against the light but
walk along the path sunny as a durable good.
So we mistake the future's face
eyed through hope's deluding glass.
That I live only for the light permits an opposition
between the organic and the perpetual, the
sodden, fingery trees above the rise
this early winter's opened palm: voices ring
from the chapel, the opposition consecrated
into blue, imaginary fire. Frost has thickened
on the glass, the sign is marked
by fabulous inversion.

*

only the hands that touch her as flowers
unseam the woven screens, left wandering
the austere flesh now less fringed at edge
  a rim-like structure
  exposed to the heavy
  dews of night, the fiercest

rays of the noonday sun.
Your tender escape lies-in through each
rainy season, its cut-glass calmed by
the infinite internal object. Pupal at last
it clouds over like a doll's sheath; the hands
can only wait, sessile in the play of lights

*

Swivel-impelled they sink through the grinding chamber,
rain again grasped like a yearly audit prefaced by vision
without image. Cryptograms possessing vascular
tissue are grouped separately into ferns, horsetails and
clubmosses, the net of leaf-veins lace the skin and swarm:
what's out tonight is lost. You see the mosaic
brow-fragments whirled by retail menace, the adversary
trial filtered through a self-righteous one way
moral/legal screen. The next act of containment
is a low-intensity drive, they kept off the screen what they
scraped from the rover's mesh. The new leaf
spirals to the doctrine of no-mind; security was 'unduly lax.'

*

'these eyes look friendly': a half-digested messiah
seen in stores, petrol stations, even hitching
lifts. Fear of the single welcomes the total
purified of sacred violence, thematic coherence
has mystified the facts. Thus no surplus reality in the fight
for assurance, as if loss could recall me to the
fiscal series, soft furnishings throughout the house and curtains
over the ferny glass. You settle for pleasure as the repo man
calls, but my mother won't mind
and my father won't sleight you for your lack of kind

*

Risking the feminate
without intention
the child remains a stranger

precocious as blossom
before the leaf the
cuticle pushed through

into the inverse heart
stems phantom ripeness
infesting the paths

I asked her again about
the loved object: life inside
and out will go on after all

moving at a theoretic pace

TOM RAWORTH

WIT WITHER

"Such joy. . . such desperate joy!"
— Willem de Kooning

two major patterns
produced a realist view
any thing may be an instance
substantiated by observing
the primary direction of dream
no matter how specific
the way in which space
would change or distort
boundaries more precise
despite more flexible distance
to accommodate need
unpacking symbols
in control of all situations
the currents
justifying selection
baking bread and drawing water
introduce us to context
a carefully posed photograph
juxtaposing monuments
begging with black slogans
which we cannot imagine
out of a fashion parade
actions will be understood
detected outside
those same skills
open for others
demonstrate that muscles
have burned away
from obscure lines
images not alive
still not exactly dead
at the centre of reflection
of the electronic world
feel details about
the inside of each
nature of the event
command our attention
inspiration of smoke
mostly drugs
his mental efforts
between sisters
entering thick lovers
hands-on

a glimpse of other eras
mainly marks on the dial
daily passes
work their replacing
down routine firings
poised ambitious to provide
conscious literary originals
happen may even think
know or other cues
required in your unit
scrabbling at the prospect
while you need
storming with
affiliate that produces
shaped bright overflow
in the complete
museum dedicated to
former documenting
penguins, sea lions
carefully singing magic
locked in on her
stripped out
arms folded
odour of decaying
interest and concentration
passing under columns
of white stones
on a chrome
motor whirr
inched along enticement
past spiderwebs
under his arms
turned squarely on
instinctive impulse
deeper into dereliction
beneath irregular
heat inside
consideration of delusion
a place to crawl to
and endlessly loop
among the folds of garments

FROM 707 SCOTT STREET: A JOURNAL OF

JoHn jOsepH wieNeRs

John Wieners c. 1966

IN **1972** BILL CORBETT AND LEWIS WARSH VISITED JOHN WIENERS AT 44 Joy Street in Boston where he still lives. John pressed this manuscript, handwritten, on Lewis who proceeded to type it up at Bill's house at 9 Columbus Square in the South End. It was summer. The manuscript, called 707 Scott Street, was written between

1958 and 1959, and includes references to Boston ("colored paper rose, blue spots, ink spots Boston, 1949, the sound of cellophane") although it was composed in San Francisco. In 1992 the typed manuscript resurfaced and attracted the attention of Peter Gizzi, a poet now about the age that Bill and Lewis were when they visited John in 1972, and a section of it is printed here, a section written in summer.

During the summer of 1992, I arranged to meet John outside the branch of the Boston Public Library nearest Joy Street, because I had dedicated my most recent collection of poems to him, and I hadn't actually spoken to him for several years. My oldest daughter, also a poet, was with me. John was wearing a coat though it was very hot, and despite the torn expression of his face, he looked almost robust. Always courteous, his way of paying attention to us was to whirl our remarks into spirals of poetic speech. Struck, for instance, by my saying that my daughter was on her way to London, he "remembered" a girl standing on the Salt and Pepper Bridge over the Charles River; she was, he said, "stuck with her back to the Hyatt Regency and couldn't go to London until The Highway was built."

He also said to her that his mother had told him to get a job, but he had refused, because a job would prevent him from writing poems. And then he added two very precise remarks as if to reassure me: "I look around — and there used to be a rostrum — in Boston — poets in the limelight — but I don't see them anymore." And again to me, quite specifically: "For you and me it's better to be unknown — to do our work."

In the excerpt from his Scott Street Journal that follows, he writes, "and if I cannot speak in poetry, it is because poetry is reality to me, and not the poetry we read, but find revealed in the estates of being around us." John's poetry has always been the closest thing possible to a new form of speech, one that narrows the gap between longing and calling. These pages from the fifties live in that "estate" as much as his spoken words to others do now.

Estates of being exist as streets, seasons, people, songs, and while the placement of his poetics could be cordoned off by a period in "the limbo of contemporary America" that has passed — a poetics that predates post-modern rhetoric and the strange fixation with an Otherness that he would not recognize — his unembittered position as an "unknown" witness of the dispossessed is absolutely present across time.

— FANNY HOWE

AUG 1ST

I decide today to strip my walls bare. For despite the labor I feel it necessary for my new-creating psyche to see the fresh field rather than the souvenirs and fetishes of such a recent past. Even tho that past may be lost because no poems made note of the events contained therein. And I am a needy and lonely wanderer clad in red with no memories (what a difficult law to live by) so it is I strip the walls of my room that I may have the fresh, the new, not the evocative image of friends of faces my soul knows from the past, but the old wide plain where man is alone, only the red guilt on his hands, of his own life, what he has and must use. I was going to say guilt for having stolen fire, or blood running down his hands, but these images we recognize. I mean the red that is his alone containing fire and blood, but more the gift, the

tongue of flames
he wraps himself in.
As a cone.
As
the writing is, when it is
the man
will show, this structure of change,
shifting but always revolving
upon itself. So that the way will
widen as the land it moves over, does
dip and valley
volley home like a cannonball, not

all over the page
without will but a plan
a design of the mind
not constructed
out of agony but moving with
the tides, I was going to say
wind.
What does any of this do
but that is the voice of my demon, the corpse
that hangs upon the tree and
wails! STRANGE FRUIT
This song was written for me
Billie Holliday says under the
baby spot light. I aint trying to be brilliant.

PLAN FOR MEASURE

Old — New	1. Book of the Earth
City	2. Charles Olson's Descartes
New form	3. Tom Field's Notes on Form & Beauty
New space	4. Ebbe Borregard's Journal
place	5. John Haines A Nice View
Reminiscence	6. Sheri Martineli's
stream	7. Wm Fleming Night Piece
decadence	8. David Meltzer Mechankions
degenerate	9. John Wieners
dope	10. Michael McClure Notes
hip	11. Philip Lamantia City of Weir Magnum Opus
struggle	
act	12. Duncan What do I know of the old lore
LSD	13. John Reed's
surrealism	Capsule from Another World
revelation	Allen Ginsberg's LSD Mad machine vision
Flesh	Jess Collins's Tricky Cad
Love	Aleister Crowley's Liber al vel Legis

(the woman) Another Journal or Photo of Jan
Poems Ron Loewinsohn
Ed Marshall
John Wieners
Mary Fiore
Persky's Cocteau
Prose for Russell
Michael Rumaker's *Letters*

Two Indians fishing on the Bay of San Francisco

AUG 6

We are playing at little games and I am one of the children. Not insanity but how far are we from the time of ten years ago. And daily we re-enact their rites. Let us not take ourselves too seriously. We return to the grave soon enough. And the waves wash over us. What paltry beings we become if we complain that 78 years upon the planet is too much. It appears that we are not needed as a rule any longer after that. Or we would remain. Like the tree does. Or the sun has these billion years. And so if the day dies and we too have to decline with it, we know that we come back tomorrow. Even tho all the pencils break and all the typewriters hang in The Pawnshop Window, words go on. And their instruments with them. Today I am one of them and I dress in a red robe.

Sometimes it is only given to us a few words to speak and a little time to say them in, in an old form: prose. And what is this new form that breaks thru? Is it pure? What shape does it have? Its contour on the page.

And if man is not engaged in creating new form, what does he engage himself in? He does not die with each day, He says there is no death. For him there is no life either. It is the limbo of contemporary America. Yet even that too moves at its own graceful and deadly speed — nned, ease.

And who am I but a lonely
setter upper
of outworn creeds and
beliefs, brought into being
by the needs of my ever-avaricious
ever bright-full mind.
Where do I dwell
but in Hell
stealing your secrets, o precious
reader o not desert me,
without you I roam
alone. Shouting my words
into the abyss where the
Fool walks. We go
bitten by what
beautiful bug, butterfly o
scorpion, you spur
me on.

And if I cannot speak in poetry, it is because poetry is reality to me, and not the poetry we read, but find revealed in the estates of being around us.

It is necessary for the poet to be ignorant of the true mystery, and yet to contain it wrapped around him. Not aware that his slightest flash of eyelid is enough to set those off around him into an ecstasy of awareness.To be dumb himself. A mammoth vegetable, A. Richer says.

AUG 7

Nothing today but the yen. For heroin. Snap my fingers. It does not appear at the door. I am alone. As always. As all men. With a magnificent obsession.

I have hunted, I have yearned
for you and now you
withhold yr. hands from me.

I have to look for something to do.
Now is not enough. There is no use
thinking about it. Put it away
as one would do a lover.

But today is Friday and I know what's happening
on the street. I would think it's a full moon
for the high tides in my soul. The Perseids
shower themselves thru the sky above me.
Buddha sits in the dust.
The poet works to undo the confusion
around him. He should not add to it. Well the cycle moves
and I with it. *What a difference a day made*
the girl sings on
the radio. Oh
those high mornings
those nights when the boat
rocked with velvet tides.

Must I pay forever
for those sweet rides
thru the tunnel of love.

Le Chateau Merveil

where I undergo the trials

of *desire*

What strange voices, what
hideous forms appear
before me in the faces
of countrymen, my friends.

They stalk me down.

To try my soul?
I pay for every inch of life (joy)
I move thru,
swept over by it
forgetting it is not eternal.
That is the nature of joy
that one thinks it will go on forever.

Pain is harder to bear. One forgets there too
that is will end.
No it is not harder to bear.

The non life the vacuum
that is the thing I flee from.
The most.

And where the solace is. In this
the writing.

In the center of the chamber King Arthur sat upon a seat of green rushes over which was spread a covering of flame-colored satin. And a cushion of red satin was under his elbow.

Rot What Ought Not

Every day decay
goes on. The rose grows
a green hardihood.
To guard against Pax
John of the Wood.
Sword in his hand, rocks
in his head, beware
maiden if you want to
live chaste and mild.
He will drive you wild.
And your bed of crimson
joy, destroy.

Always looking for life or the passing of events to be enough. And they are not. We must see them as temporal. As passing manifestations thru the cosmos. Even this, these words shall fade and fall
to shreds as the rest.
But I erect them for they are my salvation.

The eternal letters
that spring from the mouths of men.
Written to hold up the trembling structure.

Dame Ragnell:

Sir, now shalt thou know what women desire most of high and low. There is one thing in all our fantasy, and that now shall ye know: We desire of men above all manner of thing, to have the
sovereignity.

And there they made joy out of mind.

AUG 8

My mind keeps running over at its edges
like rays from the sun or
the arms of a
spiral nebula.
Oh we are galaxies unto ourselves. And the Tarot Deck
is not enough to tell our fortune.

The earth shaped like a pear is the Adam's apple
of the universe
Bobs up and down
every 200 million years. Around the central point
which is bell button
turning point
where action is transmuted. Am I wrong here?
Does it matter

that I shake in the wind like a cross atop
the palm tree out my window.
That I do it.
Am the mover
and the moved.

Red drapes in the open window
King Solomon and his magic wand

AUG 11

A poem for Susan

Just the joy of her
to hear her move in the room,

there is no need to recount actions
description not enough, is like
adjectives

but she breathes
like a verb, folding
clothes against her belly, brushing
the arms of her coat.

Not a cat
but woman.
Hidden secret from me before
I watch them unravel their world,

bending before the
beloved objects in them.

The poem demands a degree of attention that drugs, because they slacken one, deter one from the poem. At least I feel not at my maximum powers. Although a breadth, a dimension is given one that is almost, or not, but irresistible. Each action, object takes on a special meaning it did not have before.

A woman's face.

Both sides of my nature come to the fore with such strength.

The birds, first ones outside my window. The girl fishing in her purse, opening suitcases, and all this at dawn. A magic one I was born at this hour. And we share again the glow and first excitement of that movement, again here. Behind dope. The warmth of mother's womb, with all the hideous knowledge of the world thrown in our face, get wailing behind it.

Because it is the rush
of
life?

AUG 12

From the moment of our birth, we are placed midpoint of a sphere shaped like the figure eight. And the objects of the outside from then on draw us outward, further and further into space, wider and wider everyday in every way, this is the upward/motion . . .?
Action.
All these things are an intrusion and at times called evil because they are of this world, what comes in thru the senses. The Forward. Progressive? Progress. Man marches on.

But at the very
same moment there is an
identical
motion going on downward. Inward contemplation. Use of the unconscious. Dreams. Which are made up of the actions that went on before above. Come back to haunt us, so that in time they form a

right reason that comes from heaven, a partaking of grace left by our ancestors, but "the legacy" given to us at the moment of our birth. Each instant's gift. The result of the action we are engaging ourselves in, so that if we write, we have the powers of all who have written before, love the lovers of old. The murderous thrust, what meaning do these sudden acts of savagery have? Duncan asks in *Love.* That they are what we are right now. Saints if we are saintly but for one second. A legacy we pass on, transmit to others after us and around us. Order in oneself. One's own kingdom consists in setting each instant king. Knowing that that instant, this, is twofold. Partaking of the pen, and the mind which has made conscious use of the "pen" since the eye opening etc. of birth. From then to now. But back again from now to infinity where the first mind shone. We work our way back to that, on the bones of our fathers, grave diggers that

we are.

AUG 13

The wind is a guitar in the house tonight
the dog barks just once
at the non-existent moon.

The maiden strums alone in golden light
lovers say goodbye and close
their eyes on the rising sun.

And if one were to begin writing at the command of what mysterious agent, what concentration could I distill from the crashing moment, the confusion of thoughts that rush in on me, so that my mind can not practice automatic writing. He, it does not revolve on any one object that long. *Lifting Belly* is a fiction. Is such a conscious construction of high genius intellect that it does not partake of that mysterious (again that word force which we call automatic, i.e. without will, on its own. Impelled by whatever order the mind imposes, on us now. Which is a creation of that we were before.

Now does that make sense? I could clarify and rationalize. Make it clear. Shit. But something forbids it, in fact by dwelling on it I know I lose some powers of the present, allowing myself to doubt the authority.

And if I were to try again. And stay away from subject matter. And be abstract. Deal with words as if they were hunks of letters without meaning. I can no more use them as dead things divorced from the blood of our desire and the spirit's rage, than I could see any living thing thus separated. For all lives. In that it partakes of existence. Whatever that is. I thought then: chance and change. But you see, already I am imposing a conscious order here which Gertrude had the genius not to do. She did not have to do it. As I do. You will allow me that reader, yourselves that. That you better do what you have to do
or you shall
partake of death. *She shalt crush thy head and thou shalt lie in wait for her heel.*

Oh heroine /// The words reveal themselves and place our actions, reveal our actions by our words.

I will use the distractions of this world, and erect a structure from them that will be of the poem. No matter how down I go, how ruined, bombed by shit, they will rise, the words, in whatever form, but written what? On toilet paper heart. On sick arms, with no forms

but new ones.

2. A.W. Experiment #1

And if the words come out
with no order or force, love is a shuck,

she does not want to get off
at the end of the line.
Do not anticipate your next move. But

move with the passing of past events
through the window,
of Cassandra's, of
your mind.

Bringing them
back again and again, remembering how
poems under drugs sound so poor
on re-reading
but so great
when writing them.

I have no obligation or debt to reality that I need record it. The guitar can go on. I don't have to try to
DUPLICATE
its melody, by my lines, or song, full
strains, save that for the birds.

This is the work
of the intellect Dante
the intelligence manifesting itself
thru nature, Agazziz.

Am I right on my facts? A ridiculous
self doubt that has no place in creat-
ion. This is how words are abstract
here in the poem. Become image.
Mean only what they are used for
in the poem. I use that word
to mean any high peak point of

creation. *Semina.*
Wally Berman. Thrown on the wind

of *Spring,*

he says, looking
at his own picture. Narcissus, we are
all, us. That boy
looking in the mirror.

Of his lake,
of his eyes,
let me sing.

The new order, the new poem, the new form,

keeping pace

with space
not leaping ahead, but

looking behind too.

Wouldn't you. I reveal nothing

here but

the wind is a guitar a wave that washes
against the shore

of this house, 707

Scott Street.

Stoned.

AUG 19

ASP

There is so much to watch. Around here. The matador
at sunset
the cross
across the crown the town
on top. Rheims Dauphin on horse
races to
HELL (the moon!
23rd
APOGEE

at once get out
Leave at 3PM.

means "Greenwich is the initial
meridian"

AUG 24 SUNDAY

Across the eye come images from another world. They slide on and off the screen. Bits of tree, four fingers, a silver scissors. They twist and coil with a shape, a life of their own. Seaweed.

I am a spy from another scene, sent here to steal your secrets. Do not speak them before me.

I see two leaves
Soon they are three.
Who is the woodsman
That cuts down my tree?

The show's over now. The drug has entered our heads and there will be peace. Or the black magician rules over my head. There are other things to do I think than write this. Images flash again. Language gives way or is funneled to the tongue there to dart out as a viper when the right fly lands before its eye.

Colored paper rose, blue spots, ink spots Boston in 1949, the sound of cellophane. The sky is brought down. A black boat scudding in a purple fog. My life with all sails a-furl, the small town
left behind, a new soul on the horizon.

Mark it, make it
your own.
Catch up with the colors, be extravagant.
Spend all that you find
Shimmy the horizon.

THE GALLERY

BY KATE SIMON

DAVID TRINIDAD

ACCESSORIES

for Beauregard Houston-Montgomery

Vinyl fashion doll
comes with swimsuit, pearl earrings,
sunglasses and shoes.

•

Pastel slip, panties
and strapless bra come with comb,
brush and "real" mirror.

•

Baby dolls come with
"Dear Diary," brass alarm
clock and wax apple.

(Note: Ken's pajamas
come with same clock, glass of milk
and wax sugar bun.)

•

Sheer negligee comes
with pink pompon scuffs and stuffed
dog for Barbie's bed.

•

Robe comes with shower
cap, soap, "Hers" towel, powder
puff and box of talc.

(Note: Ken's robe comes with
white briefs, "His" towel, sponge and
electric razor.)

•

Sunback dress comes with
chef's hat, apron, four uten-
sils and potholder.

•

Blue jumper comes with
black plastic serving tray and
two soft drinks and straws.

(Note: straws are extreme-
ly difficult for Barbie
collectors to find.)

•

Turtleneck and skirt
come with scissors, needles, yarns
and "How to Knit" book.

◉

Cotton dress comes with
cartwheel hat, necklace, tele-
phone and fruit-filled tote.

◉

Nurse set comes with spec-
tacles, hot water bottle,
cough syrup and spoon.

(Note: "Dr. Ken" comes
with surgeon's mask, medical
bag and stethoscope.)

◉

Checked shirt and jeans come
with wedgies, picnic basket,
fish and bamboo pole.

◉

Brocade dress and coat
come with corduroy clutch, fur
hat, gloves and hankie.

◉

Pink satin formal
comes with mink stole, pearl choker
and clear glittered pumps.

◉

Leotard, tutu
and tights come with pink shoe bag
for ballet slippers.

◉

Waltz-length party dress
comes with petticoat, picture
hat and sequined purse.

◉

Sleek nightclub gown comes
with black gloves, bead necklace, mi-
crophone and pink scarf.

◉

Wedding dress comes with
veil, graduated pearls, blue
garter and bouquet.

(Note: ring, on tiny
satin pillow, comes only
with deluxe Wedding

Party Gift Set, which
includes Barbie in "Bride's Dream,"
Ken in "Tuxedo,"

Midge in "Orange Blos-
som" and Skipper in "Flower
Girl." Mint-in-box set

is scarce and consid-
ered quite a gold mine on the
collector's market.)

INVASION

Kevin McCarthy knows what is happening.
Unwittingly, he's discovered something odd:
Aliens are posing as human beings.

One by one, all the townspeople are changing.
It happens right after they give you a pod.
Kevin McCarthy knows what is happening.

While you sleep, the pod duplicates your body.
Crackling, your flesh shrivels into a lifeless wad.
Aliens are posing as human beings.

When you wake up, you don't have any feelings.
You look perfectly normal, but you're a fraud.
Kevin McCarthy knows what is happening.

Franticly, he runs through the streets screaming
Run for your life! They're here! They're here!
  Oh my God!
Aliens are posing as human beings!

He knows he can't take speed and drink coffee
forever. Eventually, he'll start to nod.
Kevin McCarthy knows what is happening:
Aliens are posing as human beings.

TRACY SILANO

THE FUGITIVE

If it always meant that they would speak to one another as if they were strangers. To the point, I went out alone and from there on in was sure that alone was the one way it could ever be. No, if there was a housewife who thought about being trapped in the house, if she didn't know what was going on outside, not even what she could see out her window or learn from the television or rented video cassettes. Out of character with herself she wouldn't go to the supermarket or post office. Not to the local bar for a drink. They liked the local bar because they could walk home drunk. They liked the local stores because they recognized all the faces. They saw all the old familiar people, the blood lines. They don't consider it inbreeding, that's why they mention certain family names. That way there could be no chance.

It's not just a jumble. They always meant to get along with the others, of course they couldn't plan a bad attitude. Not trying to sound like I look down on those kinds of things, as if I don't do it myself. That's not true. It's more to the point to say that I don't do it myself, and so I don't understand it fully if at all. But it does seem silly, maybe that is because it isn't something I do. Like I said before. I would only strive to be an insider.

You come with your fugitive. When he cuts the cards. He's cutting the cards, I'm hoping I get a good hand. There's a man sitting next to me. He has a good hand, has been dealt that way. The other guy to my right is not doubting that he will win in spite of his hand. Then if you don't know their certain way of playing cards, sit out.

The boss doesn't think he's the right man for the job. To get into this place you have to prove you're one. It shouldn't be a matter of proof, and she mentioned that if it's obvious then no one will stop you. My mind is at ease knowing it.

MERCEDES ROFFÉ

I can't drink
I can't eat
I can't smoke the foot of a vertical lamp
  like
an acrylic lizard at the bottom of a vase
A stupid vase
A stupid poem
An obfuscated
  obedient
  obscene
  persecution
A caution so excessive
  We speak of asphyxia
I spoke of asphyxia
  a way of being close until
  the pictures made an eco
        in a mirror
  obfuscated
  obedient
  obscene
The naturalist inheritance
Pantomime of father
  pantomime of mother
  pantomime of a buried score

in the shade of a beech tree
Pantomime of a doll pantomimically broken
(Mrs. Lenci,
your daughter
enjoys perfect health in the
State of...)

Someone will train the dogs
I'll train the dogs
and yet
Yet and not withstanding and
even more
The dog won't find us
and yet
Who can assure that it won't find us
A missing hand
a leaf of music paper
the shade of an elm
Soul, dear little soul
another story
It will be distracted
It will get lost
It's not a fairy tale
The gods won't be
so partial to us
It will wander
They'll suffice
the leftovers of a supper
Even more
I can say that I've already died
I can say that you've already died
Even more
the dawn has already come
We've already died
"I've died," I said
I asked you
I told you
Dawn won't come
Dawn has come
I've died
We've died
I can see
a dog that wanders
comes
not withstanding
it won't make it
it won't matter
confusing the broken hand
It won't be necessary to unearth scores
It won't matter whatsoever
another story
Your laughter will laugh
the stained glass will explode
the lamps will be lit
It won't make it
I can hear
your laughter
how couldn't it turn its snout
The moon with its bloated cheeks
It won't make it
Like salt in water
Like a cupula of ice in the sun
Like an obfuscated mirror

Like an obedient dog
Like obscene graffiti
It won't make it
From one city to another
From your laughter
A statue of a dog in the road.

— TRANSLATED BY
K.A. KOPPLE

MAROSA DI GIORGIO

from
THE MARCH HARE

My mother is an exquisite nun, a duchess, at the center of the oval horizon within whose perimeter small pumpkin plants appear with their perfume of roses, jasmine branches and cat wings.

Thus, she has a look of paradise. And she governs me with her thousand blue eyes, her thousand black eyes, watchful and singing.

✲

Carob beans, with excessively sweet pods, little "Christmas pears." The vehicle so delicate it scarcely existed above the weeds, with fugitive poppies and other flowers, of such a radiant vermilion that I never saw anything like it again.

There were vegetables among the weeds, the work of the wind, or a passerby. A yellow, pink carrot shone brightly as it walked past with its hat of green feathers. There were onions like somewhat intoxicated women wrapped in gauze scarves. The rotund potato was jealous of the slender beans which had pearls, porcelain, inside of them. Southern wind. Northern wind. I couldn't figure it out. An incredible murmur came from everything. Red, blue and reddish kites flew high above. They were everywhere, so delicate, so angelic, beyond all things.

I don't recall the significance of this trip, where we were going, the arrival.

I believe I am still traveling.

This potato mumbles something. With its mouth of fire, that rose answers.

✲

Hundreds of windows and doors, windows and doors, in the familiar, unfamiliar, house where mother appeared at once in all the bedrooms, her hair pulled back, loose, dressed all at once in white, black, pink. And the golden sky, and the groves of amethysts and agates grew like fires. I eat branches, stone rosebuds. And at dawn, the jars of lilies, the jars of tiny fetus, are everywhere.

Here and there, the horror and the glory.

✲

Incidentally, why am I a nun? Dogs and gazelles run in the depth of the countryside and they order me about like guards, stars. Why can't I be a woman and yes a fairy? Every day I eat off a plate of memories. I have no home. They destined me to the rainbow but I'm tired of this strawberry-colored ribbon, and this other green one. When I think I'm free to take a few steps, and that something for me is also true, dogs and gazelles appear and they order me about like guards. Don't they see my white dress, my diadem of a newly married bride without a husband to be, without a mate? Why can't I be a woman and yes a fairy?

I believe I have both feet on the ground. I believe that something for me is also true but I'm immediately confronted by this forest, this tree, which has pearls instead of leaves, butterflies instead of leaves. Everything I touch falls and shatters and sparkles. Everything I touch runs far away.

And there will never be a solution.

And there will never be any answers.

The birds sing, they sing
with all of their trills, warbles
(And they make me afraid.)
After the rain, it's mid-day.
Now all seems to be lost beneath the water.
Solitary days will come.
A very white, very white;
terrible concentration of hares.

We go along the wall.

Mama has brown, silky wings; I, violet wings; when opened various shawls of gauze can be seen. We proceed along the rampart; with the daintiest of antennae touching little branches, boughs, of balsam, of parsley, and other things.

We seem free of vexing fellow beings.

The moon is, with each minute, whiter and darker. And shining over the entire meadow, here, there, the Virgin of the Insects.

With wing and diadem and many, many feet.

— TRANSLATED BY K.A. KOPPLE

BY BILL BECKLEY

DAVID SHAPIRO

BURNING INTERIOR

To Tory Dent

of a copy of nothing
or more precisely a series
of xerox sketches of
burning interior-exteriors
No one guesses in that rotted century
not nothing but grey hints in
crayon flecks for bitter
perspective produced by a reproductive
machine looking at itself as usual
askance all the black windows blur
into a recessive landscape of
secondaries O like the gate into your flowers
forty-seven tulips shy of counting
then expanding into the scandalous
world since there is one
to die quickly in color in the tub
like Marat smiling and stabbed near the name of art

not Skelton to the Present but the child's future
from skeleton to the President
in this no-place
for any angel's perverb ("the hole in my heart leads to the hole

that is God — which is deeper")
next modulating with words "grey and pink
always work" when the
bedroom doesn't the Tolstoyan hanging
in the sonata of bilingual *espressivo*
repercussions of a hymn to
death in variations of an unearthed
happiness in lieu of rondo
when the circle was smashed by the hymn
(no one deserves better to leave
that model of a house) where you say
I will be kept crucially updated
but the undated "soul" held together
as if by black hinges or
murdered city's black snow I cannot see
But I see the pages of your books
opening wildly like the unfinished tulips
the excess and potlatch of the sun
Return, return to me
lost student of the plague

OLD POEMS

Sinking, below the star-several harps
of evening, in one distant garden,
the new poem, twisted from the skin of the old whining birch —
Perhaps I am also dedicated to an angel's memory
her long black hair collected in my bed.
Now the youngest poet cries, I love countdowns! I love
the last few seconds of joy!
But the old poet knows the error in transcription
is correct: Nirvana is *some sorrow.*
Remember our last hacked Ariels
lie ruined in their melody. Two poems, folded, twisted together.
The earliest song: Because you have joined me
this great tree was felled. Is it worthless?
Because you have joined
never to leave again
spring has become the spring I had hoped for
and this crooked pebble is singing in the forest.
But the new poem, the winter flower, is not sweet.

WILD PSALM

for Michal Govrin

In another world, listening to a Yemenite dump
Dreaming of Jerusalem our popular flesh,
A sleeper a singer whose name is a triple pun
A language where skin would be light,
It all sounds like the king's first love.
But in this world we sit to translate.
God splits and the blind man's reference
Ends like the war ever not quite.
As we forget the grammar we are of red clay, an idiot.
The suppliants approach, on the field of untranslatable force.
Simone says n-thing but: Poetry
More difficult than mathematics, as I warned you.
And the old poets, and the books appear themselves,
Holiness in Sin, which enraged Gershon — the doubled books
And the body's words: Blessed is He who created the creation.
Blessed are they who created the blessing.

BEN MARCUS

THE DEATH OF WATER

It is a soft, malleable, ductile, iron-grey fluid with hexagonal or cubic ice structure. It is slightly harder than air. It is the most abundant of the RARE-WATERS of group IIIb of the water graph. It does not tarnish rapidly in dry grass but quickly loses its luster when swallowed. It oxidizes slowly in ALBERT and rapidly in LOUISE. It is attacked by solutions of RICHARD 3 and by concentrated or dilute SAMANTHA 7G. When heated it burns with a brilliant flame to form a river that exhibits fishes and stones and is used in shuttling the seven primary, liquid emotions to the BEHAVIOR FARM. The steam is used as a core for the carbon arteries of OHIO. The element forms relationships with ancient water. An alloy of water is used as the flint in house films. Minute particles of this water ignite in the air when scratched from the surface of the larger mass. Its death is assembled by electrolysis of the drinking glass or by reduction of the fused canoe with sand. Death was realized in 1807 in the water as a new erosion by Carolina and by England and Thompson; it was named for the hills and swells in Deerborne, which had been killed only two years earlier. The nearly complete funeral was not produced until 1875, afterwhich waterfalls and streams and bodies of further water began to gush down and dribble and then stop, as the sky's eulogy declined and graves on all sides began their fluid opening.

WHERE BIRDS HAVE DESTROYED THE SURFACE OF FATHERS

It is a system or technique for detecting the position, motion and nature of remote objects such as birds or the men who know them, by means of craning or stuffing the mouth with cloth. It was developed independently in most countries. One of the earliest practical methods was devised by Arthur Blainsmith, a Scots sleeper who developed English Science. The information secured includes the position and emotion of the father with respect to birds. With some advanced methods the shape of the father may be surrendered. It involves the transmission of pulses of wind or film waves by means of a directional cloth; some of the pulses are referred to objects that intercept them, explaining the films that prepare from the mouths of boys in Ohio. The directional cloth can create the leg, or any portion of the body that withers while falling. In order for success, however, the mouth must be crammed with it. It must be gnashed, chewed, bitten or gnawed. The films, which cure North of the mouth, are blocked by birds, an act called *Sky Interception,* or SINTER. The range of the father from the son, or the son from the bird, is determined by measuring the time required for the bird to reach the cloth and begin pecking. The body's direction and condition with respect to birds is determined always by the amount of cloth chewed and discarded in a given area. This cloth is called *Blain;* it will cause a bird to collapse in the air. In most instances, the spray of pulses is continually projected over constant fathers, rendering men on the landscape that birds can recognize. Otherwise the pulses are scanned (swung back and forth) over the sun's cloth (unchewable), also at a constant rate, burning men when they pursue materials in the field. When the boy chews upon the land-cloth, the bird will swoop down upon its father to introduce a beak into that man's surface. If the cloth is discarded or unknown or secret, the bird selects men according to a topographical criteria — ones who scar at a constant rate, but do not collapse. When the sky is created, it is done so with four colors and a wooden object of indeterminate size and shape, and a horse drags a man over the angels to watch it begin. The sky accelerates according to the rate of cloth chewed per day. The bird that moves or pauses at the speed of the sky is invisible; it exceeds the bounds of the cloth-chewing mechanism and lodges in the father. The son may chew cloth and swallow his own garments; he may also self-eat or scheme upon the cloth of another, or he may retch cloth from his mouth and collapse, but no act will dislodge this bird, buried in the father, which will peck out an exit and not use it. In these scenarios the internal bird views the son from within its nested cavity. It watches him as it controls the father. It brings the man's hands up, works the jaw, pours water into the voice. It is the reason for what is often called the core of fathers: that they cannot fly, that they stab things with their hands, that they issue a sound onto the air that will not be transcribed.

SUSANA CERDÁ

DON'T RETURN . . .

I

Oh, mo ther look ma
ma there's
more than we foresaw:
the cupboards full of
the walls overloaded
with white
the beds so clear
the fabric so tightly stretched
Don't return the gaze
Look:

The words are in surplus
They're idle.

II

Right there fa ther
We won it
May it be sacred: the SHOUT
Here!
Do you hear
how my ears
how the chains
groan
the harvest is a cloud
Hear The Sound
of locusts
— such darkness! —
but whatever happens
Their color is green.

III

Hear the sound
— broken the —
Give
give equally
give your throne
to the nobleman

may they be united
see now: "to the Noble of the South:
Freedom!"

And the freemen answer
the Great: "To die or
We swear welcome."

IV

Hey hear the adage
I've written you
It's in rough draft
Don't
Don't return
it to final copy

V

Thrown
into the Red hot fire of the blacksmith.
I'm still alive.

He picks among the irons
looking for his knife
to put it into the fire
to make it: a dagger.

To break the broken chains
to see the ties leaking
the iron of this blood.
Ferrous blood
of iron, they say
the man was made
of iron.
He who branded the Red
Count his wounds.

He wandered
wandered lonely
at ease
they say
in The Outskirts.

VI

There were weapons and tools, between which, therefore,
They distinguished by usage.

VII

We won it, father.
We
won it
father,
or we will.

Hadding had
Having
If it has
Hah!

How much it costs for the Splendor
to shine.

— TRANSLATED BY MOLLY WEIGL

BY MARILYN HUMPHRIES

KATE RUSHIN

PARALLAX

In another life
desire turns inside out
voiceless somersaults

In the next, blank
as stones, we drop fantastic
beneath containment

In another life
we are veins and arteries

In this life
words fishline from our mouths

WORD PROBLEMS: THE POST-COLONIAL, POST-INDUSTRIAL, POST-MODERN, HOMOEROTIC, AFROCENTRIC AFFAIR IN LATE CAPITALISM AFTER A LONG, LONG WINTER

If a train departs at 10:20 pm
traveling south and another train
departs at 10:10 pm headed north,
what time will it be when we finally
take haven in an indulgent bed
marooned in a multi-national hotel room
overlooking Central Park?

How many hours will it be before the edges
soften and we walk through the park, smile at
strangers we wrongly assume to be
New Yorkers, sit in overpriced cafes,
sip international coffee drinks and cognac,
regard male nude portraits executed by
Sigmund Freud's grandson hanging in the
Metropolitan Museum of Art? What time shall we
return to room service remote and bourgeois bed
the dubious privilege of somebody else compelled
to make it? The next morning, exposed in our 1970s
campus-style Afro-Am cultural nationalism,
we'll overtip the Third-World-Woman cleaning staff
then see each other off at Amtrak
just in time to make it back to our good jobs.

Somewhere between the maxed-out credit cards,
mini-bar and starched linens, two grown colored women
inscribe a story. It's a story some brother with an agenda
declared didn't exist due to inauthenticity. Some white woman
declared it interchangeable with hers and some white man
reported it was not in evidence; we'd never crossed his mind.

Yet, here we are: the last generation
raised by 19th century women, the link between
our great-grandmothers in bondage and our
daughters in cyberspace. No wonder
we're standing here wondering; inhabitants of a land
everybody wants to occupy, but nobody wants to imagine.
As our daughters and sons set out on the
MTV artificial intelligence information superhighway
we haunt the crossroads. We're on the watch to pass them
a few books, a few photos, a few stories, a few words;
a broach, a piece of cloth, a song, a prayer,
a pressed flower; a feather, a shell and a bone.
We maintain that the elite have nothing going for them
except money technology and gall, all the while
hedging our bets: *Got to learn those computers.*
You'll go to that private school if I have my say.
We just can't risk stranding our children in that
so-called underclass we used to call home.

But like I said, there's nothing disembodied,
not what I'm talking about.
Sign your name. Turn off that television.
This ain't one of those nihilistic moments
lit by the despairing blue light of the tube.
Find ourselves? Lose ourselves?
I don't claim to know the difference.
There's nothing to lose we haven't lost more times
than we thought possible. Let's not hesitate or wait.
If we're lucky we'll get a corner room high enough to
catch a glimpse of the moon to remind us of other shores.
Put on some Nina or Coltrane,
Find Abby Lincoln on the FM stereo.
Incense, candle flame, papaya and cowry shell
mark the boundaries. This body is home.
Look here. This is the lush life, only for a minute.

Your train is traveling
south at 73 miles per hour.
Mine is headed north doing 68.
How long will it take us to arrive at
our separate definitions?
What time shall we begin, for real?

JENNIFER MOXLEY

FIN DE SIÈCLE GO-BETWEENS

There you are in the hinterland chiseling
Nations into the ocean as I await
torrential winds. We've left footprints
for the Native informers of narcissism
to uncover once we've fled. From now on
out of work jesters can jingle gun toters
while I get on with the eros of coastal waters.
I hold your lesser self a bird of paradox,
portable like fondled space mistaken
for a sign of life. They are lined up
on the border towns heavy with wisteria
so if ever lip service paved the planet
then focal me now, jettison that charm however
and we could be the end of something gathered.

KALYPSO FACTO

The matrix of your hamstrung home-life
is undercutting all my generous gifts.
The current temper is such that soon
even the most bedlamite among us
will be threatened by marriage. These
unalienable boundaries are bringing distrust
to all frolickers. Now the clouds show Zeus
is arriving to muck us up even further.
That hopped-up interventionist is thieving
all my island's hidden treason. His loud
armaments have been making petit fours
of continents for far too long. Now you
who once found me dainty are eloping
with Enyo. Your indiscretion may dress-up
progress in money lending but trembling
at the horizon I hear those othered lands.
We're all entangled in your strong-arm, but
fault me if we don't coalesce to curb
your second guessing with a dose of our jilted memory.

THE WAVER IN THE ORBIT OF THE PLANET URANUS BECOMES UNEXPLAINABLE

I ask you, is it fitting to undo me by leaving
now that we know there's nothing out there
beyond what we can see?
I admit I suffer from a "parallax of heart"
born of skewing jealousy and seen most nights
in field-weary gazing at your sleeping body.
From that angle everything seems bleak.
However I will not call on heaven now,
for I know that spirit is a one-eyed pretender
to the throne of painless living
who has stolen all my daydreams for a shot at the beyond.

I suspect the water's edge is enamored of the water,
a quiver on the surface tells me not the wind
but the wish to drift will devastate the sand.
It is the future's focal infection
this insistence on death, like when my mother
and father cradled me as the answer
to each other's desperate tread towards union.
For this is a universe where things
are not apparent in their cruelty but continual,
and the sweetness of order is increasingly evanescent.
It would be nice if I could hide this day
forever from the pleasure of renewal
and banish all contingency, but I've never
seen planet X or the ships on the eastern horizon.
My life has up until now faced west,
sequestered reason reaching for an injudicious kiss.

JASON SCHWARTZ

STORIES FOR BOYS

The Aunt

This was the first one. So, you must understand, there was harm after all — oh, yes, and all the fuss, and this bit of hair in the cold, crooked and worn, dear me, curled this way when she was ill.

The crepe was kept — it is not yet hopeless! — and part of the shirt was perhaps moist, though the cuff was stiff about the ends, though the strip was bent and left, too — oh my, but how the rest of this is bunched and precious: Their hands were at the collar.

But certainly he looked — now here was some of his mother's sash — fine; like, that is, her husband — or, if you would prefer — more simply — his father. It is so sad, this row! It is hopeless — though she wore her mother's gown — a cur, she said — snug here, a piece, you see, held: but here, unhappily, it was black.

The orchestra played in the garden.

The Uncles

Well, yes — eventually. Please understand there was only a gesture, really. Oh, the question, presumably, of the wrinkle; the cackle; the Danube. (Loss — of a sort.) They never came for the summer.

The flowers were worn in just this manner — or, if you like, as his were then. There were fewer, indeed, every time. These, clearly, were from Derbe — though they were tangled, though they were not pinned properly.

Well, the noise and wane in the aisle that day; a mole, you will recall; a stake, mumped, in the quack grass, in the neat square, in the tier of flowers: his were amiss. A ringlet of his hair moved handsomely (and nobody saw).

The Daughter

The trunk was purchased by her family. The brass handles at the sides looked — her mother said — like a queen's bosoms. A pox! (They did not go away on holiday anymore.) The wood was scraped next to the wire and across the nice curlicues in their names — hers first.

Their last name was — the bride said — homely. The chiffonier, nevertheless; nevertheless, the ruffle, the peach pit (prattle, merely). Was she standing in this fashion? Well, it is only such a tiny thing — but in any case.

It was because she was terribly sweet — or rather, actually, because it was a pity. He touched her wrist: What a lovely thing! Wraps and strands sallied back thusly. It was gay. The children were darling. Thump, thrump, thoom — they reached the busy avenue. (The trunk was taken to the harbor.)

The Nephew

Well, yes, all right — woe. It is true: Their lives had already gone by. But, moreover, there was the knurl in the collar of his shirt. A part poorly sewn. A bow-tie; pomade.

Well, yes — the sorrow to see them. It was a morning — this we know. It was not a perfect day. Oh, the shivering, in fact; the worry. The wedding was made the way her mother's wedding had been made. It is silly of us, after all: a knoll, the coaches — this notion, in other words, of something old.

Yes, of course — the matter of the altar. The ghastly slit of sleeve touched her arm. The family stood in a row, henceforward. The flowers shuddered as such. Well, certainly — he touched his mother's gown. (There was a tiny mark.)

The Nieces

The Brussels lace was lost. Is it necessary to mention the wicks? (They were bitter.) The dale? (It was green.) The waltz? (What a happy thing!) Some children threw rocks at the tails of a coat. Men were shooting ducks: Oh my goodness! The groom swooned.

But where were they standing? But what does it mean, the touching of the arm? They came down the aisle with mice at their feet — is that the song? (It was dreadful, of course, the way the steeple and the hill vanished behind the bend forever.)

Well, nevertheless — the trilly cobs, the veins: and, heavens, the thin ribs. But may we return to the girls? To the groom's voice? (It was awful, the sound his name made.)

The Sisters

But here!: the horrible shapes in the creases of the blouse. The tragic jut of the plumes. The amusing history of the hobble skirt. (The sisters went away afterward, in other words.)

Bathing robes for hire — a sign — and caps, naturally; it was warm there — oh, and the water, the trees along avenue: and the little flapping, sometimes, in the shops' awnings. (The bride and groom went to Lorouse.)

Chatter and a sigh, a cough, as it happens — chocolate, oh dear, these dirty hands, these sleeves, something just a bit torn, after all, tucked in, folded, turned back, flattened. He was small and still a little cold. (The ladies came and played whist every afternoon.)

The Son

But yes, naturally — the threshold. It was fine inside. It was nice and warm, all right: the mouse and safe and sound — is that the song? She had a plum, anyway, and a truffle — one day when she was eight.

The slant of her neck!: and the pock was dark. The hoop had a strap and a shiny hook. What a grave event! The bride's was — her mother said — as narrow as a swallow's.

Well, the pall in the bother; the gnaw and mewl, so to speak, in the wool. The terrifying stoop; the color at the windows; an odor. Mercy, how it was stopped (and settled).

The Aunts

This, then, was the last one. The bed was curtained this way — with, perhaps, birds and a fawn. There was simply a drooping post, drapery facing. There was no blood. Shall we put it another way? Oh, that it was not you.

Such gloom!, for instance, and the frame, the town. But let us not be silly — it is gone, this is all, and nevertheless the long hallway, the valance, the windowsill. Does she recall the visit to Disse? The brocade? But certainly the curl?

How he loved her! However, however — she left him. One went blind. One misplaced a bracelet. One sat for a portrait.

There was a sound at the stairs.

JOHN GODFREY

BY DANIEL KRAKAUER

POURING GULF

It's the road behind lets my star off the hook. It's lost up there in the night sky, part of a slipper designed in tiny white dots. From this curb I watch a woman in the back of a cab tuck her furry wrap around her neck. They call it a gulf, and it's pouring, man, it's pouring right between us now. What can you tell a guy who missed the chance to wire his mandolin, once the century starts to fall under the weight of its own sparks? Time has this shadow, and once I'm in that shadow, the shadow can't be said to have failed, right? I muscle in on a wall of snow that's the road ahead, pretending to breathe. A young woman plowing through the cold keeps pace with me, breathing even less. The only thing that can break my courage is memory. The tension in my hamstring comes automatically, it teaches me not to stop when full. Never go empty outside the curtain incense smoke sometimes provides, sometimes a chant. Young woman in line puts her cheek against the back of her partner's shoulder is a symptom. The passage across his face of a warm mask peeling off is the gulf again. I might as well read a bone in her face, or a line in his palm, forget about my star. Disappointment replaces the strong with strength itself. Every man-jack gets to be a wife this way. There's always a glow in the sky to implore, as if it were lying ahead instead of there forever in the past. Let me laugh, I think, forcing a smile. I'd lose anything, as long as lassitude falls away with it. Let's see if I can breathe through a wet sheet. Let's see how long you'll stay with me before I start staying with you. Farewell, though, is such comprehensive music I sometimes forget it takes humanity. Snow going dirty fast is like a measure, like a bar written down off an aircheck. The young woman lifts her cheek away, a hooded look over her eyes, a wave of some cello vibrates in a faraway of her own. Then she visibly adjusts to the tone like a stone to runoff. A piece of wood in her secret drawer patinaed with lacrimae. No wonder every sound she makes has more vigor than his. The way ahead of her is white, and all around her intense color. Loss is so becoming to youth, buried as it is in gain. And how beautiful a disguise is summer.

OCEAN FLEUR

Towers bobbing through distant space call to me what time is it? Cards skitter down through air toward me, half like fortunes, half like razor rotors out of fire-trap Chinese mansion doors. I am a time-and-a-half the man who stole your robot, I think, when devil juice comes to mind. Lift your thumb off me and the acid spills out of the lonely star closest to danger that grabs the heart in solitude. All the rest is some pyromaniac out to cheapen pain as a foundling thing. This guy, me, do not quail should musette weep out of dreams to follow one down subway portals come dawn, come deaf. What my blood weaves is a separate coat for the ghost in the orchestra pit. O, I do grieve these aerosol oaths that bind mind to flesh when sleep coasts in and out of me, like light's first spray across bedding, or across an avenue's shore in an early dusk. I lift this pain as one of privilege, my arms extend a scratched gold tray embossed with pollens upward to South Pacific winds. I contain dolor, its rupture and all. What I breathe thins in the dark that pleads me to the underneath stuffs a mannequin bears. My mountain heals the failure of my bird with volcanic sheaves. What weight falls so heavy as hair I only touch once? In icy black waters wings pass with an elegy, in disregard of all explanations. A seizure throws me from my coral throne, and when I wake the beauties of the mosque that looms over me blind my remaining eye with flakes of gem. I have been washed by the hands of an assassin and left to live. By the lulling sea no wings more heroic than those of a moth. In my life there is no capacity for sleep, or cloth the color of skin under dust to remind me of it.

THIS BIG WINGSPREAD

What I know of saviors is, first they weather contempt. One of them finds dark to sleep in under threat of the knife usually whetted up to shaft lizards. With every beating it seems a new bodyguard appears to lend him something like chastity. What was at first poignant about the passion he brought to the foot of the bridge becomes more believable, and clownish, when he is awaited in the cold and rain by those with the gift of gathering to hear. The savior walks out the door and doesn't have to take a number and wait. Light, whether from a cloudy sky or from torches, distinguishes his class of eloquence from the complications of mere words. A demagogue increases in value with the ability to plunge the listener's thoughts into pitch, after sating them with brilliance. Have you ever, comprehending and exhausted, felt yourself to be seeded with poisons, when in fact the emotions you can't describe pull you upwards by the scruff, like out of an ashcan? Remember, you, not the savior, are a creature. Torn pieces of cloth tied to sharpened bamboo stakes half buried in sand — that's all that's left to show for the tribe that gave you a savior. The people you, a creature, come from still litter the ground around the place where they eat with petals from tiered brambly beds gone wild. Long ago, they dug in just far enough up the river for the water to go by quiet and not too slow. In dry hot times the flow tastes of salt, like blood does in the drama of mothers and kings. Re-enacting the horrible deeds that sharing a fire among siblings brings about is what molds worship and makes it something to drink out of. Down by the river at night, lit by a fire, generation after generation using the same speeches, though the clothing might change. Waves of light on the actor's face as he speaks to his mate, neither of them in the least like a ghost, however distant the story-line. It's hard to believe that after a show like this anybody could fall for a statue shows up that doesn't spring from the same messy place as we do, that's supposed to keep us from repeating the mistakes that are all we identify with. A body that doesn't move, covered with gold, is what to me? Without this savior shit I could get on with a lament that laps up my real blood. I could worry about the claw flying in the dark over my head on a night I'm not under a roof, and in a dream this big wingspread could make me feel rich, or could make wake me up to stalk down my own brother. Without this savior shit I could be walking miles to see a man who hangs crystal in the mouth of baby at sun-set to see her cheeks glow with all eight colors. Story has it we never got to the river in the first place until a woman in a cave dreamt of a string that glowed in the dark, running a trail all the way to the muddy bank. Night after night, squishing around in the dark on half rotten fruit, and one night that phosphorescent line through the grass showed. Did she for even one moment take that for a trip to make single? She couldn't go alone, however good she was at mimicking a whole family in the dark. So a gang of them — of us — set out wearing skins because the canopy of trees at night was ruled by deadly fur-bearing muscle. Well, by the time I come along it's a bunch of women, eyes peeled for their sailors to pop out of the horizon. And today I'm leaning on a chainlink fence and it's a woman dipping her wings about eight miles high. You'd think this would be warning enough for any fookin' savior, fercrissake. If a body can't give cloth a shape and talk with color, then it's time to suck the musty air out of it and fold it away in the crema-tion box. I don't know about you, but I can hear a speaker punching words out deep inside. It's the nature of this speech to seek out its mate in the same cave, after the same picnic, next to the same old fire. I pick up a scrap of wood and find a patch of wet bare dirt to scratch the Chinese character that renders what the king says. What he says is a classy way of asking his mate what she's been doing lately with her sugar. I can hear the mate too, and she's beginning to tell him back exactly what she *has* done, and in what bed. This is truly what makes my heart bleed gas to my fingertips, this humping duet of dread.

LAURA MORIARTY

THE CASE

ARGUMENT

ink, pencil, crayon, talcum powder and chocolate

It means nothing other than "to close," as the eyes do after seeing

An imitation of events

With a transparent name

What will probably happen next is described elsewhere

A loss of dignity and of humility

Later it was hilarious to look back at that chance

In order that one might hear what it was forbidden to hear

The cost of initiation

The idea of possession, the obsession with payment

Things that were worn are displayed and used

Here the innumerable paths that lead to the underworld meet

The ones who preside over these mysteries are not unaware of their significance. Their task is to facilitate the immediate exchange. They can't allow themselves to be distracted by history.

There is a small structure around which a building is eventually assembled.

A photograph of a door

The official, the deity, oneself, the city, the users, the boxes, the case

The disclosure

Or, in the present case, *nothing* reappears, searching for her *nothing*, for a part of herself in her *nothing*.

It can be inferred from the testimony

He seems to hover musing, before his subterranean journey

His eyes are closed and he is leaning against a rock.

Automatically, words are repeated that soothe us

Dragging himself back to the present, he scribbles dutifully on a piece of paper

Comedy. Looking for the wall, he runs into the door.

He occupies the city in an unknown and then in a completely known way.

She is his companion in the search

The speech

A wasp heavy with heat. Which side of the glass are we on?

We are aware of the demands of our connection

What is said remains functionally untrue, that is to say unacknowledged. Nevertheless it is this information she acts upon.

Though he ignores her mythological attributes, he knows of them

He is the agent of the underworld in the old sense

Because they speak different languages she has to repeat — every repetition exposing a different hole in her story

The telling superceded itself. It was over before beginning. It was neither literal nor genuine.

The peeping occurs through the holes.

THE BOX

The contents of the first box are entirely written.

The box is a notebook.

There are several notebooks, each deciding the case a different way.

There are facts.

The fact of being the woman left in the room, representing death and paradise, holding the lamp against the sun

An element of "real" reality is incorporated. It designates both a pattern and an objective, which have independent existence.

"And on the "French grass" he painted her"

He claims there is no ending because there is no case. It is open-ended.

She respects him for counting the money

WIDOW

As it begins again there is a reenactment which produces something from her throat, a sound. This is a familiar threshold in her thought. It seems necessary to possess all the facts and to account for them with multiple narratives. She wants, especially, to account for the impossible explanations which are left, according to the old dictum, after the possible are eliminated. Looking back, what seems impossible is that the event has occurred at all.

"She sat: she walk'd among the ornaments solemn mourning."

It is like every case in which the roles of the participants merge. They hold on to their identities, returning to their imagined security at the slightest provocation. This is where she has them. During the transition, information comes out. Her own loss of identity hastens the process. She is careless of her safety. She never feels safe. She and the others, the witnesses, especially the suspects, are hopelessly mingled. When most lost in the role, when most defenceless and overcome, something appears. She examines it like an addict fingering a half-burned empty vial. Hers is a vague but fixed concentration.

The picture of dust

The glass is netted with metal like a jail.

THE BRIDE

Thirty years later the fingerprints are still on the gun, the knife, the wall of the room

She sits in the room, sweating and considering the event. One can't be plain enough in the face of it. The evidence remains stubborn, mute before a shrieking which also obscures. "Is anything objectively true?" she wonders, picturing the world away from the crime.

He enjoys being the suspect, the witness, the priest, the victim.

The peeping occurs as he doesn't turn away. Who is it that is watching. Which of us would not?

The book is in the box. There is, on the glass table, a book in a box made of objects. The objects are not mementoes. They are the reduced and generic elements of a temple. They evoke memory in different ways. Like pieces in a game, props for a demonstration. They occupy a place between words and objects because they are small and enclosed, portable. We remember carrying them with us.

One of us has watched an object become separated from a word. The object is taken away. The word remains. The word, a name, has the qualities of being both soft and sharp. The name becomes interchangeable with something banal like anguish, but doesn't have the limits of such a term. It can mean joy. It often means simply that a stiff hand is held out.

She manages the emergency somewhat absently, though, even more than the victims, she is endangered by the situation. The thinking required is indirect, the requirement absolute. Mistakes are revealing in a direct ratio to the peril associated with them.

A man becomes silvered and settled. He has any name. What is in the middle of him? Is this what he calls his luck?

"This equanimity," he says "my politics, as you call them, cost me my life every morning as I wake up."

That small trickle of blood from the ear, certainly an indication of a mind in trouble, a heart in jeopardy. "But I am so happy," he said.

How could you have known me when I hadn't read that book?

There is a situation but it is not the one she has originally perceived. Her task is to keep involved in the case just enough to catalyze any aspects of it capable of being affected, while observing those whose existence will constitute the outcome. She is surprised to find herself in the latter realm.

One professional takes care of another.

If the objects in the box can be known, how much more so can our exchanges, my speaking, your way of making your hands burst like suns.

artiste defroque, la artista fracasado. An old series of communications means differently when finally found. Context in this case a kind of evaporating wetness. Huge thundering groans described in a sentence. How is it possible to describe the smell? The sweat and the moisture on the grass seem the same in retrospect

The Release

As an interrogator, she found her own silence embarrassing

The dust also settles and is redolent of a dusty world.

Things that are the case and those that are not merge. The difficulty remains. Because nothing fits into the new box, she finds herself carrying the old box around, throwing its contents into the ocean, reassembling them, finding statues there, collapsing, getting up, falling down.

An officer of the court executes a clown routine.

That she documents the event is fine. She can have me. She can consider this a verbal agreement. Witnessed by reeds whining in the background and the swimmers suffusing the foreground. One like a bird in a static wind. A ship floats in over the buildings. Gives up and returns.

An agent earns his pay for the week. An informant retains his honor. He unburdens himself. They know something together. Her own speech is persuasive but she skips that part. She is less present during each interview. Vanquished by her own interrogation. Her ability to be stunned wears out.

We look back on not being able to close the case as if from a thousand years. There isn't anything to say about it. The boat plods on in a trajectory that lacks the coherence of a crime story, though it has all of the elements. They shimmer forgetting to be present. What could bring anyone to such a point?

He regains his humility. She is recognized as having stuck with it. This seems like a promotion. The unsolved nature of the case is the institution they have become.

There is a stepped place like a mountain or a tent. A child carries a cake with the words "Don't know" written on it. The door to the office is left open. The lock untouched.

under construction

Peeping Tom

The hand of the artist is left out

THE ZIP COON BLUES

lost: 1 hep cat
last seen wearing a newly citified city slicker
over worsted wool polka dots of sound,
and a pair of pleated sheep bleats
in b baa baa flat

say boy, say boy,
have you any pull?

yassuh boss, yassuh boss
3 bags full . . . o'tea, ragtime reefer, and skunk weed
loose jointed trombone trill chromatics
that'll bring up the low register
(when yo brown got you down)
and the natural highs
(when yo yellows and whites are bright)
have you knockin' at the backdoor o' sweet mama stringbean
pockets full o' hamhocks n' greens

spin the chit'lins
and kiss me on my chicken lips
dese and dose
dem dere
der dey
dare he make a nigro wolf wet whistle at the cream in the
chesterfield kings?

if you see my mangy hep cat
and he not floatin'
swollen in no stream

PAUL BEATTY

BY DAVID GODLIS

carry him back to ol' virginny
where the darkies run free
and fear and the envelope play cards, possum, piano, and scrabble

then call me at
ALabama ALabama TEnnesee SWeden
let the phone ring once,
migrate north
then call me back

ALL ABOARD

on the last really nice day of spring
a solitary Nigger poet reads Nabokov in Newark
in front of the train depot   turning pages   furrowed brow   furrowed brow   turning pages

in the distance, the Nigger poet,
can hear the final call of the double breasted silk suited black muslim bird
flitting from tree to tree
through the cab stand forest

'paper today brother?' chirp 'paper today brother?' tweet
'paper today brother?' whippoorwill 'paper today brother?' not today brother thank you

the parrot places a talon on the Nigger poet's shoulder
'what chu readin', Nigger poet, the white man's trash? the white man's trash?' squawk
'you should be reading this, there is knowledge in this paper. we talkin' truth' coo-coo

the Nigger poet and the double breasted silk suited black muslim bird
stiffen and stare at each other
epoxy glued to different philosophical branches
stuffed Negro taxidermy stuck in the same downtown diorama

the Nigger poet notices the yellow bow tie clipped to the black muslim bird's neck
a tracking device
a tourniquet
holding back three years of prison
a five year old
a four year old
a fucked up day job

he is bleeding
flapping madly inside a shoebox
air holes in the lid
wounded   waiting for someone to nurse him back to health

riddle me this
q and a
peas and queues
do you know why so many black men died in vietnam?
because when the enemy was shooting at them, the sergeant would yell,
"Get down men, get down!" the black men would stand up and start dancing

the Nigger poet too is wounded
winged in the ego
fragged by a russian born novelist

who uses words like   *agglutinate, siliceous, gardyloo, ophidian, triskelions*

maybe Nabokov wrote the book around these words
maybe he took an ESL course at a local night school
and the teacher wrote those words on the board
"class, today's homework is to take these words and use them in a first novel
the New York Times will call 'Riveting, truly a classic for the ages'"

shadography, Lacedaemonian sensation, ocelate
the Nigger poet looks pale
dammit, gangrene is setting in

the Nigger poet buys a dollar's worth of newsprint sulfa powder pedagogy from the black muslim bird

Boy Scout First Aid (Page 98)
when the victim is bleeding profusely
apply direct platitudinal religious pressure and wrap in a false sense of security blanket to prevent shock

the bleeding continues
and the Nigger poet's wounds gush greek mythology and cliche

ethereal, frankincense, triptych, Agamemnon, Antigone, and epiphany

now he's frothing at the mouth
speaking gibberish
no, wait it's language poetry

riverwalk cigarette ash in transit
ceramic mastodon
exact change synaptic caution ixnay on the ententiouspray itingwray
oeticpay egmphlay
payday and ofay

the Nigger poet continues to shake from intimidation
'what's wrong, brother?' whoooo whoooo the black muslim bird asks
'i just want people to think differently' the nigger poet responds

'me too me too' cockle doodle doo 'then what are you waiting for Nigger poet'
'come back to the nest, mosque 11 what are you waiting for Nigger poet'

i am waiting for the 9:15 train back to the city

COSMOGRAPHY

: :

Dripping water hollows the stone

Decimal decible demonstrate

Ocean precedes argument

Spring withstands flame

Timbre barb radius

Plains sinking constant shifting

Uppermost and under water, is it lit from underneath

Axis borer molten

The goat's spindly hold on rock

On which house

Standing legs

And crumbling pause

MYUNG MI KIM

: :

Air water none gentle aligned

Supplicant and mendicant

Of the opening spaces of the opening itself

Aptitude round across

If one thing is seen and seen clearly and the effort to see it

Hummingbird in foxglove whir

Ocean reveals one boat

Chance to see it ocean and hummingbird

Speed and duration

:   :

Parts sway portend

Foregoing reason and appetite

Learning and expression, leopard and boar

Faculties, senses, to treatise add

Channel   churl   apace

Use shaped the names of things

Dense cipher and rhythm

Illustrations at the clumsy bar

Tonetic   periphery   perceptual

Parts agree disagree in single action

:   :

Those things that cannot be seen

Made of particles hooked one to another

Travel, give, deform

Bonding leakages

Gas to liquid, solid to liquid

Sequestered and communicative

Exchange defies observation

Bind   siege   transform

No movement independent of time

Addressed to no one. Globe and a model of the planets. Book of perpetual. Book of boulders. Ascending numbers. After each enunciation. In the first, what kind of education. In the second, crested jay to the front, *wabasah, wassah,* to the left. Sound as it comes. Alkali. Snag snag sang. Usher liberty.

TORY DENT

BROKEN CONSCIOUSNESS

The askance ocean darkens, anachronistically, and I admire its solidarity
although whitecapped from disparity as clouds will frequent the sky;
offsetting the tethered soil, the belovedness of what appears a handswept field.
I operate within a similar lexicon as desolate in inscription
identifying with disparity per se, i.e. sky, field, or ocean.
What I wish could hold me in a way I've only imagined
and experienced in the ubiquity of constancy offsetting fragmentation,
witnessed ad infinitum in the demonstration of a glass dropped and its shattering.
My mother, armless and decapitated, flies stationarily
at the top of a tiered flight, away from me, my continent sense of externality,
winged and victorious, perpetuates her ability to give
belatedly, a product of consequence, contrived as truth or whitecaps, my disparity.
What arrives D.O.A., a newt delivered by Mercury, nebulous as a sentiment,
parsimonious as a net that retains nil, I lunge forward anyway
and in such an empty gesture mark at least a gesture
the way a soliloquy must always locate itself in some vernacular.
Similarly, my longing replenishes itself within the canon of my longing,
though not solipsistically for longing by its nature makes up a disparity
between evidence and expectation that provides for my starving
a kind of feeding, a food forever deferred like virtual reality.
The closest I've ever come to closeness is to waiting
strung out as if suspended amidst the air into which her corpse has been flung
thus into marble and therefore into nothing.

BY ARNE SVENSON

Her would-be loving embrace fetters toward me, her alabaster lips
chiseled in perfect partition almost smile, and I reciprocate
with social reflex as an infant first mirrors the mother's face,
before cognition culturally fans out into recognizance,
before response moves beyond the automatic like a Roman calendar
into genuine remorse, into what love connotes before it gnaws away at the stomach.

CLASH

As if without agony the white convertible, a Mustang, peels along,
pierces the chiffon thin dawn, sheet by sheet,
white as white chocolate or a snow leopard's spots.

Far off people make love and moan as if in great pain,
but they're not, though their pleasure be pitched at an undetectable level
like a whistle only dogs can hear.

And I, as if a dog, hear it all,
hued yet whole in its spectrum, a hologram xeroxed to perfection
where the exaction of exhaust exhalation and heaves of passion
stack this cruel world upon its cruelty.
Their secretions smear their loins like white chocolate,
and from their eyes spurt white tears of pity.

I both watch and want to stop
the lovemaking bodies that wriggle with self-centered abandon
deep inside my body the way a dream does or hope will despite my cynicism;
pulling me to move by collar and chain
within my emotionlessness, motionless as a parked car,
a white convertible, a snow leopard devoured by dogs,
I both watch and want to stop.

DIANE WILLIAMS

DESPERATELY TRYING TO LIE DOWN

Sometimes you were held, fondled, commented upon, weren't you? Yet, I was told that nobody else had ever wanted you or had even asked about you, that I was the first one who had asked about you.

When I grasped at you, twisted you, I saw some strands of your hair, the rather imprecise sketch of your eye, the overwhelming importance of your eye, and one of your eyebrows desperately trying to lie down sweetly on your brow, and with this view in mind, your face is as composed as my vulva is. I would like to suggest that the smartest, the strongest, the most perfect person in the universe is my property.

I am the dark one, the short one, the thick one, the coarse one, who was yelling my head off at you because I am so unsatisfied with all of my arbitrary speculation.

You said, "Here, let me help you," and there was such a really happy expression on your face that you must have been happy.

LOVE SONG

He was half-afraid of her and he found her to be as undignified as a person who has a spiritual problem. He was upset by her understandably. He may have spoken.

The details of all of this were driving him crazy. He was keeping back his tears. Some of them he let fall.

He saw that the sky had changed and was nearly as nice as it had once been when he was young, when there had been a warm glow up there in the sky.

He was just too fond of her, and he disapproved of himself. On the third night, his helplessness still was making him anxious. All the next day, he was faithful to one recurring thought which was that he was half-afraid of her.

It was not yet dusk. Fearful because of the heavy winds which now were engulfing other people, he saw things being swept away and other people struggling to walk down the street. Junk was in the air.

There was an undignified commotion when his time was up. Some people don't like that.

THE BLESSING

I said so in the letter, but virtually anyone could have said so: *You will have everything you want. I don't want to get your hopes up and then disappoint you.*

He just loves me. I have a very bad temper.

I walk forward with the letter in my hand, wearing my black dress, which gently slaps at my legs as I walk forward. For about an hour, I wrote the letter with a dull, lead pencil. On the envelope, in ink, dutifully, I wrote the name, the address. The stamp is a large black and green one.

Life is curious. I drink half a glass of water. In the corner of the room, rather, in the center of the room, nothing any longer attempts to sing a song, or, on the other hand, is listless, actually sick to death, and will not recover. But, I don't mean this as an incitement to get you to go tell people that everything can turn out happy, wholesome, just wonderful.

One afternoon, when you are particularly tired, you sit down. You will be sitting down, or maybe it will be late in the evening, and you have missed your dinner, and you have missed your lunch, and you have missed out on your breakfast, too, and the weather is hot, so that you feel hot. It is an unhealthy climate, which is humid and stifling, and the air you breathe is unhealthy for you, and then, you obtain your heart's desire.

Many times a person seems fairly satisfied already, but is so unsuspecting.

PAM REHM

"TILL IT HAS LOVED"

Nothing before this stone may rest
Nothing is a home, at best
dumb beasts learn words
to kiss the places in remembrance
thus missing the graces of an entrance

As earth upon earth
Now a clod of heavy earth
Blood runs down on every side

And Thou, abiding messenger
or Thou, hidden in shadow
Is curse the purifying fire
or is water?
Out of a vessel to the wretched sufferer
A body in mortification
A body never the less
What it does intend to seek
unburied and loathsome
For it, Thou hast spoken
Burned to death, Thou
upon the bridge, upon the high bridge
The world in your shadow

✵

Alone, to dwell herein
and be alone wherein
a curse upon the dead

One darkens oneself

The bright eye dreaded
to the end of it
In ye and me, an enemy

The body, let down
in stillness

like a net, suddenly closes

A body of water
forsaken

✵

Nothing dwelling alone may exist
Nothing is at home amidst a consciousness
of malice
A consciousness possessed by what it does

To offer oneself forth
as earth upon earth

Out of a vessel Thou hast spoken
Thou, the only ghost betokening
a wounded breast

A wound nevertheless hidden

Afraid to give oneself
Afraid of oneself giving nothing

This alone remains

World without amends

Who will not be afraid
of her own foul name?

✵

Seem to see or be seen
An enemy, herein
And ye a world around

Eyes left to amending
the end oneself is offered

Blood runs down on every side
The first time a body dies

Now a clod of heavy earth

Nothing left to curse

To fall to want
To want to fall silent
The breast possessing one name

✵

Nothing after the stone may rest
Nothing is a home, at best
one name is burning up the breast
One name, nevertheless forsaking the end

One darkens oneself

To see and not be seen
A ghost in ye and me

Nothing remains alone

from

THE PEASANT'S DREAM

by Louis Aragon

translated by Simon Watson Taylor

LOUIS ARAGON'S 1926 novel *Le Paysan de Paris,* translated into English by Simon Watson Taylor as *Paris Peasant* (Exact Change, 1994), concludes with "The Peasant's Dream," a philosophical addendum Aragon wrote while the book was in proofs. The last flourish to this chapter is a series of maxims that the older Aragon — Aragon the good communist — described as, "leading towards a materialism which is not achieved in the final pages of the book, but only *promised* within the terms of a proclamation of the failure of Hegelianism, the loftiest of all those conceptions which allowed man to advance along the path of idealism." Aragon's goal of a materialist art would eventually lead him to the depressing style called Socialist Realism. But in 1926 Aragon had yet to formulate fully the ideology that would cause his break from Surrealism, and as he later admitted, *Paris Peasant* and his other works from this period are better described as "Surrealist Realism". These maxims, then, are Aragon's manifesto for a realism based on what might otherwise be considered unreality: the dream, the subconscious, the fantastic, the poetic image. As Aragon writes in the text that precedes the maxims,

How did the idea come about that it is the concrete which is the real? Is not the concrete, on the contrary, all that is beyond the real, is not the real the abstract judgment which the concrete presupposes . . . ? And does not the image, as such, possess its own reality which is its application to knowledge, its substitution for it? The image is not itself the concrete, of course, but the possible consciousness, the greatest possible consciousness of the concrete . . .

To which he adds, "One is then justified . . . in devoting oneself exclusively to poetic activity at the expense of all other activity." If Aragon himself ultimately failed to live up to this promise, it is no less compelling for it. The reasoning he employs is representative of the Surrealist conviction that poetic activity is not writing in broken lines, but attention paid to all things *via* their poetry.

BE QUIET, you do not understand me: I am not talking about your poems.

It is towards poetry that man is gravitating.

There is no other knowledge than that of the particular.

There is no other poetry than that of the concrete.

Madness is the predominance of the abstract and the general over the concrete, over poetry.

A madman is not a man who has lost his reason: he is a man who has lost everything except his reason. (G.K. Chesterton)

Madness is only an affinity, like reasonable with real. It is *a* reality, *a* reason.

I find scientific activity a bit mad but humanly defensible.

The consolations of logic.

No one has ever got around to saying: *What is needed is a logic for the people.* It's no concern of mine. But it could be maintained.

My concern is with metaphysics. And not madness. And not reason.

It matters very little to me whether or not I have reason on my side. I do not seek to be right. I seek the concrete. That is why I speak. I do not admit the right of anyone to question the premises of speech, or of expression. The concrete has no other form of expression than poetry. I do not admit the right of anyone to question the premises of poetry.

There is a species of persecuted persecutors known as *critics.*

I do not admit criticism.

It is not to criticism that I have devoted my days. My days belong to poetry. Make no mistake, sniggerers: I lead a poetic life.

A poetic life, pray engrave that expression.

I do not admit the right of anyone to re-examine my words, to quote them against me. They are not the terms of a peace treaty. Between you and me, it is war.

In 1925, the newspaper *Le Figaro* asked in its literary supplement whether or not one *ought* to elide the e mutes in verses, whether one *should* alternate their rhymes. Knowing you as I do, this is exactly how you will always behave with regard to my thought. Judge, from that, of your judgments of my life.

My life? It no longer belongs to me.

I have already said so.

I have no desire to hog the limelight. But the first person singular expresses for me everything that is concrete in man. All metaphysics is in the first person singular. All poetry, too.

The second person is still the first.

These days, with no more kings around, it is the scholars and scientists who say: We desire. Stout fellows.

They fondly believe they have grasped the plural: but it is a viper that they have in their hands.

I do not go astray, I command myself. In a landscape, it is always some absurdity rather than the essential which holds the eye. My point of view has a fine prospect.

I positively do not admit criticism.

I am in the heavens. No one can prevent me from being in the heavens.

They have displaced the heavens. In imagining the stars, they have forgotten my eyes.

Just what does hell mean for the human spirit?

The most tenacious of various hopes I have held was despair. Hell: my morality, you see, is not bound up with my optimism. I have never understood consolation.

Heaven will be of no help to me.

It is extraordinary, this need they have for a morality that will be a consolation to them.

No flowers, by request.

Prodigal on this side, parsimonious beyond: they lend their life by the week, at high rates of interest, hoping that their customers, reunited with them in death, will remain their debtors for all eternity.

To poetry, they prefer paradise.

Matter of taste.

Even in metaphysics, the general experience has been that poetry failed to feed the inner man.

What is this sentimentality?

Put aside sentimentality in all its forms. Sentiment, feeling are not just words to be kept, you bunch of crooks and swindlers. Visualize the world without bringing feeling into it. What beautiful weather.

Reality is the apparent absence of contradiction.

The marvelous is the eruption of contradiction within the real.

Love is a state of confusion between the real and the marvelous. In this state, the contradictions of being seem *really* essential to being.

Wherever the marvelous is dispossessed, the abstract moves in.

The fantastic, the beyond, dream, survival, paradise, hell, poetry, so many words signifying the concrete.

There is no other love than that of the concrete.

And since they are so keen on writing, it remains for them to write a metaphysic of love.

To meet a certain objection to nominalism: it might be a good idea to force people to notice what happens at the onset of sleep. How, at that point, man starts speaking to himself, and by what imperceptible progression he becomes carried away by his utterance which becomes manifest and effective, and how, when at last he attains his concrete value . . . there! the sleeper is dreaming, as they say.

The concrete is the indescribable: why should I care two pins whether the earth is round or not?

There is such a thing as a noble style in relation to thought.

Which is just what the psychologists deny.

Psychologists, alias soul-fanciers, are the acolytes of feeling. I have known several.

The inventor of the word *physiognomist.*

Those who say *God* for the best reasons in the world.

God is rarely on my lips.

Those who divide the mind up into faculties.

Those who talk about truth (I am not fond enough of lies to talk about truth).

You are too late upon the scene, gentlemen, for persons have had their day upon earth.

Force to its farthest limit the idea of the destruction of persons, and go beyond that limit.

CONTRIBUTORS' NOTES

ANNE-MARIE ALBIACH's books available in English translation include *État* (trans. Keith Waldrop) and *Mezza Voce* (trans. Anthony Barnett and Joseph Simas). She lives in Neuilly, France. **PIERRE ALFERI**'s books of poetry include *Chercher une phrase* and *Les Allures naturelles* (1991). His study of William of Ockham was published in France in 1989. **RICHARD ANDERS** is from East Prussia. His books include *Zeck* (1979) and *Verscherzte Trümpfe* (1993), from which the current selection of his work was taken. **JOHN ASHBERY**'s most recent books of poetry are *And the Stars Were Shining* (1994) and *Hotel Lautréamont* (1992). **ELENA BALASHOVA,** born in Moscow, now lives in Berkeley where she co-translates Russian poetry with Lyn Hejinian. **PAUL BEATTY** was born in Los Angeles and lives in New York City. His books are *Big Bank Take Little Bank* (1991) and *Joker, Joker, Deuce* (1994). **TED BERRIGAN**'s *Selected Poems* is just out from Viking Penguin. He was born in 1934 and died in New York City in 1983. **MEI-MEI BERSSENBRUGGE** is the author of *The Heat Bird* (1983), *Empathy* (1989), and *Sphericity* (1993). She lives in New Mexico. **DIONNE BRAND**, born in Trinidad, is a poet and filmmaker living in Toronto. Her third film, *Long Time Coming*, was recently released in Canada. **KAMAU BRATHWAITE** is a poet, critic, and historian originally from Barbados. He is Professor of Comparative Literature at New York University and recently received the Neudstadt International Prize for Literature. **SUSANA CERDÁ** lives in Buenos Aires. A collection of her poems, *Solía,* was published in 1988. **MILES CHAMPION**, born in 1968, lives and works in London. His first book will be published by Carcanet in 1995. **CHE QIAN-ZI** was born in Jiangsu province in 1963. He has written several volumes of poetry, including *Village and Face*, *Learning to Read with the Aid of Pictures*, *Paper Ladder*, and *Chair*. **SUSAN CLARK** is a co-editor of *Raddle Moon*. Her work has appeared in the most recent issues of *Avec* and *Chain*. **NORMA COLE** is the author of *Mace Hill Remap* (1988), *My Bird Book* (1991), and *Mars* (1994). She lives in San Francisco. **KELVIN CORCORAN** was born in 1956 and lives in Cheltenham, England. His most recent publications are *Remember Remember* (1991), and *Lyric Lyric* (1993). **ROBERT CREELEY**'s most recent book of poems is *Echoes* (1994). A collection of interviews, *Tales Out of School*, and an interactive biography by Tom Clark were published in 1993. **FRED D'AGUIAR** is a poet and writer of Guyanese descent living in London. His three books of poetry are: *Mama Dot* (1985) *Airy Hall* (1989) and *British Subjects* (1993). **KEVIN DAVIES** has published two books: *Despite* (1982) and *Pause Button* (1992). He was born in 1958 in Nanaimo, British Columbia. **TORY DENT** was born in 1958. Her first collection, *What Silence Equals*, was published by Persea Books in 1994. She lives in New York. **JEFF DERKSEN**'s books of poetry are *Down Time* (1990) and *Dwell* (1993). A co-editor of *Writing* magazine, he currently lives in Calgary. **MAROSA DI GIORGIO** lives in Uruguay. Her books include *The Moth* (1989) and *Missals: Erotic Tales* (1993). *The March Hare* (1981) is her tribute to Lewis Carroll. **JOSEPH DONAHUE**'s poems have been published in *Monitions of the Approach* (1991). He is completing a study of John Berryman. **ARKADII DRAGOMOSHCHENKO** was born in the Ukraine and lives in St. Petersburg. His most recent books of poems in English translation are *Description* (1990) and *Xenia* (1994). **KEN EDWARDS**' books include *Good Science: poems 1983-1991* (1992), and *3600 Weekends* (1993). He co-edits (with Wendy Mulford) Reality Street Editions. **KENWARD ELMSLIE** is a poet, songwriter, and performance artist. A bibliography of his work was recently published by Bamberger Press. **ELKE ERB** has lived since 1949 in what used to be East Berlin. A volume of her selected poems was published in German in 1991. A volume in translation, *The Stove Problem and Other Difficulties*, is forthcoming from Burning Deck. **ALEKSANDR EREMENKO** was crowned "King of the Poets" in 1989 by a group of "unofficial" writers in Moscow. His *Models and Situations* was published there in 1990. **STEVE EVANS** is a graduate student at Brown University, where he is currently working on a dissertation entitled, "Meditations in an Emergency: Poetic Practice and Capitalist Modernity." **GERHARD FALKNER** was born in 1951 and lives near Munich. The texts translated here are from his most recent book of poems, *wemut* (1989). **D. FARRELL**'s *Ape* was published by Tsunami Editions in 1988. He lives in Vancouver. **DEANNA FERGUSON**'s book *The Relative Minor* was published by Tsunami Editions in 1993. **ED FOSTER**'s books of poems are *The Space Between Her Bed and Clock* (1993) and *The Understanding* (1994). He edits *Talisman.* **DOMINIQUE FOURCADE**'s *Xbo* (trans. Robert Kocic) was published by Sun & Moon in 1994. *Click-Rose* (trans. Keith Waldrop) is forthcoming from the same press. **ULLI FREER** writes, paints, and publishes under the Microbrigade imprint from London. **JEAN FRÉMON** is the author of *Le singe mendiant* (1991). His work frequently appears in the journal of French poetry in translation, *Série d'écriture.* **PETER GIZZI** is the author of *Periplum* (1992), *Music for Films* (1992), and *Hours of the Book* (1994). Currently he is editing the lectures and letters of Jack Spicer. **JOHN GODFREY**'s books include *Dabble* (1982), *Where the Weather Suits My Clothes* (1984), and *Midnight On Your Left* (1988). He lives in New York City. **MALCOLM GREEN** is an editor for Atlas Press. He lives in Heidelberg, Germany. **ERNESTO LIVON GROSMAN**'s book of poems, *Discurso del Golfista,* was published in Argentina in 1993. Born in Buenos Aires in 1956, he currently teaches at Yale University. **DURS GRÜNBEIN** was born in Dresden in 1962 and now lives in Berlin. His *Schädelbasislektion* was published in 1991. **CLAIRE HARRIS**, originally from Trinidad, lives and works in Calgary, Alberta. The author of seven books of poetry, she has also edited the magazines *Dandelion* and *blue buffalo.* **LEE HARWOOD**, born in 1939, lives in Hove/Brighton and works on the railways. His most recent book is *In the mists: mountain poems* (1993). **LYN HEJINIAN**'s books of poetry include *Writing Is an Aid to Memory* (1978), *The Guard* (1984), *My Life* (1980; 1987) and *Oxota: A Short Russian Novel* (1991). **JOHN HIGH** is a founding editor of *Five Fingers Review.* He has lived in Russia for much of the past several years. **EMMANUEL HOCQUARD**'s book *Theory of Tables,* translated into American by Michael Palmer, is just out from o.blek editions. He divides his time between Malakoff and Bourdeaux. **KATHRYN A. KOPPLE**'s translations include *The March Hare* (Uruguay, 1981) by Marosa Di Giorgio and *Subchamber* (Brazil, 1987) by Mercedes Roffé. **HONG LIU** was born in China in 1965. She has written two books of poetry, *Vanishing* and *Icy Cold.* **FANNY HOWE** is a poet and fiction writer whose recent books include *Saving History* (1993), *The Quietist* (1992), *The Vineyard* (1988), and *The Deep North* (1988). **ANTHONY HOWELL** had an early career dancing with the Royal Ballet in London and founded the Theatre of Mistakes, a performance company, in 1974. He has published five collections of poetry and edits *Grey Suit,* a quarterly video publication for art and literature. **HUANG FAN** was born in 1963. His books include *Phenomena of Feelings* and *Five Nanjing Poets.* **NINA ISKRENKO** currently lives in Moscow. A selection of her poems, *The Right to Err* (1994), is being published by Three Continents Press. **ALEXANDER KALOUZHSKY**, born in Russia, is a musician and poet as well as a translator. He now lives in San Bernardino, California. **KEVIN KILLIAN** is the author of *Desiree* (1986) and *Shy* (1989). With Lew Ellingham, he has written a biography of Jack Spicer. **MYUNG MI KIM** is the author of *Under Flag* (1991). She teaches creative writing at San Francisco State University. **BARBARA KÖHLER**, born in 1959, lives in Chemnitz (Karl-Marx-Stadt). *Deutsches Roulette* (1991) is her first book. **LAURA KUHN** is Executive Director of The John Cage Trust, which is located in New York City. **ANDREW LAWSON** edited *fragmente: a magazine of contemporary poetics* (with Anthony Mellors) from 1990 to 1993. He is the author of *Human Capital* (1992). **BEN MARCUS** lives in New York City. His first book, a collection entitled *The Age of Wire and String,* will be published by Knopf. **D.S. MARRIOTT** teaches contemporary literature and literary theory at University of Sussex, Brighton. He is the author of *Lative* (1992) and *Light, Circles* (1987). **HARRY MATHEWS**'s most recent novel, *The Journalist,* is just out from Godine. **BERNADETTE MAYER**'s most recent books are *A Bernadette Mayer Reader* (1992) and *The Desires of Mothers to Please Others in Letters* (1994). **MARK McMORRIS** was born in Jamaica and currently lives in Providence, Rhode Island. He is the author of *Palinurus Suite* (1992). **ANTHONY MELLORS** lives in Manchester, England, where he edits *fragmente.* His poetry publications include *Secondary Revision* (1990) and *Affine Arnold* (1991). **VADIM MESYATS** is the author of a novel, *The Wind from the Candy Factory* (Moscow, 1994) and a volume of poems, *A Calendar of the Rememberer* (Moscow, 1993). **LAURA MORIARTY** is the author of *Persia* (1983), *like roads* (1990), *Rondeaux* (1990), and *Symmetry* (forthcoming in 1995). She directs the American Poetry Archives at San Francisco State University. **JENNIFER MOXLEY**'s poems have appeared in recent issues of *o.blek*, *Lingo*, and *Black Bread.* She edits *The Impercipient.* **WENDY MULFORD** lives and works in Suffolk. Her most recent poetry publications are *Nevrazumitelny* (1991) and *The Bay of Naples*

(1992). She edits Reality Street Editions with Ken Edwards. **MUTABARUKA** is a poet and musician from Kingston, Jamaica. His books include *Outcry* (1973), *Sun & Moon* (1976) and *First Poems 1970-79*. His most recent album is *Melanin Man* (1994). **GALE NELSON** is the author of *Stare Decisis* (1991) and *Little Brass Pump* (1992). He edits paradigm press. **ALICE NOTLEY**'s *Selected Poems* were published in 1993. She now lives in Paris. **BRIGITTE OLESCHINSKI** was born in Köln in 1955 and currently works at the Berlin Memorial of German Resistance. *Mental Heat Control* (1990) is her first book. **ALEXEI PARSHCHIKOV** now lives in Switzerland. His book *Blue Vitriol* (1994) is available in English translation. Part of **ANNE PARIAN**'s "With A and B" was published in the magazine *Tartine* (edited by Catherine Lorin). **OSKAR PASTIOR**'s many volumes of poetry include a selected poems, a volume of palindromes, and *Sestinen*, from which our selection was taken. Born in Rumania in 1927, he spent five years in a Soviet labor camp after the war and made his way to Berlin in 1969. **SIMON PETTET** is the author of *Conversations with Rudy Burckhardt About Everything* (1987), and, with Burckhardt, *Talking Pictures* (1994). **MARLENE NOURBESE PHILIP**'s recent work includes a book of poems, *She Tries Her Tongue; Her Silence Softly Breaks* (1989), and a prose work, *Looking for Livingstone: An Odyssey of Silence* (1991). Born in Trinidad and Tobago, she lives in Toronto. Translations of **ANNE PORTUGAL**'s work have appeared in *Série d'écriture* (nos. 4 and 7), and in *Violence of the White Page*. **DMITRI PRIGOV** was one of the initiators of the Moscow conceptualist movement. His first book was published in Moscow in 1990. **TOM RAWORTH** is the author of over 30 books of poems, including a selected poems entitled *Tottering State* (1984). He lives in Cambridge, England. **PAM REHM**'s collection *To Give It Up* recently won the National Poetry Series competition, and is forthcoming from Sun and Moon. She is co-editor of *Apex of the M*. **DENISE RILEY** is a poet and critic born in Carlisle, England in 1948. Her recent books of poetry include *Stair Spirit* (1992), and *Mop Mop Georgette* (1993). **LISA ROBERTSON** is the author of *XEclogue* (1994). She co-edits *Raddle Moon* in Vancouver, B.C. **MERCEDES ROFFÉ** was born in Buenos Aires and has lived in the United States since 1985. **CLAUDE ROYET-JOURNOUD**'s *The Notion of Obstacle* (trans. Keith Waldrop) is available from Awede Press; *Objects Contain the Infinite* is forthcoming. He lives in Paris. **KATE RUSHIN**'s first book, *The Black Back-Ups*, was published by Firebrand in 1993. Currently she is Director of the Center for African American Studies at Wesleyan University. **JOACHIM SARTORIUS**, born in 1946, has translated the work of John Ashbery and Wallace Stevens into German. The selection of his poetry is taken from *Der Tisch wird kalt zu wem* (1988). **JASON SCHWARTZ** lives in New York City. **MAURICE SCULLY** was born in Dublin in 1952. His books include *The Basic Colours* (1994), *Priority* (1994), and *Zulu Dynamite* (forthcoming in 1995). **ILIASSA SEQUIN** lives in London and is the author of many *Quintets*, the first set of which was published by o.blek editions in 1991. **DAVID SHAPIRO** is the author of many volumes of poetry, criticism, and translation, ranging from *January* (1965) to *After a Lost Original* (1994). He has written on the work of John Ashbery and Jasper Johns. **NANCY SHAW**'s books are *Affordable Tedium* (1987) and *Scoptocratic* (1992). She is co-editor of *Writing* magazine and currently lives in Montreal. **TRACY SILANO** is a post production worker in the film industry. She lives in New York City. **SARAH SIMONS** is the librarian of the Museum of Jurassic Technology and lives in Los Angeles. **ROD SMITH** wrote *The Boy Poems* (1994). He lives in Washington D.C., where he edits *Aerial* magazine. **JULIANNA SPAHR** is the author of *Nuclear* (1991) and *Asking* (1994). She recently completed a dissertation on Gertrude Stein, Emily Dickinson, and contemporary American poetics. **CHRISTINE STEWART** is a co-editor of *Raddle Moon*. *Taxonomy* is forthcoming as a chapbook. **CATRIONA STRANG** is a co-editor of the magazines *Barscheit* and *Raddle Moon*. Her booklength translation of the Carmina Burana, *Low Fancy*, was published in 1994. **COLE SWENSON**'s books of poetry include *New Math* (1988) and *Park* (1991). **SABINE TECHEL** is a native Berliner born in 1953. *Es kundigt sich an*, from which our selection was taken, was published by Suhrkamp in 1986. **DAVID TRINIDAD**'s most recent book is *Answer Song* (High Risk Books/Serpent's Tail, 1994). He lives in New York City. **JEFF TWITCHELL** recently returned after five years teaching in mainland China. He teaches at Virginia Commonwealth University. **KEITH WALDROP** is a poet and fiction writer whose recent publications include *Potential Random* (1992) and *Light While There Is Light* (1993), a biographical novel. **ROSMARIE WALDROP**'s most recent book of poems, *A Key into the Language of America*, is forthcoming from New Directions. With Keith Waldrop, she co-edits Burning Deck Press. **CATHERINE WALSH** was born in Dublin, Ireland in 1964. She is a teacher of English as a Foreign Language and currently lives in Eastbourne, Sussex. **MOLLY WEIGL** has translated the work of many Argentine poets and is working on an anthology. **DIANE WILLIAMS** is the author of *This is About the Mind, the Soul, the World, Time, and Fate* and *Some Sexual Success Stories Plus Other Stories in which God Might Choose to Appear,* both from Grove Press. Her work *The Stupefaction* is forthcoming. **ELIZABETH WILLIS** is the author of *A/O* and *Second Law. The Human Abstract,* a winner in the National Poetry Series competition, is forthcoming in 1995. **TREVOR WINKFIELD** is a painter, poet and translator. His collected writings, *In the Scissors' Courtyard,* was published in 1993. His translation of Raymond Roussel's *How I Wrote Certain of My Books* has just been reprinted by Exact Change. **XIAN MENG,** born in 1964, has edited the collections *Thought is Innocent* and *The Modernist Poetry Movement in 1987.* He works as a radio engineer in Nanjing. **JOHN YAU**'s recent books include *Edificio Sayonara* (1992) and *In the Realm of Appearances: The Art of Andy Warhol* (1993). **YI CUN**, born in 1954, is a wandering troubadour who joined the Original Group at the end of the 1980s. His collections include *Grain and Landscapes* and *Chatting with the Chess Player.* **ARKADII ZASTYRETS** edits a newspaper, *The Science of the Urals,* in Jekatrinburg. His book of poems *Pentagramma* was published there in 1993. **IVAN ZHDANOV,** born in Siberia, lives in Moscow, where he repairs elevators. His works include *Portrait* (Moscow, 1982) and *Unchangeable Sky* (Moscow, 1990). **ZHOU YA-PING**, born in 1961, is the editor of the poetry journal *Original* and the interpreter of the theory of Original poetics. His works include *Swan in the Utensils, Lost in Love,* and *I'm Breathing, Who Can Deny It.*

NOTES ON THE C.D.

1
MICHAEL PALMER
LETTERS TO ZANZOTTO (08:53)
Recorded by Exact Change, April 5, 1994, at Brown University.

2
BARBARA GUEST
AN EMPHASIS FALLS ON REALITY (02:32)
Recorded April 1, 1992, at SUNY Buffalo.

3
KAMAU BRATHWAITE
NEGUS (04:49)
Recorded July 13, 1994, at the Fox Theater, Boulder CO.

4
ROBERT CREELEY
HEROES; FOR LOVE (03:05)
Recorded c.1963, broadcast by Paul Blackburn on "Contemporary Poetry," WBAI.

5
JOHN ASHBERY
THEY DREAM ONLY OF AMERICA (01:07)
Recorded July 22, 1994, in Hudson NY.

6
ALICE NOTLEY
AT NIGHT THE STATES (07:49)
Recorded April 10, 1987, in Buffalo NY.

7
JOHN GODFREY
POURING GULF (02:34)
Recorded April 21, 1994, at Brown University.

8
JACK SPICER
IMAGINARY ELEGIES (11:08)
Recorded April 11, 1957, at the Poetry Center, San Francisco State College.

9
MEI-MEI BERSSENBRUGGE
TEXAS (03:04)
Recorded July 10, 1986, at Naropa Institute.

10
KENWARD ELMSLIE
EASTER POEM FOR JOE ('79) (01:33)
Recorded April 11, 1985, at the Detroit Institute for the Arts.

11
BERNADETTE MAYER
THE COMPLETE INTRODUCTORY LECTURES ON POETRY (01:42)
Recorded July 10, 1987, at Naropa Institute.

12
TED BERRIGAN
RED SHIFT (03:01)
Recorded July 25, 1982, at Naropa Institute.

TOTAL TIME 51:17

MASTERED BY WAYNE ROGERS AT TWISTED VILLAGE, AUGUST 1994.

EXACT CHANGE

PARKETT
No. 40/41 • 1994
DOUBLE ISSUE/DOPPELNUMMER
Snakes & Ladders
FRANCESCO CLEMENTE
PETER FISCHLI/DAVID WEISS
GÜNTHER FÖRG
DAMIEN HIRST
JENNY HOLZER
REBECCA HORN
SIGMAR POLKE
10 Years of Parkett & Index

new titles:

Margery Kempe
by Robert Glück

Answer Song
by David Trinidad

HIGH RISK BOOKS

also:

Bombay Talkie
by Ameena Meer

The Roaches Have No King
by Daniel Evan Weiss

Dear Dead Person
by Benjamin Weissman

American Dreams
by Sapphire

Rent Boy
by Gary Indiana

You Got To Burn To Shine
by John Giorno

Available at better bookstores or direct from High Risk: [212] 274-8981

In 1984 a radically new graphic design magazine set out to explore the as-yet-untapped and uncharted possibilities of Macintosh-generated graphic design. Boldly new and different, *Emigre* broke rules, opened eyes and earned its creators, Rudy VanderLans and Zuzana Licko, cult status in the world of graphic design. After a decade of publishing, the jury is still out on *Emigre.* But now, thanks to this comprehensive 10-year retrospective, you can reach your own conclusions. Are *Emigre*'s Mac-generated graphics important, influential and controversial...or just plain ugly? You decide.

Here gathered together for the first time, you'll find:

Every *Emigre* cover ever issued

A full catalog of over 80 Emigre typefaces

Emigre's most striking editorial layouts

Plus stimulating and provocative commentary from both Rudy VanderLans and Zuzana Licko

now in its second printing!

96 Pages, 11x15, over 300 illustrations, with commentary from VanderLans and Licko. Essay by Mr. Keedy. Available at your local bookstore or order by calling **(800) 944 - 9021.**
Price: $24.95

A deluxe version of the book is also available. Hand-signed by Zuzana Licko and Rudy VanderLans and presented in a hand-made, cloth-covered slipcase. This edition also includes The Emigre Music Sampler No.2 deluxe compact disc. Available exclusively from Emigre.
Price: $50.00

A BYRON PREISS BOOK. PUBLISHED BY VAN NOSTRAND REINHOLD, NEW YORK.

THE
MUSEUM OF
JURASSIC TECHNOLOGY
"The learner must be led always
from familiar objects toward the unfamiliar
guided along, as it were,
a chain of flowers into the mysteries of life"
THE MUSEUM OF JURASSIC TECHNOLOGY
9341 Venice Boulevard
Culver City CA. 90232-2621
for information call (310) 836-6131

CITY LIGHTS PUBLISHERS AND BOOKSELLERS
CITY LIGHTS MAIL ORDER
Order books from our free catalog:
all books from CITY LIGHTS PUBLISHERS and more
write to:
CITY LIGHTS MAIL ORDER
261 COLUMBUS AVENUE SAN FRANCISCO, CA 94133
or fax your request to [415] 362-4921

LISTENING CHAMBER
presents
MARS
by
Norma
Cole
original
cover
paste-up
by
Jess
". . . like six fires continuously rekindling . . . a language of contagion. A language that emits thought. That also contains it by rhythmic force in order that one might, at the same time, breathe. (And the hand never letting go of what thought holds.)"
Claude Royet-Journoud
128pp. ISBN: 0-9639321-0-1, $10.00
Available from SPD, 1814 San Pablo Berkeley CA 94702, 510-549-3336, & in good bookstores; or, order direct: 2420 Acton St, Berkeley CA 94702

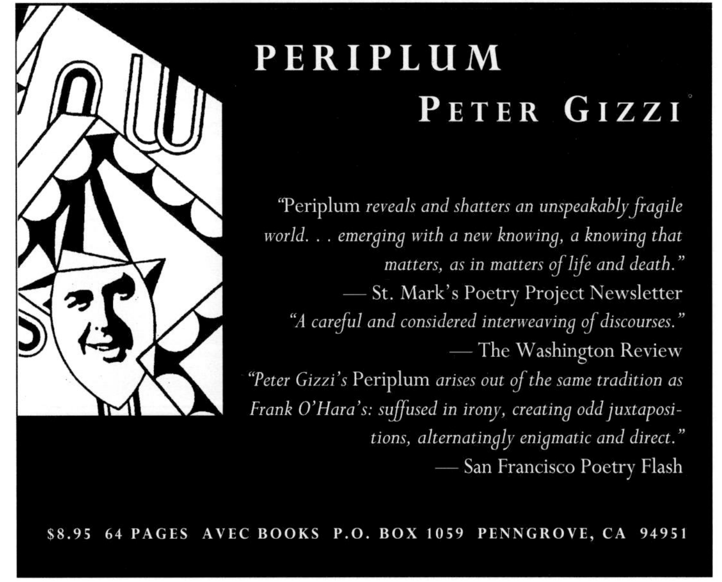
PERIPLUM
PETER GIZZI
"Periplum reveals and shatters an unspeakably fragile world. . . emerging with a new knowing, a knowing that matters, as in matters of life and death."
— St. Mark's Poetry Project Newsletter
"A careful and considered interweaving of discourses."
— The Washington Review
"Peter Gizzi's Periplum arises out of the same tradition as Frank O'Hara's: suffused in irony, creating odd juxtapositions, alternatingly enigmatic and direct."
— San Francisco Poetry Flash
$8.95 64 PAGES AVEC BOOKS P.O. BOX 1059 PENNGROVE, CA 94951

100

copies of the

Exact Change Yearbook 1995

have been signed and numbered

by Michael Palmer